PRAISE FOR KERRY

Everything We Keep

Top Amazon Bestseller of 2016 and *Wall Street Journal* Bestseller

Amazon Charts Bestseller

Liz & Lisa Best Book of the Month Selection

POPSUGAR and *Redbook* Fall Must-Read Selection

"This fantastic debut is glowing with adrenaline-inducing suspense and unexpected twists. Don't make other plans when you open up *Everything We Keep*; you will devour it in one sitting."

—*Redbook* magazine

"Aimee's electrifying journey to piece together the puzzle of mystery surrounding her fiancé's disappearance is a heart-pounding reading experience every hopeless romantic and shock-loving fiction lover should treat themselves to."

—POPSUGAR

"You'll need an ample supply of tissues and emotional strength for this one . . . From Northern California author Kerry Lonsdale comes a heart-wrenching story about fate sweeping away life in an instant."

—*Sunset* magazine

"Gushing with adrenaline-inducing plot, this is the phenomenally written debut every fall reader will be swooning over."

—*Coastal Living*

"A beautifully crafted novel about unconditional love, heartbreak, and letting go, *Everything We Keep* captures readers with its one-of-a-kind, suspenseful plot. Depicting grief and loss, but also healing and hope in their rawest forms, this novel will capture hearts and minds, keeping readers up all night, desperate to learn the truth."

—RT Book Reviews

"A perfect page-turner for summer."
    —Catherine McKenzie, bestselling author of *Hidden* and *Fractured*

"Heartfelt and suspenseful, *Everything We Keep* beautifully navigates the deep waters of grief and one woman's search to reconcile a past she can't release and a future she wants to embrace. Lonsdale's writing is crisp and effortless and utterly irresistible—and her expertly layered exploration of the journey from loss to renewal is sure to make this a book club must-read. *Everything We Keep* drew me in from the first page and held me fast all the way to its deeply satisfying ending."

—Erika Marks, author of *The Last Treasure*

"In *Everything We Keep*, Kerry Lonsdale brilliantly explores the grief of loss, if we can really let go of our great loves, and if some secrets are better left buried. With a good dose of drama, a heart-wrenching love story, and the suspense of unanswered questions, Lonsdale's layered and engrossing debut is a captivating read."

—Karma Brown, bestselling author of *Come Away with Me*

"A stunning debut with a memorable twist, *Everything We Keep* effortlessly layers family secrets into a suspenseful story of grief, love, and art. This is a gem of a book."

—Barbara Claypole White, bestselling author of *The Perfect Son* and
The Promise Between Us

"*Everything We Keep* takes your breath from the very first line and keeps it through a heart-reeling number of twists and turns. Well plotted, with wonderful writing and pacing, on the surface it appears to be a story of love and loss, but just as you begin to think you've worked it out, you're blindsided and realize you haven't. It will keep you reading and guessing, and trust me, you still won't have it figured out. Not until the very end."

—Barbara Taylor Sissel, bestselling author of *The Truth We Bury* and *What Lies Below*

"Wow—it's been a long time since I ignored all my responsibilities and read a book straight through, but it couldn't be helped with *Everything We Keep*. I was intrigued from the start . . . So many questions, and Lonsdale answers them in the most intriguing and captivating way possible."

—Camille Di Maio, author of *The Memory of Us*

All the Breaking Waves

Amazon Best Book of the Month: Literature & Fiction Category

Liz & Lisa Best Book of the Month Selection

"Blending elements of magic and mystery, *All the Breaking Waves* is a compelling portrayal of one mother's journey as she grapples with her small daughter's horrific visions that force her to confront a haunting secret from her past. Examining issues of love, loss, and the often-fragile ground of relationships and forgiveness, this tenderly told story will have you turning the pages long past midnight."

—Barbara Taylor Sissel, bestselling author of *The Truth We Bury* and *What Lies Below*

"With a touch of the paranormal, *All the Breaking Waves* is an emotional story about lost love, family secrets, and finding beauty in things people fear . . . or simply discard. A perfect book club pick!"

—Barbara Claypole White, bestselling author of *The Perfect Son* and
The Promise Between Us

"A masterful tale of magic realism and family saga. With its heartfelt characters, relationships generational and maternal, and a long-ago romance, we are drawn into Molly's world. While her intuitive gifts may be ethereal, her fears and hopes for her daughter and personal desires are extraordinarily relatable. Woven with a thread of pure magic, Lonsdale crafts an intriguing story of love, mystery, and family loyalty that will captivate and entertain readers."

—Laura Spinella, bestselling author of *Ghost Gifts*

Everything We Left Behind

Amazon Charts and *Wall Street Journal* Bestseller

Amazon Editors' Recommended Beach Read

Liz & Lisa Best Book of the Month Selection

"In this suspenseful sequel to *Everything We Keep* . . . readers will be captivated as the truth unravels, hanging on every word."

—RT Book Reviews

"A stunning fusion of suspense, family drama, and redemption, *Everything We Left Behind* will hold the reader spellbound to the last sentence."

—A. J. Banner, bestselling author of *The Twilight Wife* and
The Good Neighbor

"Love, loss, and secrets drive Kerry Lonsdale's twisty follow-up to the bestselling *Everything We Keep*. *Everything We Left Behind* is an enthralling and entertaining read. You'll be turning the pages as fast as you can to see how it ends."

—Liz Fenton and Lisa Steinke, authors of *The Good Widow*

"While *Everything We Left Behind*, the long-anticipated sequel to *Everything We Keep*, is page turning and suspenseful, at its center it is the story of a man struggling to discover the truth of his own identity. A man who is determined above all else to protect his family, a man who is willing to risk everything to find out the truth and to ultimately uncover the secrets of his own heart. For everyone who has read *Everything We Keep* (if you haven't, go do that now!), this is your novel, answering every question, tying up every thread to an oh-so-satisfying conclusion."

—Barbara Taylor Sissel, bestselling author of *The Truth We Bury* and *What Lies Below*

"With one smart, unexpected twist after another, this page-turner is as surprising as it is emotionally insightful. *Everything We Left Behind* showcases Kerry Lonsdale at the top of her game."

—Camille Pagán, bestselling author of *Life and Other Near-Death Experiences*

"Told through a unique perspective, *Everything We Left Behind* is a compelling story about one man's journey to find himself in the wake of trauma, dark secrets, and loss. As past and present merge, he struggles to confront fear and find trust, but two constants remain: his love for his young sons and his need to protect them from danger. This novel has everything—romance, suspense, mystery, family drama. What a page-turner!"

—Barbara Claypole White, bestselling author of *The Perfect Son* and *The Promise Between Us*

Everything We Give

Wall Street Journal Bestseller

"Fans will not be disappointed in this stunning conclusion to the Everything Series. With Lonsdale's signature twists and turns, nothing is a given until the last satisfying page. I cried, I bit my nails, and I lost myself in images of wild horses galloping across rural Spain as I journeyed through Ian's past and present. A page-turner about the devastating impact of mental illness and dark secrets on a family, *Everything We Give* is also a story filled with the enduring power of love."

—Barbara Claypole White, bestselling author of *The Perfect Son* and *The Promise Between Us*

"Kerry Lonsdale gives everything away in this final book in the Everything Series, *Everything We Give*. Questions involving an enigmatic woman, the mystery of her name and her identity, and her connection to Ian kick off what is a fast-paced and sensual story of suspense. Like *Everything We Keep* and *Everything We Left Behind*, books one and two in this delectable and layered series, *Everything We Give* is the frosting on the cake, delivering more than one surprise and a total knockout punch of an ending."

—Barbara Taylor Sissel, bestselling author of *The Truth We Bury* and *What Lies Below*

"Kerry Lonsdale brings the conclusion to the Everything Series to a magnificent ending. Ian's journey through past and present is a trip to remember. A fast-paced thriller with romance and intrigue. Bravo, Kerry!"

—Kaira Rouda, *USA Today* bestselling author of *Best Day Ever*

"*Everything We Give* is a satisfying conclusion to this series, which began with a funeral when there should have been a wedding, and ends with the final fallout from the mysterious woman who warned the almost-widow that all was not as it seemed. Lonsdale has woven together a tapestry of characters—Aimee, Ian, James—whose lives are intertwined in ways even they don't entirely know. [It's] both a romance and a mystery, [and] readers will turn these engrossing pages quickly to find out what their final fates [will] be. Fans of this series will not be disappointed."

—Catherine McKenzie, bestselling author of *Hidden* and
The Good Liar

Last Summer

Amazon Charts and *Washington Post* Bestseller

"An involving story weaves a tale of recovery into a mystery that embraces relationships, danger, and new beginnings."

—Midwest Book Review

"To say that this book is a page-turner is an understatement."

—Criminal Element

"This was a highly entertaining and wildly addictive read that is perfect for summer! . . . Compulsive, sexy, and tense."

—*Novelgossip*

"*Last Summer* is one hell of a ride, with a heroine who's easy to relate to and a glossy romantic mystery that holds the reader's attention."

—All About Romance

Side Trip

"Exploring a series of what-if scenarios, readers will thoroughly enjoy this road trip along Route 66 with two curious strangers."
—*Travel + Leisure*

"Swoon-worthy moments and heart-stirring drama . . . A romantic ride!"
—*Woman's World*

"Lonsdale keeps the reader guessing right to the very end . . . with a twist you don't see coming. A great summer read."
—*Red Carpet Crash*

"Lonsdale again takes us on quite a ride through love, loss, and life. Her groupie following will devour this one!"
—Frolic

"Smart, sexy, and unexpected—*Side Trip* is everything that makes a novel unputdownable, which is why I devoured it in two days. Kerry Lonsdale's latest demonstrates what fans like me already know: she just keeps getting better and better."
—Camille Pagán, bestselling author of *I'm Fine and Neither Are You*

"Route 66, a convertible, a folk singer, and fate combine to make a confection of a novel in Kerry Lonsdale's *Side Trip*. Scoot into the back seat to watch what happens. What a wild ride!"
—J. P. Monninger, internationally bestselling author

"Kerry Lonsdale's *Side Trip* is an absorbing, poignant exploration of the road not taken and the pitfalls of failing to follow one's heart."
—Jamie Beck, bestselling author of the Cabots and Sanctuary Sound series

No More Words

"Lonsdale is at her best with this multilayered story about three dysfunctional siblings and the secrets they keep. What a ride. I'm still a little breathless. This one was an addictive page-turner—impossible to put down. Fans of domestic suspense will EAT THIS UP."

—Sally Hepworth, bestselling author of *The Good Sister* and *The Mother-in-Law*

"Kerry Lonsdale is back and better than ever with this multilayered tale about three siblings torn apart by a series of tragic events. Nuanced and smart, filled with characters with real emotion and depth, *No More Words* is everything you've come to love from the master of domestic drama. A mesmerizing beginning to a new trilogy that will have you one-clicking the next in the series."

—Kimberly Belle, internationally bestselling author of *Stranger in the Lake*

"Full of suspense, romance, and drama, *No More Words* is a powerful story about what it means to be a family. Emotional and honest, it tells the story of three siblings, each dealing with demons from the past. I fell in love with all three Carson children and look forward to the second and third installments of this series. Kerry Lonsdale is a master storyteller of family drama, and this is Lonsdale at her best."

—Suzanne Redfearn, #1 Amazon bestselling author of *In an Instant*

"Kerry Lonsdale starts her latest trilogy off with a bang! Brimming with drama, suspense, and family secrets galore, *No More Words* will have you tearing through the pages to figure out what really happened to this broken family, and who is playing whom. With beautifully drawn, complex characters and a twisted plot that reveals itself layer by layer, *No More Words* is a stunning thriller that deserves a top spot on your 'to be read' list."

—Hannah Mary McKinnon, bestselling author of *Sister Dear* and *You Will Remember Me*

"*No More Words* burns and smolders with the tension of a lit cigarette. Kerry Lonsdale has created a page-turning story of family secrets and assumed truths that forces readers to ask what they would do if the buried past came calling at their door. Nothing and no one can stay hidden forever."

—Amber Cowie, author of *Rapid Falls*

"Every family has its secrets, and the way Kerry Lonsdale twists the truths in *No More Words*, you're guaranteed to lose sleep over this perfectly blended tale of suspense, intrigue, and emotional betrayal. Lonsdale has done it again, gripping the hearts of readers with her complex characters and layered story lines. This is a must-read thriller that will leave you stunned at the end!"

—Steena Holmes, *New York Times* and *USA Today* bestselling author of *Lies We Tell Ourselves*

NO MORE

LIES

NO MORE LIES

LIES

A NOVEL

KERRY LONSDALE

LAKE UNION
PUBLISHING

Published by Lake Union Publishing, Seattle

www.apub.com

Amazon, the Amazon logo, and Lake Union Publishing are trademarks of Amazon.com, Inc., or its affiliates.

ISBN-13: 9781542019071
ISBN-10: 1542019079

Cover design by Rex Bonomelli

Printed in the United States of America

For Dad.
For always being a voice of reason and
my biggest supporter.

CHAPTER 1

Jenna Mason jogs across the Washington Middle School parking lot, racing the morning bell. She absently waves at the parents huddled beside Beth Hopkin's white BMW X5. Snippets of their conversation reach her—aggressive reporter, chasing a lead—that would have alarmed her a few years ago. She would have asked what the reporter was chasing. She would have wondered if she needed to run.

Their chattering abruptly stops. They stare at her. Then Beth whispers to Leigh Duffy. Shock paints Leigh's expression, and Jenna wonders if they're talking about her. She's an enigma, newer to the close-knit community, who for the most part keeps to herself. Once, she might have felt a prickle of unease across her shoulders. Jenna is sure she's a curiosity. But right now she's rushed and irritated. Josh left his homework binder behind again.

She's enabling her son, she knows that. A sensible parent would let him face the consequences from not turning in his homework on time. Tough love would teach him to pack his book bag before bed and have it ready by the door come morning. She could drop his binder off at the front office, but then she'd have to talk to people. Socialize. Interact. Leave an impression. Things ingrained in her to avoid. Habits she hasn't quite shaken since she and Josh settled in Oceanside, California.

Some days, she envies how easily her son has made friends.

But he doesn't have a past he needs to hide from. People he's running from.

Jenna cuts through the schoolyard. Kids congregate in their cliques like dolphin pods. They fuss with their phones, snapping and tiktokking or whatever it is kids do these days. Josh has tried to explain, but since she won't buy him a smartphone or allow him online unsupervised, she hasn't gone out of her way to learn more about social media. She avoids it and intends to keep Josh off if possible. She can't risk him posting something to his profile that could lead her past to their front door.

Josh has given her an earful about his flip phone. He prefers to not use it over getting mocked for having one, which she could guess is why he didn't answer when she called him about the binder a few minutes after he left the house to walk to school.

At least she hopes that's why. Her heart beats furiously as she reins in her panic that something happened on his way to school and that's why he couldn't answer his phone. A constant fear she'll never get over, not with her past.

She beelines to the lunch tables under the green-and-gold canopy, the school's colors, where she knows Josh sits with his friend Anson before class starts. She's watched him some mornings through the chain-link fence that borders the school grounds when he thought she already left for home. He's growing up fast. Hard to believe he'll be thirteen. Even harder to accept she's been living a lie just as long.

Anson sees her before Josh does and waves. Relief floods her when she spots her son next to him. He's here. He's safe.

"Hello, Ms. Mason."

Josh swivels on the bench. "Mom!" His eyes dart to see who's watching, and his shoulders drop as he curls into himself, trying to look smaller in an effort to go unnoticed, embarrassed she's here.

"Hi, Anson. Josh." She drops the white binder covered in vibrant shades of permanent marker on the table. Josh is a doodler, though his artwork is more realistic than her quirky characters. She still can't believe her YouTube cartoon went viral several years back. Now she has a four-book contract and a movie deal. *Tabby's Squirrel* is everywhere.

Some days she wishes it weren't. It makes her a target, too visible despite her almost manic efforts at privacy. But it pays the bills and then some. She can buy Josh Vans at the Shoppes at Carlsbad rather than worn sneakers with stained soles at the Salvation Army. They can eat out at restaurants with linen napkins, like the ones her parents took her to when she was young, rather than the reheated leftovers of canned food she bought at the grocery outlet.

Thanks to her unexpected success, they have been living like real people, not transients moving from home to home within Murielle's network of angels, like they'd been doing up until eighteen months ago.

She often wishes they hadn't come out of hiding. She fears being discovered for who she really is. It's a constant struggle, fighting the urge to look over her shoulder versus just living.

Josh drags the binder toward him and stuffs it in his backpack. "What are you doing here?"

"You didn't answer my call." She clenches her hands, nails biting into her palms. Lately Josh has ignored their rules, tested her patience, and pushed the boundaries she's set to keep him safe.

He grimaces. "My phone's dead."

"You didn't charge it last night?" That's a hard, fast rule between them.

The school bell rings, the noise jarring. She can hear that darn bell from their house five blocks away.

"No, I didn't," he grumbles, standing.

"Why not?"

"I forgot." He shoulders his backpack. Anson does the same, looking guilty he's been caught in the middle of their squabble. Josh starts to back away. "Can I go now?"

"If you'd remembered to charge your phone and answered it, I wouldn't have had to grace you with my presence."

Josh's face reddens. "Mom, stop." He backs away faster. She gives him a warning look he knows too well. She'll ground him after school if his attitude continues. "Fine. Sorry. I'll charge my phone tonight."

"Have a good day, Ms. Mason."

"You too, Anson." She smiles at Josh's friend.

Anson jogs to catch up with Josh. They bump shoulders, laughing, and she feels a pang of jealousy with a brutal stab of remorse. She hasn't had a friend like Anson since she was sixteen. Her friend died the night she ran away from home.

And whose fault is that?

Bile coats her mouth like soured cream, foul and rotten. She shoves the thought aside, visualizes it dissipating. But it'll be back. Always reminding her what she's done. Always proving she's no better than her mother.

Heading home, Jenna makes it halfway across the parking lot before Leigh steps in her way. The move is sudden, and Jenna slams into her.

"I was hoping to bump into you on your way back," Leigh says.

Jenna squints at the parents' club secretary, wondering what she could want with her. Then she remembers the bits of conversation she picked up earlier and the way she and Beth had been watching her. *Aggressive reporter. Chasing a lead.* A nervous flutter behind her ribs takes flight.

Leigh's swimming pool–blue eyes are bright and her smile wickedly wide. The tip of her tongue touches the end of her incisor as her *Flashdance*-inspired sweatshirt slips off her right shoulder. She crosses her arms over her chest, pressing up her breasts, and wiggles her shoulders as if she can't contain her news. Leigh always thinks she has something delicious to share.

"Is it true?" she asks, trimmed brows lifting high.

Jenna frowns, searching for an escape route, the desire to flee fiercely beating the back of her neck. "Is what true?"

Leigh tilts her head, giving Jenna a look as if Jenna should know exactly what Leigh is talking about.

"Word on the street is that you murdered a sixteen-year-old kid."

CHAPTER 2

Jenna flinches as if Leigh slapped her. "What?"

"It's true, isn't it?" Leigh moves into her personal space, and Jenna fears her horrified reaction reveals all. *It's true!* Excitement radiates off Leigh. She doesn't care whether Jenna responds one way or the other. Jenna could have stolen a Cézanne watercolor from the J. Paul Getty Museum in broad daylight and Leigh would be bursting at the seams. She loves a good story.

The urge to put some distance between herself and Leigh clambers up her leg like a cat climbing a tree, digging in its claws. She needs to run. But she has nowhere to go. Cars block her on both sides. Behind her, Beth and Sherry close in to listen. She's trapped. Her breath comes in short bursts. She usually isn't this careless. She tracks the news, keeps tabs on the people who are after her. But between the publicity surrounding the deals for her animated cartoon, Josh's recent rebellious streak, and Kavan's marriage proposal last Friday, she's been distracted. She let her guard down when they settled here. She falsely believed they'd be safe. Her identity was solid.

How was she exposed?

A shiver slithers down her spine as awareness crystallizes. She's been naive, overconfident of their security. She never should have let Josh convince her to stay here as long as they have.

Leigh's gaze flicks over Jenna's shoulder. "Tell us. We want to know."

How in the world did they learn about Wes? How did they connect him to her?

For thirteen years she's been one step ahead of her past. But she fears that with what Leigh is about to tell her, her past has finally caught up. Tapping her on the shoulder. The same shoulder she stopped looking over because she'd grown complacent.

Jenna's pulse pounds in her ears. "Of course it's not true." *Wes drowned. I wasn't there.* Her mantra since Murielle, the woman who took her under her wing, ingrained it in her head all those years ago.

"That's not what Beth said."

Jenna looks at the woman behind her. Beth dodges eye contact and ducks into her car. She backs up quickly, forcing Sherry to jump out of the way, and leaving Jenna wondering what *exactly* she does know.

"Beth!" Sherry squeals. She slaps the hood.

"Beth told us in confidence," Leigh says. "She's not supposed to talk about it until the article drops tomorrow, but Sherry already posted about it in the parents' group."

The school falls away into the background. Voices fade until it's just her and Leigh. "What article?"

"No idea, but I'm dying to read it. Oops, poor word choice. My bad." She touches Jenna's arm with a high-pitched giggle. "Did you do any time? Don't answer that. I'll look up the case," she says when Jenna's vision blurs along the edges. The parking lot starts to spin.

Leigh leans in. They're practically nose to nose. Her voice drops to a whisper. "I listened to this crime podcast the other day. They say people have a genetic predisposition to kill. Should we be worried about your son? He does hang out with ours." Concern ripples across her face.

Jenna's heard of Leigh, how she shoots off at the mouth, unaware of how offensive she is. But her expression and the underlying tension in her voice tell Jenna enough. She thinks of her mom, what Charlotte did. She thinks of herself and what she's capable of, what she had been running from up until eighteen months ago, when she moved here.

She then thinks of her son, and what Leigh is insinuating. Josh wouldn't hurt a fly.

She needs to know more about this article. What paper? Who is the reporter talking to Beth? She hardly knows the woman. She needs to call her publicist, Gayle Pierson. Have her convince the publication to pull the article before her identity hits the wires.

A minivan pulls up behind Leigh, horn blaring. With a shriek, Leigh whirls around.

"Dammit, Keely. You about gave me a heart attack," Leigh snaps.

The passenger window slides down, and Anson's mom leans across the seat. Jenna likes Keely. Of the women who have approached Jenna at school functions, Keely is the only one that Jenna has taken to. The closest person she'd consider calling a friend aside from her fiancé since she's moved here. Keely is transparent. She has nothing to hide and says exactly what's on her mind. There's no bullshit about her. Coming from someone who swims in it, who's been hiding and chronically lying half her life, Jenna finds Keely absolutely refreshing.

And this morning she might be a lifesaver.

"Morning, Leigh. I see you forgot your galoshes," Keely quips.

Leigh looks at her sparkling-white Nikes. "What are you talking about?"

"You're walking in other people's shit again." Keely's smile is sugary sweet. She shifts her gaze to Jenna. "Need a lift?"

Yeah, she does, desperately so. She ran to Josh's school. It was quicker than fighting for a parking spot. But the sooner she can get home, the faster she and Josh can disappear.

"Excuse me." She nudges Leigh aside.

"You're leaving?" Leigh asks.

"Uh, yeah." She slides into the front seat and shuts the door.

Keely flips off Leigh and exits the parking lot.

"Thank you," Jenna says over her mounting dread. What is happening here? She ran away from home to escape her parents. She changed her name to hide from the police. And she constantly relocated to evade

7

Ryder, Wes's older brother, who tracked her up until four years ago, when he was sentenced to prison for domestic violence.

She looks back at the school as Keely drives away. Her knee-jerk reaction is to run, and briefly she considers yanking Josh from class. He'll fight her. She promised they wouldn't move again. He doesn't want to return to that life, relocating every six months, sometimes less, leaving friends behind, losing a favorite toy or game along the way because Jenna neglected to pack it. It wasn't an essential item.

And she's beyond tired of that life, too. She doesn't want to go back to it. But if that reporter has connected her to Wes, then he knows who she is. He knows what she did.

She's been exposed. She doesn't have a choice.

She takes a long breath, forces her erratic heart to slow. She needs information; then she can assess the damage and decide what to do. "What's going on with them?"

Keely's smile is sympathetic. "That's right. I forgot. You're not on social media. How much do you know?"

She assumes Keely's talking about the article Leigh mentioned. "Hardly anything."

"Whatever you do, don't read the thread on the parents' club Facebook group." She waves her hand in the space between them like she's trying to wipe away whatever's been posted.

"What are people saying?" she asks, fearing the worst. All she's run from, everything she's tried to keep hidden . . . it's all coming to light.

Keely looks reluctant to share. "You know how it is. Someone posts a snippet of gossip, and it festers into a big negative mess before the moderator can get in there and screen the comments. It's probably been deleted already. It isn't school related, so Sherry shouldn't have posted in the first place. She's the parents' club VP. She knows better." She signals left and turns onto Jenna's street.

"Beth told Leigh about the article. What have you heard?" She wonders how serious this is. Exactly what information about her is out there?

"There's a reporter with the *Oceanside Sentinel* poking around. He's young, but he's hungry. Like super, gobble-gobble hungry." She takes her hand off the wheel and Pac-Man chomps the air. "He caught me in my driveway yesterday evening after grocery shopping. He knocked on the car window. Scared the crap out of me. I would have been a lot nicer if he'd waited until I got out of the car. He obviously got to Beth. I expect he spoke to a few other parents, too."

Thick, viscous nausea sloshes in her stomach like a toddler running with a bucket of mud. Who is this reporter? What's his sudden interest in her? How much does he know, or is he just fishing?

She needs to cut that line. The urge to run burns through her, but so does her promise to Josh. There has to be a chance to salvage this situation. Or maybe she's just fooling herself. She'll have to walk away from her career, her home. Kavan.

Oh god, Kavan. Her heart is breaking already. She'll have to leave him, too.

"What did he ask you about me?" she cautiously inquires.

"The usual stuff at first. What I thought about your cartoon. Had I watched it? Was I happy for you about the movie deal? He asked how we met and about our boys being friends. That's when the alarm bells went off. Ding, ding, ding. How does he know about our kids? Who told him? Is he following them? I'll make sure his ass is grass if he's stalking my boy. He then asked me . . . uh-oh." Keely stops in front of Jenna's townhouse, a two-story modern stucco two blocks from the beach Jenna never could have leased if it weren't for *Tabby's Squirrel's* success and her attorney's signature. The lease is under her attorney's name: Samantha "Sam" Brooks.

"That's him," Keely ruefully growls.

Jenna looks out her window. Seated on the steps leading up to her narrow porch is a young man barely in his twenties. He's the same man who knocked on Jenna's door yesterday evening. She didn't answer. She thought he was a solicitor who ignored the NO SOLICITING sign clearly displayed in the door's side window.

He notices them immediately. With a wave, he stands and smiles. Golden-brown hair falls in his face, but he quickly sweeps it off his forehead with blunt fingers. Sunglasses hang from the collar of his white crew shirt. Unfaltering strides bring him closer to the car.

"Go," Jenna whispers, then louder. "Go!"

Keely slams her foot on the gas. The car lurches forward, and she pulls away from the curb. "I take it you don't want to talk to him."

Jenna shakes her head, her mind reeling, emotions chaotic.

"Don't blame you. He's an arse." Keely gently touches Jenna's arm, and she flinches. "He's not following us. You can let go of the door now."

Jenna peels her fingers off the door handle. She stretches her fingers, easing the ache from gripping so tightly.

Keely peeks at her. "You okay?"

She is far from okay. "How long do you think he'll be there?"

"Doesn't matter. You're coming home with me. I'll make coffee. You can stay as long as you like."

Jenna hates talking. The more she talks, the more people want to know about her. But this is Anson's mom, and Anson is Josh's best friend. Keely's invited Jenna for dinner more than once. She's made it clear she wants to be friends, and right now Jenna could use one.

"Okay," she agrees, praying the reporter gives up on her and leaves.

What if he doesn't? What if he pursues her until she answers his burning question?

Did she kill Wes Jensen?

10

CHAPTER 3

LILY

Lily's gaze wandered over the small selection of pregnancy tests at the 7-Eleven where she worked twice a week. She couldn't tell which brand was best. What if one said she was pregnant, but she wasn't? What if the test showed she wasn't, but it was wrong?

Her hand unconsciously fluttered to her flat belly, tight from years of competitive swim. If there was a baby in there, he was hers. Someone who would love her unconditionally. She'd never known a love like that, not even from her parents. They tacked conditions on everything like price tags on merchandise.

She could call her sister, Olivia, and ask, but they weren't close like they were when they were younger. Or like Wes was with his older brother, Ryder. They shared everything. She couldn't remember the last time she shared anything with Oliva. Before she moved out, she wouldn't let Lily near her stuff, and the only reason Lily could think of that might have caused Olivia to push her away was their dad. Several years back he started blaming Lily for ruining Olivia's things.

Once, Olivia found her prom dress muddied and hidden in their deceased grandmother's chest in the attic above the garage. Lily swore she saw their dad outside her window with something blue and glittery like Olivia's dress. But Dwight denied he'd taken the dress from Olivia's closet and dragged it through the mud before hiding it. He did blame Lily, though; said she was jealous of her sister. He was convincing enough that Olivia believed him. Olivia thought Lily was a chronic liar. And now that Olivia had moved to San Francisco for college, they'd hardly talked, except once when Lily called her. She wanted to move in with her. Lucas had moved out of the house to the apartment above the garage. She was alone with their parents. She didn't have a car, and she didn't want their father to know she was working. It would only invite his attention. Olivia could do no wrong, while Lily did everything wrong.

Dwight also didn't approve of her doing anything that cost him money, so she paid for her own swim equipment. Some days, she paid for her own meals. Her mom worked an ungodly number of hours, always eating out, and her dad would leave on business trips for weeks at a time. They didn't always remember to stock the kitchen with groceries. Lily had no choice but to work because it came down to this: she was the unplanned, unwanted child of a nuclear family that was perfect until she came along.

It explained Dwight's preferential treatment of her siblings over her. Though sometimes when Dwight did something really nasty, like the prom-dress incident, Lily wondered if there was something more behind his sabotaging her childhood and relationships.

Olivia refused to let Lily move in with her. Her apartment didn't have room for a third person. So Lily was stuck living in a home where she didn't feel loved or wanted.

The bell above the entrance chimed, and Lily spun around to face a shelf stuffed with tampons and pads. The product hardly turned over. People didn't buy feminine products here unless it was a late-night emergency run.

Lily watched the new customer beeline to the drink fridges in back, relieved he hadn't cut through her aisle. Kids from school came here all the time. What if it had been someone she knew? Better they thought her period started rather than spread rumors that Lily Carson got herself knocked up.

God, she wished she were having her period. But she was late, like, really late. Her cycles hadn't come in almost three months, and she couldn't believe she only realized that this morning. But it had been just one time, she argued, thinking back to the night she lost her virginity.

Okay, they'd had sex more than once. She and Tyler had slept together at least ten times since her first time. Yes, she was still counting. But they'd gotten much better at it—sex and putting on a condom. And she enjoyed sex with him. Like, enjoyed it a lot. Tyler adored her. He freely gave her the compassion and attention she sought. The comfort and reassurance her parents withheld from her. With him, she was content. But their first time together? If felt weird and gross and amazing all at once. They were clumsy, all awkward kissing and elbows in eyeballs and legs fumbling as they took off their clothes in the back of Tyler's car. Then the blasted condom had torn. Of course, they didn't realize that until after the fact, when Tyler went to remove it.

He'd been so upset, worried he'd hurt her. Ashamed he'd screwed up. There had been a lot of blood, and he swore he'd practiced putting on the condom. But he'd never rolled one on in front of her, and he'd been nervous. Since then they'd been overly cautious, so it never crossed her mind they'd made a baby.

"Shit!"

Bottles crashed in the back of the market, glass shattering on the linoleum floor. Lily peeked over the shelving. The customer who'd just entered stood in a puddle of broken Snapples. Lily cowered at the mess, her gaze shooting toward the back, where Ryder had gone to take a break.

This was her fault. She'd just stocked those shelves. Now he'd have that excuse he'd been looking for to fire her. She was a reluctant hire, unnecessary, according to Ryder. He hated her for reasons she didn't understand. She always caught him staring at her, only for him to look away when she'd notice. Wes had pleaded with him to give her a job and keep tight-lipped about it. She needed to earn money to remain on the swim team. She needed cash for when she and Tyler moved away after she graduated. They'd go to San Francisco like Olivia. Or maybe they'd go south, live near the beach.

The double doors to the stockroom flew open. Ryder scanned the floor, searching for the source of the disturbance. Customer guy jumped away from the fridge, hands raised, one empty, the other gripping a Snapple.

"Not my fault," he said, standing in an iced-tea puddle. He shook liquid off his shoes. "I just wanted a drink. Whoever stocked this put way too many bottles on the shelf."

Lily thought she'd been quite ingenious. She'd arranged the entire supply delivered that morning. But of course, customer guy had to grab a bottle from the back of the fridge, where they were the coldest.

"Carson," Ryder shouted, and she cringed.

Snagging the first pregnancy test within reach because she wouldn't have another chance to stash it without being noticed, she dropped the test kit into her apron pocket and rounded the aisle endcap. Guilt over lifting the merchandise put a bitter taste in her mouth. She wasn't her brother, who showed no remorse when he stole. She'd ring up the purchase when Ryder wasn't around.

"My shoes are ruined," the customer complained, shaking his feet.

Lily would have rolled her eyes if she weren't afraid Ryder would fire her or rat her out to her dad. They were canvas sneakers. Wash them and they'd dry. But she didn't tell him that, because "the customer is always right," blah, blah, blah, as Ryder had drilled into her. He'd sit across from her at the break-room table prattling on about how she should handle an unsatisfied customer while staring at her boobs the entire time. He never made eye contact. The creep.

"I'm not paying for this." Customer guy gestured at the mess.

Ryder grabbed a second Snapple from the fridge, one of the last bottles standing, because the shelf had collapsed, and handed it over.

"On the house, both of them," he said, pointing at the bottle in the guy's other hand.

The customer blinked at the gift. "Thanks, man." He took the drinks and left the market.

Ryder turned to her, fists propped on narrow hips. He shook his head. "You have got to be the dumbest employee I've ever hired. Could you not see that you overstocked the shelves?"

She looked at the mess on the linoleum floor. No, this wasn't the first time. "I stocked them exactly like you taught me," she mumbled.

"You can't have the bases hanging over the lip of the shelf. They'll fall." He pointed at the shelf above the Snapples to prove his point, and Lily's posture folded. She was trying to be efficient, but she couldn't finagle her way out of this one.

"You'd be out that door five seconds ago if you weren't Wes's friend."

The things Ryder did for his brother. He loved and respected him in a way Lily wished Olivia and Lucas did with her. But Lucas had returned a different person after serving time in juvie for holding up a minimart. Gone were his smirks, the pranks she loved. Their friendship, too. He wanted nothing to do with her. He wanted nothing to do with anyone. And Olivia? Well, she just thought of Lily as that pesky little sister who ruined her stuff, even though it wasn't true.

"One hour, Lily May Carson." She hated when he used her full name. Make her throw up already. "Clean it or I dock the lost stock from your pay," he ordered.

"You can't do that." The entire fridge was a mess. Iced tea had sprayed everywhere. She'd have to empty the fridge; wipe down bottles, shelves, and the glass door; and restock the section in addition to cleaning the floor. Her shift was up in an hour, and that was hardly enough time.

"One hour," Ryder bit out, ambling toward the checkout counter. "Mop and bucket are in the back."

She knew where they were.

Lily groaned with frustration, shook with embarrassment, but she cleaned without further complaint. She couldn't afford the lost wages. She barely earned enough as it was. Ryder took over behind the counter, helping customers in her absence. She finished just as her ride home arrived.

Ethan Miller was Olivia's boyfriend. He'd taken the semester off from USC to help his mom, who was at home recovering from an accident. He'd seen Lily walking home in the dark one night after work several weeks back and offered to drive her, knowing her dad would flip if he found out she had a job. He insisted on driving her home after every shift. He'd never forgive himself if something happened to her.

Lily liked Ethan. He treated her better than her family, and he seemed genuinely interested in her well-being. He respected her. Unlike Olivia, he noticed how differently Dwight treated Lily compared to her older sister. Olivia preferred to live her life in a shiny bubble. She was Dwight's princess and could do no wrong.

"Catch, Lil." Ethan grabbed a shopping basket and tossed her his keys. "I have to pick up a few things for my mom. You can wait in the car if you want. I'll be out in a few."

He knew she hated lingering at the market longer than she had to. She couldn't stand the smell of the fake nacho cheese simmering in the warming pot or the hot dogs rolling on a rack under a heat lamp. The smells were especially foul today, and she almost threw up twice. But the nausea had been constantly in the background for a couple of weeks. She'd been feeling queasy a lot lately, and her boobs ached. Two reasons that she wondered if she was pregnant.

She snagged Ethan's keys midair and went to wait in his truck. The cab smelled of worn leather and the spearmint gum he always chewed. The seats were still warm from the heater. She removed her apron with the pregnancy test tucked inside and stuffed it into her backpack. The driver's-side door flew open, startling her, and Tyler slid into Ethan's seat.

Lily's heart leapt at the sight of him. "What are you doing here?" She glanced out the back window, afraid they'd be seen together. She worried word would reach Dwight. Her parents wouldn't allow her to date until she was eighteen.

"My mom—" He stopped abruptly and dragged a hand down his face. He looked wiped.

"Not a good day?"

He shook his head. His mom was dying of lymphoma. She was in hospice with in-home care, but with his older brother, Blaze, away in the army, most of the responsibilities around the house fell on his shoulders.

Tyler was two years older than her, eighteen to her sixteen. They'd met when she was three and she'd sworn she fell in love with him the first summer she and her siblings stayed with their family at their lakeside cabin. The Carson kids returned each summer until that last summer eight years ago, when Lucas was caught shoplifting, and her dad somehow twisted the incident until he thought only Lily was to blame. He was convinced the toy car Lucas lifted was for her. That she'd begged him for it, pressured him to steal, even threw a tantrum. Lucas stole to shut her up.

Like everything else Dwight accused her of, it couldn't be further from the truth. But neither of her siblings came to her defense. Lucas tried, but when their dad threatened to ground him until school started, he backed off. And Olivia didn't say anything at all, even though all three of them knew Lucas was entirely to blame for ruining their summer. Their dad picked them up from the lake house three weeks before they were scheduled to leave, and they weren't invited back the next summer. But by then the Whitmans had divorced, and within a few years, Mr. Whitman died of a heart attack and Mrs. Whitman was diagnosed with lymphoma.

She missed those summers. The Whitmans were better parents to her than her own. They treated her as if she were part of their family.

"I had to get out of the house." Tyler pulled her into his arms, Lily's favorite place to be. "I needed to see you." It had been almost two weeks. Tyler had been busy with his mom and school. Lily had been busy with swim and work. He nuzzled her neck and hugged her fiercely.

"I've missed you," she said, looking over his shoulder. Through the store window, she could see Ethan talking to Ryder at the checkout counter. Her friendship with Tyler was public knowledge, but not their romance, which blossomed as they had, growing into their adult bodies. If her dad knew Tyler meant as much to her as he did, breaking them up would become his new pastime.

Dwight was always taking from her, blaming her, belittling her, as if his life's mission were to suck up her happiness. And Tyler made her happier than she'd ever felt in her sixteen years.

In that moment, she almost told him she thought she might be pregnant. But she could be wrong, and she didn't want to worry him. She'd wait for the test result.

Tyler's lips found hers, and she melted into him. Almost. She broke off the kiss within seconds, putting her forehead against his. Their breathing was heavy, their breaths mingling. "You have to go."

His hands glided up her neck, cupping her face. His fingers worked their way into her hair. "I don't want to."

"I know."

"When can I see you?"

"Sunday." Her dad was scheduled to leave that morning for a business trip. He'd be gone the entire week. "I'll meet you at two in the usual spot."

The bus stop was a block from her house. If anyone spotted her, nothing would look out of the ordinary. She knew how to drive. She had her license. But her dad forbade her from using the spare car. It was a waste of gas money, and Dwight insisted the car remain available for his use, like when his car was in the shop. He gloated that it sat unused in the driveway like a sweet treat in the cupboard, luring her to eat it.

Lily was sure he wanted to catch her using the car so he'd have an excuse to punish her. Another reason to keep her home and not wasting his resources, as he once told her. So instead, Lily took the bus unless she could get a ride from a friend, anyone but Tyler.

Tyler was hers, and she'd do anything to protect what she had with him.

"Sunday. Can't wait." He kissed her and leapt from the truck, shutting the door behind him. Lily felt the emptiness of his departure in his lingering scent and the ghost of his kiss on her lips. She missed him already.

A few minutes passed, and Ethan settled into the seat Tyler had just vacated. "Sorry about that." He inserted the key Lily had left in the cupholder and started the engine.

"That's okay." She didn't mind. It gave her a few stolen moments with Tyler.

On the drive home, Ethan asked about her day, and she told him about the mess she had to clean up. Other than that, Ethan didn't talk much, and that was fine with her. He parked the truck a block from her house as they'd agreed and left the engine idling. He didn't like letting her out at the corner. He always dropped Olivia off in front and would wait until she walked through the door.

She saw him hesitate. He wanted to argue.

"I'll be fine," she said. She didn't mind the short walk.

She thanked him for the ride and jumped down from the truck's cab, reaching for her backpack. The shoulder strap snagged on the seat-adjustment lever, and the apron fell out. The pregnancy test dropped into the foot well.

Lily's gaze flew from the test kit to Ethan. His darted to the floor before rising to meet hers. His mouth parted.

Her face flamed. "Don't ask," she said before he could say anything. She wouldn't talk about it.

She buried the test in her backpack.

Ethan reached for her. "Wait. Are you—" He stopped, dragging a hand over his head. "Who's the guy?"

She shook her head, not wanting to tell him. If he knew, he might tell Olivia, who would definitely tell their parents.

"He'd better not bail on you."

"He's a good man. I love him."

"Is he going to help you?"

She looked at the ground and Ethan swore.

"He doesn't know yet, and neither do I." She hadn't taken the darn test yet.

"You'll tell me if you are."

She didn't say anything.

"Lily." He dragged out her name. "I want to help."

How in the world would he do that without her family finding out?

"Thanks, but I got this." She did everything on her own. She couldn't rely on anyone but herself.

"Does Olivia know?"

Lily didn't even know. And she wasn't going to call her sister. Olivia would help, but her version of helping meant getting their mom involved, who would then share the news with their dad.

"Call her, Lily, or I will." He trusted Olivia to keep her secret. Lily, unfortunately, didn't share his faith in her.

Just because Ethan was five years older than her didn't mean he could order her around like a child.

"Don't tell her," she pleaded, panicked. "Please, Ethan, you can't tell anyone."

His mouth drew into a hard line. "You can't do this on your own."

She wouldn't. She had Tyler.

"My body. My life," she said with force, hoping she sounded more confident than she felt. "You can't tell me what to do. And please, please, *please* don't tell Olivia. I will when the time is right, *if* I am pregnant. Promise," she added when he didn't say anything.

His jaw tightened. "Give me your word you'll see me if you need anything. I mean it, Lily. Anything."

Was he telling her without telling her that he'd stand in for Tyler if Tyler abandoned her, which he wouldn't ever do? Tyler wasn't like that. He owned his responsibilities, almost to a fault.

Lily nodded, wiping her eyes. "I will."

"All right." Ethan pushed back into his seat and released the truck's parking brake. "Take care of yourself, Lil."

No problem there. She'd been fending for herself longer than she could remember. Self-preservation was a Carson family trait.

Lily shut the door and walked home. She went straight to the bathroom.

Her fingers trembled as she unwrapped both sticks and followed the instructions, peeing on each. She set them on the counter.

Then she waited.

CHAPTER 4

Keely Lawrence's house is a single-story ranch a quarter mile from the kids' school. She parks in the garage, and Jenna follows her through the laundry room and into a kitchen ripe with scents of a bacon-and-egg breakfast.

Jenna folds her arms over her chest, anxious to call Gayle, to get home. For that reporter to leave.

"I have to make a call." She shows Keely her phone and strides to the glass slider overlooking the backyard for privacy. She calls Gayle and is immediately dumped in voice mail. She fires off a text. Call me!!!!!

"Any luck?" Keely drops her purse and keys on a counter crowded with unopened mail and clothing catalogs. She flips on the lights and rinses the coffee carafe.

Jenna shakes her head.

Keely nods at the stools under the kitchen island. "Have a seat."

"I can't stay." She needs to start packing, put everything in motion so they're ready to leave.

"Nonsense. We'll give that guy a chance to leave, then I'll drive you home." Keely slides the carafe onto the hot pad.

Jenna forgoes the stool and paces the kitchen. Nervous energy vibrates throughout her. She can't go to Kavan's restaurant. It's too public. The reporter could find her there. And she can't go home, not yet. She could have Keely drive her to Kavan's condo, but it isn't much better than waiting out the reporter and Gayle's call from Keely's. If anything, she's safer waiting him out here, especially if he knows she's engaged to Kavan. Nervous energy vibrates through her. She cracks her knuckles, all ten of them.

Keely tears the lid off of a large plastic container. "Scone? Lemon poppyseed. I baked them this morning."

The pastries smell divine. "I shouldn't . . ." She cracks her wrists.

"Please, I insist." Keely shoves the container toward her with a sanguine smile.

"All right," she relents, if only to keep her hands busy before she breaks a finger.

Keely plates a scone and warms it in the microwave before setting it in front of Jenna. A ribbon of steam rises from the glazed topping. She barely has a chance to enjoy the first bite when Keely grasps her hand.

"I heard the news. Anson told me. Congratulations." Keely grins, eyeing the diamond ring on Jenna's finger. "Goodness, you're shaking." Her gaze lifts to Jenna's.

"Just a little anxious."

"Then let's talk about Kavan. When did he propose, last week?"

"Friday." Jenna stares at the ring Kavan slipped on her finger as if seeing it for the first time. She isn't used to it. It still surprises her when the gem catches the light.

After she went into hiding, she never envisioned getting married. Never thought she'd have the chance. It wasn't easy meeting people when she moved every six months. But then Kavan came into her life quite unexpectedly. She wasn't looking for anyone, but she wouldn't change running into him. She loves him. She wants to marry him.

But he'll drop her in a heartbeat if he learns the truth about her. That article could kill their marriage before it happens. It could destroy the life she's been building for her and Josh. A normal life, not one on the run.

Though it's a life built on lies.

Kavan will have questions. So will Josh. They'll challenge what she's told them.

She shivers at the thought that she's been exposed, and Keely notices. "Are you cold? I can turn on the heat."

It's June. Jenna forces a smile, her hand still in Keely's. Another shocker. Outside of Kavan and Josh, human touch is a rarity. Something she didn't have for many years that contributed to her brutal loneliness. Keely's warm fingers hold hers, and she relishes the contact.

"I'm fine," she says smoothly despite the hurricane roaring inside her.

Keely angles Jenna's hand so the diamonds catch the light. There are three, each a half carat. *Yours*, *mine*, and Kavan's hoping one day, *ours*. Kavan's almost ten years older than her, but his daughter is two years younger than Josh. Uma's a sweet girl who splits her time between parents. She's also become quite taken with Jenna. When you create a cartoon that appeals to kids as much as adults, you are a fascination. People like Jenna because they've fallen in love with her characters. But the feeling with Uma is mutual. Jenna adores her. She once dreamed of having a large family of her own, one where the parents loved their children as much as Kavan cherishes his daughter. She wouldn't mind having a child with him. She'd feel lucky to have the chance.

After this morning, she doubts she'll get one. She already feels the loss.

Keely settles on the stool beside her. "Where did he propose? What did he say? I want to know everything," she says as if they've been the best of friends for years. As if Jenna has all the time in the world.

Her gaze darts to the microwave clock. She can't imagine that reporter lingering too long at her house. On the other hand, he's desperate for her story. He works for a small-town paper. If he connects her dots, it'll be career-making.

"It was at his restaurant, and he invited his family," she summarizes in a rush.

"He proposed in front of his parents?"

"And his sisters, and their families, and Uma, his daughter. He even got Josh involved." And Jenna loves that he did. Josh wants a family as much as she does. A life full of friends, a house that belongs to them. A father.

"That sneaky man. Josh didn't spill the beans? Anson would have blabbed the moment he found out."

Jenna shakes her head, still shocked Josh didn't let her in on Kavan's plan. He doesn't keep secrets from her. "I had no idea he was going to propose," she says, recalling how happy she'd felt on Friday, wondering if she'll feel that way again.

Under the twinkle lights on the patio of his beachfront café, Thalassa, Kavan popped the question in front of his family and friends. Josh stood beside her wearing one of the biggest grins she's seen on him. Her hesitation was brief. Does she want to be married? Could she be married? Yes, she said. But could she sustain the illusion of who she was—a woman who ran away sixteen and pregnant because her parents wouldn't let her keep her baby; a woman who frequently moved; a woman estranged from her family? For that is all Kavan knows.

Yes, she convinced herself. He makes her happy, and after years of being lonely and alone she isn't ready to let that go. She'd make it work. She'd take Kavan's name, keep it separate from her public one.

She should have considered how easily her past could find her. How quickly she could bring danger to Kavan and his daughter, Uma, a girl she couldn't wait to call a daughter of her own.

She's grown selfish and sloppy, cocooned in an illusion of security since they moved here.

"When's the wedding?" Keely's enthusiasm lures Jenna back to the warm scents of her kitchen.

"We haven't picked a date yet," she says, again glancing at the time. Twenty minutes since they left the school. She points at Keely's phone resting facedown within reach, trying to play it cool so Keely doesn't sense Jenna's urgency and ask questions Jenna won't answer. "Is the post still up?" she asks.

"Let me check." Keely taps the screen. Her gaze scans down, eyes widening. "I can't believe it. It's still up. Admin should have deleted it by now."

Jenna's muscles tighten as if she's getting ready to run. The longer that post is up, the more people will see it. "May I?" She doesn't have access to social media on her phone, and she isn't a member of the Facebook group.

Keely presses the phone against her ample bosom. "Are you sure?"

Jenna nods. She needs to know what she's up against.

Keely gives her the phone, and she reads Sherry's post.

There's a reporter from the Oceanside Sentinel asking questions about Jenna Mason. He's talked to me and Beth Hopkins. Anyone else? He believes Jenna murdered a kid when she was sixteen. What do you guys think about that? Should we do anything? I don't know about you, but I'm a little uneasy. Her son hangs out with mine.

Jenna's stomach churns.

"I told you it was bad," Keely commiserates.

It isn't anything worse than some of the comments that follow.

Tess White: Who is Jenna Mason?

Sherry Matters: Josh Mason's mom. He's in seventh grade.

Hal Jacobsen: My daughter Ellie has him in her math class. She says he's nice to her.

Tess White: He's the son of a murderer! What if he's like his mom? I hear it can be genetic.

Ally Danvers: Give me a break, Tess. 🙄 He's just a kid.

Tess White: So was Jenna when she killed that boy.

Hal Jacobsen: Fake news. Do we know she killed him? Anyone have proof? @BethHopkins, you need to delete this. It's against group policy, not to mention slanderous. That reporter should be fired.

Mandy Roberts: Josh hangs out with the stoners by the pier. Watch out, he's going to be trouble.

Hal Jacobsen: Hey, Sherry, isn't your kid in the stoner group?

Sherry Matters: FU Hal. Like I said, I'm not comfortable about this whole situation.

Tess White: Should we do something like @SherryMatters asks? Maybe we should report this to administration.

Ally Danvers: You can't hold a child responsible for their parents' actions, people. Josh hasn't done anything wrong. FWIW, we don't know if Jenna has either.

The comments go on, many attacking Josh's character. Jenna feels sick. Heat flushes her body as she glares at the screen. "Are they always like this?" Utterly vicious. Jenna hasn't done anything to them. Nor has Josh. The nerve of them turning this on him. It was her mistake, not her son's. And, oh my gosh, what's Josh going to do when he finds out about this? Because he will. Kids will talk.

He'll know why she's making them leave. He'll assume she's guilty.

She's dreaded him discovering what she did to Wes or finding out what her own mother did to Jenna's biological father. Benton St. John was their neighbor, and Charlotte murdered him—stabbed him eight times—before Jenna was born. Josh will despise her as much as she detests Charlotte, and Jenna couldn't bear that.

At least a couple of parents came to her defense, stating that the reporter doesn't have proof. But her name is already out there. Another parent attached a link to an article about Wes that Jenna read over a decade ago. It mentions Lily Carson. She resists clicking on the link. She knows what it says. She ran away the night Wes died. Police had asked the public for more information on her.

Gayle still hasn't returned Jenna's call, though she can't see how this can be contained. It's a small community. People whisper, and whispers turn into shouts. It could reach the Seaside Cove Police Department.

Jenna is shaking when she gives Keely her phone. She wants the post removed immediately. "How do I delete it?"

"You can't. Only the admin or moderators can."

"Who runs the group?"

"Beth Hopkins. She's the parents' club president."

Jenna knows who she is. The woman fled the scene as soon as Leigh called her out in the parking lot. "Do you have her number?"

Keely smiles, her eyes sparkling. "I do. Let's give her a call. She knows me. She won't give us a fuss. We'll insist she take that shit down." She smacks the countertop.

"Thank you."

Keely pats her hand. "It'll be okay. We'll fix this. Like I mentioned earlier, gals like us need to stick together against vipers like Leigh and Sherry, and half the parents out there."

A ripple of surprise rolls through her, and Jenna understands why Keely gravitated to her. Leigh and Sherry *are* vipers, and they must have struck Keely. She's been singled out, shunned from their noninclusive group. Keely really was looking for a friend, an ally, and she hoped to find that in Jenna since their sons are close.

Keely calls Beth. "Beth, honey, it's Keely. How are you? Good, glad to hear. I'm not doing so well. I'm a little upset, to be honest. Yes, it's about the post. A lot of people are messaging you? I'm not surprised. Uh-huh. Uh-huh. I agree, the discussion has been lively, but it's slanderous. There isn't proof that Jenna is that Lily girl or that she killed that boy. Parents are attacking her son, and that blatantly goes against the group's rules and school policy. Uh-huh, uh-huh." Keely nods, listening to Beth. She looks at Jenna and rolls her eyes. She covers the mic on the phone and whispers, "She's shopping at Hobby Lobby.

"Tell you what, Beth. How about you set down that beach-scented candle, park your shopping cart, and delete the post before more damage is done or I report you to the school administrators and insist they remove you from your position. Perfect. Thank you."

Keely ends the call and checks Facebook. "She's deleting the post as we speak."

"She isn't the brightest tool in the shed, is she?"

"Unfortunately, common sense isn't a prerequisite when you run for office. And voilà! It's gone." She sets down her phone and Jenna explodes off the stool, surprising them both. She can't sit here any longer.

"I have to go."

"Oh!" Keely's eyes widen to saucers. "Are you sure? That psycho reporter might still be there."

She'll take her chances. "I have to work. Deadlines," she excuses, her mind tallying what they have to pack and where everything is in the house.

Keely's eyes light up. "That's right. You have a movie to make. I heard you're writing the screenplay. How exciting. Josh must be proud of you. Oh, coffee. I got so caught up in our conversation that I forgot. Let me pour you a to-go cup."

She starts to decline, but Keely is already digging out a wide-mouthed Hydro Flask. "How do you take it? Cream, sugar?"

"Black, thank you." Add-ins are luxuries she once couldn't afford and has since found they're an acquired taste she hasn't quite latched on to. She fears if she gets used to her wealth and stability, she'll lose everything. Her success, her money. The people she loves. It's a constant battle, the desire to have a normal life while believing she doesn't deserve one.

She fears she's lost it already.

Keely pours the coffee and screws on the top. "On loan," she says, giving Jenna the flask. "It'll give you an excuse to visit again when you return it."

"You're too kind."

Keely scribbles on a pad of paper and rips off the top piece. "Here's my number. Call if you need anything. Sugar, Netflix buddy, chitchat. I'm serious, you can talk to me about anything."

Her offer is heartfelt, but Jenna's nape tingles all the same. Keely will want to know more about Jenna's past, and probably already does. Jenna would if their roles were reversed. She's just being kind, downplaying her curiosity like Jenna's been downplaying her paranoia the entire time she's been here.

Jenna glances at the number, tucking the digits in her mind. "Drive me home?"

"You bet."

CHAPTER 5

Jenna's townhouse is one of four attached units. The front doors face the street and the second-story windows overlook the building across and a sliver of ocean beyond that. The single-car garage that fits her Subaru and Josh's bike and board is in back and accessible through a narrow alleyway. It's where she has Keely drop her off.

"Are you sure you don't want me to do a drive-by?"

Keely offered to loop around front to see if the *Sentinel* reporter is still waiting. Jenna shuts the door and leans into the window space. "I'll be fine. Quiet as a mouse. He won't know I'm home."

"All right," Keely says, unconvinced. "You have my number. Call if anyone gives your boy trouble. We'll take care of it together."

It's been so long since she's had friends that she doesn't know how to respond to Keely, so she doesn't. She lifts the flask into view. "Thanks for the coffee."

"Anytime."

After Keely leaves, Jenna enters the code for the garage, and the door lumbers open. Inside the townhouse, she goes directly to the front and peeks through the door-side window. The porch is empty. The reporter seems to have left. She settles at her desk in her studio and logs into her surveillance app from her laptop just to verify. She installed the camera above the front door within days of moving in. She checked it obsessively the first few weeks, then occasionally every month, until she stopped since she never saw anything out of the ordinary. She plays the video back, and sure enough, he wandered off fifteen minutes ago. He checks his watch, stands and stretches his arms overhead, looks up and down the road, then walks out of frame.

A shrill ring. She jolts and whips out her phone, flipping it open.

"Morning, love. I have exciting news," Her publicist Gayle launches into the call. "The announcement about Catherine O'Hara cast as the voice of Tabby runs next week in *Variety*. Both *Highlights* and Scholastic selected *Tabby's Squirrel: Going Nuts* as a children's book of the month pick. Didn't I tell you you'd go supernova? Watch out, Jim Davis, here comes Jenna Mason. The San Diego National Wildlife Refuge reached out. They want you for a series of short public-service videos. It's illegal to have a pet squirrel in California, and they're concerned kids will want one with the explosion of *Tabby*'s popularity. I regretfully declined." As Jenna would expect Gayle to do. She doesn't do in-person interviews, or prerecorded videos. She has a Facebook and Instagram account, and both handles are managed by Gayle's team. Call her paranoid, but for their safety, Jenna keeps her image out of the media. Her team never posts anything of a personal nature, including photos of Jenna. Her profile pictures are a rough caricature of the squirrel she's been doodling since she was twelve.

Gayle takes a breath. "Lastly, the *Oceanside Sentinel* agreed to do a feature on your book. The piece runs—"

"You need to stop it," Jenna cuts in, her voice edged with desperation. She leaves her studio and looks out the front window. "The reporter was parked on my porch this morning trying to get a quote from me. He's been questioning parents at my son's school."

"Why would he do that?"

"He's fishing for info." Gayle doesn't know the details of her past, and while she doesn't understand Jenna's need for extreme privacy, she respects it. She'll go to ultimate lengths to protect that privacy. It's in her contract.

"They agreed to a PR piece. I sent them the materials they'd need."

"What did you send?"

"The usual. Your bio, book cover, and a couple canned quotes you signed off on."

Jenna yanks the front blinds closed and paces the sparsely furnished room. "He's digging into my past. You can't let it publish."

"Why, that jerk. I knew something was off with him when he asked where you grew up. I told him we agreed to a feature focused on your work, nothing personal. The *Sentinel* is a tiny community publication. Who do they think they are, the *National Enquirer*?"

"You have to kill it." Before it's too late. She fears it already is.

She'll have to change her name again. Destroy the trail the reporter paved that leads to her. Give up her career. Leave Kavan. Move. Start over.

Anguish builds in her chest at the thought of leaving everything behind.

"I'll do my best," Gayle says. "But be forewarned, they might give me pushback. If they found something newsworthy, the *Sentinel* will run with it whether or not they get a quote from you."

Jenna presses a palm to her eye and debates what to tell Gayle. If the *Sentinel* verifies she's Lily Carson and publishes that article, the wires will pick it up. News about her will explode, especially since she's the *next big thing* in the animation world. It's probably already reached Seaside Cove, where she grew up.

But Gayle signed a nondisclosure agreement. She's also one of the few women Jenna trusts. The publicist was willing to work with her knowing Jenna's past isn't a topic of discussion and that she refuses to conduct in-person interviews or attend live events, including book signings and movie premieres. She's not an easy client to work with given Jenna's recent rise to fame.

Jenna met Gayle several years ago through Jenna's attorney Samantha while she was still moving every six months, back when she homeschooled Josh. When Jenna taught herself video animation and first started posting two-minute clips to YouTube as a way to make ends meet, she could easily ignore the growing number of messages from fans overflowing her inbox. That was until the day an offer came from an editor at one of the top children's-book publishing houses. Sam hooked her up with Gayle and Naomi Carr, Jenna's literary agent, after Jenna received a four-book offer from the children's book publisher Scholastic. Then Jenna started to dream. She could shop at Safeway instead of scraping coins to buy canned stew at the grocery outlet. She could take Josh shopping at the mall instead of purchasing secondhand clothes that reeked of body odor at Goodwill. She could stop worrying who would open their home to her and Josh in Murielle's network of angels because another cast-out soul needed the bed they slept on. Jenna would be able to afford a place of her own. She could start paying it forward into Murielle's network. It had been several years since she'd felt the compulsion to move—that tingle at the back of her neck had gone silent when she learned Ryder had been sentenced to prison. He was no longer a threat. She no longer felt the need to run. It was the only reason she gave in to Josh's request to settle here, to have a bit of normalcy.

Pacing back to the window, Jenna peeks through the blinds and retreats a step as if the slats burned her fingers. The reporter is back, seated on the curb just beyond her postage-stamp lawn. He's working his way through a sub sandwich.

She confides what she read in the parents' club Facebook group, information about her that's already public. "He's trying to connect me to a thirteen-year-old accident one of the victim's family members believes was a murder. It's not true, none of it is." Bile coats her throat at the lie. "But if that article prints, I'm not safe. I can't go into details, but please believe me. It may already be too late for me."

Gayle pauses. Jenna knows she has questions, and she braces for them, for the lies she must tell. But Gayle swears, then says sharply, "He's making it a smear piece." And Jenna has never been more grateful for her publicist.

"What about Sam? Can't she do something to stop them?"

"She can file an injunction, but let me try first."

"They can't publish it," Jenna says, fighting off tears of frustration as she tries not to give in to her fear. Everything she's worked for is moving out of reach as they speak.

"Don't worry, honey. We won't let them."

"Find out how they made the connection." Jenna's racked her brain and can't determine where, if ever, she slipped up. But the *Sentinel* somewhere, somehow found a lead that led them to Lily Carson.

"I'll do my best. Call you when I know more."

Gayle disconnects and Jenna sets aside her phone. A truck rattles as it drives over the speed bump out front, and she flinches. The front door draws her gaze. She wonders how much time until the paper's editor calls the reporter off the story. And if he doesn't, how long do she and Josh have before they need to leave?

Not much, she thinks. The damage has already been done.

Heartsick and scared, she runs upstairs to pack, starting in Josh's room first. She pulls out his roller case and puts it on his bed, then deliberates where to go. She'll take them to Murielle's, lie low until the dust settles and the parents stop talking. They'll figure out their next steps, steps that will cost them, and . . .

Josh is going to hate her.

What does she tell him? What does she tell Kavan?

Nothing.

Better to leave and have him hate her for bailing on him and Uma than telling him the truth.

As if he can sense she's thinking about him, her phone pings with an incoming text from Kavan. Ina has Uma for the night. He'll come over after he closes the restaurant. He loves her.

More than the sun loves the moon.

She closes her eyes and sees him, his brown-black hair and warm sienna eyes that crinkle in the corners. The smile that chased away her loneliness. The hand that always rests on her lower back when he's near, as if he has to touch her, his presence a constant reminder that she isn't alone.

She's going to break his heart. She knows this because hers is already cracking into a million fragments.

She starts to text for him not to come over tonight. She won't be here, she's leaving town. But she deletes the message and types the moon can't live without the sun's love, only to delete that, too.

Instead, she doesn't reply at all. Just tucks the phone away.

A tight knot of emotion thickens behind her ribs, making it hard to breathe. She goes to her room to pack.

CHAPTER 6

The school bell rings, and Jenna is out of her car to meet Josh at the gate. He doesn't know she's picking him up since his phone died and she can't text him. She allowed half a day to wait for Gayle's call, her anxiety increasing with every minute that ticked by, to tell her she'd killed the article. To detail who the reporter had spoken with, explain *how* he made the connection. She can't figure that one out.

Gayle's call didn't come, and she debated picking up Josh from school with the car already packed. But she didn't want to upset him more than he already would be. He'll resist. He's not the little kid who used to go along with everything she said. He'll want a good explanation why, which she has yet to come up with because she's having a hard time cutting her own cord. Even she agrees that moving every six months isn't any way to live.

She keeps her distance from the other parents. Their hushed conversations float around her. She can feel them watching. Talking about her. The post may have been deleted, but she's still a curiosity. A murderer in their eyes.

Her social anxiety breathes down her neck, hot, panting. She watches the yard, begging Josh to hurry.

Students pour from their classrooms. They trek toward the parking lot. It doesn't take long to find Josh. He stares at the ground as he walks, his hands clamped around the backpack straps. Mateo, Levi, and Brad flank him. Using Josh's backpack as leverage, Mateo yanks him backward. Josh stumbles. Anson grabs his arm to assist him up, but Josh knocks him away. Jenna recognizes his body language. The humiliation. Anson backs up, hands lifted. Mateo, Levi, and Brad reach the gate first. They keep walking past her. "Murderer," Brad coughs into his hand. The other boys snicker.

Shame moves through her like a heat wave. Her fingers dig into her triceps so she doesn't lash out at them.

Josh and Anson walk through the gate.

"See ya around." Anson parts ways with Josh, who ignores his friend, and that isn't like him.

"Hey," she says, trying to capture her son's attention as he walks by. He doesn't stop. She jogs to catch up and rests a hand on his shoulder. "You okay?"

"Fine." He walks faster.

"Josh?" She wants to know what he's heard, what he believes. What lies she must formulate.

"Can we just go?" He stomps across the grass.

"I drove. Car's over there." She points down the road.

Josh looks up and spots the car. He rushes toward it. Jenna unlocks the doors, and Josh chucks his backpack into the rear. He drops into the front, slams the door, and sulks.

Jenna settles into her seat. "What happened today?" she asks, pulling into traffic.

"Nothing." Josh crosses his arms, his attention out the side window.

"Do you want to talk about it?"

If he saw the article link, read it, he learned more today about her family than she's shared with him his entire life.

But if he had, he might better understand why she must break her promise. A risk she'll take to keep him safe, even if he never trusts her again.

"Josh," she prods when he doesn't say anything.

His eyes well up. "Is it true what they're saying?"

The weight of her past presses her deeper into the leather seat. "What did you hear?"

"They're saying you killed a kid and ran away from home. That you changed your name and that you've been hiding from the cops. Is that the real reason we always moved?"

"It's more complicated than that." She's woven such an intricate web of lies over the years that she barely knows how to unravel one without the illusion that is her life falling apart.

She never told Josh about Tyler because she didn't want to be found by anyone. And Josh would go looking for him. So she told Josh that she had him when she was young, practically a child herself. Her parents didn't want her to have him, so she left. As for why they'd moved every six months until recently? There was always an excuse. She couldn't pay the rent. The owner sold the house. The landlord rented the apartment to another family. She didn't feel safe, wanted a more secure place to live. She wove the lies to protect him. He wouldn't grow up knowing the kind of fear she's felt. The fear she's run from. And he was young enough then to believe her lies.

He won't after today.

"They're going to call the police," he says, shock lining his eyes.

Alarm prickles. "Who's going to call them?"

"Kids." He hiccups on a sob. "They're calling me murderer's spawn."

"What?" They've been watching too many crime documentaries and horror films.

Jenna sees red. Those kids couldn't have drawn a more perfect picture.

And their name-calling. She wants to Bubble Wrap her son, protect him from the bullies. More important, protect him from her past. If they call the police, she could land in jail. Where would that leave Josh?

Unsupervised. Alone.

She never thought she'd be discovered. Her identity was solid. She doesn't have a contingency plan for Josh. She just assumed she'd take care of him until he was old enough to live on his own.

Josh glares at her. Hazel eyes shimmer. "Anson let me use his phone. I saw what everyone's saying about you. Did you do it? Did you kill that boy?"

His mouth twists, and there it is, his disgust. Exactly how she'd look at her own mom. The moment she realized Charlotte had murdered Jenna's father, Benton St. John, stabbing him eight times in the stomach and chest. Her abject horror that her mother could carry out such an act and get away with it consumed her. What she'd done to Wes wasn't as horrific, but it was enough for the guilt and shame to chase her to this day. Josh could never learn that it's true. He'd run from her.

She sticks with the lie, a lie that's getting more difficult to tell the older he gets. "It was a horrible accident."

His chin quivers. A tear drops, then another. They leave silvery trails on ruddy cheeks. He covers his face and sobs.

"Josh, baby." She strokes his back, devastated he found out about her this way when she honestly believed he never would. She thought she could sustain the lies forever.

He lifts his head. "Who was he? Was he my dad? Is that why you told me you don't know who he is, because you killed him?"

"No! God, no," she says, stunned. "Wes was my friend, but he isn't your dad."

"Then why'd you kill him?"

I didn't.

The words hang on her tongue. A lie. His face is shattered, tears flooding his eyes, and she's afraid no matter what she says, she would break him. Fracture his trust in her.

"It wasn't like that," she whispers, stuck in her own web.

Josh kicks the dash, leaving a dusty sneaker print. "I want to go home."

"We're almost there." They were stuck at a light.

"Now!" he shouts.

The light changes and Jenna guns the car. As soon as she pulls into the garage, Josh bails, grabbing his book bag from the back. He's sliding on his pack and reaching for the door into the house when she hears, "Ms. Mason? Stan Clint with the *Oceanside Sentinel*. A word?"

Jenna's skin tingles at the sound of the reporter's voice. She exits the car, and Stan is right there outside her garage, holding a device that'll record whatever she dares to say. Aviators shield eyes she knows are trained on her, expectant. Hungry for her story.

"Or perhaps I should call you Ms. Carson?" The side of his mouth pulls up into a smirk.

"Mom?"

She glances at Josh. He tightly grips the doorknob, his eyes huge.

"Go inside," she says.

He doesn't budge.

Stan toes the line where pavement meets the garage concrete. "Ms. Mason, can you confirm you're Lily Carson?"

Jenna slams the door and locks the car.

"So you're saying you *are* Ms. Carson?"

"I didn't say anything. Josh, inside." Her heart bangs against her rib cage; she's appalled and livid this guy approached her while her son is with her.

"I don't have my key."

Again? Jenna rounds the front of the car, trying to keep a lid on her panic. She practically growls in frustration over Josh's absentmindedness.

Ozzy Osbourne's "Crazy Train" blares from Stan's rear. He yanks out his phone and gives the screen an impatient glare. "What?" he answers, turning away.

Hope flares that it's his editor, yanking Stan's leash. But Jenna doesn't wait to find out. She smacks the garage remote. The door rolls down. She unlocks the house. "Inside." She practically pushes Josh into the laundry room.

"Who was that?" Josh drops his pack on the floor beside the dining table. He removes his ball cap and flings it onto the couch.

"A reporter."

"The one everyone's talking about?" Josh's voice elevates, breaking at the end. She can see the whites of his eyes from across the room. "Are you going to be in the news?"

"I've been in the news before."

"For your cartoon! Not about this." He throws out his arms. "What if they arrest you?"

"They won't." As long as they stay one step ahead.

She peeks through the front blinds and finds no sign of Stan. She turns back to Josh. "Your suitcase is out. Go pack. We're leaving within the hour."

Shock unnaturally stiffens his posture. "What? No!" He gapes at her, then storms upstairs to his room as if to see whether she has indeed pulled out his luggage. Not a moment later he reappears at the top of the stairs, face red and eyes wild. "I'm not moving." His voice bounces off the ceiling.

"Josh, I know this is difficult to accept."

"You promised," he sobs.

Her heart cracks. "I know, but things have changed. You remember my friend Murielle? The woman we've stayed with a few times in between homes? We're just going to her house until I figure out what to do," she says.

"Why?" he shouts.

"I'll explain later." Her mind scrambles. She needs to come up with that explanation fast.

"I'm not going. You can't make me."

"I can, and you will. I'm not leaving without you."

Her phone chimes in her back pocket. She yanks out the device and answers Gayle's call. Behind her she hears Josh sprint down the stairs and turns to watch him scoop up his pack as she semilistens to Gayle explain that she just got off the phone with the paper's editor. Josh shoulders his pack and marches to the front door.

Alarm sluices through her. "Just a sec, Gayle." Jenna presses the phone to her chest. "Where are you going?"

"Out." Josh flips the bolt, unlocking the door.

"You're not going anywhere." He presses the latch. "Don't you dare."

Defiant, Josh flings open the door, and the floor splits open under Jenna. The blood in her head floods her feet. She sways. "Gayle," she whispers into the phone, her voice sounding as sick as she feels. "I'll call you back."

Standing on her porch, sharply dressed in a tailored suit and fist raised as if he were about to knock, is a man she hoped to never see again. Swore on her son's life she wouldn't see again. He smiles as if it's perfectly normal for him to be here.

Jenna gulps down the nausea. His teeth are stained from age, and his hair has thinned. There's more silver than the rich sable she remembers. But he looks virtually the same as he did the day she stepped between the barrel of his Glock and the boy she'd killed. He's just as fit, his looks just as striking.

Her phone slides from her grasp and drops to the floor. His gaze pivots to Josh. If her shoes weren't glued to the floor, she'd step between them, too.

"You must be Josh." His smile broadens. He extends his hand. "I'm Dwight, your grandfather."

CHAPTER 7

LILY

Sometime after dinner, Lily's mom called her into the kitchen. Lily had just changed into her pajamas and was about to crawl into bed, though she doubted she'd fall asleep. She was pregnant. *Pregnant.* And she didn't know what to do. Who to tell.

A life was growing inside her. Part her. Part Tyler. She wanted to keep it, let it grow. Flourish. And a love unlike anything she'd known bloomed for this little speck. She should be terrified. She was only sixteen, a child herself. And her parents . . .

They would go ballistic if they found out.

Which they wouldn't.

She and Tyler planned to move after her graduation. What if they left now? She'd have to ask him about that, and soon. Given how many cycles she'd missed before she considered testing that she was pregnant, she could start showing any day.

Her mom yelled for her again. Ignoring her, she set aside a sketchbook of doodles and inched her way off the bed to call Tyler. Dwight filled her doorway. Fists at his side, he vibrated with anger. Her mind reeled to the one question that surfaced when he looked ready to explode: What had she done wrong? Her hand fluttered to her stomach. It couldn't be about the baby. The pregnancy test was at the bottom of the wastebasket in the bathroom.

"Your mother's been calling you."

"I know, I was coming."

"Well, move faster."

She scooted off the bed just as he reached for her wrist. She stumbled on the floor. "I can walk," she said, scrambling to her feet. She tried to yank her wrist free.

He wouldn't let go as he led her down the hallway.

"Ow. You're hurting me." She winced when his nails dug into her skin. He was infuriated. She feared he'd hurt her. He could hurt her baby.

She hollered for her brother, praying he'd hear.

"Shut up."

Dwight deposited her in the kitchen like a sack of clothing at the laundromat. She wiped her face, rubbed her wrist. "What's going on?" Her bottom lip trembled. Had he found out she was working?

Charlotte was seated at the table, a full glass of wine within reach. She hadn't changed out of her work clothes, an elegant ensemble of silk and wool despite the late hour. She picked at her nails, mouth pinched.

"Mom?" Lily whimpered. Charlotte had a temper, but she always kept Dwight in check when he lost his, as if she knew what he was capable of when a line was crossed. He'd never struck her. It didn't mean Lily wasn't scared that one day he would.

Charlotte looked past Lily. Lily followed her line of sight. Dwight tossed the pregnancy test stick onto the island. It skidded across the granite and dropped with a plastic-sounding thwack at her feet.

Lily's fragile little world cracked underneath her.

Her hand fluttered to her stomach, already protective of the life growing inside. Charlotte's face drooped with disappointment.

"Explain," Dwight ordered in a voice that chilled.

If Lily could have foreseen how the next twenty-four hours would play out, she would have lied. She should have lied. Blamed it on a friend. Said the test belonged to Shayne or Hannah, girls from swim, especially since she'd become quite adept at lying. The people she thought loved her, who should have loved her, people like her own sister, had stopped believing her when she told the truth.

Once, their dad gave her permission to use Olivia's magazines for a class project. It was her favorite publication, an art magazine that featured her favorite contemporary sculptors and painters, and she saved every issue. But Dwight said it was okay. That Olivia wouldn't mind. She had plenty of issues to spare.

So Lily set about cutting into the stack only to have Olivia freak out when she came home and saw the carnage spread across Lily's bed. Magazine scraps covered her quilt.

Lily confessed their dad said Olivia wouldn't mind. But Olivia did, and she didn't believe Dwight gave Lily permission, especially when he explicitly denied it.

A rift started to build between them like a thin crevice in the earth's mantle, widening with every shake, every time Olivia insisted Lily was lying to her, until she no longer trusted her.

Lily began to wonder if there was a point to telling the truth if no one believed her in the first place.

But instead of lying, she heard herself ask, "How did you find it?" Did he have a sixth sense? She'd buried that test. And what was he doing in her bathroom anyway?

"Pick it up."

Lily stooped over, arm trembling. She placed it on the counter between them.

"I was out of toilet paper. Found a piece of the wrapper on the floor when I went looking for a roll in your bathroom."

She stopped breathing, stunned at her carelessness.

"Who's the father?"

She shook her head.

"You don't know, or you don't want to tell us?"

"I—" She squeezed her eyes shut, wishing the ground would swallow her whole. She didn't want them to know. They wouldn't let her keep it, this little thing that was all hers.

Charlotte quietly spoke Lily's fear. "You can't keep the baby. It'll ruin your life."

"Like I ruined yours?" She'd heard her parents arguing on numerous occasions. Lily was a mistake. Unplanned. A stain on their perfect nuclear family.

Her baby might be unexpected, but he would be loved.

"You have two choices." Charlotte held up her fingers. "You abort the baby, or you put it up for adoption."

"No!" She hugged her abdomen. She already loved this baby with every breath. He was hers. Someone who'd love her back unconditionally. No one, not even her parents, would take him from her.

"We'll go to the clinic this week. No one has to know."

A clinic. Not even her regular doctor. Someplace cold and sterile. *No one has to know.*

They didn't care about her or her baby. Her pregnancy was an embarrassment. Another blemish on the picture-perfect life Charlotte endeavored to project.

There was a family portrait in the living room. She and her siblings, along with their parents, dressed in gowns of golden silk and tuxes the color of midnight. The photo was for a magazine spread from a feature article highlighting Charlotte's real estate achievements and contributions to the community. They looked like Seaside Cove royalty.

If people only knew she often neglected the needs of her youngest daughter. If they only knew Dwight treated the neighbor's dog with more respect than he gave Lily.

But sadder than that, Lily had become used to their treatment. She'd come to expect it. She couldn't do anything to appease them, change their attitude toward her. Everything she did was wrong.

Except this. She'd make sure her baby lived.

"You can't make me." Lily had done her research. She knew her rights. She was sixteen. Her parents couldn't force her to terminate her pregnancy.

"We can if you want to live under this roof," Dwight said.

"You're kicking me out?" She looked between them. History told her arguing was pointless. They wouldn't budge. "Fine." She angrily swiped at a tear. "I was going to leave anyway." She turned to go.

"Who's the father?"

She whirled back. "You want me to get rid of it. What does it matter?"

"I want to know the bastard who knocked up my daughter. Is it Wes?"

Lily's mouth pressed flat.

Dwight's face turned molten red. "Who then?" he bellowed, slapping his palm on the counter.

She yelped, backing away.

His gaze narrowed. "Where're you going? We're not finished."

She shook her head, wondering how soon Tyler could get here if she called him, so they could leave.

"You have ten seconds to spit out a name or I will kill whoever did this to you when I find out."

Lily gaped. Even her mom gasped. "You can't be serious," Lily said.

"Ten seconds, Lily, or you'll have to live with the knowledge you could have prevented this. His death will be on you."

"You wouldn't dare," she cried, shaking all over. His threat had to be empty. He was trying to scare a name from her.

But seventeen years ago, their neighbor was murdered. Stabbed eight times and drowned just down the road. Lucas had told her Dwight was a suspect. He got off. He had an alibi. There wasn't enough evidence to charge him. And Lily didn't give it further thought. Her dad was innocent. But now she wonders if there was some truth to it. Charlotte was his alibi. An alpha wolf who'd do the unthinkable to protect her pack. And a neighbor had seen Dwight out walking that night.

His threat might not be that empty.

Lily felt sick. "I just want to go to my room," she said to her mom.

Charlotte drummed her fingers on the table. "We'll give you until tomorrow evening. But we want an answer."

Out of options and short on time, Lily ran from the kitchen.

Twenty-four hours. Hardly enough time to prepare to move out. But the two choices her parents gave her weren't options she'd consider. And she'd die before she gave up Tyler's name, not if her dad was the monster she was beginning to suspect he was.

Quickly, Lily retrieved the roller from her closet and packed. Then she called Tyler, begged him to meet her later that night. She needed to escape the house. They needed to talk.

Lily waited until her parents turned in before she slipped out her window in a hoodie and flannel pajama bottoms. She froze in the juniper bush, the shrub scratching her ankles and calves, and glanced up at Lucas's apartment. His lights were on, blinds closed. He wouldn't see her. Doubtful he'd care if he did.

She took off at a full sprint.

Tyler met her a block over. "What's going on?" he asked when she got into the car.

She shook her head, near tears. "I had to get out. My dad—" Her breath hitched and she rubbed her wrist.

Tyler noticed and grabbed her hand. He turned her wrist over. Crescent scabs from Dwight's fingernails marred her skin. Bruises darkened the region. The pupils in his eyes narrowed. "Did he do this?"

Her lip trembled. "Just drive, please." She needed to get away.

Ignoring the NO TRESPASSING signs, Tyler drove them to their spot, a gravel road that dead-ended at a low cliff, the ocean raging below. No one ever went there. They could be alone. Explore their dreams and each other.

Tyler parked the car and faced her. "What's going on?"

She started to tell him that she was pregnant, but fear kept the words locked in her throat. A tear escaped. Then another. His thumb wiped one off. "Lily," he said, his voice soft with concern. He kissed her gently until she traced her tongue over the seam of his lips; then his restraint faltered. They came together in a clash of lips and limbs.

Lily climbed into his lap, surprising them both with her boldness. Tyler gripped her waist. "Condom," he whispered, lifting his hip to get to his wallet.

She wanted to tell him they didn't need one. But the biggest secret she'd ever kept from him lodged in her throat. Dwight's threat pressed heavily on her chest. If Tyler knew about the baby, he'd come forward. Take responsibility. Then who knew what Dwight would do. Lily wouldn't risk his life.

Later, Tyler held her. He murmured sweetness into her hair, pleaded for her to share why she couldn't stop crying.

"Remember when we talked about leaving the Cove?" she whispered against his neck. She twirled a finger in his hair.

"Mm-hmm," he murmured.

"You said you wanted to move far away."

He released a sigh. "I remember saying I wanted to move to the lake house."

Wherever, she didn't care. "I want that, too."

"I promised I'd take you," he reminded. "When we're ready."

She leaned back to look at him. "I'm ready now."

He studied her face, his gaze searching. "Why the rush?" He sat up straighter. "Did something happen at home? Is that why you're crying?"

"It's terrible," she admitted. "I can't wait until graduation, Ty. We need to go now. You can find a job there. I'll finish school online. But let's go now."

"I can't leave yet. You know that."

His mom.

She put her forehead on his shoulder. "I'm sorry." It was selfish of her to ask. She couldn't force him to choose between her and his mom. It wasn't much better than the choice her parents gave her. And Tyler would choose her if he knew about the baby. He'd then resent her for the rest of their lives.

She didn't see another option. She had to leave on her own. The idea petrified her, but if it was the only way to keep her baby, she'd do it.

"Hey, Lil. What is it?"

Lily shook her head, pressed deeper into his shoulder.

He tucked a finger under her chin and lifted her face. "Is it really so bad at home you can't wait another year?"

Her eyes skittered away. "I'll figure something out."

He looked at her for a long stretch, then sighed. The muscles bracketing his mouth tightened. "Tell you what, I'll take you there tomorrow," he offered. "I can't stay, not until my mom—" He stopped, choked up, but he didn't need to finish his sentence. They both knew he wouldn't leave until his mom passed.

But this plan was better than her running away on her own. She'd be safe at the lake house until he could join her. Same with their baby. Soon they'd be together.

"Tomorrow." She kissed him. "We'll leave tomorrow."

CHAPTER 8

The last time Jenna saw Dwight Carson was down the barrel of his handgun.

"Go to your room, Josh." Her voice is soft but carries enough urgency for him to sense her alarm. The timing between the reporter's interest in her and Dwight's arrival leaves no room for coincidence. Stan must have interviewed him.

Why is he here? Does he think she told Stan about him and Charlotte? Does he plan to report her to the police? Could he have been the one who told Stan who she really is?

She has so many questions and not nearly enough time to get the answers.

Josh doesn't give her any pushback. He retreats upstairs. Jenna counts his footfalls, her eyes on Dwight. They stop four steps shy of the second floor. Out of sight, but not out of earshot.

Her pulse roars in her head. "How'd you find me?"

His weathered skin crinkles. "Well, now, that's an interesting story. May I come in?" He steps up onto the threshold, bold as ever.

Jenna blocks the doorway, clutching the door close to her side. "No." She doesn't want him in the house or her life.

Dwight grins, his tongue running along his upper teeth as he casually slides his hands into his pockets. His gaze scans the porch, lifts to look over Jenna's head, into the townhome. "Nice place you've got here. Good to see you, Lily. Or should I call you Jenna? You look good. Take after your mom. And him. I see a lot of him in you." His face sours with distaste, and Jenna realizes he can't even say his name.

"I look like Benton. His name was Benton St. John, and *he's* my father."

A shadow of anger crosses his face and quickly scatters.

"Leave," she says. "You're not welcome here." If he found her this quickly, the police wouldn't be far behind. They'll reopen Wes's case. They'll discover his death wasn't an accident.

Heart banging against her chest, she closes the door. Dwight's palm smacks the wood, holding it open. "Not so fast."

"Move or I'm calling the cops."

He lifts a brow. They both know her threat is empty. "You sure you want to get them involved? Ready to give all this up?" He twirls a finger in the air, indicating her townhome. Their lifestyle and her career. Kavan. Her son.

No, she isn't ready. But does she have a choice? Either way, Dwight's right. She won't call the police because she can't get them involved. It'll break their deal: she keeps silent about what she overheard her parents admit, that they murdered Benton St. John, and Dwight won't breathe a word about what she did to Wes.

He chuckles, calling her bluff. Then he flashes his dental work. "I wouldn't mind a cup of coffee."

"There's a Starbucks two blocks down. Don't let me stop you."

"Come now, darling. Invite me in. I'm just here to talk." He holds out an arm, the other still holding the door. "How about a hug. I've missed you."

"Go to hell."

He tsks. "Is that any way to talk to your old man?"

"You aren't my father. You stopped being my father the night you—" She chokes down the words. She was about to say the night he discovered she was pregnant and threatened to kill Josh's father. Josh might have gone upstairs, but he's still close enough to hear them.

"But I raised you."

A bark of laughter escapes. "I raised myself." He was never there for her, not like he was for Olivia and Lucas.

Dwight's eyes narrow. "Difficult as always, I see." He steps away from the door, settling against the porch rail, arms crossed.

"Why are you here?"

"I'm on my way to a conference in San Diego. Had a little chat with a reporter the other day. Thought I'd swing by for a visit."

Nausea churns in her stomach. Did Stan give away her address? Is that even legal?

"It wasn't too difficult finding you once I knew you lived in Oceanside," he says. "Given your son's age, I figured he'd be in school, so I waited around until you showed up. Followed you home."

How did he recognize her? She's worked years to blend into the background. But he plucked her out like a piece of hair in a bowl of cereal. Then she remembers. She looks like her mom. A woman she despises.

"What do you want?" she asks again, her whisper harsh. She has nothing to give him. She's done nothing to draw him back into her life.

His eyes narrow, darken. "What did you say to that reporter? He dug up my records. He asked me about him." Benton, her father, and his thirty-year-old unsolved murder case. His mouth twists, and fear moves swift as the wind through her.

"I haven't spoken to anyone. If he's asking about you or Wes, he didn't get any of that from me. And just so you know, I don't plan to speak to him either."

He stares at her for several pounding beats before he breaks into a grin. "Then we don't have anything to worry about."

He draws in close, enough to force her head back. She can smell the mint on his breath, the spice of his aftershave.

"We wouldn't want Stan to get extra curious about our family. If the police come after your mother and me, you can bet every dollar you're earning from that ridiculous cartoon you make they'll be knocking on your door, too. I still have that video. Would be a shame if your son saw it."

The recording of Wes's last breath.

She's never forgotten that video. It's what's kept her silent all these years.

Wes's death was at her hands and left a deep hole in her that constantly refills with guilt and shame and remorse like a never-ending well.

"I haven't told anyone anything, you have my word." She holds his gaze so he won't detect the lie. Murielle knows the full truth about him and Charlotte, as does Murielle's daughter, Sophie. It's the only time Jenna broke down and confessed. She was young, pregnant, and frightened. But she needed Murielle's help. More so, she needed her trust.

"Fantastic." Dwight's teeth gleam. "Which brings me to the second reason I'm here." He clapped his hands once and eagerly rubbed his palms. His eyes take a spin over the townhouse, around the neighborhood. "You're doing well. Nice place next to the beach, books, movies. Red carpets, fame. Must be lucrative. Wine consulting, not so much." He shrugs.

Her blood ices over. She knows where he's going with this. "You're not getting a dime from me." Dwight always was fixated on money. There was never enough.

"About that video . . ."

"You wouldn't dare."

"Anonymously send a copy to the police?" His bottom lip protrudes as he contemplates. He hums. "That depends."

"On what?"

"How much you want to give me. I'd say twenty K. To start," he adds after a pause for dramatic effect.

She balks. "I don't have that kind of money. And don't forget what I know about you and Charlotte. We have a deal."

"You don't have proof. The worst you can do is make my life an inconvenience. And we both know how I feel about inconveniences." He looks pointedly at her, then in the direction Josh went.

She was the inconvenience, as was her pregnancy.

A vicious tremble shudders through her.

"Think on it." He winks before stepping off the porch. He stops and turns around. "I won't be far."

Bastard.

Jenna slams the door, shaking. She can't spare that kind of money. Royalties won't kick in for months.

"Is he really my grandfather?"

She whips around. Josh stands on the bottom step, his face a mask of disbelief and worry.

"Legally, yes. Not by blood."

"Is he going to hurt us?"

She shakes her head. "I won't let him."

"But he wants money."

"I'm not giving him anything." She won't give him the chance to extort her. They're going to disappear.

Josh tilts his head. "What about that other stuff he said? About a video and you not talking to anyone? What does he mean?"

"I know things about him. He wanted to make sure I've kept my promise to not share."

"Because of that reporter?"

She nods.

His hands clench then flex open. "He called you Lily."

She briefly closes her eyes. He'd heard that.

"He did," she says, pained.

He tilts his head the other way, looking at her like she's a stranger. His mouth turns down, angry and suspicious.

"So you are her. That girl they're saying killed that boy."

56

"Josh, I—" The lie lodges in her throat. She can't deny it. She's been his world. And it's killing her how dishonest she's been with him.

"What was that about a video?" he asks. "What does he have on you?"

"Nothing that concerns you." But if that video falls in the right hands, she'll land in jail. She'll lose Josh.

"You're lying. Everything you've been telling me has been a lie." He turns abruptly and storms through the kitchen, catching her off guard.

"Josh!" She runs after him. They have to leave.

He throws open the laundry-room door to the garage and smacks the opener. The door lumbers open. He grabs his skateboard and ducks under the slowly opening door.

"Josh, get back here!" she hollers, but he doesn't stop. He's already reached the end of the alley.

CHAPTER 9

Jenna gets in her car and follows Josh to Anson's house, terrified Dwight is doing the same. And he would, just to antagonize her, show how easily he can get to her through her son.

Popping up his board at the curb, he carries the Tony Hawk to the porch, props it against the house, and rings the doorbell.

Jenna rushes from the car before he goes inside. "Josh!"

He isn't surprised to see her. "I'm not coming home. And I'm not moving."

"Come here," she orders.

"I know what you'll do, Mom. You're going to take us to Murielle's; then you won't want to come back. You never do. You'll tell me some bullshit why we can't, and I know it's not true." She can't help but cringe at his language when Anson opens the door. He watches them curiously. Josh makes to go inside.

"Fine." She throws out her arms, desperate for him to listen, but more afraid of losing him. Losing control over him. "We won't go. We'll stay."

That gets his attention. He turns back to her. "Really?" He doesn't look like her believes her.

"Just come here, please." She waves him over, worried what Anson might overhear.

He stops in front of her, head bowed. Resentment frosts his eyes. Anson hangs on the door, bounces the rubber toe of his Vans against the edge. His gaze darts from them to his foot, too curious to give them privacy.

She turns her back to Anson. "Don't hate me," she says softly, thinking of what Josh said to her earlier. *So you are her. That girl they're saying killed that boy.*

"I don't," he admits. "I just don't understand why we have to leave. It makes me think what they're saying is true, that you killed that boy and you're afraid of getting caught. But even if you did." He nudges a pebble with the toe of his shoe. "I don't think I could hate you."

A tear runs down her cheek, surprising her. She didn't think she could love him more than in this moment. He is more like his father than she's cared to acknowledge, mainly because it hurts to do so. Tyler was the most understanding person she'd known. His mom was dying, and aside from a live-in nurse he was her sole caretaker at eighteen. Yet he left his mom to drive her to his cabin by the lake when she told him she needed to get away from her parents. Regret ribbons around her, bowing, flexing—tightening. She's never forgiven herself for the way she left him.

She lied to him. And she's been lying to her son.

Maybe she can share some of what happened, skew the truth, if only to appease his curiosity so he'll do as she asks.

"What happened to that boy Wes," she says. "It was a terrible accident. Not a day goes by I don't think about him. He's not the reason we move. He's part of it. But there's more. Things I can't tell you, and please don't ask," she rushes to say when he opens his mouth. "I'm trying to protect you."

"I don't need protection. I'm not a little kid anymore."

She cups his warm cheek, lifting his face until he looks her in the eye. "Trust me. In this case, you do."

"Like those crime shows. I'll be complicit if I know?"

Her eyes narrow. "You've been watching too much TV."

"Will the police take you away if we don't go?"

Her mouth tightens. That's her fear. That's why they need to leave. "No one is taking me away from you. You're not going to lose me." They'll disappear again. They won't catch her.

"Then I don't want to go." He glances back at the house where Anson waits. "I don't want to lose my friends. And don't tell me I'll make new ones. You'll make me leave them, too. I won't have anyone . . ." His voice trails off into a mumble. His chin dips to his chest.

"You have me," she says, her voice cracking. He looks up at her, and her heart falls as realization runs clear. She's no longer enough for him. Was she ever? Because underneath his sadness is a profound loneliness. The same she recognized in herself before she met Kavan.

Contending with her own loneliness is one thing. But seeing it in Josh? Knowing she's the cause? It's too much.

Forcing him to move again might destroy him. It would dismantle their relationship. He'd never trust her again. He might even leave her, as she left her parents. She can't protect him if he isn't with her.

She cradles his face with both hands. "All right. We'll stay." For now. Maybe she and Gayle can keep this contained. It won't reach the police. She'll become old news, and the parents' club will find someone else to gossip about. As for Dwight, she might need to buy his silence.

His bottom lip trembles and he sighs with relief. But he keeps it together. Anson's waiting. "Thank you," he whispers. She kisses his forehead and he asks, "Can I stay here for a while?"

She lifts her gaze to the house. Keely's in the kitchen. "Stay in the house and don't leave. Call me when you want a ride home or have Mrs. Lawrence drive you."

He nods, and as he goes inside with Anson, she prays she hasn't made a horrible mistake by agreeing to stay.

Jenna's phone rings as she enters the house. She answers Gayle's call, locking the door behind her. "What have you got?" She double-checks that the front door is bolted. The blinds are already closed from earlier when she was hiding from Stan. "Are they still running with it?"

"As a feature piece about your upcoming picture book as we originally agreed upon, yes. And no, they won't delve into your background. Stan's been pulled from the article."

Jenna hugs her midriff and collapses over the countertop, forehead kissing the cool quartz, phone pressed to her ear. "How? Did you have to call Sam?"

"Nope. Took care of it myself. I convinced the editor, who also happens to be the paper's owner, that you'd sue for libel if they printed anything insinuating you're this Lily Carson girl or that she murdered a sixteen-year-old boy. Stan couldn't locate anyone to corroborate the Jensens' allegations, or that you are in fact her." Which means Dwight didn't tell Stan who she is. "It's a small local paper. They can't afford a lawsuit; they're already operating in the red."

"How did Stan find out I'm from Seaside Cove?" And who else did he speak with aside from Dwight? Did he interview Wes's parents?

Gayle pauses. "It's my fault, really. I didn't prep you."

Her mouth dries. "What happened?"

"Do you remember that Comic-Con piece last year in *On the Spot*? He followed a lead from there."

Jenna lifts off the counter. What lead? *On the Spot* is an online news site based out of San Diego. After she'd signed her book deal, her agent, Naomi, sent her two congratulatory tickets for her and Josh to San Diego Comic-Con. Josh wore his Wolverine costume, and she dressed up as her character Tabby, complete with a wig of frazzled white hair, gold-rimmed glasses, and a pound of makeup to make her look like an elderly woman. *On the Spot* was on location, and Gayle had arranged an interview for their up-and-coming profile. Jenna wasn't too concerned about her first and only face-to-face interview. She was unrecognizable in her costume. But the interviewer's rapid-fire questions for the publication's speed round caught her off guard. Given no choice, she rolled with it and did as Murielle advised. Answer questions as truthfully as possible so you don't get caught in a lie.

"You told them you were the youngest freestyle champion in the Central Coast Conference."

Jenna circles the island. She'd dropped her guard at that conference. She wanted to show Josh a good time. Had she really been that specific? She didn't read the profile. She rarely searches herself. She feels like she's drawing attention when she does. The law of attraction and all that.

"Stan looked it up and saw the record belonged to Lily Carson. He started digging."

He dug up old articles and went to Seaside Cove with his questions.

"Jenna, honey." Gayle's voice drops. She almost sounds motherly. "This will all blow over. Pour yourself a glass of wine, hug that handsome fiancé of yours, and enjoy the bit of good press in tomorrow's paper. I know it's local, but a tight community like yours loves when one of their own hits it big. People love your cartoon. They're going to love your books, too."

The paper is small time. The article will barely make a blip on the internet. But she fears the repercussions have been monumental. Josh now knows she's Lily. Dwight knows where she lives. And the parents at Josh's school suspect what she did.

Jenna ends the call with her publicist and calls Keely. Anson's mom picks up on the second ring.

"I was just going to call you. Josh is here."

"I know. I hope that's all right."

"It's perfectly fine. Though he seemed upset when he got here. Everything all right?"

The loneliness she picked up from him earlier tumbles over her. "He's taking the social media fiasco hard. Kids gave him a rough time at school." Partial truth, and her stomach churns slightly compared to the outright queasiness she feels when she blatantly lies.

"I'm not surprised. Poor guy. I fed the boys milk and cookies. They're playing Nintendo now. He's welcome to stay for dinner. I can drive him home afterward."

"I appreciate that. Not too late, if that's all right. Josh has homework." She feels better having him at home where she can see him.

"We'll make it an early night."

"Thanks." Jenna ends the call and retreats to her studio, aching over what her son's going through. What he must think of her.

Seated at her desk, she wakes her laptop and runs a search for Wes Jensen in Seaside Cove, curious if anything recent has been written about him that she needs to worry about. Two links from the *SLO County Press* appear at the top: Local Boy Missing and Body of 16-Year-Old Boy Recovered. The titles are a gut punch even thirteen years after the fact. This was her friend, his life cut short by her hands.

Jenna clicks on the first link and reads the brief article.

> Seaside Cove Police are searching for a missing boy. Sixteen-year-old Wes Jensen was last seen in the vicinity of 398 Sundial Court where his brother, 19-year-old Ryder Jensen, dropped him off. The older Jensen has been questioned and is not a person of interest. Police say Wes was wearing a black sweatshirt, white baseball jersey, jeans, and white sneakers. Seaside Cove Police also say this is not an Amber Alert as there is no evidence of abduction. If you have any information, call the Seaside Cove Police Department. Update: Body of 16-Year-Old Boy Recovered

Jenna clicks the update link, which takes her to the second article, the same one shared in the parents' club group. She reads it knowing Josh read the same piece just hours ago.

> The body of 16-year-old Wes Jensen, who went missing three days ago, has been recovered after a frantic countywide search. Charlotte Carson, the owner of 398 Sundial Court, found the body floating near the shore at the edge of her property during her morning walk. Initial evidence indicates Wes slipped off their dock, hit his head on the edge, and drowned.

> Neighbors claim they heard a gunshot around Wes's estimated time of death, but there are no wounds to suggest he'd been shot. There is also no evidence a gun had been fired on the Carsons' property.

> "Weather conditions weren't ideal that night. Visibility was minimal, and the dock would have been slick. We believe Wes fell off the dock, clipping his head in the process, as the location of the head trauma suggests," Officer Jim Harold of the Seaside Cove Police Department said.

> Both Charlotte and her husband, Dwight Carson, allege they didn't see Wes the evening his brother, Ryder Jensen, dropped him off at the Carsons' house. According to Jensen, Wes was visiting the Carsons' 16-year-old daughter, Lily, who also has been reported as missing. Charlotte Carson said her daughter ran away before the time Jensen alleges that he dropped off his brother, but Jensen reported

he saw Lily Carson leave the premises a short time later. No other witnesses have been able to corroborate her presence. Police have no additional evidence to support that the two incidents are related. Olivia Carson, 21, and Lucas Carson, 19, Mr. and Mrs. Carson's other two children, were reportedly not home and can't comment on either incident.

The investigation is ongoing, and Wes's body has been sent for an autopsy.

Anyone with information on the whereabouts of Lily Carson should contact the Seaside Cove Police Department.

Update: Autopsy results confirm Wes Jensen drowned after sustaining trauma to the head. Police have determined the cause of death as an accident.

"Nobody in the Carson family claims to have seen Wes on their property, and no other witnesses have come forward. The shore and dock are easily accessible from the road. The property isn't fenced in," Officer Harold said. "The fog horns are loud when the fog is at its thickest. There's zero visibility. Like any kid, Wes was probably curious."

In lieu of flowers, the Jensen family requests donations to the Jensen Family Trust to help cover funeral and burial costs. If anyone has information on the whereabouts of Lily Carson, please contact the Seaside Cove Police Department.

Jenna leans back from the screen feeling as disgusted as she did the first time she read the article years ago. Dwight kept up his end of the bargain. He lied to the authorities. He kept her involvement in Wes's death off the record on the condition she kept silent about him and Charlotte. He protected her, but only to protect himself because of what she knows and would assuredly share if she ended up behind bars.

Murielle followed Wes's case. Ryder Jensen's assumption about Lily's involvement was unfounded, according to the police. If it ever went to court, the case would be circumstantial. No murder weapon was found or determined. No witnesses. No proof that Lily was present.

But Dwight has that video he filmed with his phone that shows exactly what she did when she returned to the house and tried to help Wes.

Something crashes into the front door. Jenna jumps and swivels her chair. Heart pounding in her throat, she peers out the window. The porch is empty, and the narrow street in front is quiet. Not a soul in sight. But she swears she heard heavy footsteps retreating. Someone was running away.

She pulls up the surveillance recordings. The figure is clad in black, head down. She can't see his face. But he left something on her porch.

Jenna opens the door and finds a soiled Vans sneaker on her doormat, the laces a grayish brown. Old and dingy. Her hand trembles as she picks up the shoe and looks around. A car drives past, a neighbor she recognizes who lives three doors down, but that's all. Whoever it was is gone. She inspects the shoe, lifting the tongue, and almost drops the sneaker. Written in faded permanent ink are the initials *W. J.*

Her heart stops.

No, not possible.

She rubs her eyes and covers her mouth. The shoe is his.

Even when he was sixteen, Wes's mom made him initial his clothing because he always misplaced his belongings. He'd lose a shoe in the locker room or leave a sweatshirt on his chair in the cafeteria. He hated marking up his clothes, but if he didn't and he lost something, it was his responsibility to replace it.

And now she has one of his missing shoes.

Dwight.

I won't be far.

This is something he'd do. Torment her until she gives in to his demands.

A slip of paper drops from the shoe. She unfolds the torn piece and reads. *I know what you did to him.*

Ice settles in Jenna's chest. A violent shiver tears through her.

Jenna puts the shoe on the counter. The white Vans Wes wore the night he died. She thinks of the boy who wore it and turns to the sink just in time. She throws up.

Then she panics. The shoe is evidence. She can't have this on her.

She flushes the note in the toilet and scratches out Wes's initials on the shoe. She then tosses it in the dumpster at the end of the alley in back.

Returning to the house, she arms the alarm and backs away from the door, wishing Kavan didn't have to work so late. Wishing Josh were home so she didn't feel alone.

She reaches for her keys, texting Keely before she realizes she's doing so. She might have promised Josh they aren't leaving. But she wants him home, now.

CHAPTER 10

Josh locks his bedroom door, upset his mom picked him up early. He wasn't ready to come home. Those things that guy Dwight said about her, their deal, her real name, the video. It's blowing his mind. On top of that, she never denied she'd killed that kid.

Is it possible she did? That that's the reason they moved a lot? She's been running and hiding this whole time?

Has everything she's told him been a lie?

If so, she must be lying about his dad. She does know who he is.

Josh shakes his head. This is too hard to swallow. Unbelievable. His mom is right. He's been watching too many crime dramas.

He could ask her. But he's asked many times before. She'll tell him he's too young to understand. Or she'll just tell him another lie.

He needs to find out the truth himself.

After years of homeschooling, of having no close friends, and constantly moving, Josh needs to understand why. Why they've lived that way. Why his mom is scared. Should he be, too?

All he knows is that he doesn't want to go back to that life. To the secondhand clothes and empty cupboards. To the long nights alone in his bed with no one to call, no one to play with, while he listened to their neighbor's muffled TV through his wall and heard the steady hum of freeway traffic right outside his window. To watching other kids walk to school each morning while he was stuck inside because his mom wouldn't let him out of her sight except on rare occasions when she had to go somewhere and couldn't take him.

If he can uncover what his mom did and why she changed her name, he might be able to help. Then maybe he can avoid another day at school like the one he had today.

It was horrible. Kids he's never met called him names during class transition. Brad punched him in the locker room after PE just because he could. The dick. His ribs hurt. Shame engulfed him like a flooded engine. He couldn't go anywhere until school was out. He had to sit there and take the ridicule and pretend nothing was wrong.

He settles on his bed and removes Anson's iPad he hid under his sweatshirt. He opens the browser and brings up the Wes Jensen article he's already read at least a dozen times. **Body of 16-Year-Old Boy Recovered.** He writes down names: Dwight Carson, Charlotte Carson, Olivia, Lucas, and Lily. His mom.

His relatives. People who are strangers to him, but ones he wants to know more about. Names he needs for his All About Me assignment due tomorrow.

He then searches each one.

What he discovers churns his stomach.

His grandfather was a suspect in an unsolved murder case. Their neighbor Benton St. John was stabbed eight times.

It happened over thirty years ago, but it doesn't change the fact that someone thought his grandfather was capable of such a heinous crime.

Josh studies the victim's name, wondering why it sounds familiar. Alarm clangs around his skull when he remembers where he heard it. It was just this afternoon. His mom said to Dwight that Benton was her real father, Josh's biological grandfather. Another name to research for his growing list.

Other things his mom and Dwight said that he overheard come to mind. They have a deal, secrets about each other they've promised not to share. Does it have to do with this Benton guy and Wes?

Disgusted, Josh tosses aside the iPad. His stomach is in knots. His family history disturbs him. Is it possible his mom and grandfather are both murderers? That they have a deal to keep it secret?

No way.

His mom is the most caring, loving person he knows. She'd never intentionally take a life. She isn't evil. Wouldn't he know that about her? Wouldn't Kavan?

Did his own father?

Is that why he's not around?

Does he even know Josh exists?

Did she steal him away, and that's why she's been running?

Or is she running because she murdered Wes?

His mom is his world, and she very well may be a killer. And a liar. He *is* a murderer's spawn.

He fists his hair and plants his elbows on his thighs, feeling down on himself. He's afraid everything he's thinking about his mom is the truth. He also doesn't like the idea of going behind her back to find out what is the truth, but he doubts she'll ever tell him.

Maybe his dad will.

Josh picks up the iPad and starts a new search.

CHAPTER 11

LILY

It was almost dinnertime when Lily let herself into the house the following day. To her surprise, both her parents were home before her.

They were probably waiting for her. They wanted her answer.

She laid a hand over her belly. Her answer hadn't changed since she'd first learned she was pregnant. She was keeping her baby, and she was leaving tonight. Tyler was meeting her in less than an hour.

Harsh voices reached her as she walked the hallway toward her bedroom. Her parents were in their room arguing, the door slightly open. She heard her name.

She should turn away, not give in to her curiosity. But she couldn't help herself.

She leaned toward their door and listened.

"She's not going to get rid of it," Dwight said.

"You don't know that," Charlotte opposed, followed by the flick of a lighter and a window sliding up.

"Don't smoke in here."

"Go to hell," she grumbled. "She won't make it on her own. She's not going anywhere. She needs us. One way or another, she'll get rid of it, and you can stop complaining about having to support one more child."

"What makes you believe she will? You didn't get rid of her."

Lily covered her mouth. She knew her father didn't want her, but to hear him say it? Something already cracked inside her fractured further.

"She's exactly like you," he continued. "Déjà vu all over again." His voice receded as he paced deeper into the room.

"This is nothing like what happened before. Not even close. Know why? We did it once. *We* can't afford to do it again. We got off. We might not be so lucky next time, which is why you're going to leave the baby's father alone. No more threats. No more killing, in case that's what you were actually thinking of doing."

Lily's head drew back sharply.

"I didn't kill anyone." Through the gap in the doorway, Lily saw him move across the room. He grabbed Charlotte's wrist. She hissed and jerked her hand free. Ash from the burning cigarette flaked off. He brought his face close to hers. His voice dropped to an icy temperature. "I'm not the one who stabbed Benton eight times. I'm not the monster."

Lily's eyes bulged. She fell back against the wall, disbelief sparkling like electricity in her chest. Her mother had stabbed a man?

Benton. Her father called him Benton.

Why did that name sound familiar?

"I wouldn't have done it if you hadn't beaten him within an inch of his life," Charlotte accused. "Yes, I killed him, but you started this. You set everything into motion."

"I wasn't the one who brought the knife."

"You dragged him into the ocean. You're just as guilty. You were running for office. I was cleaning up your mess."

"Whose fault is that?" Dwight raged. "None of it would have happened if you hadn't slept with him."

Lily's breath came in rapid bursts. This was not a conversation they'd want her to hear. If they knew she had . . . She shook her head, not wanting to imagine what Dwight would do.

A mix of incredulity and fear roped her torso, trying to tug her toward her own room. But she remained frozen as a memory from their last summer at the Whitmans' lake house surfaced. The five of them—Blaze, Tyler, Olivia, Lucas, and Lily—were supposed to be asleep in the loft. It was past midnight. The lights were off, and the moon glowed outside the triangular window as they passed around a flashlight telling horror stories. It was Lucas's turn. He held the light under his chin, casting an eerie glow on his face that sunk in his eyes and elongated his nose. And the story he told wasn't a myth or a legend. It was as real as they were, and it pissed off Olivia enough that she punched him hard in the shoulder. Olivia couldn't believe he told it in a way that made them think of their father as a murderer. Lucas swore he was joking. That he'd fabricated most of it.

But it hadn't been a lie at all. Seventeen years ago, their neighbor's body, bloated from days in the water, was found washed ashore with eight stab wounds in his torso. His name had been Benton St. John. He was murdered, and their father, Dwight Carson, was a suspect. The case was never solved.

Several realizations slammed into her at once. Benton St. John was her biological father. Her mother had murdered him. Dwight had aided and abetted. And both had kept it secret for almost twenty years.

Lily struggled to breathe. Her skin tingled with a flight-or-fight reaction. Her parents were murderers.

Which meant Dwight *was* serious. If he and Charlotte killed Lily's real dad without remorse, they wouldn't hesitate to harm Tyler to convince her to give up her baby. Lily started shaking uncontrollably, terrified.

Her feet scuffed the wall, and the door creaked. She froze, mouth open, eyes darting erratically as if looking for a hiding place.

Dwight shushed Charlotte. "What was that?"

"What was what?"

Dwight shushed her again.

Heart pounding, Lily looked down the hall and wondered how fast she could make it to her room before they saw her.

"You're hearing things," Charlotte said, taking a drag on her cigarette.

"When does Lily get home?"

"Not sure. She might be in her room."

Lily took the chance. She dashed straight there. She threw her backpack on the bed and backed up against the wall. What would they do if they realized what she knew? Would they kill her, too?

They didn't love her. It had never been clear to her until now why Dwight favored Olivia and Lucas. They were *his* kids. She was the product of an illicit affair.

Unwanted. Unloved. A constant reminder of the neighbor his wife slept with. The man he helped kill. Could he see Benton in her?

She hugged her shins, dropping her forehead on her knees, wishing it was already time to meet Tyler. She had to get out of here. She didn't want to be in the same room as them, let alone the same town.

Her door flew open. She gasped, lifting her face. Dwight filled the doorway. A shudder of fear passed through her.

"Did you just get home?" he asked conversationally, so at odds with the shouting she'd heard moments ago. "Well?" he prodded, brow lifted, when she only stared at him.

She nodded, dragging a trembling hand under her nose to wipe the tears that had collected there.

His gaze narrowed on her face. "What's wrong with you?"

"Bad day at school," she lied.

He started to close the door only to sweep it open. "You really just got home?"

She nodded.

His mouth thinned. "You didn't hear your mother and me?"

She shook her head, sniffled. Wiped her nose.

He stared at her for a beat, then flashed a grin before looking at his watch. "Dinner's in less than an hour. We'll talk then."

The door closed and Lily released a breath.

She'd be gone by then.

CHAPTER 12

Jenna met Kavan over a year ago when she came across his upscale beachside café while out walking late one evening. Josh was spending the night at Anson's, a first for him, and the townhouse was too quiet for her comfort. Josh had never spent the night away from her. But she'd promised him a normal childhood. She was starting to feel less on edge after so many years of running. Josh was beyond excited about the invite. She couldn't deny him.

But she couldn't relax while he was away. She hadn't spent the night alone since he was born.

Lured by the scent of good food, something she never could have afforded before her animation was so successful, Jenna entered the café. She settled at the chef's counter where Kavan was working that night, feeling more alone than ever. Josh was all she had. She didn't have anyone she'd call a friend, and the few people she'd allowed in her life, those she trusted, had been hired: her attorney, Samantha; her agent, Naomi; and Gayle, her publicist. Her gatekeepers to keep the public at bay and her privacy secure. So she felt uneasy about sharing anything beyond a business relationship with them. She wasn't sure if she'd know how to be friends with them.

At Kavan's recommendation, she ordered the special, roasted chicken topped with cherry tomatoes and baby bella mushrooms covered in a sherry wine sauce. The night wore on and the patrons dwindled. Staff cleaned around them until the last server clocked out, leaving Jenna alone with the sparkling mini lights that adorned the ceiling,

Dave Brubeck playing softly on the speakers, and Kavan, who'd fixed himself a plate and joined her on her side of the counter. It took her some time to share anything about herself, even little half-truths, like where she was from—she'd told him everywhere—but they talked about their kids, his experience as a chef, and her art. He opened up about his previous marriage. She kept her secrets closely guarded, told him she didn't know who Josh's father was and that she ran away from home to keep her baby. But Kavan didn't seem to mind that her life was unconventional. And she couldn't tell if he suspected that she had lied. But between her son and her recent book and movie deals, she had plenty else to share. And it felt good talking to another adult about everything and nothing after going for years with only Josh and herself.

She couldn't explain it, barely understood it, but with Kavan she felt alive for the first time in a long time. And she started to feel safe. It's probably why she fell hard and fell fast.

As the hour coasted toward midnight, Kavan topped off her Chardonnay. He set the bottle near his elbow and gently touched the back of her hand where it rested on the rustic counter. His finger lightly stroked across her skin, tracing a raised vein. His eyes met hers.

"I haven't enjoyed an evening like this in . . ." He smiled appreciatively. "Quite some time."

"Me neither." Never, actually.

Jenna hadn't allowed herself to enjoy another's company because she didn't deserve to enjoy herself. And she certainly hadn't enjoyed the company of a man, let alone another human being, as much as she had when she met Kavan. Jenna was starved for affection and human companionship.

"Can I see you again?" he asked softly.

Jenna nodded, even as the voice whispered through her mind that she was unworthy of his attention.

Kavan's smile reached his warm honey eyes. He then walked her the few blocks home. At her door, after a beat of second-guessing, a moment of nervous reserve, she gave him her phone number. Josh wanted to live a normal life, and he was. She wanted the same for herself.

Too bad her and Kavan's relationship is based on lies.

But she never thought she'd be in the position to share the truth. Never imagined their relationship would have gone on as long as it has, that, as much as she wants this, she'd find herself engaged to him. And now that her original identity is out there?

He will know that her past is a bigger secret than she alluded to.

She'd planned on leaving him and everyone else just hours before. But now that she's decided to stay? She hadn't considered whether Stan might have approached him, too. Even though the article Stan wanted to write was canned, Kavan could hear about her if someone from the parents' group ate at his restaurant and her name came up. Josh could bring her up.

She agreed to stay for Josh, but she might lose Kavan either way.

CHAPTER 13

Long after Josh has retired, Kavan arrives a little after 11:30 p.m. with a bottle of wine and Thalassa takeout. He smells of coriander and saffron, strong earthy scents. Jenna is kissing him before he crosses the threshold. Seeing him now, his hair tousled after a full day, makes her feel like she made the right decision to stay. Almost. The inclination to pick up and go still hovers in the back of her mind like a storm on the horizon.

"Mm-hmm." Kavan's arm loops around her back, lifting her off her feet. He moves inside and kicks the door shut. "What brought this on?" he asks against her lips.

"I missed you." How did she ever think she could give him up? This is why she never developed attachments before. It makes it harder to leave.

But they're not leaving. She promised Josh. And her mind again fills with apprehension. Her name is out there. She's been connected to Lily. The police could come at any moment.

Jenna is only five-foot-four and Kavan is more than a head taller. Lips locked, he lets her slide down until her toes touch the floor. He lifts his head, breaking their kiss. His heated gaze pins hers. Warmth churns the honey color of his eyes. "I want more of where that came from, but I need to shower first. Have you eaten?"

She bolts the door and arms the alarm. "No, not yet." She hasn't given any thought to food after today.

"Didn't think so." His face crinkles knowingly. "Brought you some lamb. Tonight's special." He hands off the paper bag he's carrying and a bottle of pinot noir. "Open that for us." He steals a kiss and heads for the stairs.

She grabs his arm. "Are we good?" Her eyes search his, as if they hold the answers. What does he know? Has he started unraveling her lies?

He frowns. "Yes, why? You okay?"

She smiles nervously. "Fine."

"Good. Be right back." He touches her cheek before sprinting upstairs.

When she hears the shower in the primary bedroom, she realizes she's been clutching the bag of food to her chest. Heat from her meal seeps through her thin shirt. She lets the bag fall to her side. Maybe Gayle's right. She should stop worrying her life will implode because she doesn't want to give up what she has. Quit worrying and do what her publicist advised. Have a glass of wine and hug that sexy fiancé of hers.

She takes the food and wine into the kitchen and opens the bottle. She pours two glasses and plates her food. As she picks at her lamb, her gaze drifts toward the stairs, her mind circling back to her earlier thoughts. What, if anything, will she have to reveal? Are they truly still good, or could this be the end? She needs more than Kavan's words of assurance.

Jenna rushes upstairs to get lost in Kavan, to cleanse her guilt, to rinse away the horror that was today. She enters the bathroom just as he is wrapping a towel around his waist. He looks up at her, startled. She crosses the small room, removing her shirt. Rising to her toes, she kisses him fervently. He grunts in surprise even as his hands come up to cup her face.

"Jenna . . ."

"I need you."

I need this.

She removes his towel, lets it drop to the floor, and kisses him. His eyes widen before they flare with heat. His lips are warm, open.

He yanks off her yoga pants and deepens their kiss. He's then lifting her aloft, filling her, her shoulders pressed to the wall. He thrusts with force, his face buried in the crook of her neck. Her fingers dig into his hair, his shoulders, and his breath heats her skin. Her spine scrapes against the cool tile, her back burning as he kneads her breast through her bra. She tugs his hair as if she's possessed. To keep him with her so he doesn't leave. She needs to believe her past won't find her, that this will all blow over. That her secrets are still hers to hold on to despite what Stan exposed today. That she'll never be as lonely as she was before she met him.

Jenna comes quickly and Kavan follows. Lifting his head, his breathing heavy, he lets go of her legs. Using the wall as support, she drops her forehead on his damp chest, her breaths labored. His ribs expand and contract beneath her. His legs tremble. He presses a hand to the wall and drops his head, exhaling loudly. She hears a low rumble in his chest before he says, "That was interesting."

Lashes fluttering, she looks up at him, her worry back. He scrapes his thumb along his bottom lip and lifts a brow. "I mean, it felt great, but . . ."

She looks down and away, ashamed. What came over her?

"Hey," he says gently. He touches her chin, lifts her face. His eyes are soft, searching. "What's going on? Talk to me."

"It's nothing. Sorry I jumped you." Their lovemaking has been passionate before, but never an act of desperation. Today threw her for a loop. She's functioning off-kilter, and she'd better find her center fast.

His mouth pulls up. "You can jump me anytime. You just surprised me, that's all." He doesn't move to cover himself. He stands before her, skin glistening from the shower and sex, watching her. "Jenna . . . ?"

Her mouth quivers. She wants to tell him everything. To expunge her sins and reap the repercussions. Just put everything behind her. She's carried her burden too long. Shunning friendships and romance. Love.

Kavan is the first person she feels has seen her, as much as she's willing to show him. And even that isn't the real her.

Her life is a lie. Their relationship is built on lies. But unraveling the mess she's woven means giving it all up. Giving him up. And giving up Josh. Because she'll go to jail, and her son will go to someone else. Possibly Tyler, if she finds the courage to seek him out.

She picks up her clothes and turns to the door. "It's late. We should get some sleep."

"Does this have to do with that reporter?"

She stops, clothes clutched to her chest. Her limbs turn to ice. Goose bumps rise, rippling across the surface of her skin. Her arms, her back, her breasts. This is it. They're over. She was foolish to believe she could have more out of life.

"He talked to you?" she asks without turning around, afraid of what's on his face. The contempt, the betrayal.

"Tried to. He came in during the lunch rush. I had to kick him out because he was harassing my counter staff. He was a dick about it, too."

"I'm sorry."

"Why? It's not your fault. Look at me, Jen." He grasps her shoulder and coaxes her to turn around. "We don't have to talk about it right now. I already know your life before me wasn't easy."

She chews on her bottom lip, wondering what more she can tell him without risking their relationship, or herself.

He smiles softly. "I also know there's more than what you've already told me." That she ran away from home to escape her abusive and narcissistic father and to protect her unborn son. "I'm ready to listen when you want me to. Just don't shut me out."

"What if I don't want to talk about it?" Or never can.

He takes a beat to answer. "Then I have to wonder who hurt you so badly. And what I've done to think you can't trust me enough to be open with me."

Shame heats her face. She does trust him. It's what he'll think of her that keeps her silent. "What did he tell you?" she asks.

"He thinks your name is Lily Carson and that you murdered a sixteen-year-old kid."

She closes her eyes, wishing Gayle had never pitched the *Sentinel* in the first place.

"I'm not Lily anymore." She whispers the confession.

He's quiet, as if waiting for her to confirm the rest. His gaze mines her face. She drops her clothes and presses her face into Kavan's chest. She inhales his clean aloe scent and loops her arms around his torso. "Love me," she murmurs with a silent plea, wishing her past would go away.

Kavan remains still, and she almost expects him to push for an answer. But he cradles her face and drops kisses on her eyes, her cheeks, her lips. Her entire body shudders from his touch. Her eyes well with gratitude. For now, he lets it slide.

He unhooks her bra, letting the lingerie drop to the floor, and scoops her up. He carries her to the bed and makes slow, sweet love to her. He tells her that he loves her more than the pain she's holding inside. And as she climaxes, he tells her he loves her despite her past. He just fucking loves her.

If he only knew the cloth she was cut from. He wouldn't love her then.

Later, after they drink the wine and she's eaten, Jenna drifts to sleep with Kavan's lips on her shoulder and his body aligned with hers. But it's Dwight who torments her mind, and in her nightmares Wes claws her arms, his fingernails leaving grooves in her skin. She then sees his decomposing body washed up onshore. One shoe is missing.

CHAPTER 14

Josh is always running late, and this morning is no different.

Jenna smears peanut butter across a slice of whole-grain bread and glances at the clock. This morning's *Sentinel* issue should have been delivered. It's out there with an article on her. She hasn't picked it up yet, afraid if she shows how apprehensive she is, Kavan will make her talk.

She wonders if parents are still posting about her on social media. Did they talk about her with their kids over dinner last night? Has anyone reported her to the police?

She woke before Kavan and Josh this morning and spent an hour skimming through last night's surveillance for police cruisers, Dwight, anyone who may be watching, monitoring their movements. Blessedly, she saw nothing but a few stray cats and the random neighbor walking home.

Kavan sips his coffee in the corner, careful to stay out of the way as she rushes about the kitchen. He reads the latest news on his phone, and she feels a quiver of nervousness in her chest about the article.

It's fine, she tells herself. Gayle fixed the problem. No one will call the police. She's yesterday's news. Dwight, though, is another story. He'll taunt her until she pays up.

She slaps another slice of bread on top of the first and slides the sandwich into a Ziploc bag. "Hurry up, Josh. You'll be late." She's driving him to school. Dwight followed them home yesterday. She's nervous for Josh to walk alone, exposed and accessible. Dwight could approach him.

"I can't find my key." Jenna hears him above, banging around his room.

She looks at Kavan like she can't believe they go through this every morning and hollers to Josh, "Did you charge your phone?"

"Uh . . . think so," he yells back.

"You'd better!" He isn't leaving the house with a dead phone.

Kavan, kicked back against the counter, smirks into his coffee mug. "At least he doesn't have to style his hair."

A smile finds its way onto her face. Josh would never make it to school on time. Kavan's daughter, Uma, is only ten but already spends most of her morning in the bathroom. It's quite the production. And Jenna loves the normalcy of it. Uma lets Jenna style her hair in curls and bows, and Uma will dress in a frilly party-girl dress, and they dance to Billie Eilish and Halsey. Josh just rolls his eyes and drags Kavan outside to play catch.

Jenna treasures those moments. They feel like a family. They remind her of Olivia, her sister, when they'd practice hairstyles on each other. Or her brother, Lucas, when he'd invite her to shoot hoops in the drive or take her kayaking.

For a few years the siblings were close. But that ended the summer she turned eight and Dwight blamed her when Lucas was caught shoplifting. He convinced them, Jenna included, that she had begged Lucas for the Hot Wheel he'd lifted.

She glances at the clock again and swipes up her keys. "Josh!"

"Coming." His feet pound the stairs. He drops his backpack on a chair and slaps a piece of paper on the counter.

Jenna glances at it while shouldering her purse, expecting to find a form he's waited until the last minute for her to sign. But it's nothing of the sort. Josh has filled out half the fields on what appears to be a social studies assignment, and what he wrote sends a sheet of ice through her.

She reflexively clutches her keys. The metal digs into her palm. "What's this?"

"Homework. It's due tomorrow." Typical for a kid who waits until the night before to start a project. Though he's already completed half of the family-tree assignment, his father's side is blank. Her side is finished except one field: hers. He must have gleaned the others from the article posted in the parents' club Facebook group and her conversation with Dwight.

Her pulse spikes upon seeing her family's name. But her stomach twists over what's written on the maternal grandfather field: Dwight Carson/Benton St. John. She points at it.

"How do you—" She can't finish the question.

"Yesterday, remember? I overheard you and Dwight. I didn't know who to put there."

A ripple of panic crosses her chest. Her gaze darts to Kavan to see if he noticed her shock. He watches them curiously, silently. She rolls her lips over her teeth and slowly shakes her head. She doesn't like seeing Dwight's name on his project.

Her gaze drops to the empty *Mother* field. "Why's mine blank?"

"I didn't know what name to put for you either." He glares at her with brutal honesty. Overnight, yesterday's shock has morphed into anger. Suspicion to disdain.

"You know my name."

Kavan puts down his phone and crosses his arms. She's worried about what he's hearing, how he'll react, knowing she can't stop this. Her name is out. There will be questions. Both deserve answers she isn't prepared to give.

"Your real one," Josh says.

"Jenna. My name's Jenna." And it is. Jenna Mason is a legit ID according to Murielle's daughter, Sophie.

He stares hard at her before penciling in her name with a huff of disgust. He presses with force. The lead snaps. He swears.

"Hey." She touches his head and he jerks out of reach.

"Why'd you change your name? You never told me. Is it because of Dwight?"

"We'll talk about that later," she says with a nervous glance at Kavan as she tap-dances around a subject she isn't sure how to explain. She points at the clock. "You're late."

He jabs his pencil at the empty *Father* field. "What's his name?"

"You know I don't know."

"You're lying. I can tell. You lie about everything. How do you *not* know who he is? Didn't you love him?" The brackets around his mouth tighten. He doesn't want to cry in front of Kavan. And she doesn't want to explain Tyler to Josh in front of him. Not when they're rushed for time. This is a longer conversation.

For years Jenna has kept Josh in the dark about Tyler. He was always accepting of their circumstance, trusting her implicitly. But that's changed this past year. He's older. His questions are more pointed. His desire for answers more demanding. And through no one's fault but her own, she never thought ahead. Would she tell him? When? How?

Honestly, she wants to tell him everything about Tyler, so much so that the truth practically crawls out of her. Tyler is a good man, and Josh deserves to know that. To know him. And to know that she loved him. That she left him because she believed she was protecting him.

Her son looks at her with a mixture of expectation and disappointment. She can tell him now. And she can tell Tyler about Josh. Dwight's visit yesterday showed her that his threat about Tyler all those years ago was empty. He was trying to control her, to convince her to give up Josh. He wouldn't risk killing Tyler, or anyone for that matter. He'd lose too much, land in prison himself.

As for Wes's shoe? It's no different than him swearing to kill Tyler if Jenna didn't do what he wanted. Just another tactic to get her to behave. To extort money from her.

She opens her mouth but stumbles over the words. Kavan's here. They're pressed for time. She needs to clear her head and think how she'll spin this. Once one lie unravels, the entire web will fall.

"We'll discuss this after school," she repeats.

"We're studying family heritage in Mr. Scalzo's class. This is only the first part." He gestures at the chart. "Next week I have to interview one relative from each side. I'm going to fail if I don't add my dad's name."

Kavan clears his throat. "You can put me, if that's all right with you." He checks with Jenna. Josh doesn't give her a chance to agree. His face screws up.

"You're not my dad."

"Josh. Don't be rude."

He looks away, anger tinting his face.

"He's going to be your stepfather when we marry. I'm sure you're not the only kid in class with a stepfamily." She hands him his lunch with another glance at the clock. "Come on, we have to go." This conversation is giving her hives.

He takes the bag and his eyes sheen with hostility. "I'm the only one whose mom doesn't know the name of the guy she fucked."

"Josh!" she yells, appalled.

"Brad called you a slut."

"Brad can go fuck himself." She clamps a hand over her mouth. "Sorry." Shock renders Josh speechless. He gapes at her. Jenna wants to take it back. "I didn't mean—"

He stuffs his lunch and homework into his backpack and heads for the door.

"Where're you going?"

"School."

"This way." She points at the garage. "I'm driving."

"I'll run." The front door slams behind him.

Stunned, Jenna drops her purse and keys on the counter. Kavan doesn't say a word, and Jenna can barely look at him. "I've never sworn at him."

"If it helps any, you didn't swear *at* him. You just swore."

She grimaces. "Semantics."

But her son is right. Plenty of kids haven't met their fathers or aren't close to them. But what kid doesn't at least know their dad's name?

"I doubt this will be the last time. Wait until he raids the liquor cabinet."

She can't think that far ahead. Will she be lucky enough to still be around when that happens? She starts to clean the kitchen, twisting the bread bag closed.

"What did Josh overhear you say yesterday?" he asks cautiously.

"My dad and I talking," she says, shocking herself with the admission, how smoothly it rolled off her tongue. How relieved she instantly feels to tell the truth. But it's Kavan. He'll find out from Josh sooner or later. And if he didn't have questions after what just happened, she'd wonder how invested *he* was in their relationship.

"You spoke with him?" There is no mistaking his surprise. Kavan knows the partial truth. The same truth she's told Josh. She ran away when she was sixteen and pregnant because her father was an emotionally abusive narcissist who wanted her to give up her baby. The part about Wes was left unsaid. As for Josh's father, she told him he was a guy at a party. She was drunk, never got his name, and that was that.

She nods and Kavan whistles. "You haven't seen him in what, thirteen years?"

"Until yesterday," she says. Best he hear from her than Josh.

Kavan sets down his mug. "How? I didn't think you were in touch."

"We weren't. Aren't," she corrects.

"Then how does he know where you live?"

"He found me through Stan, that reporter." She worries her lip, wondering if she's telling him too much.

Kavan swears. "Why that little shit. If I'd known, I would have decked him."

Her lip quivers into a smile. She would have loved to have seen that.

He comes over to her, rubs her arms. "Are you okay? Did he hurt you?"

By *hurt*, Kavan means *threaten* and *torment*. She's told him stories about what Dwight did to her and Olivia, how he cast her in a bad light so that Olivia no longer trusted her, driving a wedge between them. Despite all that, Jenna never stopped loving her. It was hard not to love her, given Olivia's promise.

It was their last summer at the lake. Olivia was thirteen, Jenna—Lily, then—was eight. And Lucas was a terrible eleven, stirring up trouble for no reason wherever he went. Late one night, Lily and Tyler were swinging on the hammock when Lucas ran up, grabbed her forearm, and twisted her skin. She screamed, and he ran off, Tyler chasing him through the woods.

Olivia found her sitting on the dock, crying. She sat beside her, dunking her bare feet into the water, and leaned back on her hands. She looked up at the stars. The sky was full of them that night.

"Lucas is an asshole," she said.

Lily nodded, sniffling. She could agree to that. Her arm hurt. She'd been rubbing the welt, but it still stung.

Olivia lay on her back and folded her hands on her stomach. "Look at the stars, Lil. They're bright tonight."

Lily lay back just as one shot across.

Olivia gasped. "Make a promise."

Lily looked at her sister. "Wishes, not promises."

"Uh-uh." Olivia smiled. "Promises are better. Wishes, you never know if they'll come true. But with promises, you keep the power. You control whether or not they happen."

Lily frowned. "That's the lamest—"

"Shush." Olivia grabbed her hand. "Make a promise before it's too late. Shooting-star magic doesn't last forever."

She snorted, rolling her eyes, but she made a promise. "Next time Lucas hurts me, I'm kicking him in his boy parts."

A bark of laughter. Olivia grinned at her.

"Your turn," Lily said.

Olivia shook her head. "Only one promise per star. We have to wait for another."

Lily turned her gaze back to the sky. Stars glittered. She swore she saw satellites orbit overhead; the night was that clear. Peaceful, too. Soon her arm didn't hurt anymore. She stopped thinking of Lucas, wondering if Tyler had tackled him and left him to rot in the woods. Then a star blew across the sky with a tail of brilliant, sparkling ice and metal and fire.

"Oh," she and Olivia gasped.

"Hurry, make your promise." Lily nudged Olivia.

Olivia inhaled deeply. "I promise that no matter what, I'll defend Lily if Lucas hurts her again. I'll go to bat if anyone tries to harm her."

A tear beaded in the corner of Lily's eye. She rolled over and hugged her sister.

Jenna always hoped that because of Olivia's promise, one day they'd find their way back to each other.

It explains why she writes Olivia every year and sends her a picture of Josh. While the envelopes have no return address and tell Olivia nothing about her, Jenna hopes her sister gets the message. She hasn't forgotten her. She's never forgotten Olivia's promise.

"No, Dwight didn't do anything that I can't handle." For now.

She thinks of the video, his threat. His demand for money. He won't go away until she gives in.

He kisses her forehead. "Sorry about Josh."

Her eyes dip to his chest. She runs a hand down the front buttons. "It's not his fault." This is on her.

"Can I give you a bit of advice, one parent to another?"

Her mouth twists. He waits until she looks up at him. "Whatever you're keeping from him, he's going to find out. Best he find out from you."

Jenna's heart beats rapidly. She sees it in his eyes. Kavan knows she lied to Josh.

"I know," she whispers, defeated. She leans her forehead against his chest. "But I don't know how." Josh will hate her. She robbed him of a life with his dad.

"How about starting with the truth?"

CHAPTER 15

During lunch break, Josh sits across the table from Anson. Kids clamor around the schoolyard, voices loud and obnoxious. A few eighth graders he knows from math class fight over the one good basketball. Josh would usually be on the court with them, but he isn't in the mood. He's going to fail his All About Me assignment. His social studies grade will drop from a C to a D, and it'll be his mom's fault.

Why is she lying about his dad?

Whoever he is, he probably doesn't know Josh exists.

Dejected, he removes Anson's iPad from his backpack. He searched everything he could find on Lily Carson and didn't come across one mention of any guy who might be his dad, except that Wes Jensen kid, and his mom already told Josh it's not him.

Unless she lied about that, too.

Then again, she seemed weird when he asked, so who knows?

He gives his head a shake. He's so confused.

It hasn't fully sunk in that she changed her name and doesn't want anyone to know who she was. It makes him wonder if she did kill Wes, and if she did, why? He can't picture her hurting anyone. It's almost impossible to fathom she's been living a life on the run. He doesn't doubt how much she loves him. He knows she's scared of what will happen to him if she's caught.

But did she steal him from his dad?

Tears singe his eyes. He pulls up his shirt collar and pretends to scratch his face. He can't cry here.

He slides the iPad across the table just as Mateo and Brad walk up. Mateo cups the back of Josh's head and shoves his face into his sandwich, and Josh chokes down a sob, trying to disguise it as a laugh. He goes to cuff Mateo, but the jerk's already out of reach. Mateo then tugs Anson's shirt.

"Nice tire print, dork ass."

"What?" Anson twists on the bench, trying to see the back of his shirt. A bike-tire print runs diagonally down the back. Anson's cheeks blister red when he notices it. "Ah, man. My mom said she washed this."

"What happened?" Josh asks.

"My sister ran over it."

Josh's lips twitch from holding in a laugh. Anson's older sister, Elise, can be clueless.

"See you at the park, losers," Mateo shouts, walking backward. He flips them off with both hands. Brad fist-bumps Mateo, cackling.

"Assholes," Anson grumbles. "You going?" he asks Josh.

"Didn't bring my board." And he doubts his mom would let him. She's been wigged out since Dwight showed up. His grandfather. That's so weird to think about after having no one but his mom for family. But it doesn't take a genius to realize his mom can't stand the guy.

Anson drops his half-eaten bologna sandwich on his lunch bag and stuffs the iPad into his backpack. "Thanks, dude. My mom would kill me if you forgot it."

Anson almost didn't let Josh borrow the iPad, let alone take it home, until Josh explained who he was looking for. Anson thought Ryder Jensen, Wes's older brother, could be Josh's dad. But Josh doesn't think it's him. He and Ryder look nothing alike, and the guy's history creeps him out. He's serving time for beating up a woman.

"He's weird looking," Josh had said. Like he's been doping on Molly.

Anson stuffs the rest of his sandwich into his mouth. Bread fills his cheek. "Wanna go to the pier after?"

"Can't." Josh scratches his head. His mom promised to talk about his dad after school. And he intends to hold her to it.

"Bummer." Anson crumples his lunch bag and launches it at the trash can, hitting the rim. The bag drops to the ground.

The lunch attendant blows his whistle. "Pick that up, Mr. Lawrence." He points at the bag. "Try walking it to the can next time."

"Hop off," Anson groans. He drags himself to the bin as their friend David runs up to their table, basketball tucked under his arm.

"Dude, bro. There's a guy over there asking for you." He points at the fence bordering the schoolyard and community park.

"Who's asking?" Anson settles back on the bench.

"Some guy. He wants Josh."

"Me?" Josh squints at the man on the other side of the fence. "What does he want?"

David shrugs.

The guy looks slick even from a distance, telling Josh exactly who it is. Dwight. He's wearing a suit like he did last night. Why is he here? Josh's heart races like a puppy with zoomies. His palms slick with perspiration. What does Dwight want?

He remembers how he told his mom that he found her because he'd been hanging around Josh's school waiting for her. Josh feels like worms are crawling on him. He shivers. How long has Dwight been scoping him out?

Anson shields his eyes from the sun's glare. "That the guy you were telling me about last night?"

Josh nods. "Come with me?" he asks Anson. He should ignore Dwight, but curiosity gets the better of him. Maybe he knows who his dad is.

"Sure."

They cut across the basketball court and traverse the lawn to the chain-link fence. Dwight looks like that guy who works at the bank who's always trying to pitch his mom shit. There's a sheen to his gray suit, and his shirt is too damn white and bright, burning Josh's eyes. Isn't the guy hot? It's almost ninety. Josh is baking. He drags his forearm across his hairline, wiping off the sweat. Dwight squints against the midday sun, chewing on a toothpick. He removes the stick when they reach him and grins. His faded-blue eyes swing from Anson to Josh.

"Hey, there, kiddo, remember me?"

"What are you doing here?" Josh asks. His mom would be pissed.

Dwight flicks the toothpick. It spins off to the left and disappears in the grass. "I didn't get the chance to meet you properly last night. Thought I'd swing by and introduce myself."

At the back fence? It occurs to Josh this guy doesn't want his mom to know he's here. Unease slinks through him. Josh shouldn't be talking to him either. Maybe it isn't such a good idea to squeeze him for info. He'll want something in return.

"I have class. You should go." He backs away from the fence.

"This him?" Anson mutters from of the corner of his mouth.

"Yeah."

Dwight grasps the chain link and leans in closer. "Name's Dwight, son. I'm your friend's grandfather. Isn't that right, Josh?" His eyes crinkle like a wrinkled shirt Josh left in the dryer. A breeze cuts across the park, ruffling Dwight's suit. Josh can smell his cologne, something tangy like grapefruit. He can't stand grapefruit. The rind is colorful and promising while the inside is poisoned death. Worst piece of fruit his mom buys.

"What of it? My mom says you're not her real father."

"Well, your mom doesn't know what she's talking about." Dwight side-eyes him. "What do you say I meet you here after school and take you out for ice cream? We can get to know one another. I'll tell you whatever you want to know about your aunt Olivia and uncle Lucas. We'll even talk about your mom. You can tell me all about yourself and everything your mom's told you about me and your grandma Charlotte. Sound good?"

Josh squints at him. "Do you know who my dad is?"

"That's a mighty good question." Dwight rubs his jaw. "We can talk about that, too."

As much as Josh wants to find out what he knows, nothing about Dwight being here feels right. The guy's vibe is all wrong. He then recalls what he read about him last night, that he was a suspect in an unsolved murder case. Dwight's dangerous.

"I don't want to talk to you," Josh says, inching back.

"That's a shame. Here." He presses a business card through the fence. "Call me when you change your mind. I'll be around."

Josh slides the card into his pocket.

Dwight shifts his weight. He grasps the fence with both hands again. "One more thing, kid. You realize you can't trust your mother. She's a liar, always has been. You won't get answers from her. That's why you need to see me. We're family. I'm here for you."

"You're an even bigger liar," Josh blurts, leaping to his mom's defense, disgusted that's exactly what he was thinking about her before Dwight showed up. But he hates the way Dwight is talking about her, how he's saying these things out loud. He strikes back. "I know about you and that guy Benton, my real grandfather. I know what you did." As soon as the words leave his mouth, he realizes it was the wrong thing to say.

Dwight's face turns purple.

Josh doesn't know if Dwight murdered Benton. He was just guessing after everything he overheard between Dwight and his mom and what he read about the case last night.

Anson knocks his arm to get his attention. "Guy's a douche. Let's go." He heads back.

Josh doesn't stick around to see what Dwight does. He runs after his friend.

CHAPTER 16

Delivered at dawn, this week's edition of the *Oceanside Sentinel* lies in the middle of a patch of grass too small to be called a lawn next to a mound of day-old dog poop. Jenna snaps off the rubber band and unrolls the single-section publication. Her article is on page six. Local Animator Makes It Big with Seven-Figure Multi-Book Deal. Stan's name isn't in the byline. And the article matches Gayle's press release almost verbatim. It includes only the two photos her publicist submitted, the book cover to the first book in her children's series, *Tabby's Squirrel: A Maze of an Adventure*, which is scheduled to publish next month, and a caricature sketch of her that Gayle's team uses in place of a headshot. Not a blurry candid of her in sight. She could have sworn Stan took a photo when she was getting out of her car in the garage.

Jenna skims the article to the end, where it wraps up with a mention that a full-length feature animation film is in the works. Her head falls back and she utters a soft curse of gratitude. Gayle prevented a train wreck of an article that could have taken her career off the rails. But Stan's interference has already done enough damage. He brought Dwight back into her life.

He has her afraid the police will come knocking. And he has her questioning again whether she should run.

It's okay, it's okay, she repeats to herself, recalling her promise to Josh. *We're going to stay.*

Refolding the paper, she texts Gayle. Read article. Crisis averted.

She wants to believe this. Needs to believe it.

Gayle texts back, See? This time tomorrow nobody will remember who Lily Carson is.

Her heart rate spikes when she sees her birth name. She wishes this would all go away.

Her phone pings with another text from Gayle. 500 books arriving tomorrow. Which she has the weekend to sign and return for her launch, since she won't attend in-person events. She returns inside, prepared to put in a full day's work. The first email she opens is from her cowriter, Joel, asking for her edits on his latest revisions to the *Tabby's Squirrel* screenplay. They were due back to him yesterday. As if she doesn't know.

But her gaze keeps going to the window. When will Dwight come back? How long will he give her until he torments her again? And what about the police? They could show up at any moment. Just yesterday morning her house felt safe. Today it feels like a cage.

She needs to get out.

———

Twenty minutes later, Jenna is seated at a corner table at her neighbor's café, Glenny's on the Beach, with a vanilla latte. She ordered a black coffee only to change it on a whim, stepping out of her comfort zone. She doesn't even know if she'll like the drink. It smells divine, she thinks, and she blows on the frothy surface as she waits for it to cool.

The café is lively, packed with babbling toddlers in strollers and chattering mothers. Two dads at the table next to hers keep their daughters occupied with coloring books. Jenna watches with envy. She missed the playdate phase of parenting. When Josh was a toddler, she was struggling to survive off the minuscule funds she earned through advertisements on her YouTube channel, desperate to keep whatever warm bed they slept in, praying another teen runaway in a more dire predicament didn't come along, forcing Jenna and Josh to move on. Murielle's angels, people who open their homes and lease their properties free of charge to runaways like her, who once might have been runaways themselves, had only so many beds.

Despite the low points of those early years and the tragedy she left in her wake when she fled home, Jenna never regretted her decision to run away. She would have lost Josh if she hadn't.

Keely bursts into the café like a beam of sunshine, her summer dress just as bright, her hair in an array of curls piled atop her head. She spots Jenna on her way to the counter and waves with both hands. "Fancy seeing you here," she trills.

Jenna leans back, grateful to see a familiar face in a sea of strangers. "Hi."

"Is this seat taken?" she asks of the chair across from Jenna.

"No, it's yours if you want it," she says, surprising herself. She's used to sitting alone, but today she feels safer in the company of others. She isn't a target; she can fade into the crowd. If he's watching, Dwight wouldn't approach her in public. It's why she came to Glenny's.

Keely drops her large bag of a purse on the chair and peers at the table, cockeyed. "No pastry? That's a crime."

A quiver in her chest at the word. Only years of practice keep her face straight. "Just a latte this morning."

Keely's nose crinkles. "Have you tried the chocolate croissants? No? Glenny's are the best. I'll get you one." Her entire forearm disappears into the mouth of her bag to get out her wallet.

Jenna picks up hers to give Keely money.

Keely declines the cash. "I got it. You can get me next time."

A smile tugs the corner of Jenna's mouth. She likes the idea of a next time.

Would there be a next time? Her eyes drift outside the café's windows. The police won't come. Dwight won't pass along the video. She's all right. Safe.

If she repeats it enough, she'll believe it.

"Be right back." Keely floats to the counter, chatting up a storm with Glenny in between her orders, and is back at the table a few minutes later with two warmed croissants and a hot mocha for herself. She drops into her chair and slides a pastry toward Jenna before taking a generous bite of her own. Her eyes close on a sigh. "So good. I really shouldn't be eating this, but fuck it. I usually avoid this place. Too many temptations." She sucks melted chocolate from a fingertip. "But I do like to treat myself."

Jenna picks up her buttery confection and bites off an end. Warm chocolate coats her tongue. A drip laces over her chin. "Oh, my god." She moans, her mouth full. "This is good." She can see why Keely comes here. She wipes her chin with a paper napkin before taking another bite.

"Told you." Keely's eyes crinkle. She dusts crumbs off her lap. "I'm glad I ran into you. I was going to call."

"Oh?" A nervous flutter in her chest over what it could be about.

"I read the article in the *Sentinel*. A movie. Wow. Congratulations."

Jenna licks chocolate from her finger, relieved she isn't asking about what Stan wanted to pursue. Jenna will happily talk about her career any day, thrilled she proved Charlotte wrong. She is a success. She can support her son.

"Thank you," she says.

"That was not the article I was expecting to read. Did that reporter ever come back?"

Dread spills into her. "He did. Josh was with me. It was terrible. But my publicist delicately reminded the paper's editor they'd agreed on a publicity piece."

"You have people!" Keely exclaims, starry eyed. "Gotta love it when a team fights for you." She leans across the table and growls like a dog.

"I do have that." Jenna cradles her latte, letting the cup's warmth seep up her arms. It's going to be in the mideighties today once the fog burns off, but this conversation leaves her with a chill. It has the potential of veering into her past.

The only way she can describe how she felt after telling Kavan about Dwight's visit was relief, like she'd let air out of a Tupperware container before the lid popped. While Kavan doesn't know her full story, just sharing a little bit about her past lifted weight off her shoulders.

But she's never talked to anyone besides Kavan about her son. Though she feels like she needs to ask advice. Kavan told her to tell Josh the truth. She doesn't know how without him hating her, without risking losing him to Tyler. Which she might anyway if the police come. She should talk with Murielle, make arrangements for Josh in the event she is arrested.

"Can I ask you a question?" Jenna says.

Keely waves her fingers. "Fire away."

"Have you ever lied to Anson and regretted it?"

"Every day," she says, and Jenna barks with unexpected laughter. She swallows a bite of croissant. "Why just this morning I told him I'd washed his favorite shirt when I hadn't. He'd been asking to wear it all week, and I just haven't had the time to do laundry. I told him I did to get him to stop bugging me for it. Terrible, I know. He wore the shirt to school this morning with his sister's bike-tire print across the back. He didn't even notice it was still there. Serves him right, I thought when he left for school. But then I started thinking about what other kids would say, especially that kid Brad who doesn't know how to keep his mouth shut. I wish I'd said something before he left for school."

"Anson has thick skin. I'm sure he'll be fine."

"I still feel bad." Keely sulks.

Jenna looks at her hands cupped around her latte. "I was asking about something bigger, like life changing. How do you fix a lie like that? I'm afraid Josh will never trust me again," she admits to Keely what she can barely stomach herself. Her entire body is shaking, as if revolting against her openness.

"Oh." Keely sits up straighter. "That reminds me. I know he was upset yesterday with the kids bullying him about that stuff that was posted online. But Anson mentioned something last night that has me a little worried. He says Josh is looking for his dad."

"What?" Shock rattles her.

"I heard Josh asking him to use our family iPad while he was over last night. If I'd known Anson let him, against our rules, mind you, I would have put a stop to it. I know how you are with him and social media."

He's not allowed to use it. Josh fights her on it. He feels isolated from his friends. But she can't risk being found through his profiles. Or him having unsupervised access to the internet and digging up her past when she can't control the narrative, which seems to be what he's already doing.

Keely presses her index fingers to her lips. "I'm sorry. It won't happen again. I hope you'll still allow Josh to come over. Anson really likes him."

That isn't what worries Jenna. Did he find Tyler? Has he tried contacting him?

"Do you know if he found anything?" she asks.

Keely blinks. "Uh . . . no. I can ask Anson?"

"Please." Then, "No, never mind. I'll talk to Josh." If he has found Tyler, he wouldn't have asked about his dad this morning. Jenna sets down her latte, the drink too sweet on her sour stomach. She isn't afraid that he might learn of Tyler. It's what he'll do when he does. What Tyler will do when he finds out she stole his son away.

If too many people from her past learn where she is, it'll reach Ryder Jensen. He will eventually be released from prison, and he will come after her. And he may do that through Josh.

She can't protect her son if he's not under her care. And she's been fooling herself she could cling to this normalcy he begged to keep.

Keely looks guiltily at the table.

"What is it?" Jenna asks.

"I told you I wouldn't look you up. I'm sorry. I got curious when Anson mentioned Josh hasn't met his father. I guess you never told him his name?"

Unease curls around her. She wishes Keely hadn't searched her, but she can't control that. People will. They probably still are.

"I don't know his name." The lie comes smoothly.

"Oh." Her eyes widen. "Ohhh . . . Were you . . ." She bites her bottom lip.

"Sexually assaulted? No, nothing like that. I was at a party, sixteen and rebellious. Never asked the guy his name." She goes with the lie.

"Does Josh know?"

"Not the specifics." What parent wants their kid to think they were promiscuous, even if they were?

"I had a friend once. We were inseparable since preschool until she, well . . ." Keely looks sad. "She got in with the wrong crowd and started using drugs. She said a few things that led to her 'friends'"—she formed air quotes—"attacking me on my way home from school. I ended up in the hospital with several broken ribs and a concussion. And you know the weird thing? I wasn't mad at her. She wasn't the same girl I knew. Her addiction changed her. She ran away from home before I was released from the hospital. I didn't try to find her. I should have. I wanted to tell her that I forgave her. They found her body in a field behind a McDonald's two weeks later. She'd overdosed."

"I'm sorry." She touches Keely's hand in sympathy. She heard and saw many similar stories while moving through Murielle's network. "I'm curious what this has to do with Josh."

"Not Josh, really. But you. I read everything I could find on you and . . . Lily Carson," she adds, guiltily. "I thought you should know that, and that it doesn't change how I think of you. I still consider you a friend. I'm sure you had a good reason to run away and change your name."

She had very good reasons to run and change her name.

Her uneasiness and anger flares, a knee-jerk reaction. Keely's just being Keely. Honest and open to a fault. It's what Jenna liked about her in the first place.

But old habits and emotions don't disappear overnight. Jenna doesn't like having her past picked apart, her actions judged. Her mistakes critiqued. She does that to herself enough each day.

She glances under the table, then lifts her gaze to Keely.

"What?" she asks.

"You forgot to wear your galoshes." That was a low blow, but Jenna is shaking with anger and shame. She pushes away from the table. It was a mistake to come here so soon after yesterday. She abruptly leaves the café, questioning her choice to remain in Oceanside. Loathing the thought that she might have to choose her safety over her son's mental health.

CHAPTER 17

Students spill from the back gate after the bell rings. Parents scoop up their kids. Other children find their way to their parents' cars queued in the pickup loop. Some cross the street and walk home. Jenna stands off to the side behind the chain link, searching for her son. She spots him the same moment he sees her. He doesn't seem the least bit surprised, even as he asks why she's here when he reaches her.

"I thought I'd walk home with you."

He rolls his eyes. "I can walk myself."

"I know you can. But after the way you stormed out of the house this morning, I was worried. Come here." She draws him away from the crowded gate. They stop under a sycamore. Josh grips his backpack straps. "How are you doing?" she asks when they're out of earshot.

His mouth tightens and he looks away. "I'm fine."

She doesn't believe him.

"Did you find your key?" He'd been searching for it that morning.

His mouth pinches and she has her answer.

"Josh, what if you needed to get into the house and I wasn't there? How would you get inside?" She doesn't keep a spare key outside. It isn't safe.

His head whips in her direction. "Are you asking because of Dwight?"

Her eyes narrow, mining his face. He looks at the ground. She feels a pounding pressure in her chest. "Did something happen today?"

"No, why?" He shrugs, acting cool.

"Josh."

"Will you tell me my dad's name if I tell you?"

"I'm serious, Josh. Don't play games with me. What happened today?"

He stands his ground. "You know who he is." Her mouth presses into a thin line. She does, and she should tell him. But not here. He scoffs, reading her reaction. "Knew it."

"We'll talk at home," she says, fumbling for what she'll tell him when they get there. How she'll explain without him leaving her. Fearing his reaction, how it can bring her more into the open than she already is.

He backs away from her. "I want to meet him."

"Keep your voice down." She starts walking, gesturing for him to follow.

"Was he mean? Did he hurt you? Is that why you won't tell me about him?"

"No, it's nothing like that."

"Then why can't I meet him?"

"Because I don't know where he is exactly." Sort of. One Google search a couple of years ago showed her he worked in the finance department at some high-tech company in San Francisco. She could easily find his number. Make that call. Plead for Tyler's forgiveness, pray he doesn't take her to court, where they'll dig into her background and question her about Wes. They'll contact Dwight as a character witness. He'll show them the video. Then it'll be over for her. She'll legally lose her rights as a parent.

The scenario plays vividly in her mind, filling her with dread.

Josh's cheek flexes. "You never told him about me, did you?" She slowly shakes her head, envisioning a life without him. She already feels a gaping hole in her chest. His mouth screws up. "Fuck you." He takes off running, his long strides cutting through the grass.

"Josh!" She jogs after him, but he's already gone, flying across the street.

She swears, dreading the argument waiting at home. How much he'll hurt when she tells him about his dad.

Josh is on the porch when she reaches the townhouse.

She doesn't speak to him as she unlocks the door. Kavan's right. She hasn't been fair to Josh. He deserves the full truth.

Josh points at something on the ground. "What's that?"

She looks at the soiled cloth beside a dirt-filled clay pot. The previous tenant left behind a pink hibiscus. Jenna unintentionally killed the plant within a month of moving in. As for the cloth, it wasn't there when she left to pick up Josh.

She pockets the key and picks up the dingy gray item that has seen better days. Like the Vans sneaker from yesterday. She unravels it and gasps. A baseball jersey. And the name displayed across the back. *Jensen.*

Heat flashes through her. Wes's uniform.

The shirt he died in.

The material singes her fingers. She almost drops it. Josh whimpers, seeing the name. She balls up the shirt.

"Whose is that?"

"Go inside." She wants to burn the shirt. It's evidence. How did Dwight get it? Did it wash up after Wes? Did he remove it and the shoe from his corpse? Why would he hold on to these?

Jenna almost dry heaves.

"It belonged to that kid, didn't it? The one in that article online? It's the same last name." His face turns ashen. "How'd it get here?"

"I don't know."

But she does.

It's Dwight. She doesn't want to spook Josh, so she doesn't tell him.

Jenna looks up and down the street. Most of the residents are at work. Some kids are walking home from school. Nothing looks out of the ordinary. No one seems out of place.

"Wes Jensen is dead, Mom. Why's it here? Who left it?" His voice is shrill.

"I don't know." She tries to hustle him into the house, glancing over her shoulder. Is Dwight watching them? Is he enjoying his sick joke, their fear?

"Stop saying 'I don't know,'" Josh pleads, backing up into the house. "You do know. I know you do. I see it on your face. Dwight did it. Am I right?"

"I think so," she relents, wishing Josh didn't see the shirt. That he wasn't as scared as she is.

"He came to school today."

"What?" She grasps his wrist. "He came on campus?" she asks, terrified Dwight is doing exactly what she feared. Manipulating her through Josh.

He shakes his head. "The park. He was at the gate."

"What did he want?"

"He wanted to meet me. And—" His gaze dips to the ground.

"And what?" Her grasp tightens and he squirms. "Josh, please, this is important. Tell me everything," she says. Ironic, given she's withheld much from him. But how is she to protect him if Dwight can get to him so easily when she's not around?

Her heart pounds. If he can, so can Ryder once he's released from prison. He has six more years to serve, not long enough. But she hopes he'll lose interest in her by then. Unless she's easy to locate. Then it might reignite his interest in pursuing her.

She shouldn't have let Josh talk her into staying. She was foolish to believe she could keep this life. Kavan. Her home. She should pack up and leave, deal with Josh's anger once they get to wherever they end up.

"He told me you were a liar," he admits reluctantly. "That I can't trust you."

She releases his wrist. "Don't believe a word he says. Anything else I should know?"

He shakes his head. "No, but I . . ."

"But you what?"

"I might have said something."

Her mouth dries. "Like what?"

His mouth works. "I . . . I . . ."

"What did you say?" she asks through clenched teeth.

"I told him I knew about him and Benton."

Her head snaps back. "You did what?" she shrieks, and he shrinks back. She drags her fingers down her cheeks until her arms fall heavily at her sides. "What did you do, Josh?"

"I searched him last night and found an article about my grandfather, the one you told me about. It said Dwight was a murder suspect. People thought he killed Benton."

Jenna feels like a building has fallen on her. Dwight will assume she lied to him, that she did tell Josh everything. He'll send the video to the police. "What. Exactly. Did you say?"

"I . . . I . . ." he hedges.

She grasps his shoulder. "This is important, Josh. I need to know *exactly* what you said."

"I said, 'I know about you and that guy Benton, my mom's real dad. I know what you did.'"

Jenna stumbles back a step. "Why would you say such a thing?"

"I don't know," he cried. "I lied. I don't know what he did. He's got to know that. But he made me mad. He was calling you a liar, and I felt guilty about thinking the same thing, and I don't know. I just said it."

"What do you think he did, Josh?" she asks, her tone serious, deadly quiet.

Fear flickers across his face. "I—I don't know. He weirded me out, and I started thinking maybe he did kill my grandfather. It's probably not true. It was just a stupid article."

Jenna goes very still. Her limbs grow cold. Josh has no idea how true it is. And by keeping him in the dark about who Dwight is and what he's capable of, she's put him in harm's way.

Though it does explain the shirt. It isn't a warning. It's a threat.

Dwight believes Jenna told Josh about him and Charlotte. He'll wonder who else she told, even though she swore yesterday she hadn't spoken to anyone. She always lies. Why wouldn't she lie about this?

"Did he say anything else?" she asks too calmly.

"No," he whispers. "But he gave me his card."

"Give it to me." He hands it over, and, after a quick glance at his phone number, she pockets it for later. She needs to deal with Dwight, placate him, beg him not to go to the police. He has her pinned against the wall, and she hates being as helpless as she'd been as a kid. She'd sworn she would never let him make her feel that way again.

"I'm sorry," Josh admits. "I shouldn't have talked to him."

"No, you shouldn't have. But I should have warned you to stay away." She pulls him against her chest, terrified of what Dwight will do next.

She's seen him at his worst.

CHAPTER 18

LILY

Within a second of Dwight closing the door, Lily heard a tap on her window, and her heart lurched. Through the glass and in the darkness she saw the faint outline of her friend Wes. He knew to come to her window if he needed something or else her dad would punish her. She wasn't allowed visitors after dark, and Wes always got home late from baseball.

She dried her face, took a deep breath, and opened the window. "What are you doing here?" she asked in a loud whisper. That was too close. Dwight could have seen him. Lily didn't want to give him further reason to punish her.

"I need to copy your algebra homework." Wes had missed class today. He left early with the baseball team for a game. He still wore his jersey; the shirttails hung below the waist of his hoodie.

"Now's not a good time." She thought of the conversation with her parents in the upcoming hour, the packed suitcase in her closet.

"Belmont's going to fail my ass if I don't get it in tomorrow. Come on, Lil, it'll be quick."

"Can't you get it from Nolan?" Another friend of Wes in their class.

"I tried. He isn't home. Look out." He hoisted himself through the window and climbed over her desk. His shoes toppled a pile of textbooks. Two dropped on the floor. He cringed.

"Quiet." Palms down, she bounced her hands for him to lower his voice.

"My bad." Wes restacked the books Lily wouldn't crack open again.

She riffled through her backpack and gave him her assignment. "Keep it."

"It's blank."

"I haven't had the chance to work on it. I just got home."

"But it's due tomorrow." He tried to give the sheet back.

"Belmont gave me an extension."

He frowned. Mr. Belmont never gave extensions.

"I'm going away for the weekend," she said, spinning the tale. "I won't be in class tomorrow."

"Where are you going?"

"My aunt's house. Her cat died." She didn't want anyone to know she was leaving, where she was going.

"Oh. That sucks." He folded the assignment, tucked the sheet into his back pocket. "Weird, but sucks." He threw himself on her bed.

Her eyes bugged. "You can't stay," she said, glancing at the door.

Oblivious to her rising panic, he dragged her sketch pad across his legs. "What are you working on?" She'd known Wes since they fought over the sand bucket in the preschool playground. Her art had always fascinated him.

"Just some caricatures." She tried to take away the pad, but he shifted. She straightened. "Seriously, Wes, you need to go."

"Relax. Daddio doesn't know I'm here."

Nerves tingled along her arms. She moved to the window, anxiously waiting for him to get up. "Wes . . . come on."

He flipped open the sketch pad to her latest drawing, a gray squirrel high up in a tree dropping nut bombs on a very disgruntled tabby cat. Laughter bubbled from Wes. He clamped a hand over his mouth. She glanced at the door, holding her breath.

"This is good, Lil. Look at that cat's face. It's hysterical." He chuckled and tossed the sketchbook aside. "You could start a comic strip. I'm serious. You're going to be famous one day. You—"

Lily's door flew open. Wes jumped off the bed. They gaped at Dwight.

He pointed a finger at Wes, and Lily's breath faltered. She knew, just knew what he was thinking.

That Wes was the father of her baby.

She started shaking her head even before he said anything.

"Sorry, Mr. Carson," Wes said. "I was just leaving."

"Not so fast." Dwight moved into the room. "I should have known it was him. You've been friends since you were toddlers. When did it change? How long have you been together, sneaking behind my back? She isn't allowed to date; did she tell you that?" he asks of Wes.

"I—uhh . . ." Wes looked at her, confused.

"Has she told you the news yet?"

Lily's face drained. "No. It's not what you think."

Wes stole a glance at her. "Told me what?"

Dwight gave her a look of utter disappointment. "He has the right to know."

"It's not him, I swear."

"What's he talking about, Lil?" Wes asked.

"He's not the father," she pleaded, panic coursing through her as everything her dad threatened about the baby's father became too real.

Dwight's eyes shined unnaturally bright; his expression turned deranged. Rage rippled through him like a slow-moving electrical storm. Hot and angry. "Liar," he whispered, and brandished a gun she never knew he had.

She screamed.

"Jesus Christ," Wes yelped, plastering his back to the wall. "What's with the gun, man? We weren't doing anything. We were just talking."

Ignoring him, Dwight aimed the gun at her chest. Blind terror moved through her. "How much did you hear when you were outside our door?"

She gulped. He knew she'd been eavesdropping.

"I didn't hear anything," she said, too afraid to admit the truth. Shock clenched its fist around her stomach, her world turning upside down, any sense of security she had in her room, this house, vanishing. This was her dad. He should be protecting her as he did Olivia. Not threatening her. "Please, Dad. Put the gun away. He's not the father. You have to believe me."

"Then who the fuck is?" he roared.

Lily sobbed, Tyler's name stuck in the back of her mouth like a wad of gum. She'd never tell him, not when she feared for her own life.

"Please, Mr. Carson. Whatever this is, it's not me. Let me go. I want to go home," Wes cried. The sharp scent of ammonia filled the room, and Lily's heart shriveled. She looked over at Wes. A wet stain spread down his jeans. She could smell his fear, and it magnified her own. Dwight was going to kill them if she didn't say something.

Dwight moved farther into the room. She could smell her mom's cigarette smoke on him, see the sheen of perspiration coating the side of his neck.

"Lily's having your baby, that's what's going on," he said, ignoring her. "And the little slut swears it's not yours."

"Because it's not," she wailed.

"It isn't mine. We've never," Wes whimpered, shaking his head.

"Remember what I told you last night, Lily?" Dwight asked, shifting the gun to Wes.

Lily cried. How could she forget?

A name. She just had to give him a name. Any name.

Ethan flared to mind.

She opened her mouth to tell him. It would be another lie. Buy herself time. Talk some sense into Dwight. Negotiate him off that rage-fueled precipice upon which he stood.

But Wes reacted. He ran. And it was the worst thing he could have done. Dwight would never let him leave the house, let alone the property. Not when Wes could report him to the authorities before he

114

could convince Wes this was a joke. He was just messing with them, she wanted to believe that. Because that's what Dwight did. Twisted the story until he wasn't at fault. It would be all on them.

Wes shoved her into Dwight and sprinted past them. Lily screamed his name, scrambling to her feet as Dwight took off after him. Later, Lily would wonder why Wes didn't run out the front door, why he ran out the kitchen slider and into the backyard. Chased by fear, he must have panicked, gone out the first exit he'd seen. He ran across the yard through the murky fog, heading straight for the dock.

Did he plan to swim? Escape on one of Lucas's kayaks? Disappear in the fog? She had no idea what he was thinking. Perhaps he wasn't thinking at all.

Dwight ran through the house after him, and Lily chased them both, shouting for them to stop. She bumped into Charlotte in the hallway. Charlotte snatched her wrist, holding her back.

Lily shrieked. "Let go. He's going to hurt Wes."

"Then you shouldn't have eavesdropped. Exactly what did you hear?" she demanded through gritted teeth, and Lily had never loathed her mother more. This woman murdered her biological father. Stole any chance of her knowing him.

"I . . . I . . ." She tried to squirm free, but Charlotte's grip was strong, and Lily detested the feel of her hands on her.

Her mom tsked. "I did what I could for you, but you're on your own." She released Lily's hand. And Lily released her heart. Her mother was dead to her.

She heard a shout from the back. *Wes.*

Lily ran outside into the cold, damp night, the faint glow of light from Lucas's apartment barely visible. She screamed for her brother's help as she ran after Dwight.

Wes and Dwight faced off on the dock. She inserted herself between them. Wes would not die because of her lies. She couldn't live knowing she caused his death.

"Move aside, Lily." Dwight jabbed the pistol. A vein corkscrewed along his temple, straining against his skin. Spittle glistened on his lips.

Lily shook her head. Tears threatened to spill over. "No." She prayed Lucas would hear them. He'd come to her aid.

Dwight lowered the pistol to her belly and released the safety.

Something unexpected unfurled inside her, and a strength she didn't know she possessed took over, something years of emotional abuse and neglect had failed to do.

She exploded with a roar, lunging at the man who had raised her from birth, and for a split second Dwight froze, shocked she'd come at him. His eyelids flickered. His face turned ashen. His grip wobbled.

It was all the time she needed. She yanked the pistol from him as her petite body slammed into his much larger frame. The gun fired, and behind her, water splashed. Dwight stumbled backward. He fell against the rail. Lily collapsed to her knees. The Glock dropped hard on the metal decking. When she looked over her shoulder, Wes was gone.

Lily screamed. She shouted for Wes. But he'd gone under. She couldn't see him in the dark and fog. Where was he? The water was black.

Dwight retrieved the gun and pushed to his feet. He pointed at the water. "You shot him."

Lily turned colder than the damp air. "No!" She couldn't have. She was trying to save him. She prayed he'd just jumped into the water to escape him.

Dwight grabbed under her shoulder and hauled her up. He pressed the gun to her forehead. She whimpered. Tears fell unhindered.

"I know what you heard. I don't trust that you won't talk. If you ever speak a word to anyone about our involvement in the Benton St. John murder, I'll notify the cops that you killed Wes."

He lowered the gun and shoved her away from him toward the house. "Run."

She was too frightened not to.

She ran straight to her room to retrieve her suitcase, startled to find Charlotte waiting for her, her suitcase open on the bed. "I see you were already planning to leave."

Lily froze in the doorway, afraid of getting too close, uncertain what Charlotte might do. "I told you I was last night."

"It won't be easy raising a baby on your own."

Lily's fingernails dug into the wood. She trembled violently. Shock kept her speechless.

Charlotte's features cooled. "For what it's worth, I fought to keep you."

She stared at her mother as if she were a stranger. A monstrous stranger. Murderer. Psycho. A deplorable human being. She was disgusted they were related.

"You'll find five grand in cash in the side pocket. Enough to get you on your feet. The rest is up to you."

"Why?"

Charlotte cocked her head, her eyes already dead toward Lily. "Why what?"

"Why are you giving me money?"

Charlotte straightened. "Despite what you think of me, I'm not a monster."

A garbled bark of laughter. Was she serious? She'd stabbed a man eight times and drowned him. Could she not see how monstrous that was?

Charlotte zipped the case and picked up Lily's backpack. "Come along, before your father changes his mind and won't let you leave." Lily wouldn't put it past him to lock her up in the windowless wine cellar for eternity. Charlotte led her to the front door.

"Why'd you do it? Why'd you kill my father?" she asked, taking the pack from her mother.

"We had no choice."

"There's always a choice."

Charlotte's face softened, eerily so. She looked cold, unyielding. She tucked a piece of hair behind Lily's ear, and Lily shivered at the touch, revolted. "Life isn't black and white, my darling. It's not always right and wrong. There's a lot of gray in between. We live in the gray. And one day . . ." Painted lips spread into a smile that chilled Lily to the bone. "One day you'll realize there isn't anything you wouldn't do for your children. Until then . . ." She pressed a finger to Lily's mouth. "Not a peep from you about what you heard."

She nudged Lily outside and shut the door in her face.

CHAPTER 19

Guilt. Grief. Regret. She might not have had friends these last thirteen years, but these enduring emotions have been her constant companions. They dine on her memories. Sneak into her dreams. Steal hours of sleep and consume her attention during the day. They've kept her on the move months after Ryder ceased stalking her.

In hindsight, it's easy to admit everything she did wrong. She should have run to Lucas and called 9-1-1, or had Tyler drive her to the police. She should have tempted fate—Dwight wouldn't have shot her—and dived into the water after Wes.

Her actions were impulsive, fraught with fear. She should have done more. But her terror was a living, breathing beast cleaving her back, snapping at her heels. Dwight told her she'd killed Wes. She believed him. So she ran.

Josh retreats upstairs to use the bathroom, and Jenna pulls up the surveillance footage. Dwight appears in frame a few minutes after she left to pick up Josh from school. He's dressed casually in pants and sweatshirt, the hoodie pulled up—as if she wouldn't know it's him—and he overhands the shirt onto the porch like he's delivering a newspaper. He jogs away.

He hasn't changed. It's like when he destroyed Olivia's prom dress and blamed her. He wanted Olivia to hate Jenna as much as he did.

Now he's trying to scare her into giving him the money he's demanded.

She crumples the business card. Not anymore. She isn't a petrified knocked-up teen terrified for her life. And she won't let him near Josh.

Dread and denial swirl like the blending of two colors. She can't believe what her son said to him. Yes, he guessed the truth not realizing he'd done so, but he was trying to defend her, and she can't fault him for that. But how will Dwight reciprocate? What will he do next? Threaten Josh at gunpoint?

She needs to stop this before it escalates like it did with Wes.

Clearing her throat, she pushes aside thoughts of her childhood friend with the skill of one who has spent her life disassociating. If she lets the memories overpower her, they will incapacitate her. She calls the number on Dwight's card.

"It's Lily," she says when he answers. Her old name sounds and tastes unfamiliar.

There's an unexpected pause. "My word. I never thought I'd live to see this day, *you* calling *me*. Let me guess, it's about Josh."

The sound of her son's name from his mouth slithers through her. She tries not to recoil.

"Great kid," he's saying. "Got a mouth on him, though. Takes after your brother. That boy used to give me hell. I bet Lucas misses you."

Doubtful.

Lucas once meant everything to her. Just a kid himself, he was the father Dwight wasn't. He taught her to swim, which fueled her passion for water. He'd take her kayaking through the bay as dawn broke and their paddles rowed in sync. And when she turned twelve, right before he was arrested and sentenced to juvenile detention for robbing a minimart, Lucas taught her self-defense.

It wasn't planned. Lucas had been playing around as always. After they finished a morning row and beached the kayak, he pulled her into a choke hold. She couldn't get free, and when she started to panic, his demeanor changed.

"Jab your elbow into my ribs," he said. "Harder," he said when she had and he didn't budge.

When that hadn't worked, he told her to thrust her heel into his kneecap, which she did. He stumbled off balance, loosening his hold enough for her to slip free. He spent the rest of the morning and many after attacking her, restraining her, catching her off guard, and walking her through how to get free.

"Guys are assholes, sis. Don't let them dick you around," he'd once told her. He was crass, but she loved him.

Yet the Lucas she left, hardened and damaged from his time in juvie, wouldn't miss anyone, let alone her.

He'd come home changed. Lifeless. And god forgive the person who tried to touch him. Lily hugged him after not seeing him for months, and he shoved her away, her back slamming into the wall, and he didn't care when she cried out. He then moved to the apartment above the garage.

"We need to talk," she says now, and Dwight's subtle laughter lacks depth or emotion. Chills scamper down her arms.

"Give me two hours."

"One." Or she'll lose her nerve.

She names the place and goes to end the call when he says, "Heads up. Whatever you're planning won't get rid of me. We're family."

She doesn't give him the satisfaction of a reply. She disconnects.

"Josh," she hollers up the stairs. "Back in a few." Their talk will have to wait until she deals with Dwight, which isn't her son's fault. This dance with Dwight, the unraveling of her lies? That's all on her. She's a coward. But she's also a monster. And she's going to give Dwight what he wants.

Jenna stuffs Wes's jersey into a plastic bag and takes it to the trash bin at the end of the alley. She lifts the heavy metal lid. It bangs into the brick wall behind it with a loud clang that rattles her ears, echoes through the alley.

She can't see the shoe. She can't believe she'd thrown it away. How much she's let her guard down since she moved here. How impulsive and quick she'd been to get rid of it. Evidence that could implicate her should Wes's case reopen. She needs to start thinking straight. She's smarter than this.

She climbs up the side and sifts around the trash. A bag rips. Food waste spills. The odor is foul, and the shoe she's looking for isn't where she threw it.

"Shit." Her palms grow slick from nerves. With a quick glance over her shoulder, she climbs inside. Her sneakers sink until the trash is calf high. She starts her search.

"Jenna, is that you?"

Jenna turns in the direction of a familiar voice. Glenny, her neighbor, looks up at her with an amused smile. Her terrier tugs his leash, tail wagging. He barks when he spots her. "Hush, Vlad. Sit." Glenny orders the dog to heel.

"Hey." Jenna smiles tightly. "Out for a walk?"

"We sure are." Glenny glances admiringly at her dog before flinging her gaze back to Jenna. "What are you doing?"

"I, uh . . ." Jenna looks around her. "I lost a necklace."

"That's a shame. Do you want help?"

She waves a hand. "No, no. I got it. You don't want to get in here. It's pretty rank."

"I'll say." Glenny jiggles the leash, looking in no rush to leave. "I read your article in this morning's paper. Lovely feature. You must be proud."

More like relieved the article Stan wanted to write didn't run.

"I am. Thanks."

Glenny tilts her head. The faint smile touching her lips fades. She swings the dog's leash. "I wasn't going to mention anything because I don't want to be that kind of neighbor. But I thought you should know."

Unease tiptoes up Jenna's arms.

"It's about Josh."

"What about him?" She stills. Glenny has her full attention.

"He came to the café last week with some boys I didn't recognize. He's usually with that kid, the blond one."

"Anson," Jenna says, wondering what other trouble Josh has stirred up. "Did something happen?"

"Nothing too alarming. But the boys took their ice creams across the street. They shared a joint with Josh."

"Oh." There's so much going on in her head, she doesn't know what to say. Is it terrible she thinks this a minor indiscretion compared to the trouble he's created with Dwight? She wishes she only had to worry about her son getting stoned. Life would be easier. Less dangerous.

"I thought you should know before it became a problem."

"Thanks. Glad you told me." She kicks aside a bag.

Glenny clicks her tongue and Vlad perks up, ready to finish his walk. "Are you sure you don't need help?"

"Positive. I should get back to . . ." She gestures at the trash.

"Right. Of course," Glenny says. "Have a good evening."

Jenna waves, looking at the mess under her feet.

"I'd shower if I were you," Glenny tosses over her shoulder.

"Will do." Jenna hefts a waste bag over the side, and there is Wes's shoe, hanging out at the bottom of the bin with decomposing waste. Guilt coils and tightens. She'd left his shoe in the trash like she'd left him to die. Wes didn't deserve that. No one did. She grabs the shoe and climbs out.

Back at the house, she finds Josh in his room. "What were you doing?" he asks, sitting up on his bed.

"Nothing," she says so he doesn't worry. "Look, I have to go out for a bit."

"But you said you'd tell me about my dad."

"I will, promise. But let me deal with Dwight first."

Josh's lips part, astounded. "You're going to see him?"

"I don't want to, but what he did today, showing up at your school? That's unacceptable. If you ever see him again, you walk the other way."

"But—"

"I mean it, Josh. He's not a nice man." The thought of Dwight coming after Josh the way he chased Wes would be her worst nightmare come true. She glances at her watch, backing up to her bedroom door to take a shower. "I won't be long; just stay here."

CHAPTER 20

His mom shuts her door, and Josh flops back on his bed to stare at the ceiling. From his window, he watched her in the dumpster talking with their neighbor. She found a shoe and put it in a bag that he knew already had Wes's jersey.

That shirt has him spooked. He messed up. He never should have spoken to Dwight, and he shouldn't have told his mom. She's going to confront him. He's afraid she'll make them move again.

He hates that they've moved as much as they have, sleeping in beds that belonged to someone else, taking baths in tubs his mom had to scrub clean until her knuckles bled because the previous tenants left everything gross and disgusting. Homeschooled since kindergarten, he wasn't allowed to attend school. His friends, if he could call them that, were the other kids in their shared housing.

When they first moved to Oceanside, Josh was nervous about attending school. He wasn't sure how to make friends, real ones that stuck around. But Anson started talking to him one morning. Then he introduced Josh to his friends. And Josh started to feel normal. He felt like he and his mom were living like most people do, and he was happy, especially after she met Kavan, who is cool and takes him to Padres games.

Uma is annoying, but little sisters are supposed to be. He likes that he's going to get a sister when his mom marries. He'll have his own family.

He doesn't want to give up the life they have here.

Josh sits back on his heels in the middle of the bed. His hands fist on his thighs; he's worried his mom will forget to talk when she returns, or will put him off again because she'll be frantic to move since Dwight found them and won't leave them alone. But he's old enough to know the truth. He's been pressing her since he first became aware that they moved more than the average person.

He was nine at the time, and she'd picked him up at Mrs. Mueller's, an old woman who smelled of sugar cubes and lemon oil and had two fluffy cats. She lived in the apartment above them. His mom rarely left Josh home alone. But he was sick and his mom had to buy medicine, so she left him in Mrs. Mueller's care.

His mom had packed the car with the few belongings they had when she came to get him. He'd left his baseball cards in his room, hidden under the mattress. She wouldn't allow him to go back for them. They couldn't, she'd said. She ordered him to sit low.

"Why?" Josh asked, putting on the ball cap.

"I don't want you getting sick in the car." Her smile seemed forced, made him worry more about what was going on.

He glanced out the side window, eyes wide, picking up on his mom's unease.

"Are we moving again?"

"Yes." This time she wouldn't tell him why.

She picked up her phone. A woman's voice on the other end lobbed questions at his mom. "Are you sure it was him? Did you get a good look? How'd he get into the apartment?"

Someone was in their apartment?

Josh dug out the lumpy stuffed puppy he kept hidden in the bottom of his backpack, comforted it wasn't left behind, too. He hugged the dog and sank low in his seat.

"Is the place ready?"

"I texted you the address. Key is under the mat," the woman said.

His mom glanced at him, touched his chin. "Don't worry, honey. I found us a new home. It's better than the apartment we left."

Josh realizes now that his mom had seemed frightened—just like she did when Dwight showed up yesterday. Had he found them before? Is that why they moved a lot?

Josh sags against the wall beside his bed. Disappointed and a little scared, he grabs his phone to call Anson and flops back on the bed. A dark screen glares back at him. Worst battery ever.

He tosses the dead phone on the floor, only to grab it again and plug it in before he forgets to charge it. He's the man of the house, and he'd better start acting like it. Take on more responsibility. Then his mom will stop treating him like a baby. She'll see that he's old enough to know about his dad and why she's scared of her own dad.

He drops an arm over his eyes, humming some Rex Orange County.

"Josh." His mom is back in the doorway, her hair wet and combed. "I'll swing by Kavan's on my way back and pick up takeout. What do you want?"

"Not hungry." He sulks, arms crossed.

She touches his phone charging on the desk. "Call if you change your mind." She blows him a kiss and then she's gone. The laundry room door slams, and the big garage door lumbers open. He hears her drive away.

Josh kicks his chair in frustration. It hits the desk and topples over. He rights the chair and stands there, listening to the house. The silence.

He's alone.

He's hardly ever alone.

This is his chance. He runs downstairs to his mom's studio. He doesn't believe her. They won't talk. She'll find another excuse. It's up to him to find the answers.

His gaze scopes the room. Her laptop is locked. He doesn't know the password. But he can search her desk and the cabinets, which he does. He moves from drawer to drawer, unsure what he's looking for.

He'll know when he finds it. He sifts through files, opens boxes, until he reaches a cabinet she doesn't use. It's empty. He sighs, flustered. There has to be something here.

He goes to close the door when a box on the top shelf catches his eye. Decorated in magazine clippings, an assemblage of fabric, glitter, and rhinestones, it reminds Josh of the boxes he's seen in Mrs. Rose's art class. Where'd this box come from? He's never seen it.

He takes if off the shelf and lifts the lid. A journal with a pink fuzzy cover rests on top. He picks it up, looks at the back, opens it up, flipping through the pages. He recognizes his mom's handwriting, her doodles along the edges. His eyes widen when he notices the dates of the entries. The last one was thirteen years ago, six months before he was born.

He knows he shouldn't read it. Journals are private. But he tells himself it's his mom's fault. He came downstairs on a mission. If she'd told him about his dad a long time ago, he wouldn't have to snoop.

Seated on the floor, he starts at the first entry. Page after page details his mom's life—her fears and frustrations—in the months leading up to when she ran away. He gets a clearer picture of who Dwight is. Same with his grandmother, Charlotte. As he reads, he begins to understand why his mom ran away. Dwight didn't love her, not the way he treated her. Charlotte did love her, but loved herself more. And Tyler Whitman . . . his mother loved him most of all.

There isn't one mention in the journal of his mom's pregnancy. But Josh knows Tyler is his dad. He can *feel* it.

The townhouse groans as the garage door opens. Josh's head whips in that direction. She's home. He notices the time, shocked almost two hours have gone by. He slams shut the journal and tucks the book into his pants. He returns the box and runs upstairs. He shoves the journal under his mattress and shoots Brad a text. Brad is the only one Josh knows whose parent would allow them to meet before school without first calling Josh's mom.

The laundry-room door slams. Keys land on the counter. His mom calls his name, and she comes upstairs. Feigning sleep so she doesn't question what he's been up to, Josh cracks open an eye. He spots a dingy white envelope on the floor. It's addressed to Olivia Carson, his aunt, in San Luis Obispo, California.

His eyes bug. He jams the envelope into his backpack, the closest thing to him, and tosses the covers over his head.

CHAPTER 21

Dwight waits for her on a concrete bench that faces the water. Waves cycle before him, the infinite ebb and flow etching the beach the way time has carved deep grooves in his face. She noticed yesterday that the corners of his eyes fold like an accordion. His forehead and neck crease like a well-read newspaper. Everything about him has aged except his cheeks. They're firm from a lifetime of shaving, a life empty of laughter.

From the back, with his broad shoulders and schoolboy posture, his peppered hair, full and thick compared to the thinning patches along his temple, Dwight Carson is just as imposing a figure as he was when Jenna was still Lily, gun pressed to her forehead. *Run!*

Jenna shivers at the memory. The fear he could incite just through a look.

He believes she's been talking to the authorities, and there is a high probability he'll release the video of her and Wes if she can't convince him otherwise. She'll go to jail. She'll lose Josh.

Dwight startles when she nears. Lifting a hand to his brow, he squints against the setting sun. "For a second there, I thought you were your mom. You look just like her."

Jenna breathes through her self-loathing. Hearing Wes go into the water after the gun fired flashes to mind. Does Benton haunt Charlotte as Wes does her? She doesn't like being compared to Charlotte, but they have more in common than just their looks.

Dwight smiles deliberately as if he knows exactly how his remarks affect her. They share two nasty secrets twisted in a vine of lies.

She looks down at him as fragments from the conversation she was never meant to hear shimmer like glass, bright and clear as if she'd heard her parents talking yesterday.

Yes, I killed him, Charlotte had shrieked at Dwight. *But you started this. You set everything into motion.*

I wasn't the one who brought the knife.

You dragged him into the ocean. You're just as guilty.

Jenna wants to be free of them both.

She thought she was. She'd run like Dwight ordered.

She drops a thick envelope on the bench beside him.

"What's this?"

"A money order for fifty thousand and five thousand cash." She made the withdrawal on her way over. It's everything she has.

His jaw literally drops. He opens the envelope, fingers the bills as if he's counting them right then and there, which he is. The greedy SOB. His eyes are extra bright.

"I feel like I should thank you." He snorts. "This still won't buy me off."

"I can try," she says, wanting to be rid of him once and for all. He's a reminder of what she did, the type of person she is. And as long as he possesses the video that proves she murdered Wes, he will always have her under his control.

"I owed Mom five thousand. She gave me cash when I ran away."

A shadow crosses his face. Charlotte never told him about that cash. Jenna once suspected her mom kept her income separate from Dwight's, at least most of it, or else Dwight would spend it.

"Twenty thousand is the money you asked for in exchange for not sending the video to the police. I expect you to honor that."

He lifts a brow, envelope clutched in hand. "And the other thirty?"

"Good faith. Josh doesn't know what you and Charlotte did. I didn't tell him, and I never will."

"Then how did he know?" His eyes harden to cold blue ice.

"He didn't. He overheard you and me talking," she snaps. "Because you were stupid enough to bring it up when he was in earshot. So, yes, he knows we have a bargain, but not what it entails. He went online. He read about Benton's case and Wes's drowning. He knows you were a suspect and that I ran away the same day Wes died. All public information. Any conclusion he came to he gleaned from that." She stops, catching a breath to calm her racing heart. She needs to remain levelheaded, appeal to whatever amount of humanity he has. And there must be something, or he wouldn't love Olivia as much as Jenna remembers.

Dwight bites into his bottom lip, considering. "I can't tell if you're lying out of your ass or if your son is brilliant."

"I don't want to go to jail. If I do, Josh will lose his mother. He needs me. I'm the only one who can protect him."

Dwight frowns. His lips part as if to ask protection from what, but Jenna rushes on with the speech she rehearsed on the way over.

"I don't have proof Charlotte murdered my father or that you helped. But if you release that video I will make yours and Charlotte's lives miserable. I'm sure an anonymous tip to Benton's widow would be enough to encourage her to convince the authorities to reopen the case." Newspaper articles had reported Benton's wife worked tirelessly for a solution before she moved to Texas, devastated her husband's murderer was never found.

"Is that a threat?"

She shakes her head. "Just a mom who will do anything to keep her son safe," she says, echoing Charlotte's unsolicited advice from long ago. "Same as you would do for Olivia."

Dwight blinks at her sister's name.

"You and I aren't biologically related, but we're the same in that regard. Olivia is your world. Josh is mine. I know how you feel about me. That you never wanted me. But I'd never come between you and Olivia. Please don't do that to Josh. Take the money, go home to your daughter. You were a good father to her. Let me be a good mother to my child, too."

Dwight lowers his head. His lips purse as if he's contemplating the ants circling his shoes. Then he tucks the envelope inside his jacket and stands. "You always were the smart one."

She doesn't know what to say to that. But her heart is pounding, and the back of her shirt is damp with sweat; she's that frightened he'll give her pushback and still take her money. "Do I have your word you won't release the video?"

He stares at her for a long moment, then dips his chin in an abbreviated nod. He starts to leave.

"One more thing," she says. She drops the plastic bag with Wes's jersey and shoe on the bench, the last things left of a boy whose only crime was lingering too long after she asked him to leave because he loved her art. Tears burn her eyes as if she'd looked directly into the sun. No one has asked who he is, and she'll never tell, but her first *Tabby's Squirrel* book is dedicated to him. *To the one who believed in me.*

"I don't want to know how you came into possession of these, but they belong to Wes's family." Not with her, and definitely not with Dwight.

Dwight picks through the bag, a question on his face, but she doesn't wait to hear what he has to say. She walks away.

CHAPTER 22

Jenna lies in bed, staring at the ceiling fan. Kavan gently snores beside her, his arm draped over her waist. She'd seen Kavan briefly when she'd picked up dinner. The kitchen was chaotic. The restaurant was hosting a large party. But he spared her a second for a kiss and the promise he'd come over after he closed. She was grateful he couldn't talk.

Standing up to Dwight, saying her piece, had left her drained. She was shaking by the time she reached her car. She dropped her forehead to the steering wheel and cried. He agreed to leave her be. He took her money. Likening his relationship with Olivia to hers with Josh seemed to have touched him on a level she didn't know existed between them, one where he could relate to her. See her for the woman she's trying to be: a mom who wants to give her son his best life.

And she needed to pull herself together. She had to tell Josh about Tyler.

He'd fallen asleep before she arrived home. He wouldn't budge when she tried to wake him. So she ate alone. Their conversation would have to wait until tomorrow.

Light from a passing car moves across the ceiling as her thoughts drift to Olivia. Dwight loved her immensely from what Jenna remembers. She never understood how her sister couldn't see the monster below his surface.

But love can be blinding. Make one do unexplainable things to hold on to it. Like lie, as she does to Josh and Kavan. Or write letters to a sister who has probably forgotten her, except once a year when Olivia receives Jenna's cryptic notes.

Josh's birthday is soon. It's almost time to write Olivia another letter. Because Jenna can't let go of her sister, of what they once had. She dreams that the three of them—her, Olivia, and Lucas—will be close like they once were. Is that even a possibility?

Jenna eases from bed, careful not to disturb Kavan. Barefoot, she pads downstairs to her studio and opens the cabinet where she keeps a shoebox of Lily's things and the stationery she uses for letters to Olivia tucked back on the top shelf, unseen unless you know to look.

But she finds the box quite visible, the corner hanging over the lip of the shelf, which she finds alarming.

That's not how she left it.

She'd packed the box in her suitcase earlier when she thought they were leaving. She wouldn't have been that careless when she put it back, not where anyone could see it.

She takes down the box and gasps when she lifts the lid. She feels blood drain from her face. The journal is gone.

"Hey."

Jenna startles, fumbling the box. She catches it and slaps on the lid.

Kavan stands in the doorway, hair tousled, sleep pants clinging low to his waist.

She returns the box and shuts the cabinet. "Hey," she says, turning to him.

"Can't sleep?"

"No." Her heart pounds as if she's been caught opening someone's safe.

He leans a shoulder against the doorjamb. "Want to talk about it?"

She shakes her head.

"Jenna . . ." Concern thickens his voice.

Her hands flex at her sides. Her walls are weak. He's steadily chipping them away through love and compassion. She can't hold it all in.

And Kavan has been nothing but supportive of her. Done nothing but love her.

"I met with my father today."

He approaches and gently moves her hair over her shoulder. "I knew something was up with you when you came by earlier. You seemed . . . disturbed."

She was. And bless him for not questioning her then.

"I'd just left him."

His thumb caresses her cheek. "How'd it go?"

"As well as can be expected. You don't know him, Kavan. He's . . ." She shakes her head, remembering how shaken up she was after she'd walked away. "He's difficult to talk to. He doesn't love me, never has. And he never listens, but this time I hope he did." She looks up at him. His warm honey eyes meet hers. "He showed up at Josh's school today."

Kavan's brows lift. "He did what? Why?"

"I imagine he wants to drive a wedge between Josh and me like he spent years doing with me and my brother and sister. It was his life's mission to isolate me from the family. He told Josh I was a liar."

"Bastard." Anger flares, darkening his eyes to a rich molten brown. He'd be furious if someone approached his daughter, Uma. It still amazes her how passionate he gets on behalf of her and Josh. No wonder Josh adores him. Like her, Josh just couldn't help falling for him.

"He has no business calling you that, especially in front of Josh. Why would he? What's the point?"

Because she *is* a liar. And he lives to torment her.

"It's what he does."

"There's got to be more to it," he says, biting the inside of his cheek, shaking his head. "He found you because of that reporter. Does that have anything to do with him?"

She shakes her head, not because it doesn't have anything to do with Stan, but because she doesn't want him to continue thinking along those lines. It'll lead to Wes, and she's not brave enough to admit that truth.

"What about those old articles? And yes, I read them. How could I not when I learned you used to be Lily Carson? Was he trying to tell Josh what that asshole tried to accuse you of was true?"

As in, she killed Wes.

A chill runs through Jenna as she turns her face from his hand, stunned at the way Kavan's mind works, how quickly he figures out exactly what's going on. It's why she hasn't told him much about her past, even the lies. He'll piece it together.

But her past has caught up to her. Every hour Josh learns more. She feels compelled to tell Kavan more. And she'll only hurt him and Uma both when everything comes out.

Maybe she shouldn't be so focused on losing Kavan. Maybe she should come clean and break it off.

"Dwight's good at twisting the truth." She stares at Kavan's chest. "Even better at making you believe what he says," she explains, thinking back to that time at the lake when Dwight picked them up at the Whitmans' cabin after Lucas was caught shoplifting. By the time they arrived home, he had Olivia, Lucas, and her convinced it was Lily's fault Lucas stole the toy car.

Kavan lifts her face with a finger. "I've never met the guy and I can't stand him." His gaze mines her features. "Have you considered getting a restraining order? I think you should."

"I can't," she says, thinking she should tell him about the money, but she can't muster the courage for that either.

He frowns. "Why not?"

"I just can't." She moves out of reach, and his arm drops to his side.

He stares at her. "I'm sorry, but can you please explain why? This guy approached your son. I'm kind of worried he might do the same to Uma once we're married."

"He wouldn't," she says in a rush while recognizing she can't guarantee that. Dwight did go after Wes, and he had nothing to do with her and Tyler. "I have my reasons for not filing. Please don't ask me to explain."

"Jenna, darling." He lifts his hands as if to cup her cheeks, but he pulls back. "On this matter, I think I do need an explanation. You're going to be my wife. There are things we're going have to discuss. And I personally would very much like to understand why you wouldn't do everything possible to keep that bastard away from you and your son."

Away from my daughter.

The words hover unspoken between them, and it hits her just how much she's put Kavan and Uma in danger. Ryder will eventually be released from prison. There's a striking good chance he'll come after her. He probably already knows where she lives if Stan spoke with his parents.

What was she thinking accepting Kavan's proposal? She can't marry him. If one more person dies because she doesn't have the courage to tell the truth, to own up to the truth . . .

"I can't marry you," she blurts, shocking them both.

"What?" he asks as if he hadn't heard her right.

"I shouldn't have said yes." But she'd been caught up in the moment when he proposed. She'd gone with the first answer that came to mind, what she desired most. Because she wanted to believe a life with him was possible. But she hadn't thought it through, considered the danger to Kavan and Uma should she marry him.

Kavan's face shutters, and her heart breaks.

She's never seen him as hurt as he looks in this moment. The pain of her rejection is there, along with his astonishment and disappointment.

She did that to them. Let him believe in them. That they actually had a chance to share a life together.

She starts to take off the ring, and he stops her, rests his hand over hers.

"What did I do to make you believe you can't trust me? That you can't open up to me?"

"Nothing," she says. "This isn't your fault. It's me. It's all on me."

Kavan glances toward the door before looking back at her, his face ravaged. "I'm going home."

She reaches for him. "Kavan—" He needs to understand it's over between them.

He holds up a hand, stopping her. "We're too emotional. It's late and I'm exhausted. I can't think straight. I'll call tomorrow. We'll figure out what's happening here. But right now I need to leave."

He does, and she lets him go.

CHAPTER 23

Despite the marine layer shrouding the playground, Josh is sweating when he reaches the park, his shirt drenched where it's sandwiched under his backpack. He's early. School doesn't start for another hour. He'd yelled at his mom while she was in the shower that he was meeting up with friends to finish a group assignment. He took off before she had the chance to stop him. But he texted when he reached campus to say he was there so she wouldn't chase after him.

Aside from a random jogger, the park is empty.

He stands under the palm beside the playground where Brad told him to wait. It's also the part of the park nearest the school's computer lab without being on campus, where the Wi-Fi signal is strongest. Brad doesn't have a phone Josh can borrow, but he'll let him use his laptop.

Palm fronds rustle overhead, barely visible through the mist. He leans a hand on the tree, his thumbnail picking at the grooves in the bark. Names and expletives have been etched into the trunk with the switchblades Josh knows some of the kids keep hidden in their packs.

Wiping his brow, he kicks up his skateboard and taps the rubber toe of his sneaker against the board's tail. He hears Brad before he sees him. One leg pumping, Brad skates across the parking lot's rough asphalt. He pops up his board when he reaches the curb, tucking it under his arm, and crosses the lawn toward Josh without breaking his stride, slinging back his hair with a shake of his head. Just as confident as ever.

"Hey, dudebro." Brad kicks Josh's shin, announcing his arrival. He slides his palm against Josh's and bumps his fist.

"Did you bring it?"

"Wouldn't be here if I didn't." Brad props his board against the tree, slipping the backpack off his shoulder. He opens the pack's wide mouth. "You owe me."

"I know." Brad's laptop came with strings. He would have used a computer at school, but they aren't allowed to access the internet unless it's during class, and only for an assignment. Josh doesn't want to risk getting caught, especially since he's searching for his dad.

"You're lucky your grandmother got you this. My mom won't even get me an iPhone."

Brad sneers. "She didn't. I picked it off a neighbor."

Josh gapes, fingers lifting off the keyboard. "You stole it?"

"What's it to you?"

"I—I'm not sure . . ."

"Do you want to use it or not?" Brad reaches for the device.

Josh jerks it away. "Yes."

"Then hurry up so we can bail."

Josh powers on the laptop, his fingers drumming the back of the device while he waits for the screen to wake up.

When it does, he types *Tyler Whitman Seaside Cove* in the search bar. Several pages of hits result. He clicks on the first few links, going with the third, a staff page for a Tyler Whitman, VP of Finance at Global Aim, Inc. There's a photo of him. He kind of looks like Josh, maybe. Sort of. Oh, who the heck knows. But there's an email address. Josh copies it to the Gmail account his mom doesn't know he has and types the email to Tyler Whitman he wrote in his head and spent the night fretting about.

Dear Mr. Whitman,

My name is Joshua Lucas Mason, and I am twelve years old. I'll be thirteen in September. You don't know me, but I think you know my mom, Jenna Mason. Her name used to be Lily Carson. She was your girlfriend in high school, and she ran away from home when she was sixteen and pregnant with me. I think I am your son.

I like to skateboard and I'm really good at math. I'm learning to surf. I love to read graphic novels. Hellraiser and Scott Pilgrim are my favorites. My mom wishes I read more books, the kind without pictures. I laugh when she tells me that because she draws pictures all day.

If you think I'm your son, too, will you write me? My family tree is due today, and my mom won't tell me about your side of the family. She hasn't told me anything about you. I think she's scared. We've moved around a lot. But her dad found us, and he isn't being nice. He kind of scares me. Maybe you can help.

Please write back. Bye.

Josh

Josh hits the send button and unleashes a long exhale. He did it. He emailed his dad. The letter isn't eloquent, nothing like the poetry his mom would have penned. He isn't even positive he wrote to the right Tyler Whitman. But if he did, maybe Tyler will want to meet him. He'll want to see Josh's mom again. He can help so they won't move again. And maybe they can be a family, a big one, since his mom is marrying Kavan. That would be the best, especially since he's never had family other than his mom. But if Tyler responds and doesn't want that, Josh tells himself that that's okay. Just knowing where he comes from is good enough.

Josh closes the laptop, thanks Brad, and Brad drops it in his pack. He looks around, noticing how busy the park has become since he started typing his email. Kids crowd the playground, and cars circle the parking lot. The county bus pulls up to the curb, making that loud *phhsst* noise as it comes to a complete stop. The door swings open, and a busload of kids spill out like the coins in his money jar when he's searching for quarters at the bottom. And suddenly Josh doesn't want to go to school. His assignment is unfinished. He's too upset about what he's learned of his family to sit in class all day. What if Dwight shows up again? He doesn't want to be around for that.

Josh kicks up his board and slaps Brad's shoulder. "Wanna ditch?" He points at the bus, his heart hammering. He's never skipped school. But it's Friday, and his assignment isn't finished, so what's the point? And if he sticks with Brad, he can check his email for Tyler's reply.

Brad grins with delight. "Dude, you are way cooler than I thought." He bumps fists with Josh. "Let's bail."

They run to the bus.

CHAPTER 24

The call comes at nine thirty while she's on the phone with Joel, her cowriter, working through edits on the script to the *Tabby's Squirrel* feature animated film. Thinking it's Kavan, nervous about the call he mentioned he'd make this morning, wondering what he felt about her when he woke, she ends the call with Joel only to find a voice mail from the school. Josh never made it to class.

Her heart hammers.

She doesn't understand. He texted her he was there.

In those few seconds between Josh shouting he was leaving for school and her shutting off the shower, running after him dripping wet, trying to get a towel around her, he was gone. They hadn't talked about Tyler last night, and her journal was missing. If he has it, he'll figure out who his father is. She was just getting into her car to follow him to school when he texted that he'd arrived. She'd been prepared that morning to explain why she left his father, that she was afraid for his life. As for what happened next—do they contact Tyler?—she and Josh would take it one step at a time. Once again, their conversation would have to wait.

Surely, though, this message from school is a mistake.

She texts Josh. Are you in class?

She then calls the school.

"Washington Middle School attendance. This is Haleigh Greer. Who's calling?"

"Haleigh, it's Jenna Mason, Josh's mom. I received a message that he's been marked absent. Are you sure? He left for school this morning. Texted he was on campus."

"It's possible he was marked in error. It's been known to happen. The kids are transitioning to second period. I'll send a runner when they get settled."

"Thank you." Jenna circles the room.

"I'll call as soon as I know."

"Appreciate that." Jenna ends the call, and a thought flares in her mind. Dwight is retaliating. He picked up Josh on his way to school. She confronted him and he's punishing her. She thought they'd come to an agreement. He'd leave her alone. She eyes her keys on the counter, impatient for the school to return her call.

Swiping up the keys, she drives to Josh's school. She reaches the attendance office just as a runner returns.

"Haleigh, Jenna. We spoke on the phone," she says, breathless, to the woman behind the counter with the plexiglass divider.

Haleigh's brows jump with surprise. "Hello there. Yes . . ." She glances around the small office, spotting the girl who just plopped into a chair. "Emily, dear, what did you find out?"

"He's not in class, Mrs. Greer."

Haleigh turns back to Jenna. "Sorry, he doesn't seem to be here today."

Jenna's knees buckle. She holds on to the counter.

"You sure?" She addresses the girl with braids and braces. A chill races across her skin. The hairs along her arms lift. Josh has to be on campus. Dwight couldn't have reached him so easily. Josh wouldn't have made it easy. He knows how she feels about her father. She warned him to stay away.

Emily nods. "Yes, ma'am."

"Is there anyone I can call for you, Ms. Mason?" Haleigh reaches for her phone.

"No, that's all right." Jenna abruptly leaves the office as a bus passes in front with an advertisement for the local hospital. Terror slashes into her. What if Josh can't text? What if he's hurt?

Jenna stops breathing. After a quick search, she dials the hospital's number.

"Tri-City Medical Center. How may I direct your call?"

"I'm wondering if my son, Josh Mason, has been admitted," Jenna says with a shaky voice.

"One moment."

Heart thumping in her throat, Jenna starts her car.

"Ma'am?" The operator comes back on the line. "We have no patients under that name."

"Thank you," Jenna says with a mix of relief and hysteria. She disconnects, quickly thumbs off the tears beading in the corner of her eyes. If he's not at the hospital, then where is he?

Where are you? she texts again. Then she calls and is immediately dumped into voice mail. He either turned off his phone, or the battery is dead. She growls in frustration, promises herself to buy him a better phone, and calls Dwight.

"Hello there. This is a pleasant surprise. Didn't expect to hear from you again."

The sound of his voice curdles her stomach. She gets right to the point. "Where is he?"

"Who?"

"You know who. Where's Josh?"

She hears the rhythmic click of a turn signal. Dwight's in his car. He's taking Josh away. He can't do this to her. She gave him every cent she had. They have an understanding.

"Did your kid run away from you, too?" His chuckle is deep. He thinks this is funny.

"Where are you taking him, you bastard?"

"Watch your tongue, young lady."

"Bring him back. Please. What do you want, more money?" She'll borrow from Murielle, get a loan from the bank. "Just tell me where he is."

"I don't have to kidnap him to extort money from you. We both know that."

"Then bring him home."

"I can't do that, Lily."

"Why not?"

"I don't have him."

"You're lying."

"I'm staying at a hotel for a conference. Where the hell would I put him? And if I did kidnap him, how would I have snuck him into my room? There are too many people around. Be smart, Lily. Think. Where is your boy?"

If Josh knows about Tyler, he might have gone to Anson's to look him up. He used Anson's iPad before.

She abruptly ends the call and throws the car into reverse. Tires squeal as she peels out of the parking lot.

Keely's car is in the driveway when Jenna arrives at the Lawrences' house moments later. She can see Keely through the kitchen window as she parks. Jenna runs up to the house and bangs on the door, watching as Keely cuts through the dining room. Keely's eyes go wide with alarm when the door flies open. Jenna must look a sight. Mussed hair from running her hands through it. Face pale with panic. Ratty bathrobe hanging off her shoulders. She'd thrown it over her shorts and tank after her shower because there was a chill in her townhouse.

"Goodness," Keely says, drying her hands on a dish towel. "Are you okay?"

"Is Josh here? Please tell me he's here."

"He's not at school?"

Jenna shakes her head, hugs her ribs. "I don't know what to do."

Keely steps onto the porch. "What happened?"

"Josh is missing."

CHAPTER 25

Keely grips Jenna's hand. "My goodness. Was he taken?"

"I don't know. Things haven't been going well at home. We've been arguing, and he's been acting out." And that was before the *Sentinel* drama and Dwight showing up. Jenna flaps her hands in a panic, unsure how much to tell Keely but afraid she must divulge everything to get the help she needs. "Maybe he just skipped school to get back at me." Or maybe he went to look for Tyler. But then why would he have texted her he was at school? He knows he'd be marked absent and the school would call her if he wasn't there. He also has no way to get to Tyler. He works in San Francisco in finance. She's followed his career, just as she's followed Olivia and her skyrocketing popularity as a graphic novelist. "I can't think straight. I have no idea where to begin. I mean, should I call the police?"

"There, there, it's all right." Keely squeezes her hand, pulling her into the house. "Kids disappear all the time. They usually turn up within a few hours."

Jenna slings her a look and Keely's mouth twists.

"Except, uh . . . except you," she stutters, stating the obvious. Jenna did not turn up within a few hours after she'd disappeared. "You're right. Call the cops. I'll get my purse and keys. We'll drive around and look."

Keely retreats to the kitchen and Jenna calls the local authorities. This will work out. Josh will be okay. He'll turn up. It's a simple misunderstanding.

"Oceanside Police Department, how may I direct your call?"

"I want to report a missing child."

"One moment, please."

Jenna holds her breath. Her heart pounds in her ears. The line stays quiet forever until it isn't.

"Officer Kentala. How may I help you?"

"My child is missing. He's supposed to be at school, but he isn't. They called me, and I don't know where he is." Panicked, anxious, and scared, she paces the foyer.

"Do you have reason to believe he was abducted?"

Her pulse spikes as he vocalizes her worst fear.

She thinks of Dwight; then she thinks of Ryder. Dwight denied he has Josh. Ryder is in prison. Josh texted he was at school.

"Yes, maybe. I don't know." Jenna explains to the officer that Josh was meeting friends on campus to complete a project, that he texted he was there. She can't believe Josh would have left the safety of school given everything that's happened.

"All right, ma'am. Tell me your and your son's names, and we'll see what we can do."

Ten minutes later Officer Kentala has a full description of Josh and his possible whereabouts.

Keely returns, keys in hand and a purse under her arm. "What did they say?"

"They'll put out an APB for Josh. They wanted to dispatch a car to my house to get a more detailed statement, but I told them I wasn't there, that I'm out looking for him."

"Then we'll look first and go to the station after. Unless you want to go there now."

She shakes her head. She wants to look for her boy, not sit in an office talking to a cop.

"Where do you want to start?"

Josh rode his skateboard to school. "The skate park."

Keely rattles her keys. "You look, I'll drive."

They settle into Keely's minivan, and Keely's phone trills at full volume. Keely shrieks. "Sorry about that." Her hand disappears into the mouth of her bag. "I didn't want to miss Anson's text."

"Is it him?" Hope flares that he knows where Josh is.

Keely reads the text. "He hasn't seen or heard from Josh since yesterday afternoon."

Jenna's chest concaves. She chews her cuticle, wondering if he could be with Kavan. Josh might be at the restaurant. But Kavan would have called if he was there on a school day. She calls him anyway while Keely drives, but he doesn't answer, and she doesn't give herself the chance to wonder if he's not picking up because of last night. She leaves a panicked voice mail and follows up with a text.

They arrive at the park within a few minutes. Jenna is out the door before the van has stopped. She runs to the chain-link fence that encloses the concrete course of ramps and hills, calling Josh's name. But the park is empty. Kids are in school, exactly where her son should be.

Why isn't he here?

Panic digs into her back. This isn't like him. Where'd he go? Why would he have left? Is he that angry with her? This is exactly what she feared he'd do when he learned about Tyler. He'd take off without warning.

She runs back to the van just as Keely is getting out. "He's not here," she shouts, yanking open the door. Keely scrambles back into the vehicle. "Try the beach," she orders.

"On it," Keely says.

Morning traffic has thinned, and they make it to the shore in little time. The marine layer hasn't lifted, leaving the beach gray and barren. Still, Jenna combs the area near their townhouse, taking a route that brings her near Glenny's. Benches are empty. The palm trees she's seen him sit under with Anson to escape the sun are deserted. A few runners jog by on the beach walk. A couple of skateboarders roll past. Across the street, Glenny's café has a full house. Behind her, Keely waits by the parked van, calling for Josh.

She looks at her phone. Kavan hasn't called back. She tries again. No answer.

Thinking he's ignoring her calls, she wants to take back everything she said last night so he'll pick up the damn phone.

Jenna waves at Keely, catching her eye, and signals that she's going across the street.

Inside Glenny's, the café is loud, alive with toddlers shrieking, parents chatting, and speakers blaring. A barista shouts an order. Jenna shoulders her way to the front of the line as irritated customers grumble their complaints.

"Glenny," she says, reaching the counter, interrupting a woman's order. "Have you seen Josh? Did he come in this morning?"

"No, dear, I haven't seen him in a while. Did you ever find what you were looking for in the—"

Jenna doesn't hear the rest. She leaves the café, racing back to Keely, dread coating the inside of her mouth. "He's not here."

Keely takes a slow turn, searching the beach, the road, the building across the street. "Is there anywhere else he likes to go?"

Jenna shakes her head. When Josh isn't at the park or beach, he's at Keely's house with Anson.

"Does he hang out with anyone besides Anson?"

"He was meeting some kids to work on a project. He didn't say who." But she remembers the other day. Mateo and Levi have been giving Josh trouble since before that reporter from the *Sentinel* stirred up her past. There's also Brad, another kid she's seen hanging out with them. Could they have anything to do with Josh's whereabouts? She pictures them roughing up her son.

"There's this kid Brad. I don't know his last name."

"Wusthoff," Keely says with distaste.

"You know him?"

151

"Of him. He's a troublemaker. He was expelled from his last school. He's got issues with rules."

"Do you have his number or know how to get hold of him?"

"No, but I know where he lives. Anson had to drop off a home-work packet last winter when Brad was out sick. He lives with his grandmother."

"Take me to her," Jenna says, getting into the van.

Ten minutes later, Keely is knocking on Brad's grandmother's sec-ond-floor apartment door. The building is old, dating back to the late seventies, with more weeds than shrubs growing in the front planter. Half of the lettering is missing from the signage on the building, as if the building itself has been forgotten in time.

"I don't know her name. We haven't met," Keely says of the grand-mother. "Anson ran up on his own to deliver Brad's homework."

"Is this the right apartment?" Jenna looks around. Keely knocks.

No sounds come from within the apartment. Impatient, Jenna takes over. She pounds the hollow door. "Hello? Mrs. Wusthoff?"

Keely glances over the banister to the courtyard below. She twists her fingers. "This place is sketchy. I shouldn't have let Anson walk up alone."

"It's not that bad." Jenna's lived in worse. Though the complex is a dump. Cigarette butts litter the ground. The tenant across the way displays his bongs on his windowsill. Glenny's remark comes to mind. If Josh skipped school to smoke pot with Brad . . .

She pounds the door again.

"Coming!" A bolt flips and a chain slides. The doorknob turns. Jenna backs away from the door that cracks open the width of a security chain. An elderly woman's pale face emerges from the darkened apart-ment like a half-moon in the night sky. Faded gray eyes behind thick lenses seated high on a wide nose stare out at them. "Yes?"

"Mrs. Wusthoff?" Jenna says, taking a chance on the name. "My name's Jenna Mason. My son, Josh, is friends with your grandson, Brad. Are they here?" She tries to see into the apartment.

Mrs. Wusthoff's gaze finds Keely, who smiles nervously, face tight, hands twitchy, before flowing back to her. "Today's a school day."

"We know. But by chance are the boys here, or somewhere else? Could they have skipped school today?"

"Brad wouldn't do such a thing."

Jenna's heart drops. She so hoped she'd find him here. She tears off a corner of a receipt she finds at the bottom of her purse and scribbles her cell number. "My number." She gives Mrs. Wusthoff the torn end. "Call Brad if you can. Ask him where Josh is."

The older woman squints at Jenna's number. "Your son skip school today?"

"We aren't sure," Keely says.

"Possibly," Jenna answers at the same time, catching Keely's gaze.

"Your boy means trouble. You need to keep a closer eye on him. My Brad would never skip class." She backs away from the door.

"At least call him about Josh. Please," she begs before the door closes. The bolt flips.

Keely exhales loudly. "That went well."

Jenna grimaces, roughly running a hand over her scalp, pulling her hair off her face as she holds back the tears. She needs help, more people searching.

"Can you drop me off at Kavan's?" she asks right as her phone rings. She scrambles to answer it. "Josh?"

"Mrs. Mason?"

Jenna starts at the unfamiliar voice. "Speaking."

"I'm calling from the San Diego Children's Hospital. Your son was just admitted and is being prepped for surgery. How soon can you get here?"

CHAPTER 26

Jenna blasts into the hospital like a Category 5 hurricane making land-fall, the sides of her ratty robe flaring like wings. When security directs her to the front-desk receptionist, who then directs her to the neurology ward, she's about to cause as much devastation as a superstorm if someone doesn't immediately show her where her son is when a nurse kindly calms her down and patiently leads her and Keely to the surgery waiting room. Where waiting is the absolute last thing she wants to do.

Where is her boy? How bad are his injuries? Was he conscious when they brought him in?

Nobody has been able to answer her questions.

The nurse just told her to wait. The doctor would be along shortly.

Jenna paces the small room. It's just her, Keely, a vending machine, two rows of empty chairs along the wall, and a window that looks out onto a smoking patio.

Keely selects a vinyl chair along the middle of the wall opposite the window. She wrings her hands. Over the intercom, a doctor is paged. Nurses converse at their station just beyond the threshold.

All that noise fades to the background as thoughts whirl around the eye of the storm in her head.

Her boy is broken. He's alone. Why won't they let her see him? Does he know where he is? Has he asked for her?

He needs her.

And she needs to see him. To assess his injuries. Hold his hand.

He's never been in a hospital. She's petrified. She can't imagine how frightened he must be.

"Where is everyone?" she asks the room. It's been twenty minutes since the nurse left them here.

Keely makes a face as if she's worried she'll say something that'll upset Jenna. "I'm sure someone will be along soon."

As if the universe answered Keely, a midsize man in teal surgery scrubs enters the room. His gaze shifts between Keely and Jenna. "Mrs. Mason?"

Jenna abruptly turns to the door, anxious for answers, to see Josh. "Where's my son?" She crosses the room to him.

"He's with my team." The short man extends his hand. "I'm Dr. Nunez, your son's neurosurgeon."

Jenna's face falls, his specialty indicative of how serious Josh's injuries must be. She takes the doctor's hand. Her own is noticeably trembling. "Neurosurgeon? Exactly how injured is he?"

"He suffered a blow to the head."

His remark slams into her. She feels like she stepped in front of a bus. "What happened? No one's told me anything."

"He fell down a flight of stairs. I don't know the specifics. You'll have to ask the police investigating his case."

"The police?" She whispers the question. She can't breathe.

Keely takes her hand. Jenna clutches her fingers, trying to not fall apart. Her boy has been injured, and it's her fault. This never would have happened if they'd left. She shouldn't have given in to Josh.

"His CTA scan shows a large subdural hematoma on the side of his head spreading over the frontal and temporal lobes. He's also still bleeding, which is putting pressure on the brain. We need to get in there to relieve it before it causes further damage."

"Goodness," Keely whispers, breathless with disbelief.

Terrified and speechless, Jenna gapes at the doctor. The risks involved. The seriousness of it all. What if he doesn't recover? What if he never wakes up?

Dread floors her. Regret floods her. Grief assaults her. Her baby. She presses a hand to her chest. It's hollow and hurts.

"At the very least, we need to drain the hematoma," Dr. Nunez explains. "We'll drill a hole and see what happens." He touches his scalp toward the front, his explanation a blow to her own head. "If the bleeding has slowed or shows signs of stopping, we'll attach a catheter through the skull, so it continues to drain while he recovers postsurgery."

"What if it doesn't stop?"

"Then we'll cut out a piece of his skull, clamp the vein, and clean the area."

He talks about Josh's surgery like he's about to wash his car. But what Jenna hears is worse than her nightmares. Beyond frightening. Her son could die.

Keely draws an arm around her shoulders. Jenna slumps against her, grateful Keely's here and that she isn't facing this alone.

Dr. Nunez touches Jenna's arm. Their eyes meet. Compassion fills his. "Brain bleeds are serious."

"Fatal?"

"They can be, yes. But my colleagues and I have studied his scan. We're familiar with his case. He's in good hands, Mrs. Mason."

"Jenna," she says dully. "Name's Jenna."

He smiles with the patience of a general on the eve of battle. "A nurse will be along with some paperwork. She'll answer your questions. I have to go. Your son is waiting." He gives her arm a squeeze and strides from the room.

As soon as he's gone she turns to Keely. "My boy—"

But she doesn't have the chance to shatter.

A nurse approaches with a clipboard. She introduces herself as Megan and rapidly explains the forms for Jenna to sign, flipping the pages, showing where to add a signature or initials. She goes into detail about Josh's procedure, which will take two to three hours, followed up by several hours in post-op recovery. From there he'll be moved to the ICU, where he'll stay for a week or more. They have her number. The hospital will call her as soon as she's able to see her son.

Jenna can barely focus on the nurse's instructions. The forms blur in front of her. Everything about this is awful.

"Anything else I can help you with?" the woman asks with a polite smile despite the severity of the situation.

"What happened to him? The doctor said he fell down the stairs, that the police are involved. Was he pushed? Did he trip?"

The nurse's smile fades. "I don't know anything more than what the doctor said. You'll have to call them." She points beyond the waiting room threshold. "I have to process these papers. If you need anything, I'll be right out there."

The nurse leaves, and Jenna immediately calls the police. She's directed to the Carlsbad station and informed the officers are still on the scene interviewing witnesses. They'll contact her after they report in.

Jenna drops into a chair feeling helpless, guilty, and confused. Sobs roll through her as she thinks of her son. She could lose him. He could die on the operating table. And the only thing she can do is wait.

Keely rubs her back, and after some time, Jenna lifts her face, her vision blurry. She's sure her eyes are red and swollen. Keely asks if she's all right, to which Jenna shakes her head.

"Josh might die, and it's my fault."

CHAPTER 27

LILY

Lily stood back while Tyler fitted logs into the cabin's wood-burning stove that he said would heat the twenty-one-hundred-square-foot house within an hour. She rubbed her arms, wishing she'd packed a heavier coat than the thin puffer she wore. Thank goodness she'd put it in her case. Her mom had rushed her out the door before she could think to grab something more suitable from the coat closet. Lily had only visited the lake house during the summer months. She didn't realize the temp could drop this low at their elevation. Then again, the house hadn't been used in over a year. Tyler said so when he unlocked the door.

She shivered uncontrollably. Her teeth clacked louder than her knees. The temperature inside had to be at least ten degrees colder than outside. Though the chill racking her body could have been from shock.

She'd killed her best friend. Murdered him. Left him.

Acute sadness slammed into her like the violent waves off the coast she'd spent her life watching. A hum buzzed in her head as a heaviness settled over her. She was drowning in guilt, and there was no escaping the pain. Unless she confessed.

Which she couldn't.

Where would that leave her baby? Jail wasn't an option. They'd take her baby from her.

On the drive up, she'd told Tyler she needed to move out because Dwight had found out she had a job. He was so mad she believed he'd get physically violent. She had bruises on her wrist to prove it. She couldn't live there anymore.

Tyler had agreed to stay with her one night; then he'd have to return to his mom. He hadn't told her why he'd left or where he'd gone, and he worried she'd need him. Once she passed—and he'd choked up when he said it, even though they both knew it was inevitable and soon—he'd join her here. Then they'd plan what to do next, where to go. Meanwhile, she'd be safe, far from Dwight. She could stay as long as she liked. He still thought she might want to return home.

Lily didn't know what her plans were, but they weren't that. She'd left home for good.

With Tyler's back to her, she guided a hand over the belly that had started to round, also hidden under a thick layer. He brushed wood particles and soot from his hands. "That should do it. Give it thirty minutes to warm up," he said, swiveling on his knees to face her.

Her arm dropped to her side as if touching the babe inside had scalded her hand. She forced a stiff smile, hoping he wouldn't ask how she was holding up, which was barely.

He showed her how to stack the logs to keep the fire burning. He then stood, lifted her chin so that he could study her face. Concern swirled in his eyes like the waves of warmth radiating off the stove.

"Don't look so scared." He kissed her nose. "You're safe now."

She nodded, her gaze darting away before he could see the darkness building there. She wasn't the girl he'd fallen in love with. Yesterday, she was Lily. Today, she was a mother and a murderer.

"I wish I could stay," he said.

"Me too." But she wouldn't ask him to. His mom needed him. He'd also discover she was pregnant. At some point she wouldn't be able to hide it. And then she wouldn't be able to protect him. He wouldn't leave her side. He'd confront Dwight for terrorizing her, risking his baby.

Who knew what Dwight would do? After the way she saw him go after Wes, she wouldn't risk Tyler's life.

"You're freezing." He vigorously rubbed her arms, and she sank against his chest. For these few moments she let him hold her. She could pretend tonight never happened, that Wes would wake up tomorrow and go to school. He'd pass algebra and play baseball.

Needles pricked her eyes. She squeezed them tightly to staunch the flow of tears or they wouldn't stop. She couldn't cry in front of Tyler.

"Unpack the groceries. I'll turn on the water," he said. He left to tinker with the water heater in the garage. Cold seeped across her like a lake freezing over where his warmth had been.

She went into the kitchen and put away a week's worth of food for one person. Tyler would be gone before morning, back to his ailing mom. But he'd return next week with more groceries, seven days from today.

He wouldn't find her here.

She'd be gone by then. She was a danger to him, and it was too risky to stay. If the police did come for her, she needed to disappear.

Her stomach growled, releasing a monster-size craving for sugar as the adrenaline from earlier rushed from her system. She tore open the Oreos, eating a third of the package by the time Tyler returned from the garage.

"Those won't last a week at the rate you're eating."

She inserted an entire cookie in her mouth, too exhausted to care. He didn't know she wasn't just eating for one. She ate her guilt, her grief.

Closing the Oreo bag, she yawned loudly.

"Let's go to bed."

Her mouth snapped shut. The bag slipped from her hand, landed with a thud on the floor. She quickly picked it up, put it on the counter.

Would he want something from her tonight? He might notice the swell in her belly that wasn't there last week. That her breasts were fuller than just a couple of days ago.

That sex was the furthest thing from her mind given what had happened with Wes.

The memory of them on the dock plagued her. She couldn't get what had happened, what she'd done, out of her mind. She wanted to curl in a ball and pray for it to go away.

At her hesitation, he tugged her hand. "I know that look. It's late and I'm tired. I just want to sleep."

"Okay." Her exhaled relief was as loud as the rafts they deflated when they summered here. He led them into the downstairs guest room.

He didn't question the thick sweatshirt she wore to bed. The back rooms were still cold. Her breath hung in the air in misted puffs. But she let him hold her through the remainder of the night and struggled not to cry when she woke in the morning with a hole carved in her chest. He was already gone, and she ached from him leaving. From Wes's death. From a future that frightened her. She would never see Tyler again.

Wrapped in a blanket, Lily padded in sock-clad feet to the main room, which was still warm. Tyler had added logs before he left. She added another two, since it had been a few hours; then she poured milk over Froot Loops for breakfast and ate the bowl by the back window overlooking the lake. It was snowing. Flakes gracefully fell on the placid water as thoughts of the previous night stung the front of her mind like yellow jackets buzzing in her face. What would happen when the police found Wes's body? Would they start looking for her? She imagined a manhunt like those she'd watched on television, pictured her face on a wanted poster, and almost threw up her meager breakfast.

The night replayed in her mind, every minute, every horrific detail, the scene vivid despite the cold and darkness.

Over and over it played until she bent over, pulling at her hair, and wailed. She wanted it out of her head.

She wanted to go back and undo it. She never should have lunged at Dwight.

But that wasn't possible. Her actions, her choices, they'd torment her for life. More than that. It would be part of who she now was. A murderer.

Over the next few days, Lily subsisted on cereal, PB&J sandwiches, and fish sticks with tartar sauce. With only a few hundred dollars to her name, and a strong aversion to using the money Charlotte had packed, she had to watch every penny.

But she needed a car, or a ride to the bus station. And she needed a place to stay far from home. Where no one would find her.

But she didn't know anyone up north or out of state, and now that Lily was pregnant, Olivia wasn't an option. She never had been. Were there shelters for people like her, pregnant teenage runaways who'd murdered their friends? Would the police find her if she stayed in one? Was there anywhere she could go without feeling like she had to keep running? The horror of her actions and the scant resources at her fingertips kept her rooted in place for days.

Then the fifth day came. Time was running out. So she mustered the courage to walk to the market. From there she'd find someone who'd drive her to the bus station. She'd go wherever the next bus took her.

Bundled in a large coat she'd found in a closet, leggings that did nothing to keep her thighs warm, and canvas sneakers, Lily packed the pockets with minimal belongings. Her wallet and Charlotte's cash, the journal that revealed too much about her and Tyler, and extra socks and underwear, leaving her luggage of clothes behind. She wanted to travel light.

She trudged through several inches of snow, regretting she hadn't left the previous day. Ominous clouds hung thick, fat with moisture. Wind blasted into her, biting her cheeks. More snow was coming.

But the impending weather didn't stop her. Head down, she kept walking.

She made it three houses up from the Whitmans' cabin.

"Hello. Hello!"

Lily looked up, startled to find a woman shoveling her driveway, waving at her. Leaning on the shovel, she wore a beanie and rubber boots. "A bit cold for a walk this morning?"

It was, but she didn't have a choice.

"I have to go to the store. Out of milk," she lied, concerned the woman knew the Whitmans and would mention her if she called Tyler.

"If you wait a few, I'll give you a lift."

Lily glanced up the road before peering at the woman across from her. She might be able to convince the woman to drive her all the way to the bus station. Tyler might find out, but he wouldn't know where Lily bought a ticket to. Lily could even lie to this woman about her destination.

A snowflake landed on Lily's nose, another on her forehead. She looked up at the unusually dark sky.

"All right," she said. She'd take the woman up on her offer.

Lily crossed the road.

CHAPTER 28

Keely's hand on Jenna's back goes still. "How is any of this your fault?"

"After I read the post on Facebook, I wanted to leave town. Josh begged to stay. I gave in. Then my dad came to town. He gave me trouble, and I told him to back off."

"Do you think he has anything to do with this?"

"I don't know. Maybe. But he said Josh wasn't with him when I called before I saw you."

"And you believed him?"

She shakes her head. She'd never trust his word. But what good would calling him do now? It's too late. Josh is seriously injured, and Dwight is well on his way home to Seaside Cove or to his conference or from whatever cave he crawled out of.

Tears flood her eyes as exhaustion sets in. She feels it in her bones.

She's tired of running and hiding. Tired of lying, weaving webs that threaten to unravel.

And to what end? Protect her son?

She scoffs. Who's she kidding?

Everything she's done since she ran has been to protect herself.

She couldn't handle losing the one person she believed would love her unconditionally. Her son.

To realize this now, to see what she's been doing for years, is another staggering blow. She would have folded to the floor if she wasn't already sitting. Nausea swirls around her middle. She can't help but think of Charlotte. They are so alike.

Jenna covers her face. Her shoulders shake with self-disgust.

"Have you called Kavan?"

"Oh, gosh." With everything going on, she forgot to check her phone. Jenna flips open her phone, shocked he hasn't returned her call from earlier. She tries again. The phone rings, then dumps her in his voice mail. Distraught, she leaves another message about Josh. Tells him where she is.

A tear leaches off her chin when she ends the call.

Her boy. She just wants to hold her boy.

She looks at the clock. He's under the knife now. A drill is burring through his skull.

Nausea sloshes in her stomach.

"You okay?" Keely asks.

Jenna shakes her head, swipes at her nose. "Surely you have other places to be."

"Trying to get rid of me?"

"No, it's just . . ." She shrugs. "Sorry about the other day at the café," she says. Keely was just trying to be a friend.

"No apology necessary. You were under a lot of stress, what with that reporter and the parents' group. Want a sweater? I have one in the van." Keely tugs Jenna's robe sash.

Jenna looks at herself and groans. She can't believe she's been wearing it all morning. No wonder security downstairs thought she was out of her mind.

"Do you mind?" she asks the same moment movement at the door snags her attention. She grasps Keely's arm.

Two uniformed officers stand just inside the doorway.

"Mrs. Mason?" asks the taller of the two. His gaze darts between her and Keely, unsure who is who. "We need to talk to you about your son."

Jenna's heart pounds against her rib cage. "I'm Ms. Mason."

"Ma'am, I'm Officer Velazquez, this is my partner Officer Horn. We're with the Carlsbad PD." He tilts his head at the man beside him. "Do you mind if we ask a few questions?"

"Not until you tell me what happened."

"That's what we're trying to figure out." Officer Horn retrieves a notepad and pen from his breast pocket. He flips to a blank page. "Is your son often truant?"

"Excuse me?"

"Is he truant often?"

"What does that have to do with anything? I want to know how he fell down the stairs. Where was he?"

Horn shifts uneasily. His gaze veers to his partner before Velazquez jumps in.

"Witnesses report your son and several other boys were seen skateboarding and smoking pot in the parking lot at the Shoppes."

"In Carlsbad?" Shock ripples through her. How'd he get there? It was a fifteen-minute drive from their house.

"The kids proceeded inside when the mall opened. One that we know of lifted merchandise from a couple stores. We found the items in his backpack."

"Was it Josh?"

"No, ma'am."

"We didn't find pot on him either," Horn adds. "Nothing but notebooks and pencils."

"Then what does this have to do with his injuries?"

"We have reason to believe your son was deliberately pushed down the stairs."

Jenna clutches her robe lapels as a sharp coldness sweeps through her.

"Who pushed him? Was it one of the kids?"

"No, ma'am," Horn says. "The boys claim it was someone else."

"Who, then?" Her pulse pounds in her head, anxious for an answer.

The officers stare back at her.

"Surely something had to have been captured on the security cameras."

"We haven't seen the security footage yet. We're headed back there next," Velazquez says.

"One of the kids"—Horn flips through his notes—"a Brad Wusthoff—he believes they were being followed."

Her heart freezes.

"By whom?" Keely asks.

"Some guy with a medium build, around five-ten. Short dark hair. He was wearing black pants and a gray sweatshirt. Sound familiar?"

Jenna goes absolutely still.

Keely looks at her expectantly.

Jenna's mind reels back to the footage caught by her security camera, the description too close a match to be coincidence.

Keely nudges her. "Tell them about your father."

Horn looks up from his notepad. "What about your father?"

Jenna tucks hands damp with nerves into the robe pockets. "My father recently came to town. We're estranged. Haven't seen him for years. He's been giving me trouble."

"What's his name?" Horn asks.

"Dwight Carson. But I don't think it was him." She never thought she'd report him to the police, no matter the reason. He might even retaliate and release the video. But this is bigger than her and Dwight.

She gives them a physical description along with his phone number.

"We'll still follow up with him," Velazquez says, giving her his card. "I'm sorry about your son."

Jenna thanks them, then turns to the window when they leave, visibly shaken, afraid she was wrong about who left Wes's shirt and shoe on her porch.

Dwight hasn't been the one tormenting her.

CHAPTER 29

"Are you all right?" Keely asks.

Jenna gathers the lapels of her robe with trembling hands. "It's cold in here." Has it always been this chilly?

"Jenna." Keely touches her arm. "You okay?"

She looks at Keely's hand on her arm, then up at her. Keely's gaze is soft, concerned.

"No." She isn't. Her son has a brain bleed, and Ryder Jensen, the person she most fears, might have pushed him down a flight of stairs.

Impossible, her mind argues. He's in prison.

"Why do you think Josh was in Carlsbad?" Keely asks.

"Wish I knew," she says, half listening to Keely. She tries picturing the man caught on tape at her house. Could it have been Ryder? Her pulse pounds in her ears. She needs to find out where he is. "How long did she say the surgery was?" she asks of the nurse.

"Two to three hours."

Jenna looks at the clock on the wall. "It's only been ninety minutes." Almost lunchtime.

The bell at Josh's school will ring shortly.

Her son should be there, playing hoops during recess. Eating lunch with Anson.

And she shouldn't be worrying the man she thought had another six years to serve could have been released.

But here they are.

"He'll be okay," Keely says.

She nods. A tear jogs over her cheek. She brushes it off.

He will. He has to be. And then they have to run.

"Are you hungry?" Keely asks.

Food is the furthest thing from her mind.

"You should eat. You'll need your energy when you see Josh."

"Can you grab us something?" She doesn't want to leave. "And can you get that sweater?" She twirls her robe sash.

"You bet. I'll get some sandwiches." Keely picks up her purse and hugs Jenna, and Jenna throws her arms around Keely, grateful for her kindness as she wonders if she'll ever meet someone like her again.

As soon as she leaves, Jenna calls Dwight. She knows he wasn't at the mall, can feel it in her gut. Still, she needs to hear his confirmation that he gave her Wes's shoe and shirt. Because if he didn't . . .

The phone rings. A voice in her head warns she shouldn't tip him off about the police. He might go into hiding. Or he might screw her and turn over the video. But that seems minor given that Ryder might be free.

Her call goes into voice mail. She skips leaving a message. He'll see the notification. He'll be too curious not to call her back. She then calls Murielle.

"It's Josh," she says to the woman who kept her off the streets, then explains what happened to her son. Murielle's worry comes through the line. She offers to help Jenna where she can. "I have to find out if Ryder has been released," Jenna says, telling her about Wes's clothes, how the description from witnesses at the mall match the man caught on her camera.

"I thought he had six more years," Murielle says.

"Same here." Jenna glances over her shoulder to check if anyone is within earshot. She could be wrong. She hasn't felt that shimmer of awareness across her shoulder like she usually does when Ryder draws near. But she needs to be sure. California restricts access to inmate information to witnesses, families, and victims only. Release dates aren't in the national database the public can access, otherwise Jenna would have set up an automatic alert upon his impending release. But Murielle and her daughter, Sophie, have connections.

"Just look. I feel better knowing," Jenna says.

Murielle agrees, and Jenna ends the call.

She stares out the window, afraid for her son. That Ryder is waiting for them. That Josh's injury will prevent them from leaving, and they'll be stuck at home. His life is in another man's hands, and their lives might be in danger. She feels more vulnerable now than when Stan exposed her identity.

Keely returns a short time later with sandwiches and drinks. Jenna takes a seat beside her and picks at her food. The wall clock ticks the day onward. Her stomach sours with each bite. She can't stop imagining what's happening to Josh. The drills, the surgical knives, the strangers invading his skull. She can't stop picturing Ryder lurking outside the hospital, reveling in his handiwork. An eye for an eye. She sets aside the half-eaten sandwich and returns to the window, bundling Keely's sweater around her. It's too large, the sleeves too long. But right now it's exactly what she needs. She touches her forehead to the window and closes her eyes.

A delicate touch on her shoulder startles her.

"I have to go." Keely glances back at the wall clock. Jenna balks at the time. Hours have passed. She must have dozed off. "School's almost out. Seth is stuck at work. I have to pick up Anson."

Jenna's mouth forms a circle. "Oh, right. Right."

"I'll get Anson situated and come back. You shouldn't be alone."

"No, I'll be fine."

"Try calling Kavan again."

Jenna nods, disappointed and concerned he hasn't called back.

"Call me when you get word on Josh?"

"I will."

Keely hesitates.

"Go. It's fine." Jenna nudges her away.

Keely squeezes her hand and leaves.

Jenna sits in the chair Keely vacated and stares at nothing in particular. The room is shockingly empty of people.

She wonders how she can be the only one here. Why is it *her* son that's in surgery.

"Ms. Mason?"

Jenna whips her head in the direction of the voice. A nurse stands a few feet away.

"Your son is in recovery. If you'll come with me."

A harsh breath leaves Jenna relieved even as her stomach tightens with nerves. She pushes off the chair, wondering how extensive his injuries are, what condition he'll be in, and tails the nurse at a quick clip.

"Is he all right?"

"Yes," the nurse says over her shoulder.

They pass curtained recovery rooms with patients looking beat up and passed out. The nurse stops at the fourth room and pushes aside the curtain. Jenna stops up short, her breath catching. In the middle of the bed lies Josh, and nothing in her life could have prepared her for what she sees. Tubes and cords are a tangle atop him. Monitors glow. IVs drip.

And the smell. Astringent and iodine. They burn the sensitive skin inside her nose.

But what troubles her the most is his head. Dear god, what did they do to him?

Half his head has been shaved. An angry incision arcs over his smooth scalp, held closed by a row of staples.

"Ms. Mason?"

"What?" Jenna snaps her head to the nurse.

"Your son's surgery went well. Dr. Nunez will be in later to give you a full report."

"So he's okay?" Her heart pulses in her throat.

The nurse smiles. "He's okay."

Tension unravels within her.

Jenna's gaze drops to her badge. Roselle. She looks back at Josh, to the tube inserted in the incision. It leads to a small plastic vial taped to the side of his head. Her eyes widen until they hurt.

"That should be out by tomorrow," Roselle says.

"That thing in his head?"

"The catheter, yes. It's catching the residual fluid."

Jenna's throat closes. A tremor ripples down her legs. She hadn't expected it to be so big and obvious. It's just there.

"You can go in." Roselle tilts her head toward the bed.

Jenna bites down her fear and goes to Josh's side, her gaze sliding down his body, almost afraid to touch him. She doesn't want to hurt him.

She slides her hand under his, relieved that he is alive, and weaves their fingers. They're warm to the touch. His breathing is steady. But her mind is reeling as she worries what he'll be like, what he'll feel, when he wakes up.

She takes a breath to steady herself.

"I'm here, Josh," she says. She presses a palm to his face. Her thumb sweeps across a brow. His eyes are closed. She wishes she could see them to see if he was in pain. But he sleeps the sleep of those who've gone to war and back. Who've fought for their life.

Roselle keeps busy around the bed. She checks Josh's IVs and pulse, takes note of the numbers on the EKG.

"His vitals look good. We expect him to wake shortly." Roselle unwinds a cord from the wall and lays a remote on Josh's lap. "I have other patients to check. I'll be back to look in on Josh soon. If you need me, just push this button." She tips the remote to show her the red bell icon then leaves the room, closing the privacy curtain behind her.

Alone with her boy, Jenna pulls up a chair, rests her forehead on Josh's forearm, and lets her composure slip.

Quiet sobs strain her lungs. In the back of her mind, she knows she needs to pull herself together. Josh will wake soon. He'll need her. But right now she needs to apologize, even if he can't hear her. She needs to hear it.

She lifts her head, kisses his hand. "I'm sorry."

If she hadn't given in to Josh and they'd have left Oceanside, he wouldn't have gone to the mall.

If she'd told Josh about Tyler, he wouldn't have been angry. He wouldn't have acted out.

And if she'd told Tyler about Josh, maybe . . .

Maybe . . .

Maybe she should have given Josh to his father.

Every decision she's made—killing Wes, running—hasn't stemmed from trying to do what's best for her son. It's been driven by her desire and determination to protect herself. And to realize this only now on top of his injuries crushes her.

Tyler would have given their son a better life than she could.

But she can't change the past. It is what it is. Yet somewhere along the way—maybe when she was sixteen and her life imploded—she started putting herself before her son. She lost perspective.

And it's cost her horribly.

Wes's life. Tyler's knowledge of his child. Josh missing a father.

All because of her.

She needs to fix this. Right what she's done wrong.

Holding his hand between hers, she kisses his fingers. "You're my number one." He must always be her priority.

She yields a breath, and her gaze trails up him, worried he has long-term damage, wondering when he'll wake. He hasn't moved since she arrived. He's so . . . still.

Voices beyond the curtain reach her. Machines click their numbers, and feet clad in white sneakers visible below the curtain rush by. The intercom crackles, alerting staff to a code blue. Somewhere in another ward there's a patient in cardiac arrest. Someone has flatlined.

Jenna turns back to Josh, and he is staring up at her. She blinks, stunned. "Josh, you're awake."

His eyes open wide. Panic dilates his pupils.

"Honey, it's okay," she says on a rush of air. She gives him a smile. "You're safe."

His gaze jostles around the room like a bird trapped in a cage. His legs squirm under the sheet. An anguished moan rumbles from him. The sound rips her open.

"Careful of your IV." She steadies his arm where the needle disappears into his skin.

He jerks his eyes back to her, and the monitor beside the bed pings with his rising heart rate. He whimpers, and the sound goes straight to her heart, twisting the organ because she doesn't know how to help him.

"Are you in pain?"

He just stares at her. Her pulse throbs with unease.

"You hit your head. You just got out of surgery," she explains. "You're in the hospital." He blinks at her. Dread forces its way into her as she fears he's worse off than the nurse let on. "Do you remember what happened?"

He whines, his face crumpling.

"Josh. Darling." She cradles his jaw and glances over her shoulder. Where is the doctor?

The curtain swoops open. "Look who just woke up," Roselle announces with a cheery smile. She enters the room, followed by Dr. Nunez. Jenna reluctantly moves from Josh's side to give him access to her son. She pulls at her bottom lip, impatient for the doctor's assessment.

Nunez greets Josh, and Josh stares back. Then he stares at Roselle when she asks if he's warm enough.

Jenna clutches her sides. Why hasn't he said anything?

Nunez praises Josh, telling him he was an excellent patient. He checks the incision and seems pleased with how it looks. He flashes a light in Josh's eyes, then does a series of other tests to check his vitals. All the while, Josh remains silent. He's shy, but to not answer the doctor's questions? That isn't like her son. Something has to be wrong.

"Looking good, Josh. You'll be back on your feet in no time." He squeezes Josh's knee and turns to her. "We can talk out there." He tips his head toward the corridor.

"I'll be right back." Jenna tenderly touches Josh's cheek.

Dr. Nunez closes the curtain behind them, leaving a gap so she can still see her son. "Surgery went well," he begins. "We didn't run into any complications, but we did decide to cut into the skull and clean up the area. I'm glad we did because we had to seal the vein. It was still leaking."

"You were able to stop it?" she asks.

"We did. We'll keep an eye on him over the next few days, but I'm pleased with the outcome."

"How long will he be here?" She glances nervously at Josh, worried about the danger he's in, and not just from his injuries.

"Four to five days, I expect. A week, tops. He'll be moved to ICU when the anesthesia wears off. I'll check on him again when he gets settled."

"Should I be worried he hasn't spoken yet?"

His eyes darken under a slight frown as he glances toward Josh. "I'm sure it's nothing. Give him a chance to get oriented. His injury was traumatic, and the anesthesia is still wearing off." He smiles pleasantly, but it doesn't reassure her. She needs to hear Josh's voice. If he can't talk, he can't cry for help.

After he promises to check in on Josh later, he zips away, his white coat billowing behind in his rush to see another patient. When the heavy steel doors separating the recovery room from the rest of the hospital close behind him, she realizes she forgot to thank him for saving her son.

CHAPTER 30

Jenna sits in the lone chair in Josh's hospital room. It's a recliner, and Quin, the young nurse with kind eyes and bunny decals on her name badge who took over from Roselle, told Jenna earlier she could sleep there for the night since Josh has a private room. Jenna almost burst into tears of gratitude. She doesn't want to leave Josh, not with his injuries, and not with the possibility that Ryder is out there. But it's almost seven. She hasn't eaten and needs to shower, collect some of her own things from home, a toothbrush, maybe a pair of sweatpants. Josh will want his stuffed puppy when he wakes. Perhaps a book.

Josh has been in and out of consciousness since he was transferred to his room and is finally sleeping soundly. If she's going to leave, now is the time.

But what if he wakes up and she's not here? He was frightened earlier. He was in a new room and had felt his head for the first time. Jenna watched as awareness seeped into his eyes only to cloud over with panic when he felt the staples and catheter. She wanted to hug away that fear. Tell him he'd be all right. But she honestly didn't know if he would be, which made her feel worse since she is the cause. And she couldn't stomach lying to him, not anymore.

Quin had asked how he was feeling and if he was hungry. She could order up a sandwich. Josh's response was quick and startling. "I want to ride the blue balloon." Her reaction was a mixture of relief he'd spoken mixed with alarm that he'd said something outrageous as his eyes went wide. He then buried his face in his hands and sobbed.

Dr. Nunez checked on Josh during his rounds, and when Jenna described what had happened, he told her Josh's confused speech wasn't common with a head trauma but also wasn't too concerning. It should clear within a couple of days. Still, Jenna worried. If he couldn't make sense when he spoke, he couldn't explain what happened, who pushed him, or why he was at the mall.

Her phone chimes with an incoming message, and she blinks in surprise that she's just now hearing it. She's been focused on Josh. She fishes for her phone in the sweater's large side pocket. Nine new voice mails and multiple text notifications crowd her screen, most from Kavan. Some from Keely. Others from numbers she doesn't recognize. Not one from Dwight. Murielle hadn't called back either.

Heart thudding against her ribs, she listens to Kavan's latest voice mail that came in not five minutes ago.

"Jenna, I'm here. They won't let me up. Please come down when you get this. If you can't leave Josh, I understand. But call me. I'll wait. Just . . ." He pauses, and Jenna pictures him pacing, shoulders tight with worry. Scared for her and Josh. And nerves skitter across her skin. Kavan and Uma could be in danger, too, because of her. "Call me, okay?" he said before the message ends.

Jenna pushes up from the chair. She gathers her purse and the clear plastic bag holding Josh's belongings, the clothes he put on this morning and the Vans she bought him last week. She kisses his forehead, the skin warm from his body healing, and leaves the room, pausing at the nurse's station to let them know she'll return shortly and to call if Josh wakes.

She spots Kavan as she exits the elevator. He sees her at the same moment and rushes over. Even knowing she must break off their engagement, put some distance between them for their safety, her legs weaken. She cries out at the sight of him. She's in his arms before the doors close behind her.

"I've been out of my mind worried about you," he says into her hair. Grasping her arms, he leans back to look at her. Hair disheveled, the white button-down shirt he always wears at the restaurant is untucked and stained with grease, and not the food kind. Dark bags weigh down his eyes. He looks positively wrecked. "Tell me what happened." He gently touches her cheek.

"Where were you?" she asks. "I called several times." Her first inclination is to tell him that she needed him. But that selfishness landed Josh in the hospital. It could hurt Kavan and Uma.

"I'm sorry. I should have been here for you." He pulls her back in for a hug. His chin rests on her forehead. "A pipe burst at the restaurant this morning. I forgot my phone at home. I've been on-site since this morning. We've been closed all day." She doesn't have to ask if the damage was extensive. His arms tighten. "Of all days . . ."

"I know," she says into his shirt. He smells of bergamot and amber. Autumn. She's going to miss the scent of him. His friendship, smile. The warmth of him when he's near. She already aches over the loss.

"How's Josh?"

"Asleep. For now." She steps from his embrace. "Can I get a ride?"

A pause. He wants to see Josh, but her son needs his rest so he can heal, and it'll only be harder to break things off with Kavan if she does invite him up, so she doesn't offer. "Yeah, sure," he says, and she starts walking toward the exit. "Jenna . . . ?" He stares after her, brows knotted in the middle.

"Please? It's been a long day." If she stops moving, she'll pass out before she can get back to Josh.

Kavan catches up to her and takes her hand. He walks with her to the car, waits until she's seated and buckled before closing the door and going to his side.

"My car is at Keely's." She then tells him what happened, how she found out, and what the police said. How she doesn't know who pushed Josh, but the police will question Dwight. She chews her lip, debating what to say about Ryder and decides to wait until she hears from Murielle. She could be wrong about him.

When they reach Keely's and he parks his car behind hers, his anger fills the car. Hot energy rolls off him. His grip on the steering wheel is tight, as if he wants to strangle his own neck. "It kills me I wasn't there. If I hadn't left my phone at home—"

She lays a hand on his arm. That seems to calm the rising storm in him. "There's nothing you could have done."

"I could have been there for you."

Tears threaten like impending rain, and her heart cracks open. "Kavan—" Her gaze drops to her hand on his arm—the contrast of their skin color, her fair to his dark—before leveling with his. "I've been thinking about what you said last night."

He shakes his head. "We don't have to talk about it now."

"You were right. Everything you said, you're right."

His hand falls into his lap. "I was angry, and"—he tilts his head side to side—"I'll admit, hurt."

"Justifiably so." She reaches for the hand in his lap only to pull away. She'll have to get used to not touching him, not always reaching for him. She takes a deep breath and braces herself for what she's about to confess with Ryder possibly on her heels. "It doesn't take a genius to realize I changed my name because I didn't want to be found. That I did something horrible and have been on the run since. I'll never admit what out loud," she adds when he opens his mouth to ask. "I'll probably never tell you what happened that night. I've never told anyone. Except one person, and she—" Jenna stops before she launches into a discussion of who Murielle is. She needs to say to Kavan what she must before she loses her nerve. "My dad knows what I did. He has proof. He won't report me, never will, because I . . . I have something on him." And she paid him $50,000 for his silence.

Her heart races fiercely. Nausea coils in her stomach. She's sweating everywhere, her palms, her back, under her breasts. She's never revealed this much.

Kavan's head is cocked to the side as if considering the enormity of what she's telling him.

She wipes the back of her neck. "I'm not going to say any more, and please don't ask. I don't want to put you in a difficult or dangerous position. I won't do that to you, or to Uma." She also doesn't want Ryder to go through them to get to her like he might have done with Josh.

Rage, compassion, and uncertainty darken the shadows on his face. "Dwight went after Josh to hurt you. You know that's true. You have to get a restraining order. Jenna—"

She holds up a hand. "Don't say anything more. Please don't." She squeezes her eyes shut, resisting the urge to tell him everything. Dwight isn't the one she's worried about, not anymore. "I can't imagine what you must think of me."

"Right now I don't care what you did when you were sixteen. I love you," he says without hesitation. "Your past doesn't change—"

"But it does. It will. You don't know the full story, and it will change how you think of me. Trust me. And telling me you love me . . . It only makes it harder for me to say what I have to say."

"Which is what?" He leans back, cautious.

"You're right. I have a hard time talking about my past because I won't talk about it."

"I'd say you just did a pretty good job talking about it. I'm still here."

"I'm not done." She squeezes the back of her neck. "I've lied to you. I've lied to a lot of people. I can't promise I'll stop. But what I do know is that I got caught up in making a life for us here, for me and Josh. A life with you. And it's built on lies. I lost sight of why I ran in the first place—to protect my son—because I wanted your love, to be loved. I wanted a normal life, too. I put my needs and wants before his safety, and I almost lost him today. He's my world, Kavan. He has to be my priority. Everything I do, every second of the day, needs to be for him."

"Josh should be your priority as Uma is mine. I'm not trying to take his place. I want to be your partner." His gaze meets her, his eyes swirling with emotion. He takes her hand, resting his thumb on her engagement ring.

"You want to spend your life with a liar?" She shakes her head, unnerved by his unswerving loyalty. "I don't think you do, Kavan. Over time, you'll start to feel like you don't really know me. Then you'll hate me."

"Jenna?"

Jenna startles and both she and Kavan look out the window.

Keely stands on the sidewalk, hands jammed in her tunic's pockets. Jenna breathes loudly through her nose, frustrated by the interruption. But she can't spare the time to talk longer, not with Josh in the hospital.

"Talk about the worst fucking timing," Kavan grumbles under his breath.

"Look, Kavan." She turns back to him. "I'm starving and exhausted, and I need to get back to the hospital. We'll finish later." She scrambles from the car before he stops her.

Keely waves to Kavan and smiles at Jenna. "I saw you from the kitchen window. Want dinner? I have plenty of leftover lasagna."

Jenna shifts uneasily as Kavan watches her for a drawn-out moment. She doesn't think he'll leave until he shakes his head and drives away. She lets go of the breath she was holding and turns to Keely.

"Thank you, but I want to get back to the hospital before Josh wakes."

"How is he?" she asks. Jenna had texted her an update after Josh was moved to his room.

"Resting. We'll know more tomorrow." She hopes he'll talk tomorrow. She has so many questions.

"Any word from the police?"

"Nothing yet." She's impatient to hear about what they saw on the surveillance video.

"Well, you'll let me know if there's anything you need?"

Jenna promises and drives home.

She pulls into the garage and comes in through the laundry room at the same time Kavan enters through the front door. She shrieks, and he almost drops the cardboard box from her publisher. The white bag on top slides to the side. Kavan lunges, tipping the box to stop the bag's momentum before it drops on the floor.

"Whoa. Close call." He chuckles, awkwardly. "Almost lost your dinner."

She puts down her keys and bags and meets him in the front room. She wipes her palm up her forehead, pushing back her hair. "What are you doing here?" she asks.

"I brought some of yesterday's leftovers from the restaurant when I went to the hospital. Figured you wouldn't have eaten yet."

And he used the key she gave him over a month ago.

Remorse wells with a slice of caution. She's breaking up with him, and he's still being so damn nice.

She frowns at the box he's holding. "What is that?"

He sets it down. "Not sure, but there are twenty more just like it on the porch. I hardly fit through the door."

"Shit." She forgot about the books her publisher sent for her to sign over the weekend and ship back. Which is so not going to happen, not after today. She can't focus on her career now. She might even have to give up her career. Another loss that weighs on her. She loves her characters and stories. Losing them along with everyone else will feel like she's lost a piece of her soul.

Kavan's eyes soften. "Go eat and shower. I'll bring them in."

She nods, hugging her chest, and turns away from him. His eyes basically tell her he's struggling not to pull her into his arms. She feels his desire pulse off him as she walks up the stairs. It takes everything in her not to turn back and run into those arms.

She showers and dresses without fuss, and packs a small overnight bag, grabbing some of Josh's things along the way. A toothbrush and comb, his stuffed puppy. She can't find the book he was reading and figures it must be in his backpack, which she doesn't have. It's probably with the police.

Kavan has stacked the boxes in the front room and set a place for her at the counter.

"I don't have time to sit." She planned to bring the meal with her.

"Eat." He points at the food. "I know you. You'll get to the hospital and forget. Josh isn't going anywhere," he says bluntly.

"That's cruel."

"It's reality." He gentles his voice. "You can't take care of him if you aren't taking care of yourself." And it annoys her that he's still trying to take care of her after all she said.

He holds her gaze, daring her to turn up her nose at the delectable spread. Grilled rib eye with a lemon-and-oil marinade topped with fresh oregano and a tomato-and-cucumber slaw as a side. The dish would have a fancy Greek name on the menu. Her stomach growls, and his mouth twitches. He pulls out the counter chair, and she settles on the seat.

Kavan removes her house key from his key ring and slides it over to her, his face a blank mask, hiding how much she knows this simple act hurts him as much as her. He's losing her. The love of his life, he once told her.

She looks at the key, shiny from lack of use. She had it made at the local hardware store. Her heart pulsed in her throat when she gave it to him. It was a big step in their relationship. An enormous step for her. He knew she didn't easily trust, that she was independent. She'd spent the entirety of her life watching out for herself, then watching over Josh. But she was excited about sharing her home with him. She wanted him and Uma in their lives. He made their world bigger. It had been small for so long.

Now he's leaving her world. And he's giving the key back, making her decision more real. The life she created for Josh is slipping through her fingers, and there isn't anything she can do to stop it.

She sets down the knife and fork she picked up upon sitting and slides off her engagement ring.

"No." Kavan covers her hand before the ring is off. He grips her fingers. "I'll give you space and time, but we're not done." He nudges the ring up her finger until it settles in the crease. "Focus on Josh, and when he heals, we'll talk."

"Kavan—" She starts to object when he interrupts.

"If your dad gives you trouble, you call the police. Or you call me. Don't answer the door if he comes by. If you don't want to deal with him, I will." He squeezes her hand and pockets his keys.

She shakes her head. "You need to forget about me." And she needs to start fighting her own battles and stop running from them.

"I could never." He cups her neck, kissing her forehead, then walks out the door.

Jenna watches him from her porch, feeling a hole in her chest his presence once filled. But when his car turns the corner she hurries inside to review the surveillance recordings over the past couple of days. She thought the man in the hoodie was Dwight. It made sense given the timing of his arrival and past behavior. But now she isn't sure. Whoever it was intentionally kept his face averted. He knew about the camera.

She plays the recordings again, then again. Dread lurks along the edges of her mind. He doesn't move like Dwight. He isn't dressed like Dwight.

She should have noticed that before. Looked harder.

Her phone rings. Murielle's on the other end. Her tone is pressing. "Ryder was released last month."

Jenna feels a sharp stab of terror. "What?"

"He's out on parole for good behavior. He can't leave the state, but you should be on the lookout. He—"

Jenna doesn't hear the rest. The phone slips from her fingers.

CHAPTER 31

Josh lies in the hospital bed doing nothing. He's been here two days? Twenty? He can't remember.

He faces the window. He can only see blue sky. But if he looks elsewhere, he'll end up staring at his mom, and he doesn't want to look at her. She's been on edge since his surgery. She'll bombard him with questions. It's not that he doesn't know the answers. But when he talks, the wrong words come out. Best not to say anything at all, because it freaks them both out when he does.

A cloud creeps across the window, and it's the most fascinating thing he's seen all day. A bird lands on the sill only to fly away, and he almost bursts into tears. *Come back, little bird.* He wishes he could take off, too. Just fly out of here. His mind is chaotic one minute and empty the next. Confused. And Dr. What's-His-Face wants him to stay until the end of the week. Dr. . . . Dr. . . .

Josh frowns, the name eluding him once again. He's not going to ask his mom his doctor's name either. He's already asked her enough times to make it embarrassing for both of them. She'll get that panicked look in her eye like there's something seriously wrong with him other than the stitched-up hole in his head that makes him look like . . .

He frowns again. What's the name of that monster whose body is sewn together from other people's body parts? He knows what the character looks like and can even recite lines from the book, but . . . but . . .

The name is right on the tip of his tongue. *Fred? Frank?*

Josh groans out loud.

The doctor wants him to stick around for observation. Apparently he didn't like Josh's response when he asked him this morning which side of his head was operated on. Josh knew it was his left. He even pointed to the left side of his head. But the word that came out of Josh's mouth was *horse*. He didn't even think that word. It popped out, startling the doctor, and Josh wanted to cry. What's wrong with him? Will he get better, or will he be like this for the rest of his life?

His mom has been here over an hour, sitting in the same chair, waiting for the doctor. He doesn't have to look at her to know she's chewing off her cuticles. He can hear her. She only does that when she's super nervous or stressed, and he feels horrible that he's the cause.

If she's this worried about him, then his injuries must be bad.

He didn't mean for any of this to happen. He couldn't help that he was upset because she left him the other day to see Dwight when they were supposed to talk about his dad. What was his name? It starts with the letter . . . What letter does his name start with? Josh clenches his sheets. He can't remember that either.

He was embarrassed to hand in his project, upset about what he read about his grandparents in his mom's journal, and nervous his dad—or the guy he found online that he thinks is his dad—wouldn't reply. Ditching school with Brad seemed like the better option.

The bus dropped them off at the mall, where they ran into two guys Brad said he knew. They were older, Josh figured sophomores in high school, and the four of them messed around in the parking lot for a bit, comparing tricks on their boards. One of the guys brought weed. Brad smoked. Josh didn't. He just wanted to skate. But when the mall opened, he followed the guys inside. That's when everything spiraled.

Josh swore he saw Brad's friends lift a shirt from one store and a pair of sunglasses from another. It was wrong. Josh knew that. But their sticky fingers weren't what bothered him. A guy in a gray hoodie was tagging behind the whole time. Josh first noticed him in the parking lot, watching them on their boards from his car. Josh thought he was an employee waiting for the mall to open. But when he just followed them around, Josh knew he was a creepster. He was giving off weird vibes, and Josh wanted to lose him. So did Brad. They took the stairs to leave. But at the top, hands slammed into his back. It's the last thing Josh remembers.

He tried once to explain to his mom what had happened, and he spoke gibberish. The nurse gave him a magazine to read, and the words leapt around the page until the sentences didn't make sense. He gave the magazine back and tried watching TV, but the actors spoke too fast, and he couldn't keep up with the story. So he turned off the screen and turned his face to the window. He's been looking out that window for most of the day. It's exactly how he spent yesterday. And the day before. And the day before that.

CHAPTER 32

Two to three days. The time frame Dr. Nunez had given Josh. If his garbled speech didn't clear up by then, it likely wouldn't resolve for months. Be prepared, the surgeon advised. Josh could struggle for upward of a year. And that's just his speech issues.

Dr. Nunez advised Jenna to keep close throughout the summer months, at least until September. Josh has to return for follow-up appointments. The staples have to be removed in three to four weeks. But there is also a risk the hematoma could return and surgery repeated. No biking or skateboarding for six weeks. Josh has to be watched closely for memory problems, seizures, or a worsening of his speech problem.

The news devastated Jenna, especially when the doctor gave Josh's condition a name. Aphasia, as Nunez explained when he'd discharged him. Although rare, it is an unfortunate side effect of BTI, brain trauma injury. The brain blocks words or retrieves the incorrect one. Writing could be difficult because the mind shifts letters and numbers out of order. Whatever he writes would look like a foreign language. The same when he tries to read. His mind will replace sentences with unrelated words. Most cases resolve on their own. Patients show no signs they ever had an issue. Others need therapy. He referred Josh to a speech pathologist.

Josh has been home for a week. Kavan and Uma have visited. Keely came by with Anson. Josh wasn't interested in seeing anyone. His speech impediment embarrassed him, and Jenna aches when he struggles to talk. She feels his frustration as though it's her own.

In another week, he meets with the pathologist. His staples will be removed a couple of weeks after that. They can't travel for another ten to twelve weeks. They are literally sitting ducks. And there isn't anything Jenna can do but wait, watch, and pray Ryder doesn't come back.

Officer Velazquez reached her by phone while Josh was still in the hospital. Video surveillance captured Josh and Brad getting off the bus. They met up with two other boys and hung out in the parking lot before going inside.

A car did park near where the boys were skateboarding, and the driver did follow them inside. His description matched the one Brad gave him. The license plate on his car didn't match the one they obtained for Dwight Carson of Seaside Cove.

According to Velazquez, Dwight wasn't on the premises. It couldn't have been him. It also could have been a case of mistaken identity. One of the older boys has a drug issue, the other previously arrested for shoplifting. They've been in trouble before. Whoever pushed Josh, he explained, could have been trying to hurt one of them. Josh simply was in the wrong place at the wrong time.

But Jenna has a strong feeling otherwise. Ryder is out of prison.

They've questioned all three boys and are following up on several leads. He'll call her when he knows more.

Velazquez was about to hang up when she said, "Wait."

"Yes?"

"I, uh . . ." Nerves fluttered in her chest. "I know of one other possible suspect."

"And who is that?"

"Ryder Jensen."

She gave Velazquez a brief description of the man who's stalked her for almost fourteen years. "He's my old boss. He's given me problems before. I just found out he's been released from prison," she says at the risk she could be arrested, too, when this is over. But she needs to stop thinking of herself and protect her son. Kavan and Uma, too.

"All right, ma'am, we'll look into it."

Josh sits beside her on the couch staring at a blank TV screen. Pretty much what he's been doing since he was discharged. She wonders how much time she has left with him. A thought that keeps repeating as she struggles each day, wondering if it's their last together. She cries herself to sleep at night behind closed doors, her face buried in a pillow.

Just give her the summer. Let her help Josh until he heals. That's all she asks.

Then she'll take him to Murielle's and give Tyler custody. It's the right thing to do, she's realized. Because as long as Ryder is out there, their lives are at risk. But she won't force Josh into a life on the run. Not anymore. He deserves a life better than the one she can give him.

Weeks pass, and Josh continues to struggle with his speech. He visits with the pathologist and follows up with his neurologist. He holes up in his room drawing, she assumes, or sits on the porch to watch his friends board. He doesn't talk to them unless he must. He loathes mixing words in front of them. He keeps his scar hidden under the Padres ball cap Kavan bought him last spring.

It doesn't take long, a few weeks at the most, for his friends to stop coming over. Just as long for Josh to stop drawing. He even stops trying to talk with her.

Worried about how depressed he is, she starts looking for a psychologist. She dyes her hair a shocking burgundy red so they both have crazy hairstyles. He isn't impressed. He doesn't laugh. He doesn't seem to care at all.

The only things he's shown interest in is when she checks the security footage, which she's become manic about, looking constantly for Ryder. And he gets excited when her phone rings. He stumbles over his words, asking if it's the police. Have they caught the person who pushed him?

This goes on until one day, as summer is drawing to a close, Josh answers a knock on the front door.

CHAPTER 33

A plainclothes officer stands on the porch. Tall with a thick mustache, dark Ray-Bans shading his eyes, and a gun holstered to his hip, he flashes his badge.

"I'm Detective Weaver with the Carlsbad police." He looks over Josh's shoulder to where Jenna stands behind him, farther back in the house. "Are you Ms. Jenna Mason?"

"I am," she says with unease, wondering if he's here for her about Wes's case. Wondering if her time with Josh is up. She approaches the door. Josh moves aside to give her room, but he doesn't leave. He's eager for his case to be closed, to find the guy who shoved him down the stairs. She knows some of his depression stems from not knowing, and she feels guilty not telling him about Ryder. But she isn't positive it was him. It's been quiet. They haven't heard from Officers Velazquez or Horn in weeks. It's already early September.

"What's this regarding?" she asks.

"I was hoping to talk with you and your son about what happened last June." Detective Weaver's upper lip slips under the mustache as he talks. He hooks the sunglasses on his shirt collar.

"What happened to Velazquez and Horn?"

"I've taken over the case."

Her heart kicks up a notch. "You found something." Or someone. Her mind jumps to Ryder. Has he been talking? Will they take her in for questioning?

He shakes his head. "They weren't getting anywhere with the leads they gathered, so it landed on my desk." His gaze falls to Josh. "I know they tried to talk with you before, but I thought I'd try again. Think you can help me?"

"He still can't talk," Jenna speaks for him.

Josh grasps her arm, meets her gaze. His face is bright and earnest, his eyes beseeching. He wants to help.

Jenna relents. "Whoever pushed him, pushed him hard." Fresh rage flares. "He's lucky he didn't break anything else." Aside from his head, which was the worst of it, Josh came away with a few nasty contusions and a sore shoulder.

"Trust me, we want to catch this guy. Keep you and your mom safe." He looks pointedly at Josh. "Anything you can show me helps."

"Show you?" she asks.

The corner of his mouth lifts, disappearing into his mustache. "I bet he can draw. Your friend Brad told us about you, Josh. I understand you're quite talented. What do you say, will you help me solve this?"

Josh nods with enthusiasm. He opens the door wider.

"Are you sure about this?" she asks. He's been reluctant to draw for her or the pathologist all summer.

He nods again, and, after a couple of beats, gets out the word, "Yes."

Jenna lets in the detective. "Please have a seat." She gestures at the dining table, but he follows her to the kitchen, Josh tailing. "Coffee, tea?"

Detective Weaver shakes his head. "Water's fine." He settles in a chair at the counter and removes a notepad and pen from a pocket.

"Go get your sketchpad and pencils," she tells Josh. He runs upstairs, and Jenna fills a glass from the fridge fountain. She glances at the detective over her shoulder. He watches her. More like studies her, and nerves quiver in her chest. She can't help it. Does he know about her? Did he uncover evidence? Can he see her guilt?

She sets the glass in front of him as Josh rushes into the kitchen. He slaps the drawing pad on the counter and drops a handful of pencils alongside. One rolls toward the edge. He smacks it back.

"How familiar are you with forensic science?" Weaver asks Josh. "Watch any crime shows on TV?"

He nods.

"He used to," Jenna supplies. "Before this." She points at her head. "He doesn't watch much anymore. It's hard for him to focus."

Weaver nods, noting what she said. "Have you ever done an eyewitness sketch?"

Josh shakes his head.

"I could use one for this case. We didn't get a good look at the guy your friend says pushed you. Do you recall being pushed?" Josh flinches at the memory. He nods. "Did you get a look at his face?" Josh's shoulders hunch, his arms limp. He tips his head side to side. Sort of.

"Think you can sketch what happened? Anything you give us will help. You might surprise yourself and remember small details when you do."

Josh starts sketching, and Jenna asks the big question, pushing around the knot swelling in her throat. "You mentioned that the leads Velazquez and Horn had dried up. Do you have an idea who pushed him?"

Josh looks expectantly at Weaver.

"No, ma'am," he says. But there's a note in his voice that indicates otherwise. His tone isn't quite neutral. A liar can spot a liar. The back of her neck prickles. He knows more than he's letting on.

"Velazquez told me he wasn't captured on the surveillance footage. How is that possible? There are cameras everywhere."

Weaver picks up his pen. "The camera pointed at the top of the staircase wasn't functioning at the time. There was an open work order to have it replaced."

"So there's nothing?"

"Another camera caught something, but the angle isn't ideal. We see a man similar to what the other boys described walking away from the scene as Josh took a tumble."

The prickle on her neck creeps down her arms. "You saw him fall?"

He nods slowly.

Wide eyed, Josh swallows and returns to his sketching.

Jenna looks at her hands flat on the counter, visibly shaken. She doesn't ever want to see that footage.

"What about the other cameras? He followed the kids around the mall. Surely something was captured."

"He kept his face averted."

"He knew where the cameras were."

"Or that he was on surveillance. Everyone at the mall is. He wore a hoodie, which obscured his face."

Josh sketches like Usain Bolt racing to the finish line. He hasn't sketched all summer, refused when Jenna asked, and she wonders if he feared what he'd draw. For a while he wasn't sleeping. Headaches plagued him, but it could have been something more like nightmares. It pains her he hasn't told her. That he could be embarrassed he has them. She'd be surprised if he didn't. Unless he doesn't know how to tell her. But she knows he's ashamed about what happened. He seemed glum whenever she asked why he'd gone to the mall.

Jenna looks down at Josh's sketch, and her eyes widen. The scene is detailed and harrowing. Josh has drawn himself looking up the staircase as he tumbled. At the top are Brad and the two kids Jenna doesn't know. And all three stare after the figure walking away. The man in the gray hoodie. He's looking down at Josh, but Josh has blocked out his face with a slate-gray pencil.

Who is that guy? She can't tell if it's Ryder or some other random person.

"You can't show me anything about his face?" Weaver asks, his disappointment obvious. Josh shakes his head. "Any distinguishing features you can remember? Tattoos? Jewelry?" He shakes his head again, and Weaver's mouth presses into a thin line. "May I have it?" he asks of Josh's drawing.

Josh rips out the page and slides it over. Weaver folds the sheet in quarters and slips it into his breast pocket.

"Did you find anything new from that?" She nods where he put the sketch.

He shakes his head then angles his lean body toward Josh. "Would you give your mother and me a few minutes?"

Another jolt of nerves tightens her chest. Josh stares at them both, unsure what to do.

"Go up to your room," Jenna directs Josh. "I'll fill you in later."

Josh hesitates before leaving, grabbing the paper and pencils.

"You gave Velazquez a name." Weaver flips through his notepad. "Tell me about Ryder Jensen. What makes you think he pushed your son?"

Jenna's eyes close. Nerves push her chest in. Just the sound of his name sets her off. Always afraid he's found her while they've been stuck here as Josh recuperates. He's still under medical care. She refuses to jeopardize permanent damage to his brain. She's also petrified they'll take her away before Josh is fully recovered.

Meanwhile, these past weeks have been agony. Ryder could have shown at any time. She's spent hours watching her front yard through the window and her camera, wondering if she's protected Josh enough behind locked doors and an alarm system. They've been on lockdown all summer. She even has her groceries delivered, afraid something would happen to her if she left the house.

She grasps the edge of the counter like she's holding on for dear life and takes a breath. "Ryder Jensen was my boss at 7-Eleven when I was sixteen. His younger brother, Wes, was my friend. He believes I killed him."

Weaver shows no reaction. "Why does he think that?" His gaze dips to her hands. She lets go of the counter, flexes her palms.

"I ran away the day Wes died. He thinks that's why."

"Why did you run away?"

Jenna's nose flares as she says, her blood pumping swiftly, "I was pregnant. My parents wanted me to give Josh up for adoption or abort him. I refused."

He takes notes on his pad. She wonders what he thinks about her being pregnant at such a young age.

"My father's also a narcissist who emotionally abused me, and my mother neglected me."

Weaver's brows lift. After a beat, he flips to another page of notes. "You ran away, and then what? Changed your name?"

"Yes," she says, coming clean, at least partially. And to the police, no less. She's scared about what will happen to her, worried how Josh will fare once Weaver knows about her. But she must reveal some things if she wants them to help protect her son.

He frowns and flips through more notes. "Does Jensen know where you live?"

"I don't know. It's possible." She looks at the countertop, clenches her hands. "I'm an animator. I just published a book and have a movie in production. A reporter from the *Oceanside Sentinel* uncovered my birth name while doing a write-up on me and interviewed people from my hometown, including the Jensens. Ryder might have learned where I am through him."

"What's this reporter's name?"

"Stan Clint. The article Stan wanted to write never ran. It was supposed to be a publicity piece. My publicist convinced the editor to pull him off the assignment."

Weaver holds the ends of his pen between his hands. "I imagine Stan wouldn't have been too happy about that. I searched you. Some would call you a celebrity. That would have been quite the article for a small-town reporter."

"I imagine so," Jenna murmurs.

"Enough that he'd go after your son to get back at you?"

She blinked. She hadn't considered Stan. "I barely spoke to him."

Weaver's pen scratches across a blank sheet. "I'll look into it. In the meantime." He puts away his pad and pen and looks around the room. "What kind of security do you have?"

Jenna folds her arms. "An alarm system and a camera in front. It's on the porch. Why?"

"You can never be too cautious." He drops his card on the counter. "Have a good day, Ms. Mason. I'll be in touch."

CHAPTER 34

The door closes behind the detective. Sweat drenches her armpits, the back of her neck, and under her breasts. Weaver will dig into her past, and shockingly, she isn't frightened. Just anxious. Her confession is inevitable. It is the only way to fix this. She'll be sentenced, but Josh can stop running. Live the life he wants with Murielle, or his father, Tyler, if he'll take him.

She pulls at her shirt to move around the air. Surely Weaver noticed how nervous she was. He must wonder about it. He wouldn't be a detective if he hadn't sensed there was more to her story.

Josh runs downstairs. "Where?"

"The detective? He left."

"No." He arrows to the door and throws it open.

"What's wrong?"

"I—I . . . Gah." He pulls at his hair.

"Take a breath," she instructs before he gets too flustered and can't talk at all. "Did you want to ask him a question?"

He shakes his head.

"Then what?"

He stomps to the kitchen, throwing a hand over his shoulder, dismissing her.

"What's going on?" she asks.

He yanks open the fridge. Condiments in the door rattle. He stands there and stares as if waiting for something to jump out at him. The temperature in the room drops.

"Get what you want and close the door," she says, her patience wearing.

He throws bread on the island and the jelly next. The jar slides across the granite. Lunging, Jenna snags it before it topples over the side. "Josh." She gives him a look to chill.

He slams the fridge closed, grabs peanut butter from a cabinet, and slams that door, too.

She catches his gaze. "Stop what you're doing and talk to me."

He slams the peanut butter on the counter.

"Fine. If you won't talk, then draw. Like you did for Detective Weaver. Like I've been asking of you all summer. Show me."

She'd be ecstatic if he picked up his pencils. For whatever reason, he's been reluctant most of the summer, no matter how often she and his pathologist have encouraged him to do so.

"No."

"Why not? And what are you doing?" she asks when he smears peanut butter across a slice. "I'm ordering pizza for you guys." Anson's on his way over to celebrate Josh's thirteenth birthday. She has yet to bake the cake.

"No," he repeats.

"No, you don't want pizza? No, you don't want Anson to come over?" She gestures with her arms, for him to find his words.

He stares at the half-made sandwich. "No."

"Dammit, Josh, you have to give me more than that. I can't help you if you don't." She opens a cabinet and lines up the baking ingredients on the counter.

When she gets out the mixing bowl, he grabs the edge, stopping her. "No."

"You don't want cake either? Anson's coming. So's Kavan and Uma. It'll be fun."

"No, I—Argh." He swings his arm over the counter, knocking the bread loaf onto the floor. "No! No, no, no, no. Fuck, no."

"Josh." It comes out as a startled yell.

He kicks the island and runs to his room. The door slams.

What is going on with him?

She sets down the bowl and goes upstairs to knock on his door. "I don't understand why you're upset. Help me understand."

A muffled grunt reaches her as if he's talking into a pillow. She tries the doorknob. It's locked. "Josh, open up." No response. "Do you want me to call Anson and cancel?"

She hears a rustling on the other side of the door. "Goal!"

Goal? She frowns. "Josh?"

"G-go! Go!"

Go away.

The doorbell rings.

She groans at the ceiling.

"I'll give you a few minutes to think, but your friends are here. It'd be nice if you came down."

Flustered, Jenna retreats downstairs and answers the door. Uma rushes into her arms.

"Jenna!"

"Hello, honey." She kisses Uma's cheek. Her skin smells of bubble gum and summer grass, and she feels herself tearing up. Uma returns her kiss and Jenna's heart melts. She's missed her.

She's missed Uma's daddy more.

Uma goes into the house and Jenna is left on the porch with Kavan.

Their eyes meet. His are soft. Hers nervously dart over him, her heart in her throat.

She's seen him only a few times in the last couple of months, when he's delivered food from the restaurant. A new dish he wants her to try. An order she's placed in the hope that he'll deliver. But they haven't spoken about their relationship since the night of Josh's accident. True to his word, he's giving her space. They aren't together, and they aren't separated. Just in limbo. She still wears his ring. He's probably picking apart everything she did and didn't say about her past, deciding whether he wants to remain involved.

But he and Uma wanted to celebrate Josh's birthday.

"Where is he?" Uma shouts from within the house before they can say hello.

"Want to come in?" she asks him.

He smiles, crosses the threshold. Their arms skim when he moves by her, sending a shock that curls low in her stomach. He stops, meets her gaze again. "Hi."

"Hi," she whispers, shy, embarrassed, and undeserving of his interest.

He gives her a wrapped box. "For Josh."

"Oh." She looks at it, unnerved at how badly she wants to kiss him despite it all.

"Jenna," Uma complains. "Where is he?"

She closes the door. "Upstairs. Go let him know you're here."

Uma flies up the steps, her party dress flouncing at her knees.

Kavan gets a look at her face. "Rough day?"

She didn't have the chance to freshen up. "The police were here." She tells him about Detective Weaver's visit and Josh's outburst after he left.

Concern etches his brow. "I knew I hated that reporter. Does Weaver think he's a threat?"

"Right now he's just a name."

"Stay with me. I'd feel better if you both were—"

She presses fingers to his mouth, shaking her head. "Thanks, but we're okay here."

His eyes narrow. "We don't have to share a room."

That's not what worries her. She doesn't want to draw Ryder to Kavan and Uma. She also needs to keep her focus on Josh, no matter how much she wants to sleep under the same roof with Kavan.

"We're fine, honestly. It's been quiet all summer."

She hasn't heard from Dwight. He took her money and left. And she can't say if Ryder ever has been in town. He's on probation. He'd have to report in.

Besides, Josh is uncomfortable enough as it is already. He'd rather be in his room than an unfamiliar bed.

"That's what worries me." He gives her a look.

She squeezes his fingers. "We'll be all right." It'll be over soon. Josh will improve, then she'll take him to Murielle's. Turn herself in. And if she's arrested, Murielle knows to contact Tyler, give him custody of Josh.

Sadness weighs her down. Kavan's gift grows heavy in her hands. She tried to give Josh a good life. She really did. But she must take responsibility for what she's done.

Kavan studies her face. "What is it?"

"Nothing." She forces a smile, then amends, "A lot on my mind, that's all."

Uma returns and flops onto the couch. Arms crossed, her bottom lip pops out. "He isn't coming."

"No?" Kavan lifts a brow. "Mind if I try?"

"Be my guest." At this point, anyone is better than Jenna banging on his door. He's sick of her by now.

Kavan is back downstairs a few short minutes later, unsuccessful in convincing Josh to come out of his room. Anson can't convince him either, when he arrives, so he and Keely leave right after pizza.

Jenna still bakes a cake, hopeful Josh will make an appearance. Uma helps, and Jenna finds herself longing for a future she can't have. One with Uma baking at her side and Kavan rounding up the ingredients, watching the cake bake to perfection. But when Josh won't come down for a slice, Kavan takes a disappointed Uma home.

Jenna knocks on Josh's door as soon as they leave. "I have cake. Want a slice?"

"Go."

"Everyone's left. Party's over. It's just me."

He doesn't answer.

It's late, well past dinnertime, and he's kept himself locked in there most of the afternoon. Concerned he might do something to harm himself—she hasn't seen him this upset all summer—Jenna retrieves the key pin and unlocks the knob. She pushes open the door, startled by what she finds.

Hunched over his desk under the glow of his desk lamp, Josh furiously sketches. Charcoal covers the paper, no area left untouched, and stains his hands. Dark smudges blemish his forehead like bruises where he's held back his uneven hair while he draws.

Josh doesn't stop drawing or show any sign he knows she's here.

He drags a charcoal stick across the paper in long, impassioned strokes. The paper rips and he still doesn't stop.

Jenna is shocked and saddened and confused. "May I see?" she asks gently so she doesn't startle him.

Josh abruptly stops. He leans back in the chair and his forearms slide off the page to the side. He leaves them resting on his desk.

Jenna rotates the sketch pad so his art faces her. She can't tell what she's looking at, but it is troubling.

Barely decipherable in a slate-gray color field, the featureless face of Josh's attacker glares back at her. He doesn't have eyes, just a slit for a mouth. His stare is intense. His intent malicious.

Jenna lifts the page to find a similar drawing underneath. Then she notices the wavy sides of the sketch pad. Paper only does that when it's been used or water has spilled on it.

She flips to the next page, then the next. Page after page is filled with the same fearsome image.

"Is this it?" she asks when she reaches the last sketch, emotion thick in her throat. The image doesn't frighten her. She's frightened for her son. For what's going on in his mind.

He leans over and slides open the bottom drawer. He scoops up four similar sketchbooks and drops them on his desk.

She flips through the top one and stops halfway. She doesn't need to see more to know it's the same thing.

Life beyond Josh's room slows down. A heaviness settles in her chest. She has never felt such sadness for him. The nightmares that must plague him.

How has she missed this? How could she not have known?

She looks at his face. Lamplight glistens off his cheeks. He's been crying, suffering silently all day. Possibly all summer, given the unbelievable number of drawings he's done. He must be waking up at night because she hasn't seen him drawing during the day. Not around her, anyway.

Her heart breaks over his misery.

"Why didn't you tell me?"

He shrugs. His chin falls to his neck.

She gets on her knees so they are at eye level. She lifts his chin. His guilt over ditching school is drawn in his eyes. His frustration that the police haven't found the guy who pushed him is sketched in the downward turn of his mouth. His fear that his speech won't improve is seen in the tight grip of his pencil. And his terror that this bad man will come after him again is revealed on every piece of paper.

"It's not your fault. What happened to you, you're not to blame." She's told him before but feels he needs to hear it again.

Fresh tears spill over his face.

She clasps his cheeks. "Why haven't you shown these to me? I could have helped." She knew he'd been emotionally traumatized. That his injuries weren't just physical. But not to this extent. He hadn't shown her the signs.

He hid his pain from her. Buried it.

Because he didn't trust her to help him.

She's lied to him, and in turn, failed him.

"What has you so frightened? Are you worried he'll come back? Are you afraid you won't get better?"

Easily it could be both.

Josh nods at the sketchbooks. "Gas—" He sighs heavily. "Go."

"You want me to leave?" No way is she leaving him alone in this state.

He shakes his head.

"Then what? I don't—"

She stops before she tells him once again that she doesn't understand. She does, actually, all too well.

"You thought we'd move again if you showed me these."

She'd freak out, like she is trying hard not to do now. She'd break her promise and take him away from everything and everyone he's grown to love: school, the beach, Anson, Uma, and Kavan. Exactly what she intends to do when his doctor has released him from care.

That's why he wanted to help Detective Weaver. Had probably been wanting to help for a while and didn't know how to express that. Once the police catch the culprit, Jenna won't insist they move. Josh will no longer be afraid.

"Josh, I—"

A loud noise rattles the house. She and Josh jump. His arm disturbs the pencils. Several drop onto the floor.

"Wh-wh-what . . . ?"

What was that?

Jenna stares down the staircase toward where the noise came from. Her heart pounds in her throat. "I don't know."

CHAPTER 35

Josh is out of his seat and running down the stairs before Jenna can stop him. But she's right behind him.

"Stop," she says when he reaches for the door latch. "We don't know who's out there." Warning bells clang inside her skull. His sketches have her on edge, petrified about Ryder's release. "Let's check the video first."

He tails her into the studio. She logs into the surveillance app and scrolls through the most recent recording. She plays back the last few minutes. About a minute into the recording, a figure clad in jeans and a hoodie, hands stuffed in the sweatshirt's pocket, cuts across the yard. He walks right up onto the porch and stares up into the camera lens. Recognition explodes through her. Shock slams her back in her chair.

Holy mother. It is Ryder Jensen.

Jenna stares at the image frozen on screen. He's the one who's been tormenting her since June. The one who pushed her son. To pay her back for killing his brother. He tried to kill Josh. She knows that better than the characters she draws. Feels it strong as each second ticks by.

Her hand trembles on the mouse. She plays the rest of the video. If Josh had a reaction when Ryder showed his face, she'd missed it. But they watch Ryder step off the porch. He pulls an object from the hoodie and pitches it toward them. It blurs before the camera, then the video goes dark.

He's trying to get her attention. As if the shoe, jersey, and pushing Josh down a flight of stairs hadn't. He's upping the ante, trying to draw her out since she's been holed up all summer.

Josh makes a noise. She looks up at him. His face has paled.

"Josh?" She reaches for his hand.

He backs away, pointing at the screen. "Hit . . . ham . . . *him*."

The faceless man in his sketches.

She replays the footage to see the object he threw. There's something familiar about it.

Jenna pushes away from the desk and goes outside. The night is cool, the air heavy with a damp fog. A horn blows off in the distance, and Jenna is reminded of another night where the weather was much like this. Where everything went wrong.

Dread and foreboding saturate her senses. She cautiously glances around before stepping off the porch. Grass crunches under her shoes. Whatever Ryder threw, it landed under the bush.

She squats and feels around in the dirt until she finds it. Her hands latch on to a ball.

She holds it up to the light, and her chest caves in.

Wes's ball.

His faded initials are visible.

"Shit." She swears under her breath.

A piece of torn paper is attached, wrapped around the ball with a rubber band. She slips the band on her wrist and reads the note.

I know it was you.

Her breath comes rapidly.

She crumples the note before Josh can see.

"M-m-mom?"

She turns around. Josh stands on the threshold. She jams the note into her back pocket and shows him the baseball.

"His?" he asks after a bit of effort. As in Wes.

A pool of sweat wells in her lower back. "I think so."

Josh dashes into her studio and gets her phone. He struggles to talk. Then he spins two fingers pointed upward, and sings "*Whirrr-whirrr.*"

"You want me to call the police?"

He nods earnestly.

Jenna stares at the device in her hand. She swore to protect him. She tried to end her engagement so she could put him first.

Raw emotion, knotted and twisted, expands in her throat.

She dials 9-1-1.

———

Turnbull and Ruiz, two officers with the Oceanside Police Department, are the first to answer dispatch. She also called Detective Weaver after she'd called the police and has just finished describing to the officers what she and Josh heard outside and saw on the security footage when Weaver pulls up in his sedan. He unfolds from the car and lopes up the walkway. "Evening, officers. Ms. Mason." He dips his chin. "Josh, how're you doing?"

Josh shakes his head, rubs his upper arms.

"Spooked? That's understandable," Weaver says before addressing Officer Turnbull. He shows him his badge, explains the Carlsbad PD has been working on a case for her and that tonight's incident might be related. "What've we got?"

Turnbull brings him up to speed. Weaver asks for the baseball Ruiz bagged and tagged for prints. He holds the bag up to the porch light. "This is all you found?"

"Yes," Jenna says, the note burning a hole in her back pocket. She flicks the band on her wrist. His gaze drops at the noise, and she folds her arms. "Yeah, that's all." She'll confess more when she gets Josh somewhere safe. She'll drive straight to the Seaside Cove PD and confess if she must. To hell with Dwight and his video. Ryder tried to kill her son. Her life isn't worth saving over his.

He holds her gaze for a split second more, then points at the camera. It dangles by wires, the lens shattered.

Weaver whistles. "He did a number on that. Got any footage?"

"Yes. He looked right at the camera."

A wisp of a smile tugs at his mouth. "Excellent. Show me?"

Jenna takes Weaver into her studio. Josh follows. She angles the monitor for them to see and replays the snippet she and Josh watched.

"Mmm." Weaver taps his mustache. "Play it again, if you don't mind, and freeze on his face." She does and Weaver smiles, hands on hips. "Well, hello there, Ryder Jensen."

A noise of despair from Josh.

Her gaze darts to her son, and Weaver arches a brow. "This the same guy who pushed you?" he asks.

"Tank . . . Think." Josh motions that it's a possibility, but he isn't positive. He looks at his mom. "Ship . . . Tape . . . Tell him."

About the shirt and shoe. That it started before the incident at the mall.

He wants Ryder caught.

So does she.

Weaver folds his arms over his chest, watching their exchange. "Care to tell me what's going on?"

CHAPTER 36

LILY

Lily crossed the road. Dirty snow crunched under her shoes. The woman's smile didn't falter as she inspected Lily from head to toe. She tsked at Lily's wet sneakers. "You could've lost a toe if you'd kept walking. I'm Murielle." She thrusts out a hand.

Lily took it with some hesitation, hung up on the danger she'd almost put herself and her baby in. "Lily," she muttered, swallowing her shame. Her mother's voice was in the wind biting at her ears. *It won't be easy* . . . If she intended to raise a child she needed to make wiser choices.

She needed to ensure her own survival.

"Lily. That's pretty. Delicate, like the flower. Though I suspect you're anything but." She jammed the shovel into a snow pile alongside the drive. "Let's go inside. I'll fix us hot cocoa while you defrost." She smirked, and Lily's gaze darted to the side, unamused.

"How soon can you drive me?" She needed to arrive at the station before dark, and before the last bus left. And if she couldn't convince Murielle to drive her once they were in the car to the market, she'd need time to persuade someone else.

"We'll go when my daughter returns. She has the car."

Lily followed Murielle into the A-frame house. The lofty ceiling rose above, the stone chimney reaching the central beam. A fire crackled in the hearth, more for aesthetics than heat. The central heater rumbled through a cycle. She felt the air from a nearby vent and envied that Murielle didn't need to set an alarm for three in the morning to add logs to a woodstove so she wouldn't wake up as a frozen popsicle.

The house was homey, though. Nothing like the Whitmans' cabin or Lily's house in Seaside Cove. She liked it. One day she wanted a home like this for her and her baby.

"Make yourself comfortable," Murielle gestured in the general direction of a four-seated table under a window. "Sophie won't be long." She went into the kitchen, opened cabinets, and turned on the stove. Lily wondered how long Murielle had been here. Watching from the upstairs window, she'd recognized some of the neighbors from the summers she spent at the cabin. But she didn't remember Murielle.

"When did you move here?" she asked, settling onto a chair in her thick coat with the overstuffed pockets. She was instantly warm upon entering the house and now bordered on overheating.

She should remove it, but the coat held her meager possessions, and she was anxious to leave.

Murielle shaved a chocolate bar into a pan. "We bought this place several years ago. You're the first person we've seen in that house you're staying in. It's always been empty. I've watched you standing out front. Waiting for someone?"

Lily blinked, dismayed someone noticed her. Who else had? But the sun the other day had drawn her outside. The lake the day before that. Both times she'd been contemplating how she'd leave and how far she'd get. Where she'd start. Where'd she go. She almost left both days, then lost her nerve. Maybe she couldn't do this. Maybe her mother was right, and she'd fail. Maybe she should give Tyler the benefit of the doubt and trust he wouldn't risk his life and confront her father. It wasn't until this morning, when the weather threatened a longer delay, that she worked up the courage to walk beyond the driveway.

"The house belongs to a friend. He's letting me stay here. I used to come here during summers when I was younger. I don't remember you; that's why I asked."

Murielle's eyes slightly narrowed, contemplative. "What brings you up this time?"

Lily looked at her hands flat on the table. They contracted to fists as a memory lit up. Wes's face as he tried to strangle her. Dwight's gun. His laughter.

"Just needed to get away," she murmured.

"Are you here alone?"

She picked at her fingernails, removing dirt from the firewood she'd handled that morning. "For now, yes." She lifted her head toward the door. "When's your daughter getting back?"

"Soon. Unless the weather holds her up. She could be waiting for the plow to clear her way home."

Lily chewed on her bottom lip. Outside the snow fell in small flakes. *Tiny flakes, big storm* her mother once told her when she and Dwight took her and her brother and sister skiing. They'd had lessons when they were younger. Lily was five and ready for her own lesson, but Dwight couldn't be bothered. The game was on. He spent his time in the bar. Charlotte spent the day reading a novel and pouring Manhattans down her scarfed throat. Olivia and Lucas took turns teaching her how to position her skis in the shapes of a pizza slice and French fries. Until Charlotte took her inside the lodge and they left her to ski bigger hills. Lily still remembers it as one of the best days. They didn't often travel as a family.

Lily tapped her foot, watching the door like a puppy waiting for its mistress to come home to let it out.

Murielle set a steaming mug before Lily and sat across from her. Lily drank without paying mind to what she was doing and scalded her mouth. She gasped, and almost dropped the mug.

"You all right there?" Murielle observed, and Lily had a feeling she was seeing more than a girl swimming in an oversize coat.

She nodded. Winced again when her tongue touched the burned roof of her mouth. "Fine." She loosened a breath. "This is good. Thank you."

"How far along are you?"

She choked on her own saliva and cleared her throat. "I beg your pardon?"

"I'd guess seventeen to eighteen weeks."

Lily's hands involuntarily fell to her belly. Here she thought she'd misheard Murielle's remark outside. Surely people couldn't tell yet that she was pregnant. She layered her clothes.

"How'd you know?" she heard herself asking.

"Pregnant women carry themselves differently. I saw you standing at the end of the driveway a couple times. You kept running your hands in circles around your stomach."

Lily's hands clenched the coat.

Murielle planted her elbow on the table and rested her chin in her hand. "Did I guess right?"

Lily would have lied, but she'd already given herself away.

"Three months." One week. Three days.

"And you're alone?"

Lily nodded.

"With no car?"

She shook her head. "That's why I need a ride." She looked out the window. The driveway below was coated in new snow.

Murielle drummed her fingers on her cheek. "Are you taking prenatals?"

Lily blinked. "Vitamins?" She'd read about them. She couldn't afford them. Murielle nodded and Lily mumbled, "No."

"Have you seen a doctor yet?"

She bristled. "I don't see how that's any of your business."

"It's not. I'm curious. Not much excitement happens around here."

Lily laced her hands and ducked her face. She couldn't look Murielle in the eye as shame tingled up her neck to her face. She shook her head. Again her mother's warning. It wouldn't be easy raising a child on her own. No home. No job. No medical insurance. No future if she was caught and arrested. Just a pregnant teen with a secret that was shredding her insides as if she were made of paper.

"Do your parents know you're here?"

She tightly clenched her hands together, her heart thudding. "No," she whispered.

"Does the father know about the baby?"

Lily lifted her head as fear for Tyler's life tore across her face. "No!" she exclaimed. "He can't. And my parents can't know I'm here either."

Lily breathed heavily as Murielle watched her. Lily knew she was an enigma, a curiosity to the middle-aged woman. Terrified she'd insist on calling her parents. But whatever Murielle saw in Lily, her face softened. She reached across the table as if she were the grounding rod to Lily's lightning.

Lily stared at her hand. Her parents had never extended a hand. Lily had always fought for herself, fended for herself. Had always been alone.

She wanted to reach for that hand. Had never wanted anything more in her life. But Murielle was a stranger. And Lily wasn't trusting.

Murielle's hand retreated. Her mouth tipped down. "Who are you running from, Lily bud? What's your story?"

That story filled her mouth faster than a tank of gas, ready to be lit. Maybe she'd been alone too many days after a tragedy she didn't know how to cope with. Or maybe she simply didn't have anyone but herself, which was a frightening realization. But she couldn't singularly carry the weight of what she'd done to Wes.

She stared at her hands as if they belonged to someone else.

Those hands fisted.

No, she wouldn't tell anyone, not even this stranger. Who knew what she'd do to her and her baby.

"I should go." She pushed from the table. She'd find another way to the market or the station.

A car pulled into the driveway.

"That's Sophie. She can take you wherever you want to go. Though I don't know if the roads are clear. You might have to wait."

Lily settled back into her chair. Lightheaded, she unzipped her coat. She was sweating, nervous she wouldn't get away today.

The front door opened, letting in chilled air, a mini snow flurry, and Sophie. Flakes dusted the threshold. She carried a grocery bag in each arm and kicked the door shut behind her.

"Did you get a fresh baguette, darling?" Murielle asked her daughter.

"The last one." Sophie stopped by the table midstride, noticing Lily, who looked up at her like a startled doe. Tall and slender, Sophie didn't resemble her mom. Rings adorned almost every finger. Studs marched up the shell of her ear. A curly mass of brown hair burst from under a gray beanie like an overcooked marshmallow. Her eyes bookended a freckled nose, and like Murielle, Lily suspected they saw through everything, including her.

Sophie smirked. "Pick up another stray?"

"Soph." Murielle glared over her shoulder at her daughter, who didn't look much older than Lily's sister, Olivia. "This is Lily, our neighbor," Murielle introduced. "She's staying at the house across the way. Lily, my daughter, Sophie."

"Hi," Lily mumbled.

"She needs a ride to the market," Murielle announced.

"Actually," Lily started, fearing her window was rapidly closing with every snowflake that fell. "Can you take me to the bus station?"

Murielle's brows disappeared under the hair swept across her forehead.

"Knew she was a stray." Sophie then had the audacity to wink at her.

Murielle inhaled a steady breath. "We can, but we'll have to wait until this storm blows clear. We can get you there but wouldn't be able to get home."

"Who knows when that'll be," Sophie says. "I saw Jeff's truck parked at Larry's."

Murielle groans and rolls her eyes. "Jeff runs the snowplow, and Larry's is a bar," she clarifies for Lily. "You're welcome to stay with us."

"I need to go, really." Tyler would be here tomorrow, assuming the roads were passable by then. There had to be another way to the station.

"Good timing," Sophie said, looking out the window behind Lily. "Looks like you've got company."

"What?" Lily looked outside and froze. Parked in the Whitmans' driveway was Dwight's car. A noise of distress escaped her throat. How'd he know she'd be here?

"Everything okay?" Murielle asked gently beside her. Lily hadn't heard the woman leave her seat.

"No." She hugged her sides.

Murielle rested a hand on her shoulder. "I didn't think so. Here, let me take that." She helped Lily out of her coat, and Lily didn't resist. She was too shocked Dwight had found her and so soon. Why couldn't he leave her be?

Murielle handed the coat to Sophie, who'd put down the grocery bags in the kitchen. "Hang that in the closet. Lily has something to tell us."

CHAPTER 37

Jenna closes her surveillance app. "Ryder was released from prison in May."

Stan interviewed the Jensens. They would have told Ryder. For all she knows, Dwight led Ryder right to her. He hasn't been this close to her since Indio. She'd arrived at her apartment and known someone had been there. She had that feeling you get when someone has gone through your things. It slammed into her as soon as she entered the place. The scent was slightly off, foreign, like cheap men's cologne. Nothing was out of place, but she could picture him tampering with her drawers, rubbing the clothes in her closet on his skin. Smelling the insides of her shoes. She felt disgusted and violated.

Then she'd seen him waiting in his car in the parking lot across the road. Watching. Just watching.

But Jenna had been watching him, too. She left with Josh after dark when Ryder slipped inside the market to piss or whatever he was doing.

She was terrified. He hadn't managed to get that close to her for a decade. She didn't think she'd get away. Headlights trailed each direction she took on their way to the next apartment Murielle had arranged on her behalf. She'd never had to sign a lease, leave her name on a paper trail.

Her gaze had darted from the road to the rearview mirror. She couldn't tell if Ryder was behind them. She didn't see his car. She believed she had lost him.

That was four years ago. It was the last she'd seen of him. She'd naively thought she was free of him when Murielle called to say he'd been arrested and sentenced. Since then she'd grown complacent, overly confident.

Weaver settled a hip on her desk. Hands clasped loosely in his lap. He leaned toward her. "What are you thinking?"

"I think"—her gaze jumps to Josh—"that he started harassing us in June. I thought it was my father."

"Dwight Carson?"

She nods, thinking of the years Dwight did torment her. "It's something he would do."

"Throw baseballs at surveillance cameras?" A humorless smile hides under the mustache.

"No." Weaver looms over her. She pushes from the desk and stands, needing space.

Josh gets her attention and plucks his shirt, points at his shoe.

"He—as in Ryder, it would seem—left a jersey and sneaker on my porch a few months ago."

"Are they his?"

She shakes her head. "They belonged to Wes, his brother. His initials are on them." She doesn't tell him Wes was wearing them when he died. She wouldn't know that.

"Where is this shirt and shoe?"

"I gave them to Dwight. Like I said, I thought he'd left them."

"Wouldn't he have told you it wasn't him when you gave them back?"

"You'd think, but no." She'd left before he could say anything.

"And Ryder left these here because . . ." He arches a brow, waiting for her answer.

"Exactly what I told you earlier. He believes I killed his brother." Her voice warbles with nerves from talking about him in front of Josh.

Josh shakes his head hard. "She didn't fat him." His eyes widen, and both of Weaver's brows shoot up a creased forehead.

"I think he's trying to say that I didn't kill him."

Josh nods vigorously, and her heart sinks into her stomach. She struggles not to correct him.

Weaver folds his arms. "Did Ryder witness his brother's death?"

"I don't know. I wasn't there."

The lie spreads thickly across her tongue, sours her stomach. The truth sticks with her until she can get Josh somewhere safe.

"You ran away before Wes perished?"

He read through the articles, but unease pulses through her at his tone. It's no longer neutral.

"Yes, I just told you that. Are you questioning what I'm saying? Because it sure sounds like it."

Josh frowns at the detective, sharing her displeasure.

Weaver's smile doesn't reach his eyes. "No, not at all. I'm trying to understand Ryder's motives." He stands and, arms still folded, arches his back. Vertebrae pop.

"Isn't his belief I did it motive enough?"

"It is. He believes you killed his brother, so he goes after your son, assuming it was him at the mall. Why now?"

Easy answer. "I didn't give him the chance before." He's been stuck in a cell for four years, preoccupied with Wes's murder. With her.

"You moved a lot."

She nods.

Josh clutches the ball cap to his head, his elbows flared like wings. Fear swirls in his eyes. He must find this conversation disturbing. His eyes are calculating. He's figuring out she's lied about more than his father. That she lied about why they kept moving. She's been running from Ryder all this time.

She puts an arm around him. Josh clings to her. "What next?" she asks the detective, anxious for him and the other officers to wrap this up, her own plan formulating. Get Josh to safety, then turn herself in.

"We'll issue a warrant for Jensen, but we'll question him regardless of the mall incident. He trespassed and vandalized your property. Do understand we haven't placed him on-site with your son. The car our suspect used was reported as stolen, and we don't have a clear image of his face. Unless a witness identifies him, or he confesses, an arrest for pushing your son would be difficult to justify."

Josh tenses and Jenna looks at him. He wants the faceless monster in his sketches to be Ryder. Then this will be over. He'd relax, and hopefully start to heal.

She'd bet her future royalties it was him.

She cups his jaw and kisses his cheek. "It'll be all right."

"I'll keep you posted. Other than that"—he stretches out his arms as if he's about to yawn—"I'll say good night."

"'Night, Detective." Jenna gives him a tight smile when he offers his hand. She keeps her arm around Josh, ignoring the hand. Hers is damp. Weaver knows she's nervous. He doesn't need to feel how much.

The officers leave, and Jenna bolts the door and arms the alarm. She turns to instruct Josh to pack. They're leaving for Murielle's. They'll stay with her until Ryder has been caught. What she doesn't tell him is that she plans to leave him under Murielle's protection while she goes to the police. If she is arrested and sentenced, then Murielle will know to give Tyler custody, if he wants his son, and only if Josh feels safe with him. Otherwise, Josh will remain with Murielle.

It's a plan. It will work. And it's the only way she knows how to get Ryder off her back. But more important, Josh deserves a better life than the one she's given him.

She expects Josh to argue about leaving. He's been adamant about staying, has kept his stress and fear hidden from her the entire summer, burying himself in his dark artwork. But he approaches with a picture from the fridge. A photo of the Whitmans' cabin, taken from the lake one of the times she and Josh had stayed with Murielle until another place opened in the network.

She looks at the picture in his hand. She'd taken Josh kayaking. She'd told him that place—Murielle's house, the lake, the small community high in the Sierras—would always be their safe spot. If they were ever separated, if he couldn't find her, he was to go there. Murielle would help. She made him memorize the address.

He pushes the photo in her hand. He's frightened. But he easily retrieves the word. "Go."

CHAPTER 38

The garage door lumbers open, the noise reverberating through the silent alley. A thick fog settled over their complex in the predawn hours. Misted air haloes the streetlamps so they look like angels watching over their departure.

Jenna glances up and down the alley as the Subaru's hatch opens. He's out there, watching. Now that she's tuned in, she feels him. The tightening behind her neck, the quiver of nerves down her arms. The voice whispering in her head. *Run.* Warnings she's heeded for years when it was time to move. To stay one step ahead. The same warnings she ignored for months until she stopped feeling them. This time, she isn't running. She's coming back. And she's going to put an end to this. To everything. She'll drive to the SCPD, give them her statement, then let them take it from there, and bring her in. Ryder wants her confession. He'll get it, just not the way he wants—her at his mercy.

Unfortunately, it'll come at a sacrifice: the joy of raising Josh until he's a man, a life with Kavan and Uma, a career she can be proud of. Her freedom.

She's willing to give it up, even her deepest desire of knowing the love of a family, if it means her son can have what he wants most—a normal life. He'll be safe.

She drops her roller into the back as a deep sadness drapes over her. Josh does the same. Then he stuffs his fists into his hoodie's pockets. He's impatient and overly tired. He wanted to leave hours ago, but

Jenna had them wait until the sky was dark and the roads free of traffic so she could see if Ryder was following.

"Got your phone?" she asks.

Josh spares the backpack slung over his shoulder a glance and drops into the passenger seat.

Behind her, the jingle of dog tags approaches. Terror rockets through her at the noise. Fearful it's Ryder, she presses a hand to her breasts and lets a relieved breath go when she sees Glenny. She's always up and about early to open her café. Her neighbor's gaze slides over the contents in Jenna's trunk. "Hello there. Going on a trip?"

"Visiting a friend." Jenna closes the hatch.

"How lovely. Will you be gone long?"

"A few days," she says, unsure when exactly she will be back. *If* she'll be back.

Vlad whines, anxious to continue his walk. Jenna opens her door, antsy to get on the road.

"I can pick up your mail if it's not on hold. You can leave your key with me. I'd be happy to watch your house, too."

"Thanks, but we're good."

"Have a good trip then. Come, Vlad." Glenny clicks her tongue for the dog to heel.

The skin across her shoulders tingles.

"Glenny," she says. "Call the police if you notice anything suspicious."

Glenny pulls the dog closer to her side. "Is everything all right?"

"Someone vandalized my porch last night."

"Goodness." Glenny tugs on the gold chain at her neck. "I will most certainly call them if I see anything."

She leaves, and when Jenna settles into her car, Josh is slumped in his seat.

She grasps his hand. "You okay?"

He nods and points at her.

Her nerves are firing. Sadness and a deep sense of failure hover close by. She's giving up her son to keep him safe, and she doesn't know when she'll see Kavan again. No, she's not okay.

"I'm scared," she tells him honestly.

He taps his chest. "Me . . . turtle. Too."

She cups his cheek, smiles sadly, then reverses from the garage. She doesn't look back.

For the first hour, Josh stares out the window, listening to the music she helped him download to the iPod Kavan gifted him yesterday. He'd wrapped the box with a navy-blue bow Josh tore into after the police left last night. He charged the noise-canceling headphones and iPod while he packed.

By the second hour, Josh is squirming. She's taking side roads and less-traveled highways. A longer route, but one where she'll notice Ryder if he's behind them.

When they reach a long stretch of barren highway, Josh gestures that he has to relieve himself. Like immediately.

Jenna groans in frustration and pulls off the road. "Be careful, it's dark," she says, worried he'll stumble and reinjure his head. Keyed up that Ryder isn't far behind. She glances over her shoulder, checking and rechecking the mirrors.

He rummages through his backpack for a penlight and clamps his mouth around it. He pulls up the hoodie over his headphones and gets out.

"Don't go far," she hollers when he keeps walking up a slight hill. A thin strip of light bounces off the slope, guiding his way. He disappears behind a hedge of bushes.

Leaving the car running, Jenna gets out to keep a better eye on Josh. Even though she can't see him from the road, the penlight peeks through the bushes.

A glimmer of light crests the hill up the road, luring her attention. The light grows brighter, separating into two headlights. And they're coming fast.

Her neck tightens, and she starts to back up. *No.*

It can't be.

But it's him. She knows it's him.

She screams for her son, pivots, and runs, but she isn't fast enough.

The car clips her hip, and she is airborne, flying over the hood. She hears the car skid to a stop as her back slams into the ground. Her head smacks the asphalt.

Pain lances through her.

Darkness envelopes her.

And then nothing.

CHAPTER 39

Josh trudges through calf-high weeds. Stickers cling to his socks. He can feel them poke his ankles. The penlight arcs back and forth across the ground like a bloodhound, searching for divots or other hazards that could make him faceplant. His mom is paranoid he'll fall, and he doesn't want to stress her out more than she already is.

His sketches disturbed her. She probably thinks he's losing it. And maybe he is. He wakes up every night with the sweats and can't fall back asleep. He keeps seeing that face that isn't a face. A face he's just found out belongs to Ryder Jensen, a man who's been chasing his mom for years, forcing them to move. Josh should be angry. His mom lied to him. Maybe he'll feel angry later, but right now he's just frightened and anxious, which makes his condition worse. And he hates that.

He hates that he struggles to talk. Worse than a baby learning to speak. And after what he heard last night, he has questions he can't ask because the words won't come. When he tries to write them, the letters spin in circles, like mixing up a deck of cards that don't land in order. They don't make sense.

And he really wishes he could ask about Wes and Ryder.

His mom swore she didn't kill Wes. She's said that twice now, and he believes her. She wasn't there when her friend died. But Ryder believes she was, and he's been chasing her since Josh was born.

What Josh doesn't understand is why his mom has been running from Ryder if she didn't kill his brother. Why not go to the police and get a restraining order?

Josh suspected Weaver wanted to ask her, but for some reason he backed off. Maybe because Josh was there. The detective will ask his mom later.

Weaver also doesn't know about the agreement his mom has with Dwight. It somehow involves Wes, and the way Dwight reacted when Josh confronted him at school tells Josh it also involves Benton. There's something his mom isn't telling anyone. Which makes him wonder if she did kill him. That she was there when Wes died, that she lied to Weaver. She's been lying to everyone.

Josh swats his calves and plucks the stickers from his socks. He skips to the next Vampire Weekend track on his new iPod.

Best gift ever from Kavan and Uma. He adjusts the wireless headphones over his ears and taps up the volume. He's scared and exhausted. He wants his head to get better, and he wants all of this to go away: Ryder, Dwight, the police. For his mom to come clean and tell him the truth. He doesn't want anything to happen to her.

Sick to his stomach, he turns up the music even louder and ducks behind a large bush. He keeps on walking until he's far enough up the road his mom can't see him whiz. Then he unzips his fly and relieves himself, looking up at the stars as he goes.

Vampire Weekend's "A-Punk" comes on, and Josh starts banging his head. He yanks up his fly and fumbles the iPod. It slips from his hands and disappears into the grass.

"Fuck."

He swings his penlight back and forth. He moves aside the grass. He nudges his foot. There. The iPod screen lights up. It took him a few minutes, but he found it. His mom is probably screaming at him to get back.

He picks up the device and unintentionally pauses the music.

A weird sensation creeps up his spine. He slides off the headphones and hears . . .

Nothing.

Penlight swinging, he tramps through the grass to peer around the bush. He can barely make out the outline of her car. He sees the head-lights, but not his mom. The car interior is pitch black.

"Mom?"

She doesn't answer.

He starts walking toward the car, and when he still can't see her, he starts running. "Mom!"

He reaches the car, and his heart seizes. Her door is open, but she isn't there. He turns full circle. She isn't anywhere.

"Mom?" he hollers, then shouts, "Mom!"

He backs away from the car into the middle of the road. "Mom! *Mom!*" Beyond freaked out, tears come fast and heavy.

She can't be gone. She wouldn't have left him.

He hugs his chest. She'll be back. She has to come back.

Josh backs up, and something crunches under his foot. He picks up a shattered phone and whimpers. It's his mom's phone.

Maybe she was hit by a car, and someone took her to the hospital.

Maybe Ryder got her.

White-hot panic singes inside his chest. He hears a buzzing in his ears as he wildly looks around, screaming for his mom. But she's gone.

Gone, gone, gone.

What should he do? Where should he go?

He scrambles across the front seat for his backpack and roots for his phone. He'll call Murielle. He'll call Kavan. But his hand finds an empty pocket. His phone isn't in his pack.

Then he remembers.

He fucking forgot his phone.

He left it charging on his desk, right beside his wallet. He'd put both there so he'd remember, and he hadn't. He'd been distracted. Too fixated on his new headphones and iPod.

Josh crawls into his seat and hugs his backpack. He slaps his head, shaking loose more tears. What's the point of having a phone when he couldn't use it anyway? He sees the digits in a phone number, and they spin out of whack. He enters them out of order.

A car drives by, then another. He leans over and shuts his mom's door, locks the car. Notices the key is missing. So is her purse. Did she take them with her, or did someone steal them?

Petrified, he hunches low in the seat, unsure what to do next. His mom will come back. Someone will stop and help him.

He waits an hour, then two. Scared beyond reason, frightened his mom has been taken.

Then he realizes that if Ryder does have his mom, he might come looking for him.

He needs to find a way to Murielle's. His mom made him promise if they were separated, they'd meet there.

Josh cautiously gets out of the car. He shoulders his backpack, locks and closes the door. He then starts walking.

When he reaches the first rise, a car pulls up beside him. His heart lurches into his throat; his first thought is that it's Ryder. He's come back to finish him off. Josh turns to run but notices the car is a boat, old and in pristine condition. The woman behind the wheel is even older. She can barely see over the dash. And he's never been more relieved to see a stranger. She stares at him, easing down the passenger window. She's an odd sight to Josh, dressed like she's going to church.

He must look an odd sight himself. A thirteen-year-old kid alone in the middle of a bleak highway.

She peers at him over her glasses. "What are you doing out here by your lonesome?"

Josh clenches and flexes his hands. His mom's stranger-danger warnings scream in his head. But he can't very well walk all the way to Murielle's. He doesn't know how to get there. He tries to explain.

"Mom—She . . . pat . . . lamp." He squeezes his eyes shut; his speech is worse when he's nervous. Then he visualizes the word and slowly speaks. "Mom . . . left."

"She left you?"

He nods and fresh tears flood his eyes.

"Dearie me. Let me call the police. Do you see a highway phone nearby? I don't have one of those mobile things."

He shakes his head.

Her mouth pinches in thought. "We'll have to find a pay phone then."

He shakes his head harder. He's supposed to go to Murielle's if they're separated. Murielle will help him find his mom.

"Know where you want to go then?"

He points at the mountains, at a loss for words.

"That doesn't help me, honey."

He scratches his head under the ball cap, wondering how to explain. He memorized Murielle's address long ago. He tells her, and he can hear how he's not making sense. Her mouth scrunches in confusion until her upper lip touches her nostrils. He doesn't have it written down. Nothing to show her.

There must be something . . .

Then he remembers the envelope addressed to his aunt Olivia.

Josh opens his backpack and flips through his notebooks until he finds the old envelope from his mom's journal. It's been in his backpack since he found it.

He can't read the address. To him, the words are jumbled, out of order. But this woman should be able to make sense of it. He holds up the face of the envelope. She squints at the faded ink. "San Luis Obispo. You're in luck, honey. It's on my way. Hop in." She unlocks the doors.

With a last glance at the mountain range beyond them, Josh gets in the car.

CHAPTER 40

The first thing Jenna notices is the birdsong. There must be a flock nearby, their chatter edged with urgency. *Help, help,* they crow, sending their notes to the heavens.

The second thing she notices is how detached she feels from her body, and that she's the one crying for help.

But her voice is weak, barely audible to her own ears. She takes stock of her body, the dull pain in her hip, a sharp burn in her ribs. Chilled, she shudders. Then she opens her eyes.

Josh.

The sun is high in the sky. Tall blades of dried grass tickle her face. She can't tell where she is, so she sits up, her movements fluid, and she cries out, grabbing her side. Her head feels like a cracked egg. Gingerly, she touches the back. Her hair is crusty, matted, and her fingers come away slick, covered in blood. Her stomach cramps. She leans over and retches in the dirt.

Gasping, she wipes her mouth with a dirty hand, resisting the urge to sleep. She needs to get to Josh.

She struggles to her feet and almost loses her balance. Bracing her legs, she lifts a hand against the glare and looks around. The two-lane highway is in front of her, her car a ways down. Josh must be frantic.

Pain slices across her head. Her eyes squint until they burn. She must get to Josh.

Memories return like the speeding vehicle that knocked her down. The silhouette of the man inside as she was thrown across the hood of the car. Ryder Jensen. She has no idea how he found them, but he did. And he hit her.

He tried to kill her.

Josh.

Terror strikes her like a blade down her middle.

"Josh," she croaks. Golden hills sprawl for miles around her. "Josh," she calls louder. "Josh!"

Perspiration beads on her forehead. Her body shivers. She makes her way to the road, shouting for her son, afraid Ryder took him when he doesn't answer.

A car approaches, and she cries out, flags down the driver as she collapses to her knees. She lands hard on the asphalt, folding onto her side. She doesn't want to sleep. Josh needs her. She has to get to him. She struggles to stave off the approaching darkness. Her eyes close, and she feels herself go.

———

"Is she alive?"

Cool fingers press the pulse in Jenna's neck. "Yes. Call 9-1-1, Chlo."

Gravel crunches under shoes as someone moves away and makes a call. Her voice is rushed and anxious, worried. Jenna fights the weight of sleep and opens her eyes, staring up at the sky and into the face of a stranger. His eyes widen in surprise.

"She's awake," the man tells the woman.

He peers down at Jenna, touches her shoulder. "Hang in there. Ambulance is on its way."

Jenna groans. "Josh."

"Sh. You hit your head. It looks serious."

She tries to sit up, and both the man and the woman named Chlo press her shoulders back to the ground. "Don't move. We don't know if anything's broken," the man advises. Weak, Jenna doesn't resist. Her body melts into the ground, her thoughts scattered, emotions chaotic with fear and pain and rage.

"She's pretty banged up," Chlo says.

"She was probably hit by a car. What's your name?" he asks.

Jenna looks wildly around. She can't make sense of what happened. Where's Josh? She groans his name.

"What?" He leans over, angling his ear by her mouth.

"My . . ." She exhales, and her head spins. Bile wells in her throat.

"Anything in that car about who she is?"

"I'll check." Jenna hears Chlo leave. She moves her head back and forth. She tries to reach for the man. She must tell him about her son. Ryder has him. They could be far away by now.

But she has no strength. Her arm thumps to her side.

"Sh-sh," the man urges. His grasp tightens on her shoulders, holding her still.

The woman returns. "The car's locked."

"Check her for the key fob. She might have a phone."

Jenna feels the woman search her pockets.

"No, nothing's on her."

"That's a shame."

"The ambulance is almost here," Chlo says.

Jenna hears the siren off in the distance, and then she doesn't hear anything at all.

———

Jenna opens her eyes and sees a white wall with a television and whiteboard across from her. The name on the board is "Samantha Brooks (?)." Whitney is listed as Samantha's nurse. Jenna lifts her left arm. An IV is embedded in her forearm. She touches it to see if it's real, then she touches her face. A tube runs under her nostrils. She pulls at it.

"Good morning," a voice says cheerily beside her. "Now, now. We don't want to do that." Hands move hers from her face. Jenna looks up at the nurse, then down to the badge clipped to her shirt. Whitney. "It's good to see you're lucid. How are you feeling?" Whitney smiles.

Jenna frowns. How long has she been here? Where *is* here? She touches the dull ache at the back of her head. Her fingers brush over a neat row of stitches. Her heart rate spikes.

"How's your head?" Whitney asks.

Her frown deepens. She was going somewhere. Her son was with her. She looks around the room for him. Worry digs into her chest. Her hand lands there amid a tangle of cords. She looks down at her chest. "What—"

"Don't pull on those either. We need your readings." Whitney nudges Jenna's arms aside. "On a scale of one to ten, what's your pain level?"

Jenna looks toward the door, wondering if Josh is out there. "What . . . what happened?" Memories clutter her head. She has difficulty making sense of them, putting them in order.

"That's a good question. We're hoping you can tell us. How about we start with your name. Can you verify this is it?" She points at the board. Samantha Brooks is her attorney. "There wasn't an ID on you or a registration in your car. The police ran your plates. We tried calling the number the car's registered to, but it's disconnected." Like the lease on her townhouse, the car's registration is in Sam's name.

"Lily," Jenna volunteers her name, only to frown. That isn't right. "Jenna. Name's Jenna Mason."

"What a pretty name. It's nice to meet you, Jenna." Whitney erases *Samantha Brooks* from the whiteboard and replaces it with her name. She caps the dry-erase pen and returns to Jenna's side. "Your doctor can give you more specific details about your condition when you're ready. But you're at the Beaver Medical Clinic. An ambulance brought you in five days ago."

Jenna's mouth parts on a gasp. Her heart drops into her stomach. *Five days?* "Where—" she croaks through her rising panic.

"You suffered a severe concussion," Whitney is saying, "which explains why you're feeling a little out of it. You have three cracked ribs and extensive contusions on your left side. Thankfully, nothing is broken. But we've been keeping you sedated. The couple who found you on the roadside think it was a hit and run. Do you remember anything?"

"My son, Josh. Where is he?"

Whitney shakes her head. "There wasn't anyone with you."

"What do you mean?"

"You were alone. It was just you."

Impossible.

"You don't understand . . ." Jenna starts pulling at the electrodes stuck on her chest, disconnecting wires. The monitor beside her starts screaming. She needs to get out of here. Find her son.

Tears cloud her vision as Whitney grabs her wrists to hold her still. The nurse is shockingly strong.

"Please calm down. You'll hurt yourself. Now what's your son's number? I'll call him for you." Her eyes level with Jenna until Jenna exhales like a defused bomb. She'll call him. He'll pick up, and he'll tell her he's okay, that he's safe. He has to be all right. She nods, and Whitney slowly releases Jenna's wrists. She shows her the industrial mobile phone clipped to her side.

Jenna dictates Josh's number and waits with bated breath for her son to answer. Whitney shakes her head when the call rolls into voice mail. She leaves a message instructing Josh where his mom is and how to reach her. When she ends the call, Jenna is sobbing. What was she thinking? Josh hasn't been able to use a phone since his injury. Numbers move around on him, jumping out of order. It would be a miracle if he figures how to listen to Whitney's message and return the call. If he even can.

Memories flood her. *Ryder.* He hit her.

What if he has Josh? What if he's killed her son?

Tears flood her eyes.

"Oh, honey." Whitney hands her a tissue. "Is there anyone else I can call? Family? A friend?"

When she gets herself under control, Jenna asks to use the phone. Never has she been so grateful for her sharp memory. One look at a business card, and phone numbers are permanently etched in her brain.

She calls Detective Weaver and leaves a hurried, panicked message when his voice mail answers. She next calls Keely for a ride.

Then she calls Kavan.

CHAPTER 41

She's been in and out of consciousness for almost a week. She remembers, barely. They kept her sedated as the swelling reduced in her head. She had no clear indication of the passage of time.

Anger at herself boils her blood. Terror for her son holds her heart. She clutches the room phone on her lap, waiting for Weaver to call back. She's already spoken to the local sheriff's department. A car is being dispatched to the scene. An APB has been issued for Josh. A BOLO for Ryder.

What she doesn't understand is why she'd let herself lie here for so long. She'd been so out of it. Why didn't she fight off the drugs? Josh is long gone by now. But where, and with whom? She prays Ryder doesn't have him, but accepts she must assume he does.

The doctor has ordered another CT scan. She needs to get out of here before that happens. She doesn't have time. Her thirteen-year-old son is out there, helpless and alone. He could be hurt or—

"He's alive," she whispers. She can't accept that he could be gone forever.

The phone on her lap buzzes. She snags the receiver. "Hello?"

"Ms. Mason. It's Detective Weaver."

She loosens a breath, relieved he's called back. "Josh is missing," she says.

"I know. I'm sorry. I'll do what I can."

"It's been five days." Panic roars behind her ribs, caged and untamed. They've lost time.

She tells him where she's been and where they were going. She explains they stopped for Josh and that's when she was hit.

"Did you get a good look at the driver?"

She recalls his face, the brief glimpse she caught as she shot across the hood. "Yes, sort of. It happened so fast."

"The license plate?"

"No. Will you issue an Amber Alert? Josh is missing. Ryder could have abducted him."

"I wish I could, Ms. Mason. But unless you can specifically ID Jensen as the driver, we have to consider this could be a simple case of hit and run."

"There's nothing fucking simple about this. The driver came right at me. It was Ryder. Who else would it be?"

"I understand." His tone is neutral and she bristles. She wants action. "You said someone found you in the grass. It's possible Josh didn't see you. It was dark. He could have found a ride somewhere. Thirteen-year-olds are resourceful. When they go missing, they have the tendency to wander off."

"That's not what happened," she yells into the phone. She knows her boy. He wouldn't take off with a stranger. He wouldn't wander. Unless he was taken, he'd stick close to the scene.

Or he'd go to Murielle's.

He could already be there.

"Possibly, but we need to consider all angles."

"Issue a goddamn Amber Alert. Please. You have to find him."

"I can't," he says, apologizing.

Pause. Her heart pounds once.

"Why not?"

"We don't have enough descriptive information about the suspect or the abduction if there was one. Not to mention it's been five days. I'm very sorry," he says when she groans, aggravated. "But Amber Alerts are issued immediately upon a known and witnessed abduction. If they were issued for every kid that goes missing, they lose their effect. But given what we know of Ryder—"

"What do you know? Did you hear something?"

"I drove to Seaside Cove and read Wes Jensen's file. I also spoke with the parents. They don't believe Wes was murdered. It's just Ryder. They haven't seen him since he was imprisoned, and that was four years ago. They did show me the box of photos Ryder left behind when he moved out. They're pictures of you. Lots of them. Dating back thirteen years."

Jenna's skin crawls. Had he been that close that often?

"There's more. The woman he assaulted has an uncanny resemblance to you, as does his ex-girlfriend. The police were dispatched to their apartment five to six years ago for reports of domestic violence. She never filed charges."

Dread gnaws her insides. "How does that relate to what he's doing to me?"

"I'm not a psychologist, but I've been a cop long enough to see the signs. Ryder has an unnatural obsession with you. It's why he stalks. Based on what you've described to me of his behavior, he's playing cat and mouse. He's showing you how easily he can get to you, whether through your son, or leaving clues at your door, snapping photos."

The shirt, the shoes. Tampering with her apartment in Indio.

It could explain why he left her on the road instead of coming back to check that she was dead. He's taunting her. If he wanted to kill her, he would have hit her head-on. Unless he's waiting for another opportunity. Or it's Josh he wants now, not her.

"Where is he now?"

Long pause. "We don't know. He wasn't at his apartment in Santa Maria."

Jenna turns stone cold. "Which means?"

"We haven't been able to locate him. There's a warrant out for his arrest. He missed his check-in with his parole officer. Police in three counties are actively looking for him."

They'd better find him with that many people after him.

"We'll file a missing person report for Josh and enter him in the national registry for the missing. Meanwhile, I'll contact the local sheriff's office and ask they dispatch an officer to take your statement."

Meanwhile, she can't wait here and do nothing. Her words mean nothing without the details of what happened, and she missed the whole thing. She was fucking unconscious.

"I'll be in touch when I know more."

Keely's on her way over. She gives him Keely's cell to reach her since she lost her phone.

Within seconds of ending the call with Weaver, Keely blows into the room like a summer storm in a heat wave. A fresh, electric relief.

Kavan follows her into the room.

Jenna's mouth falls open.

"Don't blame me." Keely holds up her hands.

"I didn't give her a choice," he says, rushing to her side.

Kavan said so much when they were on the phone. Her call stunned him. He'd been trying to reach her for days. She begged him not to come. She wanted him home in Oceanside in the event Josh found his way back. But he was adamant he wanted to see her when she mentioned she'd asked Keely to pick her up and help her look for Josh. She doesn't have the strength to do so on her own.

"He showed up at my house right after you called," Keely explains.

Kavan cups her cheek and presses his forehead to hers. Her fingers are trembling when they weave through his hair, and she shuts her eyes, squeezing out her tears. "Jenna, baby, I've been going out of my mind with worry. I needed to see with my own eyes you're okay. How could I not come?"

"I'm sorry." The apology slips from her mouth. She should be mad at Keely. She wanted Kavan to stay in Oceanside. But now that he's here, to see him, feel him. To hold him after she was going to leave without so much as a goodbye. She sobs.

Kavan cradles her face. He kisses her eyes, her cheeks, tasting her tears. "What can I do?" he asks gently. "Where do you hurt?"

Everywhere.

Her ribs, her shoulder, her hip, her head.

Her heart.

She inhales a shuddering breath and buries her face in the curve of his shoulder. "I've been so scared."

"I know," he whispers. "I'm here now. Tell me what happened."

"I told him what you told me," Keely volunteers. She stands to the side, her gaze nervously darting about the room as she looks away from their reunion to give them some semblance of privacy.

Jenna only gave Keely the highlights over the phone.

"I'll tell you everything. Just help me get out of here." She's too weak to do so on her own.

She kicks off her covers and closes her eyes, pausing as a wave of dizziness passes over her. Bile creeps up her throat. She breathes through it until her stomach settles.

"Hand me my clothes," she asks Kavan, pointing at the folded pile atop her sneakers on the cabinet below the window.

Keely watches her, concerned. "Have you been discharged?" Jenna shakes her head. "What about your head? Shouldn't you wait for your doctor?"

"Josh is missing," she snaps. "He's alone and frightened. He can't communicate and god knows what else." Emotions gather like a whirling storm. "A med team is on their way to take me down for a scan. I don't have time, and if anyone sees me leaving, they're going to try to talk me into staying. If I still insist on leaving, they'll discharge me against medical advice and that requires time and paperwork. I refuse to sit here—" She yanks out the IV, hissing in pain, and tosses the needle aside.

"What are you doing?" Keely's face pales at the trail of blood seeping down the inside of her forearm.

Kavan drops her clothes on the bed beside her and presses a tissue to the wound. His gaze lifts to hers. "Okay?"

She nods.

"Keely, stand over there." She points at the end of the bed. "To the left a bit," she says, and Keely steps to the side. Jenna glances behind her. She can't see the camera, so the nurse's station shouldn't be able to see her. Last thing she needs is to attract their attention. "Don't move; stay there," she says.

Keely wrings her hands, glancing out the door. "Please tell me we aren't going to just walk out of here."

"That's exactly what we're doing," Kavan says, helping her pull on her jeans under the hospital gown. She winces as pain flares along her cracked ribs. "Careful," he says so gently that she feels moisture in her eyes again.

She keeps the portable EKG device tucked in the gown's pocket and shoves her feet into her sneakers. Kavan ties her shoes when she has trouble bending over.

"You're taking that?" Keely asks of the device.

"Yes, we are," Kavan says, growing impatient with Keely's second-guessing.

"If I unhook it, a nurse will show up within seconds. Hold these." She gives her shirt and sweater to Keely. Kavan takes her elbow. "Don't look at the staff. We're just going for a walk." She's seen patients circle the floor all morning.

Jenna squeezes Keely's hand. "You're doing great. We'll be fine."

Out in the hall, she pushes the button, and the elevator opens. Inside Jenna removes the electrode tape and wires. Kavan helps her into her shirt. Every movement shoots pain through her body and reflects on Kavan's face. "I'm fine," she tells him, breathless. He doesn't believe her. But he finishes helping her dress.

"Where's your car?" Jenna asks when they reach the ground floor. She's breathless from lying in bed for five days. Weak from her injuries. Her body shudders, chilled. Her skin feels pasty.

"You okay?" Kavan asks.

She nods, teeth gritted, and forces down the rising nausea.

Keely doesn't look so sure. "Where are we going?" she asks when they reach the van.

"Back to where I left my car. The last place I saw Josh." She needs to see the scene herself. Josh could have left a message, a sketch. A clue in the direction he'd gone.

Kavan helps Jenna into the front seat. He takes the back. Jenna gives Keely directions to the accident site.

She then calls Murielle.

CHAPTER 42

LILY

Lily couldn't see Dwight through the curtain of snow. But his car was in the drive. He was there, and she imagined him peeking in windows, pounding the front door. He would even have tried the keypad for the garage. She'd locked the doors and closed the blinds. The rooms were barren of her belongings. Not a single grocery item had been left on the counter. And the logs in the woodstove had burned down to embers. If he could see anything through the blind slats, he wouldn't find evidence of her. The house appeared empty, closed for winter.

She shook with fear, remembering his rage.

Her mother had warned her he'd change his mind.

His temper would have cooled. He'd regret what he'd said, as he always did after he exploded. He would have regretted ordering her to run away. He'd want to keep her close because of what she knew.

What shocked her was how quickly he found her.

Then again, where else would she have gone? Dwight brought her here for summers. He knew she loved the lake and hated it when those summers away stopped.

In hindsight, she never should have come here.

Dwight gave up his search and left. Lily sagged where she stood by the window, relieved she wasn't there when Dwight showed, and shivers at that thought. She can still see his malice, the evil burning in his eyes. His resolve to control everything she did. All down the barrel of the gun he'd aimed at her.

"My dear, you're shaking."

Lily jolted when a hand cupped her shoulder.

"Who is he?" Murielle asked.

"My dad," she says, releasing the breath she'd been holding. "He's not really my dad."

That admission, spoken out loud for the first time since she learned about her father, cracked something inside her. Her gaze then met Murielle's, and she lightly gasped. Never had she seen such compassion directed at her.

Lily's resistance faltered.

She thought if she hid what she'd done to Wes, it would feel like she didn't do anything at all. But she'd been alone for days with nothing but her dark thoughts. She kept seeing Wes go into the water. Over and over again.

It kept her up at night. Followed her every waking moment.

The guilt and remorse and fear were bigger than her. She couldn't keep it to herself any longer.

She confessed everything.

Charlotte and Benton. Dwight and their deal. Wes's death. She killed him.

She told Murielle why she couldn't tell Tyler about the baby—that she feared for his life should Dwight discover he was the father.

Murielle listened, and when Lily finished, she leaned back in her chair. Sophie had joined them at the table. A look passed between them. Sophie pushed up from the table and put on her coat.

"What's going on?" Lily cautiously watched them both. She'd taken a risk. They could turn her in. Were they doing that now?

"I shouldn't have said anything." She stood to leave.

"No, no. I'm glad you told us. It was the right thing to do." Murielle clasped her hand. "So was running away. You can't return home. Your baby's life is at risk." She then nodded once as if her mind was made up. "You're staying with us, at least until your baby is born. Your father will never know you're here."

Lily stared at them both. They were crazy. They couldn't be serious. "Why would you do this?" They'd just met. They didn't know her.

Sophie tilted her head in Murielle's direction. "It's what she does, fusses over strays."

The label rankled, but Lily looked at Murielle for confirmation.

Murielle clasped Lily's hands. "You're a mother now. Think of your unborn child. Where were you planning to go? How do you expect to support him? Keep him safe?"

Lily was dumbfounded. People didn't just help people and expect nothing in return, especially people like her. Murderers.

She also didn't want to be a charity case. She'd practically raised herself. She was capable of raising her own child.

"Trust me," Sophie piped in. "You'll get your chance to pay us back, if that's what you're worried about." As if she'd read Lily's mind.

She thought of the cash in the coat. It wouldn't be enough. "I don't have anything to give."

"Not now. But if we set you up right, you'll be in the position to do so one day. And just to be clear"—Murielle gave her daughter another look—"we don't expect to be paid back. We pay it forward around here."

"Can I leave anytime?" She didn't want to be trapped.

Sophie rolled her eyes.

"If you want," Murielle said.

Lily chewed her lip. She could still find a way to the bus station if it didn't work out with Murielle.

"I won't be a freeloader. I expect to help around here."

"We wouldn't have it any other way. Go with Sophie and collect your things."

"Come on, flower girl," Sophie said. "Snow's getting heavy."

Lily put on her coat and tailed her down the road, waiting for a shoe to drop. Her fortune was too good. Things never came to her this easily. And that made her feel uneasy, phantom fingers skating across her shoulders.

The snowfall had grown heavier in just minutes, a thick curtain that obscured the sparse neighborhood. Lily unlocked the front door, thinking how she would have been walking in these conditions. She could have gotten lost.

Sophie shot out a hand when Lily tried to enter the house. She cocked her head, listening. "Should be okay. Where are your things?"

Lily pointed down the hallway. "Last room on the right. There's stuff in the bathroom, too."

"Got it. Wait here."

Lily stayed in the entryway, nervously shifting from one foot to the other as she looked at the cabin for the last time. This was it. She was leaving for good. She'd never see Tyler again. He'd never know about the child she'd bring into the world. And that broke her heart, what she'd done, what she was going to do to him. He'd be devastated when he learned how deeply her betrayal went. But she wouldn't change her mind. She was leaving. And whatever she did, she'd strive to ensure her and her baby's safety. Going forward, she'd remain vigilant in keeping herself out of bad situations.

The front door flew open with a crash, and a heavy weight slammed her against the wall. She opened her mouth to scream, and a bear-size hand clamped her neck, lifting her several inches off the ground. Her feet dangled. The rubber soles of her canvas sneakers flailed against the wall. Pressure built in her lungs. She couldn't breathe. Her fingernails scraped at the hand around her neck. Ripped into his flesh. Her gaze lifted to her attacker's face.

Wes's eyes stared hard into hers.

No, not Wes.

Ryder.

Blind terror punched into her chest.

"Confess, bitch. You murdered him."

When she didn't answer him, couldn't answer him, he started squeezing the life out of her. Her vision darkened along the edges.

It wasn't her time to go. She had to do something. Her baby needed her. If she could just get her knee between his legs.

Color flashed in the corner of her eyes. A blur.

His eyes rolled back, and he dropped like a stone.

Lily landed on her knees and gasped.

Sophie stood above her, a pot gripped in her hand.

"I could have handled him." Lily coughed, feeling weak and incompetent.

Sophie arched a brow. "Sure, you could." Then she grabbed Lily's hand and hauled her to her feet. "He's twice your size. Unless you know how to defend yourself, don't be stupid. I'll teach you. We'll have time."

Lily looked at the way Sophie held herself. She knew things, like how to survive. "Okay." Lucas had taught her some basic moves, but she wanted to learn more.

"Who is he?"

"R-Ryder." Lily coughed, trying not to freak out that he had found her. That he'd tried to kill her. He must have followed Dwight; how else would he have known to come here? "Wes's brother. He was in front of my house when I ran away. I think he saw me. Is—is he dead?" She dared to look at him sprawled on the floor.

Sophie crouched and checked his pulse. "No, but he's going to be stinkin' mad when he wakes. We need to go." She wiped her prints off the pot and dragged Lily's luggage from the house. "Lily died here tonight," Sophie said on their way back. "Best you get that in your head."

It took three days for Sophie's remark to sink in. From the safety of Murielle's house, Lily watched Tyler frantically search the lake house's grounds. Through the trees, she saw him call for her over the lake.

He called for her from the drive, and he knocked on neighbors' doors asking after her. Sophie answered when he came to Murielle's while Lily listened from the other room, her cheeks drenched with tears. She hugged a pillow, nearly ripped it to shreds to keep from running to him.

Defeated, Tyler left the lake a couple of days later. Lily felt like he took a piece of her soul with him.

"You're doing the right thing," Murielle reassured her.

Agony was a bear mangling her chest. She'd never see him again, her first love.

But Tyler was alive, and she needed to survive. To keep herself and her baby safe, Lily had to die.

CHAPTER 43

He isn't here.

Murielle's words sink in. But Jenna shouldn't be shocked that he hasn't made his way to her. How could he? Assuming he isn't with Ryder and someone else picked him up, he can't describe where he needs to go. She doubts he can draw the directions either. He's never seen Murielle's house on a map.

Jenna feels a sudden heaviness. She cups her hands over her face, agonizing over how helpless she's left her son.

"Jenna," Kavan says behind her. "It would help if Keely and I knew exactly what is going on."

Jenna drops Keely's phone in the cup holder, and, doing her best to maintain her composure, she brings them up to speed. She tells him about Ryder, who he is, how he's been following her, and how she thinks he's the one who pushed Josh. She explains the clothing articles from Wes she thought were Dwight's doing. How she learned that Ryder had been released from prison, and they couldn't run from him because of Josh's injuries. He was still under medical care. She'd been frightened all summer, diligently watching for him through her windows, on her surveillance. Then she mentions the baseball to the surveillance camera that convinced her and Josh to leave.

When she tells him she was hit by a car and spent five days in and out of consciousness only to wake up in the hospital and discover Josh wasn't with her, Kavan takes her hand. He repeats her name over and over, his thumb caressing the back of her palm.

Maybe she's exhausted. Maybe the residual painkillers in her system have relaxed her tongue. Maybe she doesn't have the strength to do this alone anymore. But she keeps talking while she has the courage. Her past pours from her like water through a cracked dam.

She tells him what Weaver told her about Ryder. His cat-and-mouse games. That he won't stop until she's dead, he's caught, or she admits that she killed his brother. How he's missing, too. The police can't locate him.

Kavan is quiet for a long time. Beside her, Keely doesn't say a word.

Then he inhales. "You've been running from this guy over thirteen years. He's a bona fide stalker. Why didn't you ever go to the police?"

The last fragments of the dam crumble.

"Because I did kill him."

Keely sucks in a sharp breath.

Kavan's hand slips free of hers, leaving her palm cold. Her heart empty.

Let her be judged on what she did when she was sixteen and pregnant and feared for her life, and not who she is now. She doesn't care. She just wants her son back, safe in her arms.

Jenna buries her face in her hand and falls apart. "It was an accident. A horrendous, awful accident. I wanted to save him. But everything went to shit. I was sixteen, had just found out I was pregnant. I didn't know what to do without getting myself hurt. So I ran."

"Oh, my gosh," Keely whispers.

"I never told you. Either of you," she says, her gaze sliding to Keely, looking over her shoulder at Kavan, whose face is a blank mask as he takes it all in, and it's not even the full story. There is one piece she'll always hold back. "I've never told anyone but Murielle," she says, for reasons she now explains to them. She was young and impressionable. She let Murielle take over, make decisions on her behalf. She does wonder if she would have run as long as she had if she never fell into

Murielle's network. Would she have turned herself in long ago? But Murielle gave her an excuse to hide.

"I didn't think I deserved your love," she admits to Kavan. "Or your friendship." She looks at Keely again.

Jenna's judged her own actions since the day she ran.

"Jenna," Kavan says with more feeling than she's ever heard come from him.

He unbuckles his seat belt and leans forward. His arms come around her.

Then he says the most beautiful thing he's had to her, given what she just shared with him.

"I wish we weren't driving."

"Why?"

"So I can hold you, kiss away your pain."

Jenna stills. He must be in shock. He should hate her. Tell her he never wants to see her again, and to stay away from his daughter.

Then he should report her to the police. That's what any good citizen would do.

But relief, her awe for this man, moves through her, settles in. That he'd be so understanding, so accepting when she's feared how he'd react. That he isn't outright rejecting her, it leaves her stunned. A shaky sigh loosens from her chest. Her head drops and she cries.

"I'm sure there's more you have to tell me. I won't lie, I have questions I hope you'll answer. But, no, I don't hate you. I also think it was an accident, just like you said. A horrendous, awful accident."

Keely vigorously nods. "I agree."

"You didn't set out to kill him."

"It doesn't change the fact I did." And the guilt of her actions has settled in deep, made a home. She'll always feel it.

"It doesn't change the fact that I still love you," he murmurs, folding his arms over her chest. He rests his chin on her shoulder.

Keely is flying down the highway, and he's unbuckled. If they get into an accident, he'll go through the window. But she doesn't want him to let go, not yet. She grasps his hands and holds him there, grateful he's here.

She then glances out the window and notices the change in scenery. "Here. Pull over." She points out the window.

"Where's your car?" Keely pulls to the side of the highway.

"Not sure." It was probably towed days ago. "We need to find it. Josh could have left a message."

"I'll call the sheriff and find out where it's been impounded. What's the license plate?"

Jenna gave her the number and steps down from the van, catching herself as she's overcome with dizziness. Kavan's hand lands on her back. "Take it easy." She nods, breathing through the waves of pain in her side, and walks around. She isn't sure what she's looking for or expects to see.

Kavan watches, a cautious observer.

A car passes, and she crosses the road, stopping abruptly at a dark stain in the middle of the opposite lane. A memory clicks on like a television. Ryder clipping her side. Her body thrown over the hood of the car then falling hard on the asphalt.

Her fingers faintly trace the stitches on the back of her head.

Kavan is at her side. "What is it?"

"I think that's from me." She points at the dried blood. His face pales. Neither of them realized how badly she'd hit her head.

For the first time since waking in the hospital, she remembers getting up, stumbling to get to Josh. Ryder had stopped. He'd gotten out of his car. She recalls him taunting her, laughing, following her across the road where she fell into the tall grass and passed out. Something like a passing car must have spooked him off because why leave her? Why not make sure she was dead?

Jenna glances in the direction Josh walked when she last saw him before looking back across the road where Keely is standing, watching her. She looks up at Kavan.

Eyes narrowed, he studies her. "What are you thinking?"

Jenna clenches her hands, squeezes her eyes shut. "No," she whispers.

Stunned by the impact, she'd gone to the wrong side of the road, opposite where Josh was. It was dark. He wouldn't have seen her. He wouldn't have known to look for her there.

"Josh," she hollers, grabbing at the sharp stitch in her side. Shouting for him is fruitless, but she does it again. Then again.

"Josh," she shrieks, hugging her ribs as she bends over in agony.

Hands gently touch her back, lift her upright, pull her into a broad chest. "He's not here," Kavan murmurs into her hair.

"I know." She cries, grappling his shirt. "I know."

A car passes, blares its horn.

"Let's get back to the van," he suggests, leading her across the road.

Jenna gestures at the phone in Keely's hand. "Anything?"

"Found where your car's impounded. They're closed till morning."

Jenna feels a tightness in her chest. More waiting. So much waiting. Meanwhile, Josh could be hurt. He could be . . .

She squeezes her eyes shut, refusing to believe he's dead.

"They open at seven. We'll call first thing." Keely pulls on her seat belt.

Kavan shuts her door and gets in back. "Where to next?"

"Murielle's."

CHAPTER 44

"Pull over," Jenna says halfway to Murielle's. She'd been thinking about the night Tyler had driven her to his family's cabin. How scared she'd been, how disgusted she'd been with herself. She'd just killed her friend and couldn't tell him.

She'd lost everything that night—her family, her home, Wes, Tyler—and she can't help comparing her circumstances then to now.

Josh is missing. He could be gone forever.

God, she prays he stayed hidden behind that bush and that Ryder didn't see him.

She just wants to find her son. Please, please let him be okay.

Keely swerves to the side of the highway, gravel popping under rubber, and nausea sloshes in her stomach. Jenna lurches from the car, crying out when she jars her ribs. She gulps the cool mountain air, cringing through the sharp pain. Kavan is immediately at her side, but she pushes him away and gets sick on the pavement. She hears him retreat to the van, and a moment later, his hands hold her hair, and a cool, wet cloth brushes her forehead. She takes it from him and wipes her mouth. Then she hunches over, breathing through her teeth until the sickness subsides.

"You okay?" Keely asks behind them.

"Yeah—Yeah, I'll be fine," Jenna says. "Needed some air."

"Are you sure you don't want to go back to the hospital?" Kavan asks, his face strained with worry.

Jenna shakes her head. "I won't go back. As long as Josh is out there, I'm here." She needs to keep looking for him.

"Keely, would you give us a moment?" Kavan asks. He tosses the soiled cloth onto his seat when Jenna is done with it.

Keely looks between them and makes a decision. "Sure." She returns to the van, and Kavan faces her. He traces a finger down the side of her face, moving hair away from her eyes. "You know I'm going to insist you check yourself into the hospital after we find Josh."

Her lower lip trembles. He said *we*. It's always been her, just her. Running.

After everything she's said to him, after breaking up with him, he's still here. It's no longer just her.

She looks up to read his face, and his eyes tell her that she isn't alone. That he's the family she and Josh have been looking for, despite who she is, what she's done. She needs to tell him more, that she did murder Wes. It wasn't an accident. But the courage she had earlier has deserted her.

"How are you holding up otherwise?" he asks.

She presses her lips flat and shakes her head, looking at the ground. "This is my fault. We should have left as soon as Stan exposed me."

A slow, disbelieving shake of Kavan's head. "You were going to leave without saying goodbye."

Guilt tugs her stomach. She nods, and hurt darkens the sienna in his eyes.

"Is that why you broke off our engagement? You thought I wouldn't want you if I knew you killed that boy? It was an accident. You didn't mean to kill him. It's tragic and unfortunate, and yes, you have to live with it. But look." He throws out his arms. "I'm still here. You don't see me going anywhere."

She looks away, her jaw tight. "There's more to it, Kavan." More she's ashamed to admit, more than what she's already told him, what only she, Murielle, Sophie, and Dwight know. What he caught on video. "Ryder tried to kill Josh because I killed his brother. He tried to kill me. If he knew about you and Uma . . ." She shakes her head. "I can't risk him hurting either of you. I love you both too much." Her voice is unsteady. She looks at the ground.

Kavan squeezes the back of his neck. "Tell me what happened after Wes died. Where did you go? Who is this Murielle?"

His voice is calm, belying the urgency of their situation, his anger now that he knows she'd left him without saying goodbye. But she also knows he's asking to keep her from panicking. To help him understand, and to keep her focused. So she tells him about Tyler taking her to the lake house, her fear he'd discover that she was pregnant. Her fear for his life. She explains how she met Murielle and that first frightening step off the grid.

Kavan patiently listens. He doesn't comment or judge, which makes it easier to talk. Like earlier in the car, everything rushes out of her as if her secrets have been penned up for too long. As if telling him is the right thing to do.

"Did Murielle really take you in, no questions asked? She helped you through your entire pregnancy?" he asks when there's a break in her story.

"And for years afterward." Murielle's generosity was boundless, and Jenna initially had been just as incredulous as Kavan, suspicious even. It took months to accept Murielle wasn't going to rip it away and leave her with nothing, worse off than before she met her.

Kavan thumbs off a stray tear. He could never not touch her when they're near. And the rest of Jenna's story pours out.

"Murielle has a network of angels, as she calls them. People who open up their homes, apartments, off the books, for people like me who need to live off the grid but don't have anywhere to go, no money, no resources. Sophie once described it to me as witness protection for when you needed to hide from even the government. She'd been a lost soul once like me. That's how she met Murielle."

"Sophie's not really her daughter?"

"Not by blood, but they are family. I stayed with them a couple months until a house opened up in San Diego. I was seven months pregnant, and Murielle drove me there to live with an older couple. Hoyt Criswell was an attorney, and his wife, Ilona, was a retired college professor. I remained with them for almost a year. They were like grandparents to me, the first adults outside of Murielle who were kind. Ilona helped me get my GED, and Hoyt, well, let's just say he wasn't as confident as his wife that Murielle's network could keep me and Josh safe. Murielle had told them of what happened to me before I got there. They knew people were looking for me: Dwight, Ryder, possibly even Tyler. Hoyt had seen enough during his career.

"He insisted I have a backup plan in the event I went missing or . . ." She sighs heavily. "Died. He didn't want Josh to get lost in Murielle's network without me, or without any connection to who he is or from where he's from. Hoyt was sentimental. He believed family was important, and asked if there was anyone I trusted, not for my own sake, but for Josh.

"I couldn't pick Tyler. I suffered from PTSD for months, no thanks to Dwight, and still feared for Tyler's life. So I thought of my brother, Lucas. He hated Dwight as much as me. I figured he'd protect Josh with his life because I knew he'd feel guilty not being there for me, especially now that I was gone. But Lucas wasn't in the right headspace. He could barely care for himself. And he was still living at home. I didn't want Josh anywhere near my parents. Ever. Even with me gone, knowing they'd have no purpose to harm him, I didn't want them to have any influence on how Lucas raised him. So I chose Olivia, my sister. She was living away from home and didn't plan on returning. She told me that several times, and once Olivia set her mind, god help the person who tried to change it. She was dating Ethan, who I liked and respected."

He was the only one who came forward to help when he saw that she needed it, the only one who knew both her secrets—that she was working and might be pregnant—and swore to keep them. If he'd kept that from Olivia, he might have been able to convince her to keep Josh from their parents. "Hoyt drew up a power of attorney giving my sister custody. I think that's why I started the letters."

"What letters?"

"To Olivia." At Kavan's surprised look, Jenna adds, "I never wrote about me, only Josh, and just generic things, like his favorite books and games, things like that. If there was the slightest chance Josh could end up in her custody, I didn't want her going in blind. I wanted her to know him, as well as she could from what I told her. I wanted Josh to trust her.

"I started the letters the day he was born. Then our papers came, thanks to Sophie, and Josh and I had new identities, invalidating the POA. We were no longer Lily and Josh Carson, and I never bothered to update it because Murielle moved us to a new house. But I kept sending Livy letters, every year around Josh's birthday, and—" Jenna falters. She swears under her breath.

"What?" Kavan's hands flex on her arms. "What's wrong?"

"I didn't send one this year." She'd started to last June. But she'd been shocked to find her journal missing. Then Kavan startled her when he came into the room.

Then Josh was pushed down a flight of stairs.

"Is that bad?" He sounds worried for her.

She dives deep into her thoughts. She should have stopped sending letters after that initial one. But she didn't, couldn't really. Something prevented her from severing the one connection she had to who she used to be, where she was from. She wanted a sense of family even when she was unable to have one. And she found that connection, as thin and fragile and one sided as it was, with a sister she still loved. One she never stopped loving and who she hoped, despite the betrayals, abandonment, and cold shoulders, might still love her. As Lily.

Jenna wondered what Olivia thought of those letters. Did she burn them? Toss them? Read and treasure them? Had she tried locating her? What did she think when this year's letter didn't come? Was she worried? She probably didn't care.

After what happened to Josh at the end of the school year, Jenna's worry and fear overwhelmed her. She forgot about their annual day trip. In years past, she'd take them to a national park, a new museum to explore, anywhere far from where they currently lived. Then she'd find a mailbox wherever they were and slide the sealed envelope with the note and Josh's photo, and no return address, into the narrow slot.

"Josh and I moved every six months or so for years, anytime I got a feeling Ryder was closing in. It was weird. I'd get this sense it was time to go."

"Survival instinct. Like animals when predators are near."

"Perhaps." Jenna looks at Kavan curiously. "Eventually I made a career out of my art, carving out a way to support us." And contribute to Murielle's network of angels. Her way of paying it forward. "That's how we ended up in Oceanside. Josh was tired of moving. So was I, if I'm being honest. Ryder had already been in prison for a couple years, but Josh didn't know that. It made it easier for me to decide to stay. Josh made friends. I met and fell in love with you. I got comfortable, complacent, and selfish. Naively thought we were safe. And look where that got me." Jenna tosses out her arms.

"It got you here, with me."

"Murielle's network saved me," she says, thinking how she could have ended up on the streets, selling her body for food, a common fate for teenage runaways.

Kavan tugs one of her shoulders, then her other one, inching her into his embrace.

Silence stretches between them where Kavan holds her like he wanted to do in the car, and for a moment, she lets him, feeling her body absorb his strength, his energy and love, until she manages to lean away, a thought crystalizing. Earlier, she recognized that she'd lost perspective over the years. She'd put herself first—self-preservation—rather than Josh, and in turn put her son's life at risk.

Murielle's network might have saved her. But it also made it easy to keep running. To not take responsibility and face the consequences of her actions. If she didn't have a place to go, she might have reported Ryder sooner, alerted the police about Dwight, and turned herself in.

She looks back at the van, the open doors, the engine running. Keely waiting. "We should go." They need to find Josh, and then she needs to finish this.

CHAPTER 45

"Jenna . . . *Jenna!*"

Jenna wakes to a bleary-eyed Keely holding a phone in her face. They arrived at Murielle's well after dark and went to bed in the room Jenna once briefly shared with Sophie, with its twin beds separated by a Craftsman-style nightstand, adorned with a Tiffany lamp that never lit the room brightly enough.

But dawn is breaking, its muted glow casting the room in a magical light.

Last night Murielle reached out to her network to be on the lookout for Josh. If he could manage it, he might return to one of the places they'd lived. When Jenna's painkiller from the hospital wore off and she had trouble focusing, she tasked Sophie, a woman who possesses a skill set Jenna has never fully understood and isn't sure she wants to, to search for Josh within an expanding radius from the accident site. Kavan wanted to help Sophie; then she'd take him back to Oceanside, and he'd look for Josh there. They left in the early morning hours.

All four of them, Kavan and Keely included, were adamant that Jenna remain at Murielle's. Jenna could wind up back in the hospital if she didn't mind her injuries. Josh needed her healthy and alert. Jenna needed to heal. She could make calls from there. She also wanted to be here for Josh. She's still holding on to the hope that he'll find his way.

Jenna wanted to stay awake with them through the night. An update might come from Weaver. But nerves and injuries had pulled her under.

"Detective Weaver's on the phone," Keely says to her now.

"Oh." Jenna comes fully awake, hope flaring. Throwing off the covers, she wraps a quilt over her shoulders and takes the phone to the front room.

"Detective?" she says, anxious for news on Josh.

"Sorry to disturb you so early, Ms. Mason." His voice is alert. All business.

"That's all right. Did you find him?"

Short pause. "I don't have news on Josh," he says in a gentle voice, knowing his lack of information would upset her.

White panic and hot rage singe. "Nothing? What the hell are you doing then? Josh is missing. Ryder could have him."

"We filed the missing person report. Officers are actively looking for Josh. We issued a warrant for Ryder's arrest."

"A lot of good that's doing."

"Believe me, Ms. Mason. I want him off the streets as much as you. We're doing everything we can."

Jenna pinches the bridge of her nose. "Why are you calling then?"

"It's about your father. Dwight Carson."

Her blood turns cold. "What about him?" she cautiously asks.

"He's dead," he says, sympathetic.

She blinks. "Excuse me?"

"His car rolled into a ravine. Alcohol was most likely a factor. There will be an autopsy, but I wanted you to know."

Her arm falls to her side. The quilt drops to the floor. Dressed in a thin shirt she snagged from Sophie's closet and boy-short underpants, Jenna should be cold. But she only feels numb.

"When? Where?" is all she can manage.

"A commuter called it in, east of Carlsbad."

Jenna stares out the window at nothing specific. Dwight was in SoCal again. Was he there on business or looking for her? Did he come by the townhouse? Damn Ryder for damaging the security camera. Now she'll never know.

Not that you care. He's dead.

No more bargain. No more threats.

But it doesn't change what she did.

"Thanks for telling me, Detective."

"I'm sorry about your loss."

"Don't be." She isn't. Not for Dwight. One day, maybe. But not today.

"Anything you need? Anyone I can call for you?" he asks after a stretch.

"No. Thank you, though." She does wonder how Olivia will react to this news. She and Dwight were close. If Jenna feels anything, she grieves for her sister.

"I'll check in later with an update."

"Appreciate that," she says and ends the call, then tries Kavan. His voice is drowsy. He's been up all night.

"Any news?" he asks.

"Nothing on Josh. You?"

"No. I figured I'd try his school today, talk to the teachers, ask around. How are you feeling?"

"Scared for Josh. Sad we haven't found him yet. Dwight's dead." She tells him what she knows.

"I'm sorry, Jen. Do you want me to come back?"

"No. I need you there for Josh. I just wanted you to know about Dwight. I'm not sad, not for him. Relieved, if anything."

"I can imagine." A pause. "I love you more than the pain and grief you carry."

Water fills her eyes, and a warm glow expands through her body. "Love you, too," she whispers.

Kavan hangs up, and she picks the blanket off the floor, returning to Sophie's room to dress.

"What did he say?" Keely asks hopefully when Jenna gives back the phone.

"Dwight's dead." Keely gasps. "Auto accident," Jenna adds, slowly putting on her clothes from yesterday, flared jeans and a shirt. Her ribs complain. Her head throbs at the site of her stitches. The room spins.

"That's a good thing, right?"

"I haven't had the chance to think about it."

"I know he wasn't the father you wanted, but I'm still sorry. Sorry for you, not that asshole. He had it coming."

Jenna flashes a smile, digging out a thick hunter-green sweatshirt from Sophie's dresser and pulling it over her head. She doubts she'll ever tire of Keely's fresh, uncensored honesty.

Keely sits up in bed. "Where are you going?"

"Outside." She needs air. Dwight's dead. Gone. The relief. "I won't be long. Or go far. The impound opens soon. I want to call first thing."

Jenna leaves the house only to make it to the end of the porch. Eyes shut, she throws back her head and takes in three deep breaths.

She won't cry over him, but the grief still hurts. This man controlled her life, shaped it, even when he wasn't in her life. Even before her life started. He aided in the murder of her father.

And now he's gone.

But so is Josh.

She doesn't spare Dwight another thought as she imagines what Josh is going through. Alone, disoriented, starving, dirty. Possibly hurt and frightened, or even worse if Ryder has him.

Unless he saw Ryder and hid. Maybe he walked the highway toward town. Anyone could have picked him up. Jenna would have if she passed a kid on the highway.

Wouldn't Josh have given someone his phone to call her? They would have found her number.

But he hasn't. Jenna checked her voice mail on the way to Murielle's. She also left frantic messages at Josh's school, asking the administration to be on the lookout for Josh. Keely posted messages across social media.

People are looking for him, but he has yet to be found.

Where could he have gone? Where could Ryder have taken him? Has he hurt him? Killed him?

A wail of anguish swells in her throat when movement down the road behind the Whitmans' cabin snags her attention. Hope and uncertainty shimmer to life. Murielle told her last night the lake house hasn't been used. She hasn't seen Tyler or his brother, Blaze, on the property in years. She wasn't sure if they still owned it.

Before she registers what she's doing, what she'd say if Tyler is there, she's crossing the road. She rounds the cabin to the lake's edge.

Whoever she saw is gone.

She walks to the edge of the dock. How many times did she jump off it as a kid? Holding hands, she and Olivia would run the length and leap off. Lily pretended she was flying.

A twig snaps behind her.

Jenna whirls. A man stands on the shore. Tawny hair. Blue eyes so vivid the color is unmistakable despite their distance. They match his jacket.

His eyes widen with surprise. He stares at her, stunned, his mouth partially open. Recognition sets in.

"Lily?"

Her hands fall out of the pocket. "Tyler," she breathes.

He visibly swallows. "Where's my son?"

CHAPTER 46

Jenna flinches, taken aback. Time slows. Tyler is here. And he knows about Josh.

"His name's Josh, isn't it?" Jenna stares at him, dumbstruck. He asks, "Is he mine?"

"How did you know?"

His jaw tightens. A cheek throbs. "Guess that answers that question."

Seriously, how did he find out?

"Did Dwight—"

"Josh wrote me."

Her chest seizes. "What?" Then she remembers the journal. Josh had found him.

"He sent me an email in June. The fourth, to be exact."

Dear god.

The day he was pushed.

"What did he say?" she asks Tyler.

"That he thought he was my son. He told me you changed your name. I only just read it last week. My assistant thought it was a hoax. He'd deleted it. I found it in my trash folder when I went looking for an old email. I replied. He didn't write back."

He wouldn't have because he couldn't, not with his aphasia.

"Lily . . ." Tyler moves closer, rests a booted foot on the dock. *"Why?"*

So much emotion in that question.

And what a loaded question it is.

Why didn't she tell him about his son? Why did she disappear? Why didn't she say goodbye?

"I've been trying to reach you for days. Your publicist refuses to forward my calls."

Because Gayle was under strict instructions not to. If Tyler had mentioned he was Josh's father, she wouldn't have believed him. Tyler wouldn't have been the first guy alleging he knew Jenna. Gayle has heard some outlandish stories from fans desperate to reach Jenna. Hence, the reason she has a gatekeeper.

"I haven't been up here for god knows how long." He gestures toward the house. "But I read Josh's email, and I couldn't stop thinking about what had gone wrong with us. What I did and didn't do. I found myself back here." The creases above his brows deepen. "I looked for you. For years."

She knew he would have. Tyler doesn't easily give up.

"When I came back here after that first week and you weren't here?" His throat chokes on the last word so that Jenna barely hears it. A flush creeps up his neck. "I went to the police. I combed the lake, Lily. I thought you . . ." He rakes a hand through his hair, his mouth pressing flat.

He'd thought she committed suicide. Drowned.

And he blamed himself, has probably been blaming himself all these years. He's the one who left her here by herself.

Ending her life never crossed Jenna's mind. She was in survival mode, but she'd also acted rashly, giving no thought to anyone but herself. And she kept on running because Murielle's network made it easy and convenient to do so.

Hands clenched, Tyler's eyes burn into hers. "Aren't you going to say anything?"

She has too much to say. Even more to apologize for. And the impulse to lie dangles from her tongue. But she doesn't have the luxury of time. And it's long past time for the truth. It's the only way she knows how to stop Ryder. To stop the insanity of running.

"Josh is missing."

Tyler's features turn stark. "I'm not following."

She opens her mouth to explain.

"Jenna . . . is that you?"

With a hand shielding her eyes from the morning glare, Keely peers down at them from the road. She waves her phone. Tyler twists his head, looking up at her. "Who's that?"

"Detective Weaver called again," Keely shouts before Jenna can answer him. Then she notices Tyler. "Is that—" Both her arms fall. "Oh, my gawwwwd." Keely is running, down the driveway, around the Whitmans' cabin. Her arms pump. Breasts heave side to side. She slows down enough to pick up a dead tree branch. To Jenna's shock, she swings it like a sword.

"What's she doing?" Tyler asks.

"Stay away from my friend," Keely shrieks, her voice warbling as she runs. She skids to a stop between Jenna and Tyler, flapping the branch, forcing them apart. Tyler lurches out of the way. "Stay back. Don't come near her. Don't even touch her."

Tyler defensively lifts his hands. "What the hell?"

"Where's Josh? Where is he?" Keely lunges at Tyler, stabbing the stick. She barely misses his abdomen.

"Keely." Jenna grabs at her arm before she can injure Tyler.

Tyler's face darkens. He yanks the branch from Keely's grasp and wings it over the lake.

"Oh!" Keely backs up into Jenna. "Oh, dear . . . Run," she barks.

Jenna holds on to Keely's arm before she can go anywhere. "It's okay. It's Tyler."

Keely's head whirls. She gapes at Jenna. "*The* Tyler?"

"Yes." Keely's charge to her defense would have been comical if the circumstances weren't so dire.

Keely slouches with a relieved sigh. "Oh, good. But god." Her eyes widen to moon size. She turns to Tyler. "I'm so sorry."

"Who did you think I was?"

"This guy Ryder."

"Ryder Jensen," Jenna clarifies at Tyler's frown. The name fills her mouth with urgency. A fresh wave of anxiety and fear rises. She prays with every ounce of her being they find Josh today. "It's a long story."

"He's the guy who pushed Josh down a flight of stairs. He also hit Jenna with his car."

"Keely . . ." Jenna warns.

"There's a massive manhunt for him happening *right now*," she says.

"Keely," Jenna snaps.

Keely gapes at her, then at Tyler, who has folded his arms. Keely inhales sharply. "He doesn't know. Gosh, I—" She backs up, pulling herself from their circle. "I'm sorry," she mutters.

"I was planning to tell him when you came running." She wants his help. The more people looking for Josh the better.

"Now would be a good time to start." Tyler turns fully to her.

"Right, right," Keely says. "Before you do, though"—she tugs her phone from her back pocket—"Weaver wants you to call him."

Jenna snatches the phone. "Did he say what for?"

Keely shakes her head.

"Excuse me a sec." She walks a few steps away without waiting for an okay from Tyler.

Anticipation he found Josh beats a steady drum in her head.

"Hi, I'm Keely Lawrence. Jenna's friend," she hears Keely say before Weaver picks up his phone. Every call from him could be good news or the worst. Please don't be bad news. She's already had enough.

"Tyler Whitman." He takes Keely's proffered hand, but his attention is on her and this call.

Detective Weaver answers on the third ring. He found her car impounded at a lot an hour's drive from Murielle's. Just the confirmation she needs. She's planning for Keely to drive her as soon as she's off the phone. Impound has two pieces of luggage, Weaver explains. No purse or keys. Her phone was found shattered on the road. He wonders if the other items are with her. They aren't, she tells him. Ryder had stopped. He must have snagged them before Josh returned. It hadn't crossed her mind to cancel her cards when Weaver asks for her to check recent charges. If Ryder did take her purse, he thinks it might give them a lead on his trail.

"He can't be that stupid."

"You'd be surprised," he says. "We did speak to Chloe and Liam Thornton, the couple who found you and called the ambulance. They confirmed you were alone. And that your vehicle was locked."

He pauses. "Check your records, and call me if there are any suspicious charges. I wish I had more to report, but that's it for now."

She gets off the phone and covers her face. Her shoulders shake with an onslaught of tears. "Where is he?" she shouts, frustrated with the lack of leads, the lack of everything.

A sudden sharp pang stabs her rib cage, and she cries out.

Tyler's gaze drops to the hand pressing her side. "You're hurt."

"A few cracked ribs and bruises." She wipes her forearm across her face.

"And a major concussion," Keely supplies.

"Nothing I can't handle."

"You shouldn't be on your feet," Keely says.

"I don't have a choice," she snaps, then apologizes. She hurts, and Keely's only trying to help. "I need a ride to the impound lot. Can you give me one?"

"I'll take you."

Jenna and Keely look at Tyler.

"We're talking. And if we have to do it while looking for Josh, so be it. And you need my help. Josh is my son. Let me do my part."

Jenna wants to cry with relief. Tyler might despise her after she explains everything, but he won't let his hatred come between him and his son. She should have given him more credit in the beginning. Then again, she was only sixteen. What did she know?

"Are you sure?" Keely asks. "I mean, that's why I'm here."

Jenna agrees with Tyler. They need to talk. And she needs all the help she can get.

"Can you stay here with Murielle in case you hear something?" she asks with a flare of gratitude. "Tyler, give her your number," she says when Keely agrees. "We need to go."

They load into Tyler's truck and barely make it out of the driveway when he says, "Start at the beginning."

So she does. She tells him about Dwight and what she did to Wes. She talks about Josh and how they've been running from Ryder for years.

She's nervous as she talks, full of remorse and disdain for herself, especially since she doesn't tell him about going back for Wes, and the video. But no matter how scared she was for her life, or how much at the time she feared for Tyler's life, she explains it doesn't change the fact that she took Josh away. She never gave Tyler the chance to raise his son.

The irony hits her hard.

Her parents tried to take Josh from her. She did exactly that to Tyler.

No amount of explanation makes her deserving of his forgiveness. But she apologizes, anyway. "I'm sorry." She will be for the rest of her life.

Tyler parks in the impound lot and cuts the engine. He asked some questions as she spoke, showed his shock when she told him Dwight had chased her with a gun and that she accidentally killed Wes. But mostly, he is angry. Very angry. She can see it in the tight set of his jaw, his firm grasp of the wheel. Feels it in the abrupt turns he took to park. The slam of brakes and sudden stop.

Silence hangs between them after her apology. But the urgency to find her son—*their* son—has her reaching for the door. She's anxious to search her car. Josh could have left a note, a drawing pointing where he went. Something.

"I should file for full custody for what you put me through after you left, not to mention risking *our* son's safety given the way you've raised him." His voice is deadly calm.

Chills scamper over her arms.

But she doesn't argue. Instead, she feels the weight of every word. Her decision to run and hide. The lies to protect herself, to keep Josh from everything she'd done. Whether right or wrong, she'd made a judgment call that led them to where they are now. Her with Tyler, and Josh on his own.

She shoves open the door, wincing at the pain in her side.

She doesn't have a choice but to grapple with the consequences, to reckon with her sins. And there are plenty of them. But right now she needs to think of her son. There will be time later for judgment.

Tyler gets out and locks the truck. They enter a small building where a woman by the name of Danyette with poodle-pink lipstick and frosted hair hauls over her and Josh's suitcases like a hotel concierge.

After talking to Jenna's attorney, Samantha, as the car is registered in her name, and after Jenna describes the contents of the luggage, Danyette gives Jenna a room to search through their suitcases, and then directs her to her car in the dusty, fenced-in lot.

"What are you looking for?" Tyler asks.

"Something from Josh that tells me where he's gone."

But there is nothing.

She circles the car, and keeps circling, panicked. Her chest hurts. Josh's absence tugs at her. Where is he? Her arms shake and teeth chatter. A pang deep inside throbs from the giant hole his disappearance has left. At her sides, her fingers grapple with air, desperate to hold him.

She needs to do something.

"May I borrow your phone?" Tyler hands it over, and she calls Murielle. "Anything?"

"No. Sophie and I are still working our grid. Nothing's turning up."

The phone slips from her ear and she cups her eyes. She won't lose hope.

"All right. Call if you hear something."

"You'll be the first to know."

She reaches out to Keely, who's been calling neighbors and parents at Josh's school. There haven't been any sightings. No word on her son.

She calls Kavan. He's been to the Oceanside Police. They've been alerted about Josh and Ryder, but nothing's come up yet.

Nothing. Nothing. Nothing.

Jenna returns Tyler's phone and almost loses her balance. The impound lot tilts, and her stomach drops.

Tyler grasps her shoulder to steady her, then snatches his hand away as if he doesn't want to touch her. "You all right?"

She presses her fingers to her eyes and takes an unsteady breath, hanging by a thread. Kids go missing every day. They're abducted and are never heard from again. She will not, *will not* lose hope. But it's easy to believe he's gone forever.

"I need to sit down."

"Go sit in the truck. I'll get your luggage." He also paid to have her car towed to Murielle's, he explains when they're back on the highway.

Weighed down by her injuries, stress, and acute sadness, she feels herself drifting off when Tyler says, "Blaze called the other day. He asked after you."

She's instantly alert. "Me?"

"Something about a Carson family emergency. Olivia had called him."

"You're just telling me this now?"

His eyes slide to her, then back to the road.

"Did she say what it was about?"

He shakes his head. "Could she have been calling about Josh?"

"They've never met, and Josh doesn't know where she lives. And wouldn't Blaze have mentioned him?"

"You'd think."

Olivia was probably calling about Dwight. She doesn't know his exact date of death. Could have been a few days ago and the news only just crossed Weaver's desk.

"Call back and check." And get Olivia's number.

"Yeah." Tyler calls Blaze, only to put down the phone. "Voice mail's full. I'll try later."

She leans her head against the window, fighting off the desire to sleep when Tyler grasps her hand.

"We'll find him."

She nods, wiping her eyes. It's all she can manage without falling apart, worried about what condition he'll be in when they do. He's already experienced enough trauma.

Jenna doesn't remember the rest of the drive back to the lake, and barely recalls Tyler helping her from the car to his couch.

"Rest," he says, as she lies down.

"No." She tries to fight him, tries to sit up, but her eyes are closed before her head hits the throw pillow.

CHAPTER 47

Jenna wakes up with a start. She tries to catch her breath, but she can't inhale deeply enough. Her cracked ribs ache. She sits in bed, panting through the pain. The tail end of a nightmare scrapes its fingers across her mind.

Ryder had Josh pinned to the wall like he'd once done to her. Josh couldn't breathe. His face was blue. And every terror Jenna has felt since she first learned Josh was missing reawakens.

Jenna rubs her eyes and looks over at Keely, who's been too generous with her time with two kids at home and a husband watching over them. She's still asleep. Outside, dawn is breaking.

They were up late working every angle they could to bring Josh home. After her nap, Jenna called Weaver for an update. He didn't have news, but said if Ryder doesn't have him, there's a likely chance Josh has wandered far from his last known point. Perhaps hitched a ride.

So they widened their search. Sophie hung posters at markets and gas stations. She talked to anyone who would listen, people at restaurants, in parking lots. Keely continued to call parents at Josh's school to be on the lookout, then called them back again to incite them to keep looking. Jenna used Tyler's phone to call the local hospitals. She left a message for Glenny at her café, the only neighbor she knows how to reach. And then she called Kavan, who talked her back from the edge as her fear tried to consume her.

Meanwhile, Murielle kept her fed, and Tyler found a private investigator. They have a video conference with him later.

They accomplished much, yet Jenna doesn't feel like they've made any progress. Her boy is still missing.

Shame, remorse, fear, and despair hang over her.

Every decision she made when sixteen and pregnant has led her to this.

She put her son in harm's way, and she feels powerless to help him find his way back.

After a quick shower, she changes into a crew-neck shirt and an old pair of silver leggings she found in the back of Sophie's dresser.

Keely is dressed and in the kitchen drinking coffee when Jenna finishes.

"I have to go," Keely says. Anson is beside himself with Josh missing. Her kids need her. "I'll come back tomorrow. Want me to bring you some clothes? What about a spare key for your car? I'll get that, too."

"That would be great. I'll call a locksmith to let you in. I don't have a house key lying around." She grasps Keely's fingers. "Thank you, for everything."

Keely smiles. "You'd do the same for me."

A warmth Jenna recognizes as friendship, something she hasn't felt in years, unfurls in her chest.

Jenna walks with Keely to the van, and after she leaves, she goes to Tyler's. She finds him on the dock. One hand in his pocket, he drinks a coffee and takes in the lake.

He turns when he hears her approach. "Morning."

She comes up beside him. "Anything?" She returned his phone late last night.

"Nope." He puts a hand on her shoulder then lets it fall. Fingers go back into his pocket.

No callbacks from the hospitals. No word from Glenny or Kavan. Sophie would have called if someone saw anything, as would Keely.

He's just gone.

And that pulls on her. The emptiness in the center of her chest. The hollowness that's been present since she learned of his disappearance. The hurt is greater than the pain in her ribs, the throb behind her head. She just hurts.

The urge to return home where Josh's things are—his clothes, his scent, the ghost of his presence—is strong. But she needs to stay here. This is where they were headed. He knows to come to Murielle's if they're separated. She needs to be here, to see his face when he gets here. To hold him. She won't lose faith.

"I'm sorry," Tyler says.

She looks up at him. His jaw is tense. The creases around his eyes deepen as he squints against the sun reflecting off the water. "For what?" she asks.

"I'm still sifting through what you told me. Not sure I'll ever come to terms with it. But . . ." He grips the back of his neck. "I should have been aware there was more going on with you. That it wasn't simply your dad being an abusive asshole. There were bigger reasons behind you leaving. We talked about some of it, I know that. But all I remember is you wanting to leave, and you had to leave right that moment. So I brought you here. When you left, why didn't you ask me to go with?"

"You had your mom to worry about. She was dying. I couldn't force you to choose between us."

He nods slowly, eyes narrowed, as he processes what she says, tries to understand.

She moistens her lips and faces him. "I don't expect this to make a difference, or to change your opinion of me and what I did, but I am sorry. For you and Josh. For cheating you both of your time together."

Her eyes well. "I was young and scared, more frightened than I'd ever been. Things with Wes happened so fast, and I had to make some very hard choices in the moment."

He inhales deeply through his nose, chest rising, his frown deepening. His gaze moves over her face. She pushes on.

"In retrospect, it's easy to say they weren't good decisions. I hurt a lot of people. Risked my own safety and Josh's. Charlotte neglected me. Dwight tormented me to no end. My parents didn't love me as parents should, and they didn't want me to have Josh. The singular, prime thought on my mind was to survive, at any cost. I believed I was the only one who could protect my baby. No one would love him as much as me. I see now how wrong that was. And I would do anything to change that. But I would give my life right now if it meant Josh was here. That he was safe."

Tyler looks devastated. "I loved you."

Her eyes close. His pain is too much to witness, yet she accepts it. Takes responsibility for it. "I know." She loved him, too.

Wind cuts across the lake. She crosses her arms to stave off the chill. "I'm not asking for your forgiveness. Only for you to understand. And if you can't, I have to live with that."

Tyler finishes his coffee and drags a hand down his face. "I want to see him, after we find him. I want to be in his life."

"I want that, too." Tyler would have been an amazing father. He still can be.

When Tyler doesn't say anything further, she turns back to the shore. She wants to regroup with Murielle, follow up with Sophie, talk with the local sheriff's department.

She makes it to the end of the dock when Tyler stops her.

"I'll try. To understand," he clarifies when she tilts her head, questioning.

She nods once and Tyler turns back to the lake.

———

After Jenna meets up with Murielle, and Murielle forces her to eat, Jenna returns to the lake house for the video conference with the private investigator Tyler hired. They've just finished the meeting when she hears a car pulling into the driveway. Gravel pops under tires.

"Expecting anyone?" She briefly wonders if Keely came back.

Tyler shakes his head and pulls back the curtains to look. Then he's out of his seat and opening the front door.

"Who is it?" She hears car doors slam, the murmur of voices.

"It's Blaze," he says, incredulous. "I never got ahold of him."

She joins him at the door. "What's he doing here?" she asks. But all she sees is the kid rushing toward her.

Raw disbelief and profound joy slam into her.

"Josh? Josh! Oh, my god."

Then she's running, reaching the bottom step just as Josh launches into her arms.

Her ribs protest, bruises complain. But she doesn't care. Josh is here. Josh is in her arms. She hugs him, hugs him some more, and bursts into tears. "I thought I lost you."

"Okay, Mom. Okay. Okay."

I'm okay. We're okay. It'll be okay.

She hears the tears in his voice, and a watery laugh breaks free. *He's* trying to comfort *her*.

"Let me look at you." She leans back, cups his face. Thumbs wipe off his tears. Fingers touch the silky hair under his ball cap. She strokes his arms as if she doesn't believe he's real. That he's really here.

"Are you hurt? Injured?" She feels his arms.

He shakes his head.

"You're so brave," she tells him.

He gives her a shaky smile. God, she's missed that grin.

He's brave and beautiful. Full of life. Whole.

"I missed you so much." She pulls him into another hug, tears soaking her face. She wasn't sure if she'd ever hug him again. Ever see him again. "I was so scared."

"Me . . . too."

"How?" The question tumbles from her. *How, how, how?*

How did he find Blaze? How does he even know about Blaze?

She can barely comprehend Josh is here with Tyler's brother until she lifts her gaze to the woman Blaze has draped his arm around, who is watching her and Josh's reunion, eyes glistening, lips trembling.

Olivia called about a Carson family emergency.

"Livy?" Her voice croaks.

Olivia wipes her face, lifts a hand in a short wave. "It's me," she whispers. Olivia. Her sister.

Here.

It seems impossible.

"How did he find you?" Jenna asks.

"I'm not entirely certain. He told me some. I guessed the rest. What about you? Where've you been? We've been so worried about you. Are you okay?"

Jenna thinks of her injuries, of Ryder's mind games, his pursuit. She wonders what they know. *How much* do they know?

"I'm fine now. Wonderful, actually." If that's even a word strong enough to describe the emotions filling her. Deliriously happy, she thinks, taking a good look at her son. She cups his face, her love bursting. "It's a long story," she says, hearing the crunch of gravel behind her. "I'll tell you everything. But first—" She glances over her shoulder. "Come here, Tyler."

Tyler approaches cautiously, nervous, his smile shaky, unsure. Water lines his eyes.

No more half-truths. No more lies.

Jenna whispers in Josh's ear. "Do you want to meet your dad?"

Josh whips his head to Tyler and gawks at him.

She puts her arm around her son and offers Tyler a big smile. "Josh, meet your father."

CHAPTER 48

For the first time in over a week, Josh feels like he can breathe, that he can grasp hold of his words before they change on him or dart from reach. The terror that consumed him every waking moment, that he'd never find his mom or know what happened to her, vanished the instant he found himself in her arms.

He shouldn't have had her stop on the highway for him. He should have looked harder for her around the car. And he should have left her a sketch showing where he was going and who picked him up in case she came back.

He thought to do that an hour after that woman gave him a ride. Nervous and scared, he had trouble explaining why he needed to go back. That he wanted her to turn around. She just smiled and bobbed her head and kept on driving, so he stopped trying to talk to her.

She didn't seem to mind. She turned up her church music and sang along, driving the entire trip in the slow lane. They practically crawled to his aunt Olivia's house. Seemed like forever, but then there he was. And there she was. His mom's sister.

Fear kept a tight grip on his words for most of the week. But it hadn't occurred to him until he arrived that Olivia could be mean like Dwight. That there was a reason his mom didn't speak to or talk about her. But he needed to find his way to Murielle's and find his mom, and Aunt Olivia was all he had.

So he made the most of it, grateful his aunt wasn't anything like his grandfather. But he wished he'd listened to his mom and the speech therapist and done his exercises over the summer. He'd be able to talk better. He wouldn't struggle to draw what he was trying to say—pencil sketches of his home in Oceanside where his mom could have returned; charcoal drawings of Murielle's house, where they were supposed to meet if they were separated; storyboards of what he thought had happened to his mom, that Ryder hit her and kidnapped her. He needed his aunt to understand his mom could be in danger.

But Olivia isn't like his mom. She didn't understand what he drew, and it took her a while to realize he talked through his pictures. She also couldn't understand what he said when he struggled to talk, or how to prompt him to find the right words. They were both frustrated until he realized Olivia was as scared as him. Then he stopped feeling so alone.

Then they started working together, which brought him to his mom and . . .

Dad.

He's meeting his dad.

Something warm and electric wells inside him, a mix of joy and relief and nerves.

The first thing Josh notices about Tyler is that he's tall. Taller than Kavan, and he unconsciously scoots back toward Blaze, a cool guy Josh hopes he'll see again.

The second thing he notices is that Tyler seems just as nervous as him, which puts Josh at ease.

Tyler squats until he's eye level and Josh doesn't have to crane his neck. He smiles, and it's a little shaky. There's even water in his eyes, and Josh is awed a big guy like him isn't embarrassed to show his emotions.

Tyler looks at him from the Padres cap hiding his uneven hair to his dirty Vans. Josh hopes he doesn't ask to see his head or make fun of his speech. His gaze then moves over Josh's face, and Josh tries not to squirm under his scrutiny. Because Josh is doing the same to Tyler, curious to see if they look or act alike.

Their smiles are sort of the same. Tyler's eyebrows are bushy like his.

Tyler clears his throat, and his face turns serious. Josh feels a tug of nerves in his chest. "Three questions for you, Josh," he says.

Josh shifts from one foot to the other, afraid he'll stumble over the answers. Blaze's hand lands on his shoulder, and Josh is grateful for that extra bit of support. He tries to relax so his words won't lock up.

"Favorite sport?" Tyler asks.

Easy. Baseball. Josh points at his Padres cap.

Tyler shows Josh his SF Giants shirt under his windbreaker, and Josh rolls his eyes. Not his favorite team. Tyler chuckles, and Josh feels a smile spread to his cheeks.

"Favorite subject in school?"

"Bear." Josh huffs. He shakes his head, then shows Tyler two fingers on each hand, hoping he understands. Two plus two.

Tyler's brows lift. "Math?" he guesses, and Josh nods. "That was my favorite, too."

Josh grins. This guy is cool.

"Last question." Tyler takes a breath like it's a doozy, and Josh braces himself for the worst. Tyler doesn't want to be his dad. Josh is too much of a surprise to him. But the corner of Tyler's mouth pulls up into a half smile. "Can we hang out? I'd really like to spend time with you. Think we can do that, catch a game or something?"

Josh goes utterly still, allowing Tyler's words to penetrate. They fill him with joy, relief, and a sense of belonging he's never felt in his life. He nods vigorously, and Blaze claps his shoulder, laughing with delight. Josh would very much like to hang out with his dad.

Tyler holds up a fist for a bump. "I think we're going to get along very well."

Josh lets his tears fall, too ecstatic to care that he's crying in front of the guys. He bumps Tyler's fist. "Me too."

CHAPTER 49

Jenna walks with her sister to the dock, not quite believing she's here. That Olivia is the one who brought Josh. That Josh found *her*.

How unreal to be with her again, here, after so many summers spent on the lake.

A lifetime ago.

And how terrified Josh must have been when he didn't find Jenna at the accident site. Had his journey to Olivia been a nightmare? She can't fathom what he did, what must have been going on in his mind.

"We made a lot of good memories here," Jenna begins, bursting with questions about Josh's time with her, what Olivia has been up to, their brother, Lucas, and life in Seaside Cove. She drags her fingers across a tree trunk where the hammock used to be. Olivia's favorite spot to draw. She spent hours swinging in that hammock. "It's really great to see you again, Livy." And it is. Jenna wonders if Dwight's death plays into that. He isn't around to influence Olivia's opinion of her. It's just the two of them.

"I have so many questions," Olivia says.

"Me too." She looks back toward the house where Josh, Blaze, and Tyler are talking. Josh has inched closer to Blaze, more comfortable with him than the father he just met. A man he's been wanting to meet since he learned as a toddler that he didn't have a dad.

Jenna's chest clenches. She regrets all the lies. The hurt, the damage.

Blaze rests a hand on Josh's shoulder while Josh talks to Tyler. The familiarity in the gesture leaves her wondering. What happened to Ethan? She assumed they'd be married with kids by now.

"So, uh . . . you and Blaze?" she asks, unable to disguise the mild shock that they're back together. Olivia's features tighten, and Jenna winces. "Sorry. That didn't come out right. And that's not what I meant to ask."

"It's fine." Olivia's hand flutters to her hair, pulls the length over a shoulder. "Mom told Dad that Ethan was Josh's father."

Jenna looks at Olivia, stunned. "That doesn't make sense. I never told them who his father was."

"Mom wanted me to hate you so I wouldn't go looking for you. She said you were safer away than at home."

Charlotte literally pushed Jenna out the door.

"That woman." She shakes her head, plucks a leaf from a bush they pass. Does Olivia know about Benton? Does she know what their mother did to him?

"She was trying to protect you, that's what she told me. I only learned about it yesterday."

"You thought *I* told her it was Ethan?" Out of spite for her turning Jenna away when she begged Olivia to move in with her. She'd wanted to escape her parents, but Olivia turned her down when she needed to get out. Of course Olivia would think Jenna was out for revenge.

"At first, yes, I believed that. And I hated you for years because of it."

Jenna's annual letters probably fueled Olivia's hatred. There Jenna was, mailing photos of Ethan's son like she was saying, *in your face*.

They reach the dock. Scents of autumn fill the air. Painted clouds sweep across the blue sky. Jenna pushes up her sleeves, feeling warm, and drops the leaf she'd plucked in the water. Both she and Olivia watch it float under the dock.

"I'm sorry about Ethan. I liked him. But you and Blaze?" Ethan was levelheaded and steady. Responsible. Quite simply, he was good for Olivia. He counterbalanced her wild streak. But when she dated Blaze, Olivia shined. Jenna remembers that last summer at the lake when everything changed between them. Olivia was electric, and Blaze enamored. He always was. "You're better together."

Olivia tilts her head. "Why didn't you ever say anything?"

Jenna shrugs, hands dipping into the kangaroo pocket of the sweatshirt she borrowed from Sophie's closet. "We didn't tell each other a lot of things. I should have," she realizes. Maybe their relationship would have risen above Dwight's determination to keep them apart. To keep them from leaning on each other.

"Are you, though? Together?" Jenna asks, and Olivia smiles. She nods, her smile spreading wider. "Good. I'm happy for you."

"What about you and Tyler?"

"I'm not sure what we are," she answers truthfully. "We haven't seen each other in a long time." But they'll never be together again. She's in love with Kavan. But she and Tyler will have to figure out a custody arrangement once the dust settles. Once Ryder is caught and she's given her statement about Wes.

Nerves take flight while she wonders what will happen to her.

She turns to face the house. Josh has moved onto the deck. Tyler and Blaze are off to the side talking. Josh waves. She and Olivia wave back. She can't believe he's here, safe and unharmed. How lucky she is that he made it back to her.

Inside the kangaroo pocket, her thumb plays with Kavan's engagement ring, and she elects not to tell Olivia about him. Not yet, when she isn't sure where they stand. But a front of longing moves through her, settles in. She needs to call him about Josh as soon as they're done talking. She wants him here. He'll want to see Josh for himself, to know that he's all right.

"This is going to sound terrible." Jenna rubs her forearm, glancing back at her son. Tyler and Blaze have joined him. She takes a breath. "I never told Josh much about you. I was going to. He was asking about his dad and my family. Then he had his accident and—" Her throat constricts, choking on the words.

"Hey, it's okay." Olivia touches her shoulder, and her eyes brighten as if she's made a sudden decision. She hugs her and Jenna gasps. Not from the pain along her side, but from the ache in her heart. She can't recall her sister ever hugging her, not since their summers here.

Seems fitting that this is the place they start mending their relationship.

Jenna steps back, palms her face. "How did he find you?"

"He has an envelope from you addressed to me. I found it in his backpack."

She frowns. "What envelope?"

"It's old. Josh's birth certificate and a power of attorney were inside." The paperwork Hoyt Criswell advised her to sign and notarize. The one she'd hidden in her journal.

She forgot it was there.

"I believe he showed the address on the envelope to the woman who drove him," Olivia says.

"What woman?"

"Some old lady. She dropped him off at my house and left before I could get her name. My guess is he hitchhiked."

Her heart lurches. "Josh!" She whirls toward the house, shocked he'd been so bold and brave.

"He's safe," Olivia says at her untethered reaction. "He's been with me the entire time. All I wanted was to find you and get him back to you. I owed you that much."

"You owed me? For what?"

"I should have let you move in with me when you asked. I should have stood up for you when Dad was being an ass. I'm sorry I didn't. I didn't realize . . . No, I refused to acknowledge how bad it was between you. But he had me believing you destroyed everything you borrowed from me when it really was him. He was manipulating us both." Her eyes shimmer with remorse. She wipes her fingers under her lashes. "I'm sorry I wasn't there for you. I'm sorry I made you think I didn't love you."

"I didn't hate you, Olivia. You were Dwight's favorite, and he didn't like me. He scared me. I wasn't trying to keep my distance from you. I was trying to stay away from him."

Josh's laughter reaches the treetops, and Jenna's heart soars with the sound.

"What happened? How'd you get separated from Josh?"

"Someone is after me." Jenna hugs her ribs. A ripple of fear tightens her skin. Josh is here, but Ryder is still out there. They're far from being out of danger. "We were on our way here when I pulled over. Josh had to go to the bathroom. I was hit when I got out of the car. When I came to, he was gone."

Olivia's expression is horrified. She grasps Jenna's arm. "Geez, Lily."

Jenna tugs her shirt collar, unused to her given name. "I've never been so scared." More afraid than she felt when Dwight threatened to shoot her.

"Was it Dad? Did he hit you? Did he push Josh? Oh, my god, Lily. I can't believe he'd do this to you. What did he want from you?"

"My silence. I know things about him and Mom. But it wasn't him. He's not the one who's after me."

"Who is, then?"

"Ryder Jensen."

Her brows pull together, then disappear under her sideswept hair. Jenna sees the instant Olivia remembers. Her eyes go wide. Ryder mowed their lawn one year when he was a kid. He and Olivia went to the same high school, two years apart. He was in Lucas's class.

"Why?" she asks.

The truth slides off her tongue as easily as the lies used to do. This is her sister. Their dad is dead. It's time to reveal all. "I murdered his brother."

Olivia's mouth falls open. As she gapes at her in stunned confusion and disbelief, Jenna tells her every blistering detail.

She'd gone back for Wes.

CHAPTER 50

LILY

Tyler was waiting for her a block away. Lily flung her suitcase into Tyler's back seat. He started the engine.

"Wait! I have to go back," she said, petrified she was already too late, praying she hadn't shot him. That what happened on the dock was nothing but a horrible nightmare she still hadn't woken up from. She had to see Wes for herself, know exactly what she'd done. And if he was still alive, he'd need her help.

"Lil, we need to get on the road."

"Please. I'll only be a minute." Tyler wouldn't be staying with her at the lake house. He had to get back to his mom. She needed to go back for Wes. She couldn't just leave him. He couldn't be dead. She had to believe that. He was hurt, and he needed her help.

Lily raced back to the house, overcoming her fear that Dwight would be there, that her mom could see her from the window. She'd never forgive herself if she didn't check whether Wes was alive.

Dwight wasn't in the yard, so she sprinted to the dock. To her amazement, Wes was there, slumped against the rail. *Alive!* Relief spilled into her. How he'd pulled himself up, she didn't know. Maybe she hadn't shot him.

"Wes! My god," she said with urgency. She needed to get him out of there fast.

She grasped his shoulders, startling him. His clothes were drenched. He shivered violently. His eyes were at half-mast, his hair plastered to his forehead. His movements were confused, disoriented. But she couldn't find any blood.

She hadn't shot him.

He must have hit his head when he went in the water. It's the only reason she can explain why he's so out of it.

"You're hurt." Lily's fingertips grazed the side of his neck, his head, checking for wounds. Then she thought better of it, and snatched her hand back, afraid she'd hurt him more.

Wes lifted his face and looked at her, unable to focus on her. He groaned, and his head lolled to the side.

Lily glanced over her shoulder. She should have had Tyler park closer, even at the risk of Dwight catching them. She considered screaming for help. Lucas would come.

But so would Dwight.

"We need to hurry." She had to get them out of there.

She pulled at his shoulder, went to wrap her arm around his back to support him when his arm shot out with surprising strength and speed. He clutched her neck.

"Wes!" Lily struggled to breathe.

His other hand latched on. Then he squeezed.

It took all of two seconds to realize Wes was strangling her. Wes. Her friend since preschool. That kid in the class who wanted her to do his homework for him. The one who adored her artwork. Who believed she could succeed as an animator. He was trying to kill *her*.

Her lungs strained. Pressure built behind her eyes. Her head felt like it would explode. She couldn't breathe. She couldn't cry for help. Her shoes slipped on the slick surface.

She pounded his arm, tried to wiggle free. Wes wouldn't let go.

He probably didn't know it was her. He was confusing her with Dwight. And he wanted retribution.

Her heart pounded.

She tried to scream. Shake some sense into him.

She had to get free.

She banged hard on his arms, tried to kick his groin. She wanted him off her. Then she remembered. Lucas had taught her how.

Lily thrust her arms upward between his and slammed her forearms into his inner elbows. His grip loosened, and she did it again. He let go, startled. She pushed him away. He stumbled back, then forward as if coming at her again.

"Stop. It's Lily." She thumped his chest. "I'm trying to help you." Her throat was on fire, raw from Wes's fingers. She reached for him. "We have to go—"

He lunged at her, eyes unclear. His face was a mask of rage.

"No!" Lily screamed, and shoved him hard toward the metal rail. She wanted him to get the fuck away from her. He was scaring her.

Wes flew back, arms flailing. His feet spiraled out from under him, and his head connected violently with the rail as he went down. He fell on his side, unmoving.

Then Dwight was there.

Lily shrieked. Terror stabbed her heart. He'd told her to run, threatened Tyler's life. He would surely kill her now. He was more than twice her size. He could easily drown her.

Dwight stood beside her, messing with his phone.

"Nifty little devices, these smartphones."

She sucked down large gulps of air through a throat that felt like it had been shredded with a machete. Panic sliced her brain. Wes wasn't moving. Blood oozed from a gaping wound on his head. She sank to her knees beside him. "Help him," she wailed at Dwight.

"You already did a fine job at that."

Lily pressed her fingers to Wes's pulse and felt nothing. "Noooo. Please, Wes, wake up." She shook him. And when he didn't respond, her blood turned to ice.

My god, what did she do? She screamed for Lucas.

"Stop that." Dwight backhanded her. She landed on her palms, stunned. Her head rang.

"I haven't quite figured all these buttons. Wait, they're called apps. Still haven't gotten the hang of this thing." Dwight stood there, fussing with that blasted phone as she shook in fear, too scared to move. "I did manage to get this one to work. See?"

He crouched beside her, held the phone for her to see, and played back a video of her and Wes. Nausea rolled through her like a ship in a hurricane. What she'd done, what she could barely comprehend, sickened her. But she couldn't pull her eyes away.

"You killed him. Good thing, too; he would have gone to the cops. Save your own ass, girl," he whispered, his hot breath in her ear. "Didn't think you had it in you. You're more like your mother than I thought. Cold-blooded murderers, the both of you. What a pair."

"I didn't mean to. He was trying to kill me," she wailed, pushing to her feet, backing away. "He was my friend. He wouldn't have hurt me. He didn't know what he was doing. He thought I was you."

"Doesn't matter." Dwight straightened, stalking her. "You murdered him. And I have it all right here." He wiggled the phone, and Lily wanted to hurl it into the water when he said, "The police will be after you. Better run."

He planted his boot on Wes and pushed him over the edge. He sank into the water.

"No!"

Dwight looked at her dead on. "Remember our deal." He wouldn't report her if she didn't report him and Charlotte.

He pressed a finger to his lips and laughed. He laughed and laughed.

Afraid for her life, what he'd do if she hesitated a second longer, Lily sprinted to the front yard before she had to stop and vomit in the bushes, letting up the horror she'd witnessed, the crime she'd committed. After she expelled the contents of her roiling stomach, she looked behind her toward the road, hearing a car pass, thinking it might be Tyler. He'd grown impatient waiting for her.

Her eyes met Ryder's.

Fear slapped her. He saw her. He might have heard her, heard Dwight's gun. But Ryder kept driving.

Sirens wailed in the distance.

She wasn't going to wait to find out if they were for her.

She sprinted to Tyler's car. "Let's go," she said, landing in the seat. She slammed the door.

He looked at her, saw the tears, noticed how her hands shook. "What's wrong?"

"Nothing. Just go," she croaked, tugging up the collar of her sweatshirt to hide the bruises she could feel forming on her neck as shock slowly took hold of her, its grip tighter than Wes's.

She would never forgive herself.

She'd killed her friend; then she'd left him.

CHAPTER 51

"There is nothing I wouldn't do for Josh," Jenna says to Olivia when her story is done.

Olivia stares at her, mouth agape. Much the way she looked at her throughout Jenna's winded explanation. Other than Murielle and Sophie, Olivia is the only person she's told about going back for Wes. And she's shaking, as much from the release of holding on to the truth as the fear and uncertainty of what will happen next.

"Will you watch over Josh? Help Tyler raise him?" She pushes the request through a tight throat.

Olivia tilts her head, drilling Jenna with a look. "What are you saying?"

"I don't know what will happen to me when I tell the police. They might arrest me. I don't know for how long I'll be sentenced. But Ryder is out there. He won't stop until I admit I killed Wes. Now that Josh is here and he's safe, I'm going to confess."

Olivia's eyes narrow. "But you didn't murder Wes. It was an accident."

"I intentionally shoved him."

"To get him off you." Olivia grasps her shoulders and looks Jenna in the eye. "It wasn't your fault. Dad convinced you it was, but it wasn't. He used your fear and manipulated you like he always did."

"But there's a video." Jenna saw herself deliberately push Wes.

"You need to get ahold of it and watch it again. Watch it when you aren't feeling the intense emotions you did that night, or even now. I bet you'll see it was self-defense. But if you are arrested, I'll stand by you. Because *I* believe in you."

Jenna folds her hands over her face and lets loose the tears she's been holding on to. The possibility that Dwight had convinced her she'd murdered her friend, that she believed him, wrecks her.

Olivia soothes her, her hands rubbing Jenna's arms, but she needs to be sure.

"Dwight said he still had the video."

"It's probably on his computer. I can look for you."

"You'd do that?"

Olivia smiles, but there is a sadness to it as she realizes her offer to help Jenna is that unexpected. Rare, even.

"Do you remember the promise I made, right here, in fact?" She points at their feet. "I found you out here crying after Lucas twisted your arm."

"He was mean that trip." She can still feel the burning sensation from his prank that she'd done nothing to deserve.

"We looked at the stars, and I promised that no matter what, I'd defend you if he hurt you again. I'd go to bat if anyone hurt you."

"You remember that?" It's one of Jenna's favorite memories of Olivia. She thought her sister had forgotten, given the way they'd drifted apart.

"I didn't, though. I failed you too often to count. But never again. We'll find that video. We'll prove your innocence. You aren't going anywhere, because that boy up there"—Olivia nods toward Josh—"that brave, magnificent boy needs his mother."

Jenna wipes her tears, moved by her sister's passion.

Olivia smiles softly. "Come here." She pulls Jenna into a hug, and Jenna buries her face in her sister's shoulder as a lifetime of doubt and hurt and betrayal dissipates. In its place she feels love, and a sense of belonging.

And maybe, just maybe, she starts feeling like she can forgive herself.

———

While Josh looks on from the cabin's deck that overlooks the lake, Jenna and Olivia talk about their parents. Jenna goes into detail about what she overheard Charlotte and Dwight confess the night she ran. That Charlotte was the one who stabbed Benton St. John, Jenna's biological father.

The news ravages Olivia. "But she told me it was Dad. She lied. She lied to me." Her knees buckle and she buries her face in her hands, sobbing. Between Dwight's death and Charlotte's duplicity, it's quite the shock to Olivia.

Jenna settles beside her, and in between gasps of breath, Olivia explains that Charlotte had spent the previous night at Olivia's. How she'd invited their mother to come with them here. Olivia thought she'd be eager to see Jenna. Hadn't she told Olivia she yearned to see her youngest daughter again?

But Charlotte had received a call right before they left. She claimed it was Lucas. He was in trouble. Worried, she'd insisted Olivia and Blaze take her home. They had.

Now Olivia wondered if Lucas had really called or if it was a ruse. Charlotte didn't want to come because Jenna knew the truth about what Charlotte did and would tell Olivia.

More than likely, Charlotte took the opportunity to disappear. She wasn't answering her phone. Neither was Lucas, and that bothered Olivia more. There was something off about their brother when she left him yesterday. He wasn't himself. Something had happened with him while Olivia had been with Josh looking for Lily, and she didn't know what. Lucas wouldn't tell her.

Jenna tries to console her sister the way Olivia did her, but Blaze comes running. Olivia's in his arms, and he's rocking with her.

Jenna feels a tug on her arm. Josh is beside her. He wraps his arms around her. She cups the back of his head, keeping him close as he rests his forehead on her shoulder and lets her hold him. She revels that he's in her arms.

Over his head, Tyler watches them. She sees the wonder in his eyes, fighting for space amid the hurt and anger he'd been directing at her. He'll be involved with their lives going forward. Jenna will make sure no one Josh wants as part of his life will be excluded.

But right now, she needs to talk with her son, and they should give Olivia and Blaze some privacy.

She asks Tyler for his phone. "Give us a few?" she asks when he hands over the device.

He nods and Jenna takes Josh aside. They sit under a tree near the lake edge. She touches his face and looks at him, really looks at him. His eyes shimmer with happiness and relief.

"I missed you terribly," she tells him, and he nods stiffly, making an effort not to cry again. "I was so frightened when I couldn't find you."

His bottom lip trembles. "I'm sorry. I . . . loop . . . left."

"No, don't apologize. This isn't your fault." Her words echo what Olivia said to her moments ago. "I'm not mad at you for leaving the car. You are courageous and strong, more than I ever could be. I know you went to get help. You can draw me your story later, but I have something to tell you. This is hard for me to explain, to admit. But you deserve to know. You've shown everyone here you're old enough to understand."

Josh frowns with unease. He sits up straighter, ready for what she has to say. Nerves skitter along her arms, settle in her stomach. She hopes he'll take this in stride, that he won't hate or fear her like she did Charlotte.

She takes a breath.

"I didn't tell you the truth about anything—your dad, why we moved, why I changed my name—because I was afraid. I wasn't brave like you. I killed—" Her voice cracks. "I did kill Wes. He was my friend, and I killed him."

Josh's eyes widen, and he inches away from her, and it takes everything in her not to pull him back. She doubts he's aware he moved. He hugs his knees.

"It was an accident. I know I've said before it was an accident, but I was under the impression it wasn't. I was convinced I murdered him. But now, talking about it, telling Olivia and you, I'm beginning to see it for what it is, that I'd acted in self-defense. But I was young and scared and pregnant with you. So I ran. And I kept on running because it was easier than admitting what I'd done. I hurt a lot of people in the process. Lied to a lot of people. You, Kavan, Tyler, but especially you. I'm sorry. I'm so, so sorry."

Her voice breaks, and she uses her shirt to dry her cheeks. Josh doesn't look at her. His thumb and finger pinch the inner corners of his eyes, and he takes a breath, loosening a sob. Her heart wrenches as he turns away from her to fully face the lake. If he could talk without stumbling over his words, she wonders what he'd say. He must be holding a lot inside.

Then a warm hand finds its way into hers, startling her. He laces their fingers, and Jenna's chest constricts, bursting with love. When he rests his head on her shoulder, he doesn't have to tell her that he forgives her. He shows it by staying with her.

Josh is the bravest boy she knows. How fortunate she is that he's hers. How lucky she is to have him in her life despite it all.

Which reminds her of another man she wants in her life, who's eager for news of Josh.

"Shall we call Kavan?"

Josh nods and Jenna puts the call on speaker. "There's someone with me who has something to say."

"Hi . . . K-Kavan."

"Josh! Is that you?"

"Yeah."

Josh smiles at her as Kavan loudly sighs "Oh, my god" on the other end. "How?" A choked laugh. "Where? God, I have so many questions. You had us worried. Are you good? Is he okay?" he asks them both.

"I'm fine," Josh says. "Happy to be . . . back."

"It's so good to hear your voice. God." He sounds flabbergasted. "I need to see you. Both of you. I'm coming up. Then I'm bringing you home."

Jenna covers her mouth, else she'll gush into the phone, telling him about the video, that she'd acted in self-defense, and that she's going to the police. Then they can talk, about their engagement, about a future Jenna never imagined possible for her. Hope warms her center, spreading outward, ever expanding. "We'd like that," she says, smiling at Josh. "Very much."

They return to Tyler's cabin, where Josh shows Jenna and Tyler his story through a series of sketches. Olivia and Blaze fill in where they can. It was a harrowing week, looking for Jenna and trying to figure what had happened to her and Josh, how Josh found his way to Olivia. They didn't know if Jenna was alive, dead, missing, or had abandoned her son. Jenna would never, but Olivia admits that it had crossed her mind, albeit before she learned Ethan was not Josh's father.

Josh knew something horrific must have happened to his mom. That he had to find a way to Murielle's to get help. He struggles with his emotions when Jenna tells him she was still there, hidden in the tall grass, not more than twenty yards from where he looked.

Olivia and Blaze stay through dinner when Blaze suggests they return home. Olivia is anxious to find Charlotte. And Lucas still isn't answering his phone. They say their goodbyes and exchange phone numbers. Make promises to keep in touch.

After they leave, Tyler challenges Josh to a game of checkers. When they start on their second game, Jenna tells them she's going to check in with Murielle and see if Kavan has arrived.

She tilts her head up at the sky as she crosses the road. The stars are out, the Milky Way excessively bright. The air is autumn crisp, refreshing after a day spent indoors.

Gravel scrapes behind her. Uneven footfalls rapidly close in. She smiles, knowing it's Josh. He doesn't want her to leave his sight. She turns around, reaching for his hand. A large figure appears out of the darkness. He's on her in a heartbeat. The blow to her head sends her reeling.

She crumples to the ground.

The starlit sky is the first thing Jenna sees when she comes to. The next is Ryder Jensen looming over her. Dizziness slants the world on its axis, and she gags only to realize she is gagged. Her scream is garbled, cut off short.

"Jesus *fucking* Christ. Took you long enough to wake up. For a second there . . ." Ryder rubs his scruffy chin, shakes his head. "Would have been no fun if you were dead already."

Her eyes bug, and she notices her face and hair are wet. He must have doused her with water, shocked her awake.

She struggles to sit up, but he shoves her down. Her hands and ankles are bound with zip ties. A whimper rattles in her throat. Her gaze searches for help. The lake laps beneath. Wood planks bite into her shoulders. She's on a dock, but which one? Ryder's so close she can't see past him. Would he risk carrying her to the Whitmans' dock, or did he take her elsewhere?

Another whimper, muffled by the gag. No one knows she's gone, and it'll be a while before they realize she's missing. By then, it'll be too late.

She stares wide eyed at Ryder, fearing his plans for her.

"You went and did it. You finally reported me to the fucking cops. The po-po are chasing my ass like they want to eat it for breakfast. We were having fun, Lily May. And you fucked it up."

Jenna whines, struggles to get away. Weaver was right. This is a game to him. She's just a marker on the board, another player. And she's terrified they've reached the end.

Tears burn her eyes. She chokes on a sob. The soiled rag in her mouth soaks up her saliva and something foul tasting slides down her throat.

"Don't cry, baby girl." Ryder's fingernail scrapes off a tear, leaving a scratch on her cheek.

Jenna squeezes her eyes shut, turns away, reviled by his touch.

"Ironic, don't you think?" He sneers. "You on a dock, pleading for your life. Your beloved family within earshot. And nobody knows you're here with me. That you're about to die. I wonder if Wes was as scared as you. Did you even give him the chance to be scared, or did you murder him that quick?"

She shakes her head, fighting the gag, tries to scream. It was an accident.

She bucks to sit up, and his palm slams on her chest, holding her still. Pain from her ribs slices through her.

He sighs through his nose and crouches beside her. "Aren't you tired of this shit? I sure am. But you betrayed what we had. You got the fucking cops involved."

His words strike a match. Anger flares. *He* got the cops involved when he pushed Josh down a flight of stairs, then tried to run her over. He gave her no choice, backed her into a corner.

"I want to hear you admit you murdered my brother, but if I take this off"—he pulls at the gag—"you'll scream. Then I'll have to slice your neck. Simple as that." His blade flashes, reflecting light from the cabin. "So do me a favor, just nod."

She shakes her head. She didn't murder him. Wes slipped and hit his head after she pushed him away. It was an accident.

"Oh, Lil." He stands. "You were a shitty employee and even shittier liar. What a disappointment." He plants a boot on her hip, just like Dwight had done to Wes.

Her eyes widen until they bulge. She fiercely shakes her head. *No, no, no, no.*

It can't end this way.

She won't let it end this way.

She's done running. And she's sick and tired of dealing with Ryder.

She pulls up her knees, intent on whirling around and smashing her feet in his groin. But he's too quick. He blocks her kick, knocking her legs aside.

"Think I'll go reacquaint myself with your son, Lily May Carson. Figure he'd want to meet the guy who gave him a nudge at the mall."

Absolute horror for her son consumes her rage.

He shoves her into the lake as she swallows her scream.

She barely has the chance to inhale through her nose before she submerges. The thick sweatshirt she's wearing and her shoes greedily soak up the water, and down she goes. She doesn't register how dark the lake is, or how cold, or that she's snorting up water. And if she weren't disoriented from the blow to her head, she would have thought to try to swim away. But the only thing on her mind is stopping Ryder to save her son.

Panic and fear consume her. But she's done letting Ryder control her life. This cat-and-mouse game ends tonight, even if it means one of them dies so that her son will live.

The instant her toes touch the mossy bottom, she pulls her knees to her chin and swings her bound hands in front. She pulls down the gag, leaving it around her neck. Then she keeps dropping until her rear almost touches the bottom. When that happens, she pushes off, surging upward. Breaking the surface. Inhaling a lifesaving gulp of air.

Ryder is there, right where she expected him. Crouched on the dock, looking for her. He wouldn't leave like he did when he hit her with his car, before he knows she's dead.

Before he can push her back under, she throws her bound arms over his head, and using her body weight and the dock as leverage, she plants her feet against the side like she would for a flip turn in the pool. She hauls Ryder into the water.

Surprise, blessedly, is on her side. Off balance, he drops in like a stone. Below the surface, he struggles, trying to push her off, to get free. But Jenna's arms are bound. She clings to him like a coiling snake, dodging his flailing arms, his legs. Her cracked ribs are on fire, but she barely registers the pain. His knee catches her stomach, expelling her air. She almost shoots to the surface. Almost. But years of competitive swimming trained her how to control her breathing, hold her breath for Olympic lengths. She'll go down with him if it comes to that.

She manages to climb onto his back, to keep his head below water, her arms a vise around his neck.

She wants him to leave Josh alone. To stop stalking her. She wants him to die.

His nails shred her forearms and hands, but she hangs on. Pulling up her knees, she plants them behind his shoulders.

Then she squeezes his neck, puts pressure on his shoulders and head, cutting off the blood flow in his arteries. Just like Lucas had taught her.

Ryder jerks frantically, almost throwing her off. She holds on until he weakens, until she remembers her son. Kavan and Uma. Keely. That she's a mom, and a good one at that. A fiancé and a friend. She *is* good. She is loved. And she's not her mother. She isn't a murderer.

Jenna pushes off him. She breaks the surface, gasps for air, intent on getting free and screaming for help.

Then she's being lifted by her sweatshirt, dragged up onto the dock.

She lands hard on a solid chest. She coughs and sputters and sobs, drinking large gulps of air. Hands push wet hair off her face. Thumbs gently wipe the water from her eyes. She opens them, and there is Kavan.

Terror, panic, and an uncompromising resolve darken his features. His hand threads in her tangled hair, tilting her face up. She blinks at him, shocked he's here.

Then absolute, blazing relief flares, warming her chest.

He's here.

Tension rolls off him at the sight of her. His gaze softens until they land on her bound hands and legs, and the light in them gutters, turning murderous. She's never seen him look so frightening.

Frightened for her, she realizes, as he pulls the switchblade he always carries from his pocket, flips it open, and slices through the zip ties.

"How?" she croaks, clutching his damp shirt. How did he know she was here? Everyone is at the house.

"I was walking over from Murielle's when I heard noises." His voice rasps, unsteady. "I thought you guys were down here. When I heard splashing and saw him go in, I can't explain what I felt, but I knew . . ." He stops abruptly, closing his eyes. His hands shake as he puts away the blade. Then he holds her tight. "I'm sorry I wasn't here earlier," he says into her hair. He kisses her there.

"It wouldn't have stopped him." He would have found a way to her. To kill her. Whether here or in Oceanside.

Water splashes behind them. They both whip around. Ryder clings to the dock, coughing and gasping like the drowned rat he is. Kavan's on his feet, and the blade is out before Ryder looks up and notices he's there.

Jenna lunges at Kavan, grabs his arm before he flings the blade. "He's not worth it."

Kavan spares her a glance, his eyes narrowed. Then he relaxes just a tad. He doesn't put down the blade.

She points at the zip ties in his back pocket. "We'll tie him up." She won't let him go anywhere, not until he leaves in handcuffs. "He also has a knife. Check his pockets."

Kavan restrains Ryder and pockets the knife, and Jenna calls the sheriff. While they wait, she crouches beside Ryder. He sneers at her. "Wes was my friend," she says. "I didn't intend to kill him. I was trying to help him and . . ." She shakes her head, water dripping from her chin. Her arms start trembling and her knees wobble as the burst of adrenaline from moments before leaves her. "It was an accident. I'm sorry for your loss and for all the pain I've caused, but I'm not a killer, not in the way you think I am." The way Dwight had her convinced of. A murderer.

Ryder's lips pull back from his teeth as he growls. He snaps at her ankle, actually tries to bite it, and Kavan stomps his hand. Ryder howls.

"Fucking touch her, and I'll slice off your fingers." Kavan's blade flashes.

Jenna gapes at him, seeing a new side to him. "That's pretty gruesome."

"I'll do it."

She knows he would.

"It's over," she tells Ryder. "Cops are on their way." She then starts shaking uncontrollably and turns away.

Concern lines Kavan's eyes. He puts an arm around her. "You okay?"

She presses her forehead to his chest and takes a deep breath. "I went back, Kavan. After my mom closed the door on me, I ran back to help Wes," she says into his shirt. "He was alive. I tried to help him, but he attacked me. I pushed him. He hit his head and fell, and then my dad pushed him, unconscious, into the water, where he drowned. He recorded the whole thing and he had me convinced it was my fault, that I'd murdered my friend."

Kavan cups the back of her neck. "You believed that this whole time?"

She nods.

"We need to find that video. Prove your innocence."

We.

She slides a hand down the front of his shirt.

"We do," she says, and her arms find their way around him.

CHAPTER 52

Nine days later Jenna walks out of the Carlsbad Police Department into the midday sun. It's fall, her favorite time of the year, especially here on the coast. The fog has taken a hiatus, the rain—as scarce as it is in SoCal—has yet to come. And the air is temperate enough to truly enjoy the outdoors.

For the first time she can remember, Jenna plans to live. A normal life, the best gift she can give Josh. One without lies and based on a foundation of truth.

This morning, Detective Weaver called her in to take her statement so they could close their case on Ryder, who'd been arrested for attempted murder, trespassing, and vandalism. When sentenced, he could find himself in prison for many years. She also gave them a statement about her involvement in Wes Jensen's death. Weaver wasn't pleased she lied while they were investigating Ryder. But after he read her report and watched the video Olivia found on Dwight's computer, he said her actions that night were justified. There wasn't malicious intent on her part. She had acted in self-defense. She was free to go.

He did warn her, as she stood up and shouldered her purse, that her statement would likely reopen Wes's case when he submitted it to the SCPD. The DA might find cause to pursue involuntary manslaughter. The thought of going to trial makes Jenna anxious, but not enough to run. She'd face those fears. She's even considering a visit to the Jensens to tell them her story, give them closure. But if tried and convicted, Jenna could end up serving two to three years in jail and pay a fine. As would Charlotte for lying on her statement. Though she could face a lifetime sentence.

If they find her.

She disappeared as soon as Olivia found Jenna.

Kavan is waiting with Josh and Uma in the parking lot, and it's the best sight ever.

He picked up Uma from school. Josh stayed with him while she was at the station. She's still homeschooling him, but just the other day he asked to return to his middle school by next semester. He wants to finish eighth grade with his friends, and Jenna couldn't be more thrilled. He's been working extra hard to overcome his aphasia. Even spending time with Tyler, who's taking Josh to a Giants playoff game next week.

Kavan is leaning back against the hood of his car, his gaze fixed on her, and Jenna walks right into his waiting arms. She rests her cheek on his chest, and he kisses her head.

"How was it?"

She looses a long sigh, and the tension coiling her muscles that had built up during her statement goes along with it. Writing about what happened to Wes was one of the hardest things she's done next to rewatching the video, reliving that night. She'll never forget it. Wes will always be in her life, live on in her mind.

"It's over. For now."

"We'll face the rest together if it comes to that." He tilts up her chin, his gaze mining her face. His features are both wary and hopeful. "I love you."

Simply stated, but enough. Because it feels like coming home.

"Hey," Uma says with sass, hands on hips, when she notices Jenna has returned. "Can we get ice cream now, or what?"

Josh sneaks up behind Uma, a devious glint sparkling in his eyes. He wraps Uma in a headlock and grinds his knuckles against her scalp.

She shrieks. "My hair!"

Kavan groans.

"Josh," Jenna warns.

He lets go, laughing, and Uma punches him in the shoulder. "Ow!"

Kavan presses his forehead to hers. "Is this going to be our life?"

Jenna can't stop smiling as she watches them. "Yes. And it's perfect." Normal.

Josh opens the car door to get in, and Uma slams it shut, barely missing his fingers.

"Well, almost," she amends with a bark of laughter.

CHAPTER 53

Five weeks later, Jenna stands in the middle of her childhood bedroom in Seaside Cove. The room hasn't changed. At all. She doesn't know what she should make of it, whether she should cry or run to the bathroom and puke.

The sketchbook she'd showed Wes that last night is still on the desk. The graphite pencils are beside it.

She imagines that, after Charlotte shut the front door in her face, she straightened up her room, turned off the light, and closed the door. Never reentered.

A lump fills her throat. She picks up the sketchbook, leafs through it. Wes loved her drawings. These were the last ones he saw. She feels she needs to keep them for that reason alone.

She adds the book to the box of trinkets she's taking back to Oceanside: journals, miscellaneous photos of her and Wes and her swim team. Tyler at the lake. Josh will want those.

As for everything else, the posters of Pearl Jam and Nirvana, magazine clippings, the clothes in the closet . . . The estate company Olivia hires will see to everything.

Charlotte disappeared to who knows where, and she won't return, not with Jenna back and knowing what she knows.

She left the house in their names: Jenna's, Olivia's, and Lucas's. Along with a bank account with enough funds to put Josh through college at a private university.

Jenna has every intention of donating the money to Murielle's network of angels. She'll donate her proceeds from the house sale, too. Whenever that happens. They can't do anything until Lucas returns. He left shortly after Dwight passed. Oliva has no idea where.

Finished, she takes the box to the kitchen. She needs to get on the road. They're celebrating Uma's birthday tonight and Tyler is in town. He wants her help looking for a condo. He plans to split his time between San Francisco and Oceanside, and Josh is ecstatic to have more time with him.

She also has an interview tomorrow for her new book. Live. In person. And Gayle is beside herself. Jenna had given her the go-ahead to organize a media tour. And it was a big day—a *nervous* day—when she sat for a photo shoot and sent those photos to Gayle with instructions to swap out the cartoon head on her website and social-media platforms with her new headshot.

She was done hiding.

Gayle was speechless when Jenna first told her. Then she had the largest floral arrangement Jenna had ever seen delivered to her townhouse. It was wider than her kitchen table.

Olivia is on the back deck watching sailboats in the bay. Jenna sets down the box and opens the patio door. Olivia turns around.

"Get what you want?"

Trinkets and memorabilia. "Yes. Thanks for opening the house for me."

"It's your house, too. I'll make a copy of the key."

Jenna shakes her head. "I'd rather you didn't. I won't be back. I'll be back to visit you," she amends at Olivia's raised brows. "But not to this house."

Olivia wraps her sweater around her torso. The knit is too thin for how cold it is here. A gust of wind hits Jenna. She zips her jacket to her chin.

"I'm seeing someone," Olivia says. "A therapist."

Jenna glances at her sidelong.

"I'm trying to work out why I didn't see through Mom's lies. Why I ignored how Dad treated you, why I didn't do anything. That's what I want to figure out most—why I didn't help you when you needed me. I was selfish. I knew you needed me. I just . . ." Her face tightens with despair.

Jenna touches her arm, waits until Olivia looks at her. "I forgive you," she says.

Olivia's smile wobbles. "I'm trying to forgive myself. It's not easy."

She thinks of Wes, her decision to not tell Tyler she was pregnant, her lies to Josh and denying him time with his father, and every other decision she made in the days following Wes's death. "Self-forgiveness never is."

Olivia gestures at the smokestack trio across the bay, unused since the power plant shut down years ago. "I used to stare at those for hours," she says. "They inspired the Crimson Wave." The superheroes in her graphic novels. Three siblings. Indestructible. Their bond unbreakable. "I modeled them after us."

Jenna knows. She's seen the life-size murals of Ruby, Titian, and Dahlia in Olivia's studio. The resemblance to her, Lucas, and Olivia is uncanny. Olivia said Josh had noticed right away. "I just finished your novels. They're good."

Olivia blows in her cupped palms to warm them. "I watched your videos on YouTube. Can't wait to see the movie."

A flutter of excitement teases Jenna. She wants her entire family at opening night: Josh, Kavan, and Uma. Tyler and Blaze. Olivia and Lucas.

"I wish we were like them," Olivia admits. "Close, like we used to be. Before everything went to shit."

One day they will be. Jenna wholeheartedly believes that.

She looks up at Lucas's apartment above the garage. "How long do you think he'll be gone?"

"No telling with him." Olivia mentioned he's disappeared before, weeks at a time.

"Should we look for him? I got a gal—"

Olivia is shaking her head. "Not yet. Whatever he's dealing with, he needs time."

"But he still needs us," Jenna says, reaching for her sister's hand.

Olivia threads their fingers. "Yes, he does."

CHAPTER 54

LUCAS

Lucas kicks back in the dark on the piss-ass tiny balcony off the run-down, wallpaper-peeling hole of an apartment he rents, bare feet propped up on the guardrail. He's naked save for the jeans he dragged on when he left his bed. He didn't bother buttoning the fly. He wanted to see the stars. Count the satellites he could see passing overhead with his naked eye. They were bright tonight.

Half a beer dangles from his fingers. He tips back the bottle, washes down a mouthful, wipes his lips.

He wonders what Olivia and Lily are doing, like he wonders every night. He thinks of them all the time.

Olivia sent him a gazillion texts before he dumped his phone. Told her Lily had changed her name to Jenna.

Jenna Mason. Author and animator. Screenwriter.

He's proud of her. He then feels guilty. He doesn't deserve to feel anything for her.

Because he let her get away.

He'd watched the whole thing with her, Wes, and Dwight go down, and he hadn't done anything to stop it.

Her book was recently published. Another's on the way. And a movie is in the works. The trailer premiered the other day. He doesn't know if he can bring himself to watch it when it opens. He bought her book last week. He has yet to crack it open. Probably never will. It's still on the coffee table with the busted leg, where he left it.

Lily was his shadow when they were small, coloring on his floor while he sat beside her on the carpet, working through his history essay questions. Tagging along when he biked the neighborhood. His friends adored her. He wonders if she has asked about him. Then he accepts that he doesn't care.

He doesn't give a fuck about anyone because nobody gave a damn about him when it mattered most. Explains why he ditched Seaside Cove before Lily showed. Now he gets to live in this shithole.

The balcony light bursts on, and Lucas bites down a string of insults, squinting against the glare.

"Turn it off," he barks.

"Only if you come back to bed." She pouts.

He looks up at her standing beside him. She's nude. He's about to tell her to go back inside, put on some clothes. His landlady, an elderly woman approaching eighty, lives next door and can easily see from her balcony window. But—fuck. What's this woman's name? He can't remember. She lifts his hand and puts it on her breast.

"I *need* you, baby."

He hates that endearment coming from her mouth.

But he needed her, too. Hours ago when he met her at a bar. She's got to be older than him by at least ten years. She's attractive enough, though. And convenient. She was all too eager to come home with him.

He tips back his beer, finishes it off as he trails a lone finger down her torso. Over her breast, circling around her belly, until he reaches her center, dips inside.

She moans. He twitches. Enough to get him out of the chair.

She smiles like a cat.

He grabs her hand and leads her back into the apartment, to his room, the stars and satellites not forgotten. Just on hold. He doesn't look at his sister's book on the way. A sister he thoroughly, unequivocally let down.

What he did was unforgivable.

And he can't change that. Never make it right. Or take it back.

They reach his room, and she turns on the light. He slaps it off.

"But I want to see you."

"No," he says, grabbing the hands caressing his pecs.

It's nothing to do with her. She's beautiful. He just doesn't want to see himself.

ACKNOWLEDGMENTS

An abundance of thanks goes out to this amazing team:

To my editor, Chris Werner, whose cheerful emails always brighten my in-box. Thank you for your endless advocacy and steadfast enthusiasm for my stories. You keep me believing in me. Every story we work on together is an honor. I am so lucky.

To Tiffany Yates Martin for your microscopic attention to story details. You think of things that would never cross my mind. You are brilliant, and my stories are better because of that.

To Hannah Buehler, Claire Caterer, Nicole Burns-Ascue, and everyone from editing to production who makes my books shine, from the words on the page to the glossy covers. Thank you for putting the icing on the cake and adding the filling between layers. Holding that final book in my hands never gets old.

To everyone at Amazon Publishing, especially Chris, Danielle Marshall, and Gabrielle Dumpit, who embraced me when I stumbled so that I wouldn't fall. Thank you for the cards, the gifts, the check-ins, the gorgeous flowers, but most especially, for not giving up on me. I am stronger today because of you.

To Ashley Vanicek, Morgan Dormus, and Erika Moriarty for your publicity and marketing savviness. Thank you for the series' incredible launch, for getting the first book, *No More Words*, and this one into readers' hands. It's a joy working with you.

To my agent, Gordon Warnock, for your wisdom and guidance. I always know who to go to with questions, no matter how odd they are. You always have an answer. Thank you for your support.

To Jen Cannon, the best assistant an author can have.

To my readers in the Tiki Lounge, y'all make social media fun. I love hanging out with you in there.

To Kimberly Belle, Amber Cowie, Sally Hepworth, Steena Holmes, Hannah Mary McKinnon, and Suzanne Redfearn for helping me kick off this series with the best endorsements.

I started writing *No More Lies* in the middle of the pandemic while my daughter, Brenna, spent her senior year in high school at home. As I'm wrapping up edits, she just started college. There were tears when I left her at school. Happy tears, though. She's stretching wings she couldn't use for more than a year. I am beyond excited to watch her soar. Same with my son, Evan, who's ecstatic to be back on campus. Thank you both for letting me love you.

To my husband, Henry, who knows when to steer clear or extend a hand, for your love and patience. At the risk of being sappy, you complete me.

To my readers, thank you for picking up this book, for going on this journey with me, and for taking the time to post a review or rate this book. I'd love to hear from you. You can reach me through my website (www.kerrylonsdale.com) or find me on Instagram (@kerry-lonsdale) and TikTok (@kerry.lonsdale). Tag me (#kerrylonsdale) and the book (#nomorelies) when you post photos and videos and I'll share. Hang out with me inside the Tiki Lounge (www.facebook.com/groups/kerrystikilounge) for sneak peeks and other exclusive material.

COMING MARCH 2023
No More Secrets
Book 3 in the No More Series

AN EXCERPT FROM
NO MORE SECRETS

Editor's note: This is an early excerpt and may not reflect the finished book.

Lucas Carson rolls onto his back and stares at the ceiling fan rotating on low, its blades spinning faster than a clock's second hand, melting his waste of a life. As if the Mojave Desert hasn't already done so.

He makes a mental assessment, digging up the motivation to get out of bed. His head pounds from the six-pack of empty beer bottles on the nightstand. More from the shots of tequila. The crust around his eyes that caked overnight stings. He scrapes it off. His body aches, his right calf especially. He must have tweaked it last night when they were going at it.

He drags his hands over his face, the stubble chafing, and drops an f-bomb into his cupped palms. He shouldn't have let her in. He's weak when it comes to her, more so when he's drunk.

She stirs beside him, her body going taut as she stretches her arms overhead and purrs. The sound drips with enough innuendo that Lucas can't believe it isn't intentional.

Her eyes slide open, revealing the stunning green that gets him every time she shows up at his door in a skimpy dress, mountain-high heels, and legs that go for miles. She has ten years on his thirty-three, but it doesn't show anywhere on her.

He sits up in bed. She smiles, catlike. He swings his legs over the side. She reaches for his wrist to keep him close. He snags his hand away and shoots out of bed, moody about when and how he's touched. She pouts because he's slipping away. Body, mind. Interest. Until next time, at least.

"Baby." Faye's plea is breathless, heavy with the dregs of sleep.

"I have to get to work," he says gruffly, clearing his throat of morning phlegm. He grabs the orange Home Depot bucket he uses for trash and slides the empty bottles in with one swipe of his forearm. The noise shatters the morning's calm.

Faye flops onto her back with an irritated groan. "Lucas," she whines, now fully awake. She drags the pillow over her face.

He drops the bucket on the floor. The bottles clatter. "You should go. Rafe returns tonight." Her husband.

She groans into the pillow, then dramatically tosses it onto the floor and rolls to her side, propping up her head. She lets the sheet slide from her shoulders, revealing perfect breasts, thanks to some fancy surgeon in the valley. "He's not leaving again for weeks. Skip work. Spend the day with me." Her bottom lip pops out.

"Can't." He hobbles to the bathroom, stretching his cramped calf.

"She's lucky to have you."

"Who?" He lifts the toilet lid and seat she'd put down. They bang against the tank.

"Izzy."

"Ivy," he corrects. His seventy-nine-year-old landlady and boss. She owns the four-apartment complex along with the market on the first floor. He works when she tells him, and he's already running late. He overslept and has the hangover to blame.

"You only care about her."

He grunts and takes a piss without bothering to shut the door.

"'The simple act of caring is heroic,'" she recites.

Lucas rolls his eyes with no idea what she's going off about. He flushes the toilet, washes his hands, and splashes cold water onto his face. He leans on the sink and stares at his reflection, mustering the will to clean up and show up. His eyes are bloodshot, the skin around them swollen. He hasn't cut his hair in months. It falls shapelessly around his head, the cowlick he's had since birth more pronounced from Faye messing with his hair. He swore she pulled sections out when he was pounding into her. She can't keep her hands off his head.

I like the intimacy, she tells him, palming his face, his neck.

He shakes his head and rubs a hand over his scalp. There's nothing intimate about them or what they do in the dark.

The switchblade he keeps on the toilet tank demands his attention, as it does every morning. He scowls at it, his gaze sliding to the tub. A memory of the bath filled to the rim with lukewarm water, him in it, fades in and out.

"Edward Albert," she's prattling on about whatever from his room.

"Never heard of him."

"That actor. He was in *Falcon Crest* and a movie with Goldie Hawn. He won a Golden Globe."

Lucas shakes his head. "I don't know what you're talking about." He turns away from the blade and grabs his toothbrush, smears paste across the worn bristles.

"He said it. Don't know when, just that he did. I ache. Be a hero and rescue me. Come back to bed, baby." Her voice goes all singsong on him.

He could crawl back into bed. To hell with his responsibilities.

He could also show her exactly how heroic he isn't.

He spits foamy paste into the sink. "I ain't no hero because I don't give a shit." About Faye, anyone, or anything. He shuts the bathroom door.

He hears a muffled "Lucas" before he turns on the shower, and when he's finished and has wrapped a loose towel around his waist, he hears the front door click into place.

He yanks open the bathroom door and spills out from a cloud of steam. Faye isn't in his bed, and she isn't excavating his fridge for spoiled milk and month-old eggs, insisting she whip up a hearty scramble for him because he subsists on Coronas and Jose Cuervo.

The air conditioner hums. The ceiling fans he installed yesterday in the main room and his bedroom still spin.

He's the only one here.

Hands on hips, he exhales heavily with relief.

———

Dusty Pantry is located on the first floor of Ivy's four-apartment building, a convenience market located on a large parcel of barren land in California City, a town that never lived up to its founder's ambition of growing bigger and more vibrant than Los Angeles. Miles of paved roads lead to nowhere, baking in the desert heat. After a postwar real estate boom, its growth tapered off until it was virtually a ghost town, exactly why Lucas has found himself here.

No one bothers him because there aren't enough people to care.

It's been eight months since he bailed on Seaside Cove, a gated community on the Central Coast; his sister Olivia; his mother, Charlotte; and the troubles that haunt him—a lifetime of shoplifting, a stint in juvie seventeen years ago that irrevocably changed him, and his father's death, for which he's sure he's at fault and the cops have a warrant out for him. He got in his truck and drove, tossing his phone out the window somewhere along Highway 58.

The market was the first place he stopped when he rolled into town, expecting to drive on through. But he wanted a beer and bought twelve. A Reese's candy, a pack of Dentyne Ice, and a jerky stick that was probably as old as him found their way into his pockets when the old lady behind the counter turned her back.

Ivy Dervish. She and her husband had purchased the land and built the drab multiuse building of apartments, deli counter, and market back in the late sixties. The business has been floundering and the structure falling apart since her husband passed away five years back. She's been working overtime to keep it afloat when she should have retired years ago. She also convinced Lucas to stick around. There was an apartment above that needed a tenant. She'd lease it to him at half the publicized monthly rate if he helped her around the property.

Desperate was an understatement for her to make such an offer to a stranger, especially to him, given his track record. He's known to bail on his responsibilities. Skip town for weeks, even months, at a time without notice. Just ask his sister Olivia, who always seems to find him and somehow convince him to come back.

On a whim—he couldn't explain why other than a feeling that had come over him that this was the place he needed to be—he took her up on her offer and has since been bringing her building into the twenty-first century. He'd paid for the beer, and before he returned to his truck for his duffel of clothes, he slipped a donation into the *Feed the World's Hungry* plastic bucket beside the cash register, enough to cover the value of the items stashed in his pockets.

Dusty Pantry lives up to its name. Lucas sweeps the stockroom's floor, pushing the fine, blond-toned dirt out the back door. The parking lot isn't paved, and Ivy's property stretches far enough in back that he can only see the rooftops of several single-family homes above the waist-high shrubs scattered across the landscape. The only good thing about this place is the night sky. Stars are brighter, more brilliant in the desert, where Lucas can imagine he isn't anything more than a speck of nothingness in the vast universe.

He hears the familiar rumble of the truck from Sanchez's Produce. Mack drives south from the valley once a week and drops off several boxes of fresh fruit and vegetables, which Ivy displays in the self-serve fridge along the far wall. The parking brake drops into place and metal doors clang open.

Lucas shuts the rear door, puts aside the broom, and pushes through the swing door that separates the stockroom from the market. He walks down an aisle of cleaning supplies, past the cash register, and unlocks the front door. He props it open with a brick.

"Hey, Mack."

"Morning, Luc." Mack drops a wooden crate bursting with apples and oranges onto the sidewalk as Lucas returns to the stockroom to retrieve the empty crates from the prior week's delivery.

"Tell Ivy I got the white peaches she ordered," Mack says when Lucas returns. Lucas can smell the fruit's sweetness wafting from the truck's refrigerated box. Mack tosses the empty crates onto the truck.

"Will do, man." Lucas mechanically bumps the fist Mack holds up before he takes the fruit inside.

"See you next week," Mack hollers after he slams the rear doors. Lucas grunts over his shoulder, dropping the fruit-laden crate by the self-serve fridge for Ivy to sort when she comes downstairs. She complained the one time Lucas emptied the crate over the fruit display. A third of the apples dropped to the ground, rolling in every direction, leaving them bruised and unsellable. After a tidy lecture about moving the old fruit to the front and neatly aligning the new fruit behind, he left the task up to her. Artfully balancing apples that would likely rot before someone bought them wasn't his thing. When the drive-throughs moved in several decades ago, Dusty Pantry lost the bulk of its customers looking for refreshment on the long haul through the desert. Wrapping several sandwiches for guards on their way to their shift at the prison and selling a few six-packs to the locals is considered a profitable day.

Mack leaves for his next delivery and Lucas retrieves the other two crates from out front. Closing the door behind him, he takes the fruit to the fridge in back. The door separating the stockroom from the market swings wide and sticks, remaining open. Lucas leaves it. His hands are full, and the market doesn't open for another twenty minutes.

He packs fruit into the stockroom's fridge, tosses the crate aside, and starts on the next when the bell above the entrance jingles. "Not open yet," he yells. He's about finished with the second crate when he hears another noise, a can falling off a shelf. It rolls across an aisle.

Lucas sets down the crate, closes the fridge, and scopes the market from the doorway. There, along the far wall, he spots a dirty-blonde head barely visible above the aisle. He opens his mouth to tell whoever ignored him that the shop is still closed. But something stops him.

The figure appears around the endcap, Lucas going unnoticed. She's too fixated on the products displayed: Snickers bars and M&M's. Hot Tamales and Lay's chips. With dirt-smudged cheeks and greasy hair, wearing a hoodie too thick and big for the Mojave's heat, she keeps her eyes averted, using her fingers to show her what's on the shelf. They skim everything she passes. Every so often, her hand dips to her side.

Lucas's gaze narrows as he stares at her retreating back. He knows exactly what she's doing because he's done the same since he was eleven. It started with a Hot Wheels car that he regrettably let his younger sister, Lily, take the blame for. Next it was a candy bar, then a shirt he swiped from Big 5 Sporting Goods just to see if he could do it. Until finally it ended with a six-pack of beer and a gun that didn't belong to him. His reward? Six months in juvenile detention bunking in an overcrowded hall with five guys who'd committed acts ten times worse than him.

He wasn't the guilty party, not entirely. But his friends, his football teammates since they played peewee, let him take the fall.

He's still falling. Flailing.

And shit he hasn't paid for still finds its way into his pockets.

Face hard, he watches her disappear around the endcap. Lucas strides up the neighboring aisle to confront her. Ivy doesn't have cameras. He needs to catch this little thief in the act with the merch still on her. Maybe talk some sense into her, shake her up a bit, so she doesn't end up like him.

She comes around the corner and gasps. Lucas snatches her wrist, small and bony, startling them both at the contact, and flips her hand. Clutched in her palm is a pack of Juicy Fruit. His gaze drops to the loaded kangaroo pocket before flying up to her face. Large, hazel eyes, haunted and deep, sit atop a wave of freckles bridging her sunburnt nose. She can't be more than fifteen, sixteen at the most. Lily's age when she ran away.

Suddenly, he only sees his baby sister, not the stranger lifting Ivy's merchandise.

He lets go of her, stunned.

The girl doesn't waste a second. She sprints from the store with her loot.

ABOUT THE AUTHOR

Photo © 2018 Chantelle Hartshorne

Kerry Lonsdale is the *Wall Street Journal, Washington Post,* and Amazon Charts bestselling author of *Side Trip, Last Summer, All the Breaking Waves*; the Everything Series (*Everything We Keep, Everything We Left Behind,* and *Everything We Give*); and the No More series (*No More Words* and *No More Lies*). Her work has been translated into more than twenty-seven languages. She resides in Northern California with her husband and two children. You can visit Kerry at www.kerrylonsdale.com.